RELATIVE STRANGERS

RELATIVE STRANGERS

Val Hopkirk

LONDON NEW YORK SYDNEY TORONTO

This edition published
By BCA
By arrangement with Headline Book Publishing
A Division of Hodder Headline Group

CN 2947

Printed and bound in Germany by
Graphischer Grossbetrieb Pössneck GmbH

Acknowledgements

Our thanks to: Dr Elizabeth Letsky, consultant perinatal haematologist at Queen Charlotte's Hospital (and her secretary Eileen Gomez); barrister Tony Baldry MP; solicitor Gilbert Rowberry and his grandson Mark Rowberry; PC Kim Bray of the Hertfordshire Constabulary; Andrew Trehearne, Leukaemia Research Fund, Great Ormond Street, London. These medical and legal experts, who gave unstintingly of their time and expertise, should not be blamed for our interpretations of their knowledge. Grateful thanks, also, to Jane Reed; Judy Wade; guinea-pig readers June Hutcheson, Sandy Sidman, Michelle Hutcheson, Geraldine Dennen and Kate Seamark; Peter Venes, ever-ready computer doc; John Obank; Champneys international health resort where some of this book was created; our assiduous editor Marion Donaldson; our energetic agent Carole Blake; and, as always, our supportive families.

Chapter One

This morning Dan Hargreaves, aspiring partner in one of London's newest research laboratories, was bracing himself for a task he did not usually have to face, telling the anguished father of a terminally ill child there was nothing either he or his wife could do except wait and hope. Hope for a bone marrow match. Wait for the blood samples to come in. Wait for the tests to be done. Wait for the results. This could take up to seventy-two hours for each tissue culture plate and there were dozens. His laboratory only had so much capacity and other jobs, just as urgent to the patients involved, also had to be processed.

Dr Hargreaves had endured an intensive ten minutes with the consultant in charge of the case. The father's main complaint was that the hospital was keeping him in the dark. This was not true but the consultant thought his patient's father needed cooling down. And Dan, the lab's newest manager, was just the person to do it since he knew the father. Dan was well aware that most doctors hated dealing with emotion and were not skilled in the so-called human touch, an aspect of medicine which had been sorely neglected during his seven-year training. Judging by the eagerness with which the consultant had shoved the chore on to him, this was still the case. Dan was not pleased. He did not often have to deal with Joe Public and that was the way he liked it.

He and the child's father, Andrew Lynton, had met at med school but only for two terms when Andy had decided medicine was not his bag. He was now a car salesman. As there was no indication when, or indeed whether, they would ever find a match, all Dan could do was offer the father platitudes.

When Andrew arrived in the office, Dan barely recognised the bulky figure of his erstwhile colleague. Andrew had gained fifty pounds since their university days and seeing this made Dan proud of the exercise discipline that had kept his weight static.

1

'Andy,' he said, rising from his desk. 'Good to meet up again after such a long time.' His lab assistant gave the man a quick look before scuttling out of the door.

'Thanks for seeing me.' Andrew sat down heavily in the chair opposite and Dan waited for the inevitable small talk but Andrew began without preamble. 'I want you to cut the bullshit and tell me Sebastian's chances. Whatever they are, give it to me straight because the hospital won't.'

Dan ignored this and put on his best pacifying manner. He tapped the file on his desk. 'My people are working round the clock to find a match. Believe me, we're a long way from giving up hope.'

'So there is hope?'

'Of course,' said Dan heartily. Why add that it was like looking for a diamond in a glass factory? Hope had to be kept alive, as much for the relatives as for the laboratory staff who, when they managed to isolate a match, were as overjoyed as if it was for one of their own family.

'But the baby's getting weaker, I can see it.'

Dan tried to inject a more positive note into his voice, 'Every day we're getting in more and more samples, not only through the Anthony Nolan Trust but via that committee organised by your friends and neighbours. But the most likely match will probably come from within your family.' He rested his hand on the folder. 'It could well be right here.'

'Are you sure you've got samples from all of them?'

'We believe so.'

'May I see?' Andrew stretched out a hand towards the file.

'Sorry,' said Dan, giving his deprecating grin. 'We're governed by ethics, confidentiality. You'll remember from the old days.'

'Look, the family situation is pretty tense.' Andrew's face was twisted with anxiety. 'I know they all promised my wife they'd arrange to give blood but what if one of them didn't and it happened to be the match? I only want a quick check.'

For a few seconds Dan hesitated, then chided himself for being ultra cautious. Andy had flunked out of medical school so soon, the chances of him making sense of the hieroglyphics in the blood reports were zero. But if it gave him peace of mind to count up the relatives . . . He handed over the file and waited while Andy looked at it, the silence punctuated by the far-off sounds of an ambulance siren wailing its passage through the busy Hammersmith streets.

'You seem to have all of them,' said Andrew, and was about to give the file back when, brow furrowed, he stared intently at one of the pages. Dan felt a twinge of concern.

'I'll have that back, thank you,' he said. Andrew ignored him. Peremptorily Dan stretched out his hand and said again, 'Thank you.'

Andrew pushed the now-open folder across the desk and sat back. 'You throw up some intriguing data in this business, don't you?' he said slowly.

Chapter Two

They lay for a while without talking, slightly out of breath, damp with perspiration, until Lizzie propped herself up on one elbow and began tracing the fine hairs on his chest.

'Whatever you're taking, keep at it.' Her voice was almost a growl. 'That was great.'

Her husband gave an extravagant stretch, a contented smile curving his mouth. She kissed his cheek and burrowed her face into his neck. 'It's good to have my lover back,' she said softly.

Calum Lynton, sometime entrepreneur and doting husband, interlaced his fingers with hers. 'I'm sorry I've been such a pig lately. I shouldn't have taken it out on you.'

'That wasn't an apology, was it?' She reared back in mock amazement. 'What's the date?'

He managed a smile. 'It's been really tough.'

'You should've told me long ago how worried you were.'

'I know but I kept on thinking business would perk up.' He let his fingers trail through her silky hair. 'I feel so much better now.'

She looked at him, a pleased smile on her face. 'Thank you, sir. I thought I was pretty good.'

He nuzzled the top of her head. 'You can't take all the credit. It might have something to do with the prospect of wiping out our overdraft at long last.'

'Does that mean I won't have to come and work for you?' she asked, raising herself up onto the pillow.

'Not unless you want to.'

Calum had been trying for months to persuade Lizzie to forget teaching so she could help him in his business organising trade exhibitions. Not only was he hoping to save on a salary he could ill afford but she had been damn successful when she had worked alongside him before. So far she was resisting. She had learned her lesson. Last time it had very nearly been a disaster for their marriage.

The difficulty had been that Calum would not switch off from business, even in the bedroom. He was in the habit of going over the problems of the day and giving her a list of tasks for the next morning. But the last straw came when Lizzie, deciding he needed to be seduced, bought herself an extremely uncomfortable but sexy nightie. Shortly after 11 p.m. she had sashayed into their bedroom and posed in front of him. He had looked at her blankly.

'I can't remember whether or not I've sent the invoice to Blakes. Did you take care of it?'

She never went back to his office after that, took herself off to a teachers' training college and now worked as a supply teacher for surrounding primary schools in the south London borough of Wandsworth where they had bought a much sought-after terraced house. Calum had installed a new right hand, Tess Parker, who seemed to fit the bill exactly.

Lizzie watched as her husband's lean figure rolled off the bed. He reached for his towelling robe, discarded on the floor. It was way past their normal time for getting up but today was exceptional. In two hours her father-in-law's last will and testament was going to be read in the offices of the family's solicitor and with it, hopefully, their worries would be over.

Calum had been stunned by the speed of his father's death a month earlier but after the post mortem, doctors had told him the heart attack had been a blessing. His father had cancer and he would have had nothing to look forward to but pain and being incapacitated.

All the Lyntons had been asked to attend the solicitor's office, with one notable exception.

'Do you think Andy will turn up?' asked Lizzie, wondering how long she dare stay in bed.

Calum was examining shirts on his side of the wardrobe, trying to decide what would be best for a solemn will reading. 'He's been told Dad didn't want him there and he ought to obey his wishes.' He selected a shirt from the top row. 'I asked Ed if he could be allowed to come but he was adamant. I left a message on Andy's machine telling him I was sorry. What more could I do?' He shrugged on what he'd decided was the appropriate choice, a pale blue shirt with fine yellow stripes.

'What do you think he'll do?'

'Who knows? Apart from being furious, I don't see what he can do. Dad can leave his money to anyone he wants.'

'But you'll look after him, won't you?'

'I'm going to have to do it another way. Dad said often enough he didn't want any of his money to go to Andy and according to Ed the law says I have to abide by that. But there's nothing to stop me giving some financial security to Edina and Sebastian. They've enough on their plates, without having to worry about money.'

Since childhood Andrew's complaint was that parents and teachers alike compared him unfavourably with his elder brother. And his self-esteem suffered a further blow when early on it was discovered he was dyslexic. He was unable to accept his father's authority, constantly challenging him over things that did not matter. Calum had often tried to smooth things out between them, explaining to his father that as Andy was built in the same mould, he should be more tolerant. But it didn't seem to work.

Despite this friction between father and son, the brothers enjoyed an uneasy alliance until Lizzie entered the scene, when it had hit a serious blip. She had actually met Andrew first. He was with his parents on a visit to Calum who had been at Nottingham University for only a few weeks. Lizzie had gone into the café in the High Street where a bored Andrew was having coffee, waiting for his parents to pick him up. He gave every sign of falling in lust and for half an hour or so he engaged her in lively conversation. He was working in London and Lizzie forgot about him seconds after he left, though he phoned her incessantly. Not long afterwards Lizzie met Calum on campus and did not discover Andrew was his brother until months later when he took her home to meet his parents.

Andrew's ill-disguised jealousy only increased as the years passed. Calum appeared to have everything he did not – supportive parents, a loving wife, a seemingly successful business and a healthy child. Calum and Lizzie had decided, for the sake of harmony, to reduce communication between them to a minimum. Lately it had dwindled to an exchange of Christmas and birthday cards. Even Sebastian's illness had not led to a reconciliation, although Lizzie maintained contact with Andy's wife. When their solicitor had informed them that Andrew was to be excluded from the reading of the will, they had assumed this meant Calum would be the main beneficiary.

Robert Lynton had never been able to forgive his younger son for what he described as 'the most underhand trick Andy could play on his family'. He had been caught stealing from his mother.

7

It emerged that he had been systematically thieving small pieces of jewellery – all of them gifts from Robert Lynton to his wife – for a period of years. Robert Lynton had insisted on reporting the matter to the police and his son had been charged and convicted. He was fined and given one hundred hours of community service. The jewellery had never been recovered and nor did he give a satisfactory explanation as to what he had done with the money he made. Perhaps he genuinely could not recall. Calum was sure his brother had stolen not for the money primarily but for the satisfaction it gave him. There had been a hint of triumph in Andrew's voice when he had admitted he had been 'outwitting' his father in this way for years. His mother had suffered a massive stroke as a result of the shock of the case and had spent the remaining year of her life in a wheelchair. Calum's repeated efforts to get his parents to forgive and forget met with failure, as did his attempts to convince Andy that he was responsible for the deepening rift.

Lizzie swung her slim legs out of bed, and stretched. Aware that her husband had not taken his eyes off her naked body, she sucked in her tummy. It had been an age since he had looked at her in that admiring way and she dodged playfully round him as he attempted to smack her bottom.

The last few months had been difficult for them; worries about the business had naturally spilled over into their private life. After such a long time together Lizzie did not expect fireworks in bed and like most settled couples they had drifted into a routine of making love once or sometimes twice a week. But lately the sex had been sporadic, due, Calum reassured her, entirely to his preoccupation with his overdraft. She had readily accepted this explanation, until yesterday. Calum had rung to ask her if she could check a message on their home computer. They both used the same password, the name of their daughter, and she found it easy to access his files.

The e-mail he mentioned had not been sent but there was another one and she could not resist opening the file when she saw it had been sent by Tess, now promoted to office manager. Attractive, curvy, divorced, available. For years Lizzie had been tempted to tell Calum that Tess would jump on him if given half a chance but an in-built caution prevented her. Why alert him to a problem that might only exist in her mind?

As she scanned the screen, Lizzie experienced a flash of

annoyance mingled with unease. She couldn't imagine herself sending a man a catalogue of items headed 'Good Things About Being a Bloke'. Tess had prefaced the list with one sentence: 'Saw these and thought of you at once!' Some of the items were amusing like 'Flowers fix everything' and 'You never look at the size of a baby's head and cringe'. Others were nearer the knuckle. 'You can buy condoms without the chemist imagining you naked' and 'Hot wax never comes near your pubic area'. But a few were frankly sexual: 'All your orgasms are real' and 'Not liking a person doesn't exclude having great sex with them'. Did employer and employee, even one who had been with the company for such a long time, exchange e-mails about such things as condoms, orgasm and sex?

As soon as all this will business was over she would tackle him about it.

Lizzie examined herself critically in the wardrobe mirror. Her gleaming hair was the colour, Calum used to say, of freshly-churned butter. Thank God for highlights. Faint lines were beginning to appear at the side of her eyes. She crinkled up, imagining how they would develop. Maybe she should invest in a good eye cream but usually by the time she went to bed she was too worn out to be bothered with the beauty routine.

Her breasts were, in her opinion, far too large for such a slim frame. Yet whenever she groused about the fit of her clothes Calum told her to stop grumbling because her figure was still eminently lust-worthy. Not too bad for thirty-six, he would tease. And it was true a number of people thought she and Gabriella were sisters, which annoyed the hell out of her daughter but was flattery Lizzie secretly enjoyed.

Admiration was something Lizzie had grown accustomed to, having been the object of male attention since she was a nubile fifteen-year-old. She and her mother had survived without a male influence in their lives and this affected the way she had dealt with overtures from interested boys. She had not acquired the art of flirting, as many confident young women with adoring fathers were able to do. Hers had died when she was eleven.

As her body developed and she realised what effect it had on her male contemporaries, Lizzie took refuge in banter to keep all would-be suitors at a distance. When she did relax her guard, it was to find that most of the young men were interested only in seeking a willing body rather than someone they could relate to out of bed.

At university Calum was the first who had not argued, pleaded, cajoled or tried to bully her into bed. He had played a long game, he told her later, because he had a hunch that they were going to mean something to each other. After many weeks of going to parties, barbecues, countless films and debating societies, he had earned her trust and it was Lizzie who finally made the first move, something Calum joshed her about for years afterwards.

Right from the beginning the relationship was serious and it wasn't long before they were making plans to settle down after graduation and earn money for a home. Lizzie's dream was to have a domestically tranquil life after living with a mother who seemed to have a gypsy in her soul. They had moved ten times in the years after her father's death. Lizzie would yearn to become a part of a community and not always be the new girl at school. Much as she adored having a mother who was colourful and high-spirited and totally impractical, she vowed that no child of hers would lead such a nomadic life. Calum still affectionately called her mother The Exocet because he could see her coming but could do damn-all about it. Even now she had not changed her habits but was travelling around the Far East. With her were three companions from the Welsh commune in which she had been living these past few years. They were seeking enlightenment, she told her daughter, and they had both laughed at the cliché. Nonetheless it was true.

Marriage to Calum provided the security Lizzie craved. His mother and father welcomed her into the family with enthusiasm and they quickly settled into a routine of alternate Sunday lunches at the Hampstead home of her in-laws. Lizzie enjoyed their company and the friendship deepened as the older pair began to absorb some of the strain of dealing with their sometimes rebellious granddaughter.

Lizzie often reflected how it was that Robert Lynton could be so patient with Gaby when undoubtedly he had been short-tempered with one of his own children. She had come to the conclusion that like many men he found time to enjoy the growing-up of his grandchild when previously he had been too tired and busy to bother.

Calum was sitting on the side of the bed, pulling on his socks. Not for the first time Lizzie envied his perfect feet, thinking how unfair it was that men did not have their toes tortured out of shape by so-called fashionable shoes. When pregnant she had wished fervently that their child would inherit those wonderful limbs. But Gaby had taken after her and although her legs were passable, Lizzie had always wished they were a couple of inches longer.

Calum was wearing a dark navy suit; the colour contrasted pleasingly with the reddish glints in his curly hair. He was ageing well and still trim, though a little heavier around the waist these days. Although he had given up playing for his local hockey team he liked to keep fit and still trained with them, as well as acting as their coach, umpire and fundraiser.

He brushed some imaginary fluff from the shoulders of his jacket. 'It still seems strange not to be able to phone Dad and have a laugh with him,' he sighed. 'I miss him.'

'So do I, but we were lucky he survived that long,' said Lizzie.

Calum began to comb his hair. 'I suppose the only thing I do worry about, slightly,' he said, tugging at his thick locks, trying to get them under control, 'is that wildlife sanctuary he was so keen on. I've always wondered why he became so obsessive about animals after Mum died. Did you know he once went to Shoreham to stop a shipment of lambs?'

She looked surprised. 'No, I didn't. But I do remember the fuss about the pet cemetery in the churchyard, all those signatures on the petition he collected. He very nearly persuaded the vicar to agree to have one.'

Calum laughed. 'It was a substitute for that retirement place he once talked about, near his ancestors in Inverness.' He rubbed his chin reflectively. 'I don't think he wanted to go there because he wouldn't have been able to see us as much.'

Lizzie smiled. 'I liked your dad.'

'I know you did. So did I.' Calum straightened his tie and picked up his briefcase to check whether Tess had remembered to put in the papers he needed for an afternoon meeting. Of course she had. Thank God it looked as though he wouldn't have to make her redundant.

Calum's exhibition design company had flourished in a boom year and his firm had quickly established a reputation for attracting influential buyers, drawn by imaginative displays and the possibility of top contacts. Years before, Robert Lynton had given both his sons a cash gift of one hundred thousand pounds. Calum used his legacy to start his company while Andrew had invested much of his in a high-risk overseas property development which had crashed shortly after its inception.

Since then Calum had channelled his energies into making his company one of the most creative exhibition organisers in southern Britain. In those early, heady days there had even been talk of expanding into Europe but that dream had died when a much-heralded boom had not lasted long enough to make a difference to a new company. Although Calum's firm was one of the last to feel the pinch, he had been forced to borrow several times from the bank. Under the management of almost anyone else, Premier Promotions would have gone under. Perhaps he would have had an easier time had he allowed it to but some stubborn Scottish streak ensured he kept it alive. And he was spurred on by the need to prove to his father that he was not a failure.

The bank had been co-operative, accepting the deeds of their turn-of-the-century house as collateral. But although Calum was managing to repay the overdraft interest, he was not on target to reduce the loan, although he had one or two useful contracts on the horizon.

A couple of times he had been on the brink of asking his father to bail him out. He had almost managed it one time after Sunday lunch at the family home but then his father had said, 'There's a good side to me, son, and there's a bad and somehow Andy has been unlucky enough to pick up all the faults I've tried hard all my life to squash. And then I look at you and think I've done something right.'

The old man had stoked the fire and Calum had listened patiently as he reminisced about the tough days when he had started his own engineering business, a story Calum had heard many times. How nobody had wanted to help, how he'd had to work out of a disused garage, the long hours, the cold. He could never guarantee good fortune for his children, he said, but the qualities needed to survive and prosper in life were not dependent on luck but on the courage to face problems and lick them. Then he began complaining that once again Andy was trying to touch him for money.

'Thank God you're not a parasite like your brother,' he had said grimly. 'You're like me. You want to make your own way. Sure, I gave you a helping hand to begin with, like I did with your brother, but you've achieved your success without bothering me again.'

Calum sighed, remembering it all. Well, after today he might be able to wipe out all the debts. That would be the only good thing to come from his father's sudden death.

He closed the briefcase and let his mind dwell briefly on the company's cash flow problems. Lizzie, as a shareholder, had known he was desperately worried but only recently had he told her how perilous the situation was. Pride had prevented him from confiding in her. It wasn't only the money troubles. What he had also kept hidden from Lizzie for too long was the effort it took each day to act the part of an unconcerned businessman in the office, and outside it to clients. He was able to keep the trading figures secret from the staff but of course they guessed things were bad when their biggest client went bankrupt. Then a major exhibition had been postponed for another year. Staff salaries, however, could not be postponed and the bank was becoming increasingly hard-nosed about the rapid increase in the company overdraft.

All this had left Calum feeling listless during the day and at night his sleep was plagued by dreams of being whiplashed from one crisis to another, one minute smiling at creditors, the next trying to cope with anxiety attacks. It was after a particularly bad night when he had tossed and turned for hours that Lizzie insisted he unburden himself. It was such a relief, he wondered why on earth it had taken him so long. She had not been the least critical of his actions, understanding at once the doldrums in which the industry found itself. She accepted it was not his incompetence that had caused his predicament.

When Lizzie reappeared from the bathroom, her long neck gleaming with droplets of water above the pink bathrobe, a feeling of warmth came over him. As he laid his arms on her shoulders, he detected a faint tang of peppermint. He loved the smell of her, the feel of her, everything about her, and began to fold her into his arms. She lifted her face towards him and gently he planted a kiss on her lips.

'I don't deserve you,' he whispered.

'I agree,' she said, cornflower-blue eyes shining. He kissed her again, this time more tenderly. At that moment the door was pushed open and a teenage voice erupted.

'Yuk! Kissing at this time in the morning. Disgusting.' Gabriella, her thick mane hanging like a cloud round her shoulders, stood in the doorway, making a face. She was wearing one of the two main colour schemes in her wardrobe, glossy black and matt black.

Her parents broke apart and Calum said, 'I see you've got your Spanish widow's kit on again.'

'Dad, you always say that.' Gabriella smirked at him and did a twirl, revealing a pair of finely-shaped bare legs under the folds of the long crepe skirt.

'I think you look just right for what's going on today,' said Lizzie and was rewarded by a smile.

'Make us a cup of tea, would you, pussycat?' asked Calum. 'We have to be off by ten on the dot.'

' 'Kay.' She paused in the doorway. 'Would Grandpa think I was being horrible if I asked you to guess how much he's left me?'

'No, he'd understand that you're a grasping little minx.'

'I'm not, Dad. I miss him. A lot.'

Lizzie did not doubt this was true. One of the secrets of the friendship between her daughter and Robert Lynton was that Grandpa never criticised, never judged and was somewhat amused by Gabriella's rebellious actions. He was the only one who accepted her right to wear what she wanted. This included the nose stud (which she reluctantly agreed to take out for school), the Rastafarian plaits, the enveloping widow's weeds of black calico, and the unwieldy Doc Martens. But he had earned Lizzie's undying gratitude when he had persuaded Gabriella not to have the butterfly tattoo that was the rage that week at school.

'I'm just asking,' said Gabriella, 'because I need the dosh.'

'Why?'

'Oh, things.'

'You'll have to be patient,' said Calum. 'Something you're bad at. But you'll know soon enough.'

Lizzie sat at her dressing table, putting the finishing touches to her make-up. Without looking round she said, 'Gaby, don't you think you should tie your hair back?'

'Why? I'm not at school and besides, I like it this way.'

Calum frowned. 'It's a serious occasion, Gabs. Your mother's right.'

'OK, if you think so,' she called out merrily before disappearing out the door.

Lizzie turned her palms upwards in a gesture of futility. 'One day that girl is going to do what I ask rather than you and I'll faint clean away.'

Chapter Three

Edward Foxton grimaced. This will was going to cause trouble. In the solicitor's experience it had all the ingredients for the grandmother of all battles. Self-made millionaire his client might have been but his contentious instruction that the younger son was not to be invited to the reading showed he was singularly lacking in common sense when it came to the management of his own family.

God knows he had tried hard to change the old man's mind in the cause of justice, fair play and, let's face it, a quiet life for the law firm. But there was just so much a high street solicitor could achieve with a client as stubborn as this one was. Mind, it was that obstinacy which had made him remain loyal to the company after the retirement of the senior Mr Foxton. Robert McDowall Lynton had built up his engineering company from scratch, a source of great pride, and a fact he never ceased to point out to both his sons and everyone else. His custom had stayed put even when the engineering company went public and began to make serious money. As had their legal advisers.

Edward thought back to those early days when Calum had sought his advice to start up his new company. There had been no conflict of interest in handling the legal affairs for both father and son and at least Calum hadn't tried to hang on to his father's coat tails as his brother had but managed to build up the company on his own.

Lately, Calum's business had hit hard times, and Ed Foxton had been placed in an extremely embarrassing position. Worst of all, he was unable to warn his friend and squash partner that his father's will, on which he was placing so much reliance, was not as predictable as everyone assumed.

Calum's reaction on hearing that his younger brother was to be excluded from the reading had been characteristic. 'Dad was wrong. Andy should be there. I hope the old man hasn't cut him

15

out completely. He and Edina have been through enough these past weeks.'

Edward could only bless the fact that Andrew Lynton seemed to have accepted his exclusion. He had heard nothing from him and the solicitor had to admit that doling out the bequests was going to be made much easier by the absence of the bombastic Andrew.

Edward examined the circle of faces. First to arrive were Robert Lynton's three ageing relatives. Two were cousins, the third was the husband of one of them. His gaze moved to the deceased's eldest son. They had become pals at university and had remained close ever since. Calum was sitting with his wife on his right and teenage daughter flanking his left.

Whenever he saw Lizzie, Edward found it difficult to suppress a feeling of envy. Respect and his wife's upper-crust credentials were the basis of his own marriage, which was successful enough, but oh, to wake up with Lizzie's wonderful profile on the next pillow. He shook himself. A woman that good-looking was bound to cause worry, although to be fair there'd not been a whisper about their marriage being threatened by so much as a dalliance. Pity she and Calum had only the one child. The girl had striking hair but in Edward's opinion she was a sulky little miss. The only time Edward had seen her looking anything but petulant was when she was around her grandfather. At over eighty he had never suffered a day's illness until his sudden heart attack a month ago. It had been a tremendous shock. Until the end of his life Robert Lynton had been active and still enjoyed 'a good stretch of the legs', as he called it, around the golf course. Many times he had been accompanied by his adored granddaughter Gabriella as his caddie. Amazingly, this un-sporty young girl would spend hours carrying her grandfather's clubs; she evidently enjoyed herself.

Gabriella had been inconsolable at the funeral but Edward did not approve of the way she had shoved Lizzie aside when Lizzie had tried to comfort her daughter. If she'd been his child, grief or not, she would have felt the lash of his tongue. He did not relish the thought that his own sweet little girl would be at the same difficult age in only three years' time.

He cleared his throat and the hushed talking stopped immediately.

'Robert Lynton's will was drawn up by my father, the then

senior partner, seven years ago,' he began. 'This was before his younger son's, er, transgression and the bulk of the estate was to be divided between Calum and Andrew. However, since his death I have been handed a new will.'

The assembly exchanged meaningful glances but there were no interruptions.

'This new will,' continued Edward gravely, 'was drawn up three years ago and witnessed by two people known to Robert – his daily Mrs Brenda Perkins and her husband, Malcolm, who used to do odd jobs for him.' He caught Calum's eye and removed his spectacles, a habit when he was nervous. 'I am satisfied that this document is legal though I'm bound to say the language is not as precise as I would have wished. Suffice to say, it does reflect his intentions clearly, which is what the law demands. And as those of us who saw him shortly before his sudden death can testify, Robert Lynton was, as the saying goes, of sound mind.' He paused. 'Very sound mind.' He replaced his spectacles and began reading.

'This is the last will and testament of Robert McDowall Lynton and revokes all previous wills. Firstly, I apologise to you, Edward, for keeping this will secret from you. You would have tried to dissuade me and as I have good reason for dispersing my money in this way, I did not want to waste either my time or yours with endless discussions. But I hereby appoint you sole executor which I hope will go some way to smoothing your feathers.'

There were small bequests to the deceased's two cousins and his gardener. Edward made an effort to keep his voice emotionless as he listed the items they were to inherit, old furniture which was handsome but not of the first rank, and paintings by minor artists. The announcement of this somewhat parsimonious handout was received in silence apart from some pursed lips and Edward noticed one cousin giving her husband a sideways glance. Then followed a catalogue of several small bequests to charities Robert and his late wife had favoured, plus a more sizeable amount to the Surrey Wildlife Sanctuary.

Edward took a sip of water and risked a look at Calum, admiring his outward calm, well aware of how much he was counting on his father's inheritance to rescue his company. Slowly he turned the page.

'I leave the bulk of my estate, which includes the sale of the house and my shareholdings, estimated after tax at a net total of

17

one and three-quarters of a million pounds, to my beloved granddaughter, the only grandchild I acknowledge.'

There was delight, disbelief and shock from both the beneficiary and her parents. A flush was creeping up Gabriella's freckled cheeks and she whispered to her father, 'Grandpa's leaving all his money to me? I can't believe it.'

Edward looked up from the document at Gabriella who was bouncing in her chair with excitement.

'Sorry,' she said, looking anything but repentant.

Calum's head was bowed. Lizzie sat as if made of stone, and the rest of the room was quiet, staring at the couple.

Edward had been troubled at not being able to give his friend any warning but in his opinion if Calum had been frank with his father, this would not have happened. Robert Lynton had been an idiosyncratic man, unable to see the world in anything but black and white terms. How often had Edward urged Calum to take his father into his confidence about the state the business was in? Robert had had such high expectations of his elder son; partly because of his great disappointment with the younger one, Calum had been forced into playing the part of the son who was a success.

After a silence in which Edward imagined he could hear his heartbeat, he cleared his throat and went on, 'I believe she displays great intelligence and the sort of bloody-mindedness that has stood me in good stead. But I wish to make it clear that this money is to be put in trust for her until she reaches the age of twenty-five . . .'

At this Gabriella sighed heavily and her father laid a restraining hand on her arm.

Edward raised his voice. '. . . with ten per cent to be released at the age of eighteen, on condition that she obtains a place at university. A further twenty per cent is to be given to her at the age of twenty-one, or graduation, whichever comes first.'

Edward's gaze strayed again to the young woman who appeared to cheer up at this news. No wonder the old bugger hadn't trusted him to draw up the new will. What on earth possessed him to leave such a sum to that young madam? He turned over the page and carried on.

'My elder son will be surprised and disappointed at my decision but he is well set up for life due to his excellent business acumen which, I hope I am allowed to say, he inherited from me.

However, as a token of my esteem I would like him to have the entire contents of my library and the portrait of his mother which he's always admired.'

Calum's eyes reflected his disappointment. Edward was not surprised. While Calum would no doubt be pleased to have those personal effects and the collection of travel books would be worth something, what he needed right now was cash. Lizzie had moved close enough to her husband to touch shoulders, her expression impenetrable. But for a couple who had seen their life raft snatched away, Edward thought they were putting on a good show.

'What's he say?' The voice was shrill and petulant.

'Ssh,' said the cousin.

'We'll talk about it later,' hissed her husband.

'Dad, I did hear right, didn't I?' Gabriella's usual bored drawl had vanished. 'I just can't believe it.'

Edward called for silence. 'This won't take long, I promise,' he said and continued to read. 'As most of you know, I have been sadly disappointed at the activities, both personal and professional, of my younger son Andrew who has been given all the opportunities that a good education, sound health and an attractive appearance could bestow. Despite this he has proved a bitter disappointment to his mother and me. Nor will I ever forgive him for causing what I consider her untimely death. Andrew will deny this because he blames everyone else for his faults. But he did not see her suffering as I did. She could never come to terms with his callous theft of her jewellery. I am convinced his activities curtailed her life and nothing will persuade me otherwise. Because I specifically stipulated he should not attend this reading, I have written him a letter to be delivered after my death, explaining my reasons for leaving him nothing, apart from my Jaguar. No doubt there will be some criticism of my actions. As this never bothered me in life, it will not concern me in death.'

'Typical,' sniffed one of the cousins, to which her sister nodded vigorously.

Ignoring the comment, Edward ploughed on to the end of the document. 'On the other hand my eldest son has never disappointed me. Calum, you know how much I admire the success you've made of your life and your business. At the time I said why wait until I'm dead and gone to distribute my money and I

19

commend the way you have managed my injection of start-up capital ten years ago. Unlike your brother, you have never come back and asked for more money. I want you to understand that my primary concern in leaving the rest of my estate to my granddaughter is to ensure that it will benefit the continuity of what I consider is the good bloodline of the Lynton family.'

Edward looked up and gave Calum a sympathetic glance. He watched as Lizzie gently patted her husband's arm and then the harsh sound of the intercom caused the entire assembly to flinch.

Irritably, Edward flicked the switch on his console, nervousness making him sound aggressive. 'I said I wasn't to be interrupted,' he barked.

The voice of his receptionist was hesitant. 'Yes, I'm very sorry. But they're insisting that they see you.'

'I'll come out.'

The sound of raised voices intruded from the outer office. Lizzie tensed, recognising at once the harsh baritone bellowing outside.

'What's happening?' asked one of the cousins, fiddling with her hearing aid.

'I thought there'd be trouble from Andy,' Calum muttered.

'Do you think he knows about the new will?' Lizzie whispered.

Calum lowered his voice. 'Why should he? I didn't.' He sighed. 'I wish Dad hadn't changed his mind about dividing his money between us.'

Gabriella leaned forward eagerly. 'Is there going to be a fight?'

'Ssh,' admonished her mother.

'She's right,' said Calum quietly. 'When Andy finds out Dad's left him nothing, he'll go ballistic.'

'I'm not sure you're right,' said Lizzie. 'Your father didn't speak to him for at least three years. He didn't go to his wedding, he never even set eyes on Sebastian. What else could he expect?'

'Then why is he here? People always hope, don't they?'

She shot him an ironic glance. 'Like us, you mean.'

The door burst open to reveal the rugged figure of Andrew. He paused in the doorway with a shrug of the shoulders as if to say, 'I'm here, and there's nothing you can do about it.'

To the casual eye the brothers shared few similarities, apart from the penetrating green eyes and tawny hair of their Celtic forefathers. Andrew was heavier and three inches shorter than his brother, the difference made more noticeable by the wide-shouldered suit he was wearing. In character and ability, too, they could not be more unalike; Calum was equable and self-possessed, Andrew quick-tempered and mercurial. Silhouetted behind him was a woman with a mass of blonde curls, who lifted a sleeping child to her shoulder, for all the world like a fox fur stole.

Edina sometimes gave the outward appearance of being frivolous but she had earned her spurs in Lizzie's eyes as a formidable tiger protecting her cub. Unfailingly courteous, she had been persistent in rounding up family members wherever they were living to request blood samples. She had proved an excellent bridge between the family and the hospital registrar. Lizzie admired Edina's plucky spirit and had become quite fond of her; she did not hold Edina responsible for her husband's actions.

Andrew's appearance always prefaced trouble and a current of anxiety ran through Lizzie. He had the unerring capacity to wind up most people, including his normally even-tempered brother.

'You didn't think you'd get away with this, did you?' he shouted, glowering at Calum. 'What have you and that old buzzard been plotting?'

Before Calum could reply, Edward said sternly, 'The people here were specifically invited under the terms of your father's will. You were not. The letter your father sent you explains why.'

Andrew snorted contemptuously. 'Dad had no right to do this.'

'He had every right. It was his money,' said the solicitor sharply. 'I must ask you once again to leave peacefully.'

'I refuse.'

There was an explosion of noise as the family reacted to this intransigence.

'This isn't what I wanted . . .'

'What's he say? What's he say?'

'Calm down, everyone, it won't do any good shouting.'

'Andrew, your uncle and I think this is disgraceful. You ought to be ashamed of yourself.'

Andrew surveyed the agitated faces. Ignoring the babble around him, he led his wife to a chair and they sat down. His body was relaxed though his arms were firmly folded. Sebastian started to cry and Edina began to soothe him.

Edward's law books did not offer guidance on how to deal with a situation like this and in the short silence that followed, Andrew, well versed in the politics of confrontation, seized control.

'I've no intention of leaving this room until I hear what's in my father's will, as I'm entitled to do, Foxy.' Andrew was aware Edward Foxton hated the nickname. 'There's nothing you can do or say which will make us leave. Unless you want to drag me out by force. And you'll need help with that.' Andrew flicked his hand dismissively in the direction of his brother. 'I'm as much my father's son as he is.'

'No, you're not.' One of the old dears half rose, her voice strong with indignation. 'I saw what you did to your parents, especially your mother.'

Heads nodded in agreement.

Andrew's mouth twisted as he swivelled his head towards Calum. 'Always the good boy, aren't you, big brother? The sun shone out of your bloody arse as far as Mum and Dad were concerned. Nothing I could do was ever right,' he waved in the direction of the cousins, 'for anyone in the family. And now you're sitting here getting your reward for all those years of sucking up to the old man.'

Lizzie leaned towards her husband and said quietly, 'Ed can't sort this out. You'll have to.'

Shifting his weight on the chair, Calum locked eyes with his brother. 'Andy, Dad wouldn't want us to scrap in public. We have no objection to you staying.'

'You should never have agreed to this in the first place,' Andrew replied ungraciously.

Edward hesitated but Andrew's pugnacious expression appeared to help him make up his mind. 'I would like to place on record that I am agreeing to your presence because your brother has requested it and only because of that.'

'Whatever.' Andrew uncrossed his arms, lolled back in his chair, and addressed his aunts. 'I presume you know my wife.'

'Yes,' said one. 'We met Edna at the wedding.'

'Edina,' he said sharply. 'She's called Edina now.'

That goes with the territory, thought Edward. Edna had made it clear she thought she was marrying money and didn't take it well when her husband became estranged from his family. Edward suspected she might have left Andrew long ago if it

22

hadn't been for the tragic circumstances surrounding Sebastian's birth. The infant's pale face reminded him how lucky he was with his own healthy brood.

'Is the baby all right?' shouted the deaf relative.

Edina smiled and nodded as she rocked Sebastian. He had stopped his fussing and was soon back to sleep.

'I think it's better all round if we get this over as quickly as possible,' said Edward, shifting his chair nearer the desk and wishing, not for the first time that morning, that he had taken up another career. 'For the benefit of Andrew I'll repeat that your father has left small bequests to his cousins and to the following charities—'

'Don't bother with the small change,' interrupted Andrew. 'How much does Calum rake in?'

A look of distaste passed over the lawyer's face and he explained about the change of will. Lizzie held her breath but Andrew seemed to take the news stoically.

'So in spite of me apologising, trying to make amends, the old sod never forgave me until the day he died. Well, I'm not surprised. Calum saw to that.'

'That's unfair, Andy.' Lizzie was unable to control her anger and this time it was Calum who tried to pacify her.

'Keep your hair on, Lizzie,' said Andrew, smiling at her. 'I only want to find out if I'm getting the silver or the petty cash. OK, Foxy, get on with it.'

In a clipped voice Edward summarised the contents of the will. For a second or two there was no reaction from either Andrew or his wife. Then Andrew spoke.

'Can you beat that, Edina, we get nothing except that bloody old Jag which I can't afford to run while Calum's kid cops the lot.' His voice was suspiciously soft. He seemed too calm, too relaxed for a man who had lost his share of a substantial fortune. Lizzie had been expecting rage, fury, possibly threats of litigation but not this passive acceptance.

Slowly Andrew took Edina by the elbow and urged her to her feet. The baby, awakened by the movement, began to nuzzle her neck. Lizzie pondered on how they could look so unaffected by the events of the past few weeks.

In an almost conversational tone, Andrew turned to Gabriella. 'Just because you sucked up to your grandfather when he was going ga-ga, don't think you're going to get away with this. Half

23

that money belongs to me and I'm going to take you to court, young lady. I intend to fight for my rights.'

Edina tugged at his sleeve. 'You've said enough. Let's go.'

'Said enough? I haven't even started. There's things I know, Gaby, things your parents don't want mentioned . . .'

Calum turned to Lizzie. 'Take Gaby out of here.'

'Why?' said Andrew belligerently. 'She's going to have to hear the truth sooner or later.'

Lizzie was already on her feet. She took her daughter's arm and began steering the reluctant girl towards the doorway. Edina caught Lizzie's eye and mouthed, 'I'm sorry.'

'Why have I got to go?' Gabriella protested to her father. 'I want to know what's going on.'

'Look, darling, just for once please do as we ask,' whispered Lizzie, propelling her into the reception area.

Once his wife and daughter had disappeared, Calum turned to his brother. 'Please don't try and blame my daughter. It's not her fault.'

Andrew snorted with derision. 'That's rich coming from you. All the time you've been working behind my back. You're not going to deny you cooked this up with him, are you?'

'Damn right I am. What Dad's done is as much of a shock to me as it is to you.'

'I bet,' Andrew sneered.

'At least let's discuss it. We can work out some compromise.'

'All right. Let's compromise. I want half Dad's estate.'

'He can't do that,' intervened the solicitor. 'It's not his to give.'

'You see, Edina.' Andrew pulled down the edges of his mouth, 'I can't get justice here.'

'Let's get out of here, Andrew,' said Edina.

'I haven't finished.'

'Well, you don't need me,' she said firmly. 'I'm taking the baby home.'

'OK, Sebastian's due for his medicine. I'll see you at home. This won't take long.'

Edward took the opportunity to usher the aged relatives through the door.

'Well, big brother, don't think I'm bluffing about going to court. I happen to have an excellent case.'

Edward, who had been watching this exchange with growing unease, interrupted. 'Andrew, I assure you your father's will is

24

watertight. You could spend a lot of money you don't have on legal proceedings. But in the end you will have wasted your resources. I strongly advise you to accept your father's wishes.'

'Ah, but you see, Foxy, solicitors don't always know everything.' His voice was teasing. 'Do they, Calum?'

'What are you talking about?'

Andrew leaned against the desk and folded his arms. 'So you're going to pretend ignorance, are you? Well, it's too late. I know something you've been trying to keep quiet all these years. And when I tell the world about it, it'll rip this stupid will apart.'

'Cut the crap, Andy. Whenever your back's against the wall you come up with some shock horror fairy story. What is it this time?'

'This is no fairy story.' Andrew walked back to his seat. 'Gaby isn't entitled to that money.'

Calum felt uneasy. This didn't sound like Andrew's usual bluster. 'Get to the point, Andy,' he snapped.

'Gabriella is not your daughter.'

Chapter Four

The Italian waiter's eyes lit up when the two women pushed open the glass doors. Lizzie had left a message with Foxton's receptionist to say she and Gabriella would wait at Luigi's, a restaurant nearby where the family had eaten an occasional meal.

'Table for such beautiful signorinas? Certainly, certainly, come this way,' said the waiter, waving expansively towards the dimly-lit interior.

'My husband is joining us later,' said Lizzie to his retreating back.

He pulled out a chair. 'What a pity,' he adopted a tragic expression. 'But your pretty sister, she does not have a husband, no?'

Lizzie sat down opposite Gabriella. 'She's my daughter.'

The waiter fell back in exaggerated amazement. 'I don't believe it. You look so young.' Plucking one of the roses from the vase on the table, he presented it to her, bowing low.

He was so ridiculously over the top Lizzie couldn't help laughing. She shot a sideways glance at Gabriella. Usually her daughter hated it when people mistook them for sisters. But Gabriella did not give the waiter the familiar glare and when he left them to study the menu, she made no reference to it. Lizzie surmised she was in a daze of delight because of the bounty she would receive from her grandfather.

Gabriella ordered wild smoked salmon and duckling with cherries, the most expensive items on the menu, Lizzie noticed with wry amusement. She could not remember her daughter ordering anything other than hamburgers or spaghetti bolognese before. Bypassing the starter, Lizzie, who had little appetite, opted unenthusiastically for a plate of pasta. The waiter hovered and fussed, bringing bread sticks, then water with slices of lemon, continually asking if the beautiful ladies would like wine.

'I wish he'd leave us alone,' Gabriella muttered. 'My friends

27

don't have this problem with their mothers.'

'Take no notice. He flatters all the women who come here, especially the old married ones.' Lizzie attempted to keep her voice light. When Gabriella was in one of her moods, she could be difficult to tease.

'You shouldn't smile at him so much,' said Gabriella indignantly. 'It encourages him. And besides, you're not old.'

'I feel old, I'm nearly thirty-seven.'

'In eight months,' replied Gabriella. 'How long were you married when you had me?'

Lizzie raised her glass of water to buy a little time. So far she had been able to avoid having to admit that her wedding and Gabriella's birth were only six months apart. She and Calum had been assiduous at keeping the date of their wedding vague, and luckily Gaby had never shown any interest in seeing their marriage certificate.

'Dad and I were keen to start our family straightaway,' she said carefully, 'so we could grow up with you. It's just your bad luck we didn't have a brother or sister to take the heat off you.'

The truth was she and Calum had been very keen to have another child, perhaps two, and there was a certain amount of sadness that she had not conceived again. When they first married she took every precaution to avoid pregnancy. After all, it had happened so easily and inconveniently the first time. When Gaby was five and they felt financially more secure, they decided to try for another child but without success. They had once consulted a fertility specialist who had told them nothing was physically wrong and to try, try and try again.

After another six months of trying and still no sign of getting pregnant, Calum suggested they trust to fate and get on with life. He had concentrated on the business and she had channelled her energies into continuing her interrupted education. She became a mature student and qualified as a teacher four years later.

As she squeezed another lemon onto her smoked salmon, Gabriella's good humour returned and she grinned at her mother. 'It's the most wonderful thing that ever happened to me. Isn't Grandpa a star? Oh, the things I'll be able to do now.'

Lizzie was in a quandary. Half of her was miserable for Calum and the other half was nervous for her daughter. True, she would not have to suffer the financial hardships of her peers and she would have to be guided and accept advice, something she took

28

rarely. But Gabriella was a clever girl and the money would enable her to travel, buy her own home and generally be set up for the future. The downside was that money changed nearly everybody and she and Calum would have to work hard and trust that Gabriella had inherited her father's level-headedness and her grandfather's prudence, qualities that would enable her to withstand the temptations that such wealth would place in her way.

Gabriella looked into the distance. 'I'll buy a sports car. A Jaguar S type. Wouldn't Grandpa have loved to see me driving around in that? It's only twenty-eight thousand pounds.'

'How'd you know that?'

Gabriella's eyes slid back to the menu. 'I read it somewhere,' she said vaguely, unbuttoning her fashionable thin-knit cardigan. 'I could easily afford it out of a million and three-quarters.' She added dreamily. 'Just think of all those noughts.'

While Lizzie was smiling outwardly at her euphoric daughter, her mind was still trying to come to terms with the shock of the announcement. Never once had Calum's father hinted at what he was planning. It was so unlike him not to talk about something which would change their lives so drastically. Didn't he give a thought as to how it might change Gabriella? Not having to live with her on a day-to-day basis he must not have noticed her truculence, her stubbornness. All their friends assured them that Gabriella was a victim of her hormones. But oh, how difficult it was for her parents to cope with them.

Lizzie regretted that they had not hinted at their financial difficulties. Had Robert known about the business debts she was positive the will would have been different. Grandpa had loved them both and Lizzie was certain he would not have envisaged such a future for them, beholden to a difficult daughter.

OK, there were safeguards. But try telling that to a fifteen-year-old who already had grandiose ideas. Here she was prattling on about how she would spend her money. It didn't seem to occur to her that there would be nothing in the pipeline for at least another two years, and then only if she did well with her exams and was offered a place at university. Lizzie wished with all her heart that Robert could have trusted her and Calum to distribute the money to their daughter when and how they saw fit. But he had not and they would have to learn to live with it. They could not rewrite history.

Until a couple of years ago theirs had been an idyllic trio. Gabriella had been an amenable angel until the age of fourteen and three-quarters. Lizzie remembered well the last time Gaby smiled at her with genuine affection. It was on her birthday, when with her own hands the child had created a cake of startling ugliness, with love. Lizzie was touched and decided that much though she would have liked more children, this one would be enough.

But that was the last sweet moment between mother and daughter. Almost overnight, it seemed, Gabriella transmuted into a recalcitrant voice of discord in the house. For the first few months Lizzie had tried to ignore the rudeness and hostility, as all the 'teenager from hell' books had advised, and to remain patient and loving but ultimately she gave way to her intense irritation. After the slamming of Gaby's bedroom door, which usually followed these blow-ups, Lizzie used to chide herself. Why did she always let things build up so that she exploded with rage at an inappropriate time? As she told a sympathetic Calum later after one of these spats, 'For God's sake, surely I should be able to say what I mean and talk about it instead of storing it up until there's a major Vesuvius?'

Lizzie looked at her watch. Calum would need all the support she could muster. She would never forget the look on his face as he heard the words that might spell the death knell of the company. She admired the way he had covered up his despair but she, who understood him well, saw the signs of distress, the emptiness of his gaze. The fall-out from the will would leave them financially vulnerable. But at the moment she was far more worried about whatever threat Andrew might present. Why on earth did he think he had grounds to contest the will? It was ludicrous. His father could leave his money to whoever he wanted. They had as much reason to be upset as he did.

'I could get such a nice flat,' Gabriella was saying. 'What a splash I'll cause at uni with my own Jag outside the front door.'

Lizzie roused herself. 'You did take on board what Grandpa said about waiting for the money, didn't you?'

'No probs.' Gabriella twirled her little finger round and round in the air. 'This is how I'll get money out of Edward Foxton.'

Listen to her, thought Lizzie. She needed to bring Gaby down to earth but she didn't feel strong enough right then to tackle it. Better to wait for Calum. He was much more tactful with Gaby than she was. At least the old man had been astute enough to push her in the direction of university. Lizzie clenched her fists and told herself she should not squelch her daughter's enthusiasm. This was just childish babble. So she smiled and nodded, and stirred her coffee so vigorously that it spilled over into the saucer.

Chapter Five

'Andy! Wait.' Calum ran after his brother's retreating figure, enraged that Andrew would choose to leave immediately after his extraordinary outburst.

The burly figure ignored him, continuing to hurry along the pavement in the direction of the car park. Their footsteps were the only sound on the concrete stairs as Calum followed him up to the third floor. There he found him unlocking a dark-blue BMW.

Andrew opened the door, climbed into the driver's seat then opened the window. 'Stop following me, I haven't time to discuss anything with you. I have a living to earn.' His lips twisted. 'Selling used cars may not sound much to you but it's what I do. Go away.'

Calum forced his voice into some semblance of calm. 'You can't make allegations like that and then disappear.'

Andrew started up the engine. 'Watch me.'

Calum wrenched open the passenger door and flung himself into the seat. 'Look, I know you're disappointed about the money but a court action only makes lawyers happy. We're still family.'

His brother leaned back and slung his arm over the back of Calum's seat. 'Haven't seen much of the family this past year. Been on my uppers too. I'd have liked some support from this wonderful family.'

'We're all supporting you, trying to help Sebastian.'

'Leave him out of it.' Andrew took his arm away and adjusted his seat belt.

'I can understand you feeling bitter against Dad but why drag Lizzie and Gabriella into it?'

Andrew put the car into gear. 'You'll find out soon enough. Look, get out. I told you I haven't time to talk.'

'No,' said Calum firmly. 'I'm coming with you.'

'Have it your own way,' said Andrew. He drove the car at

33

dizzying speed down the narrow inclines of the car park towards the exit. Outside, with Calum breathing in relief that they had made it in one piece, Andrew manoeuvred the vehicle towards the garage opposite and into the 'Eazi Wash 'n' Dry' cavern.

'Got a fiver on you?'

Seething, Calum fished in his pocket and proffered a ten pound note which his brother handed to the attendant.

The woman smilingly passed Andrew a ticket which he keyed into the car-wash machine. He swiftly pocketed the five pound change she handed him and drove into the car wash cave until the front wheels hit the front barrier. Almost instantaneously the huge roller brushes whirred into life and started to move, enveloping the bonnet and snaking around the sides while water and a thick covering of soap suds rained down on the car.

Calum sat, silent, almost unaware of his surroundings. It was hard luck that Andrew was cut right out of the old man's estate and for once Calum completely agreed with his brother. He was hardly thrilled that the old man's fortune was going to his daughter. When the words had first been spoken by Edward he'd thought he must have misheard, missed some vital part of the sentence. He could hardly take it in. He'd been coasting the last few weeks, relying on being bailed out of trouble, and dared not speculate what would happen to the company. All the dreams he had begun to allow himself for paying off his creditors and perhaps expanding to America, where real growth lay, were vanishing into dust.

But really, Andy could hardly have expected to benefit from his father's largesse. The theft of his mother's jewellery had been bad enough but then his father had actually reported Andy to the police as a common criminal. Calum had disagreed with his father's actions and pleaded with the old man to keep it in the family. But his father had been adamant that Andy had to be taught a lesson he would not forget.

Calum could still remember every detail of that terrible scene outside the magistrate's court where, among other things, Andrew had accused his father of hating him and of always favouring Calum. His mother had broken down in court and never really recovered. The case had made headlines in the local paper and Andrew, who had turned self-righteous indignation into an art form, blamed the subsequent failure of his property business on that.

34

Afterwards he tried to make peace by saying the experience had made him a reformed character and that his father had done the right thing. But this made no difference to Robert Lynton. The mere mention of his younger son made him so angry, the family was afraid he would burst a blood vessel. He never spoke to Andy again and after his wife's death even Calum gave up trying to persuade the old man to forgive and forget.

Robert Lynton's death had taken them all by surprise. Andrew did not turn up at the family home in Hampstead until the day of the funeral. And afterwards none of them had heard from him until the awful day when Edina visited them one by one to beg them to donate a blood sample because her baby needed an immediate bone marrow transplant. They had all agreed immediately.

The younger members of the family were tested first. Apparently if a match was found amongst one of them it was more likely to be accepted by the baby's immune system. For once Gabriella had been co-operative, volunteering to go to the hospital as soon as it was suggested. Calum had been quite proud of how brave she had been. Not once had she complained about the procedure, though she hated needles.

Why the hell should his brother question her paternity? Calum moved his hand over his chin as he watched the soap spurt all over the windscreen. Andrew was a thief, a conman and disloyal but no one could ever accuse him of being a fool. What was he trying to achieve by peddling a fact which could so easily be proved false?

Andrew seemed to read his thoughts. 'You're wondering how I know, aren't you?'

'Know what?' Calum parried.

'Don't be smart. What I can't work out is, did Lizzie tell you before the marriage or after? And did she tell you who Gabriella's father is? Anyone I know?'

Calum took a deep breath and told himself to keep calm. 'I'm trying to work out what you hope to gain with this farfetched story. Of course Gaby's mine. I was there when she was born.'

His brother gave a harsh snort. 'But were you there when she was conceived?'

Calum did not trust himself to speak.

Andrew clicked his fingers, 'Of course. You and Lizzie got

35

married because she was pregnant, didn't you? My God, you were trusting.'

At this Calum felt an overwhelming urge to strike his brother. Hard. As far back as he could remember, he had been the conciliator of the family, the one who interceded with his parents on Andrew's behalf, who mediated between his warring wife and daughter, who acted as peacemaker between employees and clients. At school a teacher had once written on a report, 'Take the "u" out of Calum's name and that's your son in a nutshell, a good influence on his classmates.' But right now he felt capable of actually harming his brother. He forced himself to think rationally. What Andy was alleging was offensive but this was surely the act of a desperate man. He was talking hogwash.

The windscreen suddenly cleared and a blast of air heralded the wax coating. Calum tried to make his voice as non-combative as he could. 'Suppose we stop this fencing and you tell me what you know?'

'Show you the cards in my hand?' Andrew's tone was scornful. 'I wouldn't have thought that was a good strategy, would you? No, it's for me to know and for you to find out.'

The green light came on to indicate the end of the wash programme and Andrew began to ease the BMW forward, past the rows of petrol pumps to the garage exit.

'This is where you get out.' He leaned over to open the passenger door. 'I have to meet a prospect who's going to hand over some cash for this little number so I'll see you in court, big brother, and may the best man not win.'

The tyres squealed as he put his foot hard on the accelerator and it was some time before Calum could get the sound of that jeering laughter out of his mind.

Chapter Six

In the restaurant Lizzie was saved from having to negotiate a trip through a conversational minefield with her daughter by the arrival of a steely-faced Calum. As soon as he sat down the waiter, less expansive this time, approached. Waving aside the menu, Calum ordered a Scotch, then called after him, 'Make that a double.' Catching sight of his wife's surprised expression he added, 'It's been tough.'

'On a scale of one to ten?'

'Off the board.'

They exchanged the kind of glance that long-married couples do not have to translate; they would discuss the events of the day in private, without their daughter eavesdropping.

Gaby, who was daintily spooning out the last drops of her Belgian chocolate milkshake, jumped right in. 'Uncle Andy's not going to try and take my money away from me, is he?'

'We won't let him. Don't worry.' Calum's breathing was laboured. Lizzie had rarely seen him so out of sorts. She attempted to lighten the atmosphere.

'Your daughter's spent half the money already.'

'Yes, I'm going to buy Mum a whole new wardrobe of designer clothes. And what about a new car, Dad? Yours is past it.'

'Is that in addition to the flat and the Jag?' teased her mother.

'But it's not going to be all for me,' retorted Gaby. 'I have a friend I want to help as well.'

'What friend?' asked Lizzie.

'Oh, just somebody.'

Calum frowned. 'Your life's going to be exactly the same for the foreseeable future, young lady. No more money, in fact probably less. It'll take a long time for Grandpa's money to come through. Legal stuff takes forever. So don't start spending anything yet.'

Gaby pouted. 'Whenever anything nice happens you always

have to spoil it. I'm sure if I ask Mr Foxton I could get something, sort of on account.'

'Don't you dare try that.' Calum sounded harsher than he had ever been with his daughter and his glowering expression made Lizzie wonder how her husband would cope with the blow his father had dealt him.

'I will if I want to,' Gaby flared up. 'It's my money. You always try and run my life. This is one time when you won't be able to. Grandpa wanted me to have the money, not you.'

Calum beckoned to the waiter for the bill, and so furious was his expression that Gaby involuntarily hunched back into her seat. Lizzie's heart banged away in her rib cage.

'Don't speak to me like that,' Calum said fiercely to his daughter. 'Ever. Do you understand?'

It was so unlike him that Gabriella was stunned into silence. She nodded and hastily put on her cardigan.

Calum softened. 'Sorry, darling. I'm a bit wound up.' He paid the bill and followed them out of the restaurant.

During all the traumas with her daughter Lizzie had often been thankful that she could rely on Calum to keep a cool head and a moderate tone but today he appeared to have reached the limit of his patience. It was a tense trip home, not a word was exchanged with their daughter. She sat, arms tightly folded, staring out of the passenger window for the entire journey. They managed to find a parking spot in the narrow street not far from the house and as soon as Calum unlocked the door, Gaby went up the stairs three at a time and slammed her bedroom door so hard the noise reverberated throughout the house.

'I don't know how that door stays on its hinges,' said Lizzie, a remark that usually made her husband smile. This time there was no response. Calum stalked into the kitchen where he sat down heavily at the table. He looked at her miserably.

'The whole thing's gone pear-shaped.'

'What happened?' asked Lizzie, picking up a watering can to attend to the plants on the window sill.

'Andy made a very odd allegation.'

'About what?'

'About Gaby not being my daughter.'

Lizzie set down the watering can. 'That's ridiculous.'

'I told him that but he insists she's not mine.'

Lizzie pulled a face. 'Darling, what's he on about? You've been

38

my only lover since we met.' She came over to him and pinched his nose. 'More's the pity.'

Calum sighed but did not return her smile. He trusted Lizzie but felt depressed, weighed down by the conversation with his brother.

'Didn't you ask him why he was making up such a stupid story?'

'I tried. But he was at his most evasive.'

'Calum. Look at me. You didn't for one moment believe him, did you?'

'Of course I didn't.'

'Who told him such a thing anyway?'

'I have no idea, but he must believe he stands some chance of getting his hands on Dad's money. Why else is he going to contest the will?'

'What? Drag us through court? He's never going to do that. It's all bluff.' Absently Lizzie removed a dead leaf from a white hydrangea. 'He'd have to produce cast-iron proof that Gaby was not your child, and therefore not Robert's bloodline, and he won't be able to do that.'

'He says he can.'

'That's rubbish.'

Calum gulped down the remains of his tea and picked up his jacket from the back of a chair. 'I'll be back as soon as I can.'

She looked at him in surprise. 'You can't just go off and leave like that. We have things to talk about, like the will.'

He pointed out that it was Tuesday and she replied tartly that she was well aware of the day of the week. 'Couldn't you get out of the hockey meeting for just one week?'

He shook his head decisively. 'Can't. I'm chairing it and we're playing at the weekend and several of the players are injured.'

Lizzie was irritated. Where were his priorities? There was a mutinous child upstairs, she had not recovered from the disappointment of the will and all he could think about was going to choose a hockey team.

'It's what I need at the moment,' he said. 'It'll take my mind off things.'

'Don't worry about me. I'll get on with my darning.'

He could not help but smile. Lizzie's domestic skills were not her forte. If cajoled she would sew on a button but that's where it ended.

'Just as well you're good in bed.' He gave her a lopsided grin and she relented.

Bloody hockey. What had started out as a favour to the local club, helping out with coaching as an ex-college player, had turned into an obsession. And she was the one who had encouraged him, thinking that it would do him good to get out into the open air, away from stuffy offices and overheated hotels. She compensated by going to a film club with her best friend, Sarah, who shared her passion for 1940 musicals. That was six years ago and his enthusiasm was unabated. Now head coach, organising the team ate up most of his leisure hours and took over nearly every Saturday in the season, every Tuesday night and occasionally one other night. At first Lizzie had cheered the team from the sidelines but soon discovered that hockey was absorbing only if you were a player. Lately she had begun to resent his commitment. On the nights he was not at the club he was on the phone, cajoling some players, encouraging others, explaining why a particular person was not on the team. He had been approached to serve on some committee they were setting up and had instantly agreed.

Bloody hockey. He could think of little else.

When Calum returned home later that night, Lizzie was already peacefully asleep in the Victorian four-poster they had purchased as a tenth wedding anniversary gift to each other. As he lay next to his wife, Calum's mind was churning over everything but the impending hockey match.

The dark green digital numbers on the clock showed it was 12.14 and he could hear the rhythmic pattern of her breathing. She was in her customary foetal position, her back towards him, and he turned his head, watching her for a while. Could anyone relax so completely if they had a secret guilt? Of course not.

Calum had placed his trust in Lizzie from the beginning and had never had cause to deviate from that trust. Nor had he given her cause to doubt him. He recalled the brief holiday they had spent apart a couple of weeks before they married. Friends had joked that at twenty-one he should make the most of his freedom. 'You have fifty years of sleeping with the same woman ahead of you,' was the way they put it. After a particularly liquid party he had almost succumbed to temptation. But somehow when it came to the actual deed he had stared down at the inviting body stretched out on the bed waiting for him and couldn't do it. Part of the problem was the effect of alcohol and the other was a sudden realisation of how he would feel if Lizzie was being unfaithful on her holiday.

He had drawn back, made some excuse about brewer's droop to the bewildered young woman and had walked along the beach until dawn, recognising how much he loved Lizzie. He was glad she was pregnant, he wanted their baby and was looking forward to the wedding ceremony when they could commit to each other officially.

But here, in the quiet of the night, with his brother's accusations threatening to overwhelm him, a disloyal thought persisted: could his darling Lizzie have given herself to someone else after she had started sleeping with him? Immediately he answered his own question, absolutely not.

Calum turned over, trying to compose himself for sleep and hating himself for allowing Andy's poison to affect him.

When she heard her father come into the house after his hockey meeting, Gabriella forced herself to wait, watching the hand of the clock as it moved with agonising slowness round the dial. He seemed to take an age preparing for bed. She could hear the low hum of the bathroom shower well past midnight.

After another half an hour she judged it safe to move and flung off the duvet. She was already fully dressed and with boots in hand she tiptoed past her parents' bedroom and down the stairs, cursing each one that creaked.

It had been easy to get out of supper by claiming the lunch as an excuse. Anyway, they were used to eating without her. She had waited until she was certain her mother was asleep before risking a call on the hall phone. Cupping her hand over the receiver, she jiggled with impatience, waiting for the phone to be picked up.

As always when she heard his voice, Gabriella lost the indifferent tones she tried so hard to foster and changed into an excited young woman rather than the bored teenager who lolled around the house.

'I've got the money.' There was a pause. 'I'm not kidding. My grandfather's left me all his cash.' Gabriella was sure that somehow she would be able to get her hands on at least a small part of Grandpa's inheritance. She wasn't asking for much but hell, more than a mill, they could surely give her a little something up front.

After more whispers she had replaced the phone, her face alight. Then she had gone back to her room to wait until she thought her father was asleep. She didn't want to bump into him on her way out of the house.

She paused at the front door, every nerve straining into the silence, half expecting one of her parents suddenly to make an appearance and ask where the hell she was going at this time of the night. They would be furious with her if they caught her but however angry they were they couldn't take the money away. And she hadn't seen him for ages. She wouldn't be long, she'd be back before they missed her.

Gingerly she put her hand on the latch and turned it with infinite care until she could tug open the door. On the front step, she hastily pulled on her boots then with her knee pressed against the door, pulled it cautiously towards her until she heard it click shut.

Edina never thought the day would come when she'd be pleased Sebastian was in hospital. He had been so lethargic in the solicitor's office, sleeping through those heated conversations. Later that afternoon his temperature had risen and the doctor decided to keep him in overnight for observation. Normally she would have stayed with him but the doctor had taken one look at her exhausted face and insisted that her husband take her home to have a good night's rest. She would need all her strength, he said, when the child came out of hospital the next day.

On the way to their flat in Crouch End, in one of London's northern suburbs, Andy had stopped to buy an Indian takeaway. Instead of sitting in front of the TV to eat it, as happened often these days, she had taken some trouble in setting the table. First to come out of their box was a pair of silver candlesticks, little used wedding gifts. Then she'd arranged the delicious collation of dishes on a serving platter which she placed between the lighted candles. Andy seemed to enter the spirit of this unusual evening and put on their favourite CD, a selection of Frank Sinatra ballads.

Halfway through the meal she was feeling so relaxed she thought she'd suggest they go to bed and make love when she noticed Andy had stopped eating. Good God, his eyes were brimming with tears.

Edina laid down her cutlery quietly. She had rarely seen him emotional, let alone weep, but experience had taught her that if she asked questions he would clam up.

'He never loved me,' Andy was murmuring, half to himself. 'I know I did wrong. I told him a hundred times I wished I hadn't taken the stuff but he never believed me. Never understood what drove me to it.' His eyes were guilt-shadowed. 'When I went and saw Mum that last time, she didn't blame me for her illness. She forgave me but he . . .' Andrew brushed his hand angrily over his eyes to wipe away the tears. 'Till his last day he said it was because of me that she'd died before her time. How do you think that made me feel? I loved my mother.'

He leaned an elbow on the table, forehead on his hand, so she could not see his face. When he did look up, his expression was so miserable she left her chair and knelt down by his side, squeezing his arm. It was better to say nothing and let him pour it all out.

'What he said in that letter was cruel but at least we were the only ones reading it,' he said, his voice stronger. 'Then he had to put it all in his will, didn't he, so he could tell all the family exactly what he thought of me.' Andrew clenched his teeth for a moment. 'Couldn't he, just this once, leave me to think that maybe, just maybe, he loved me a little? No, he had to bang that on the head.'

Edina did not know what to say. Andrew had insisted they all go to the solicitor's office and when she'd asked what good it would do, he'd replied, 'It's easy to demonise me when I'm not there.'

'Imagine the vindictiveness of a man who says Gabriella is the only grandchild he acknowledges,' he said now, sounding choked. 'He never saw Sebastian, was never interested enough.'

Edina pointed out that his father had died a few weeks before Sebastian's illness was diagnosed. 'I'm sure he would've come round to visit us when he found out,' she said.

'Don't kid yourself. Not that man.'

Privately, Edina was inclined to agree. When Sebastian was born, Andrew's mother had come to see them but Robert Lynton had remained implacable. Edina had never set eyes on him.

Andrew pushed away from the table and began to stride

around the small flat. 'I meant it, you know. I'm going to fight that bloody will. Gabriella's not his granddaughter and she's not entitled to anything.'

'Oh, Andy, is that wise? It'll cost money and—'

'There are ways, Edina. You leave it to me. Not all solicitors are like Eddie Foxton. I've found one who'll do it on a no win, no fee basis. I've already talked to him informally.' He clenched his fists. 'I'm not going to let them get away with it. The solicitor reckons if this will isn't allowed because Gabriella has no Lynton blood, then the court will say Dad died intestate. That means they'll divide all his property and money between Calum and me, which is exactly what Dad was going to do in his original will. So that's what I'll accept. And nothing else.'

Edina recognised the set of his face. He'd had the same determined expression the night he'd returned from telling his parents they were going to be married. His mother had been ill and there had been a scene with his father. If Andy thought his father would relent and come to their wedding, he was wrong. Calum, his family, and a couple of second cousins had attended. Robert Lynton and his wife had not. Since then there had been minimal contact.

Now Andrew was taking on the family again. This time through the courts. Edina began to clear the table and stack the dishes, aware there was nothing she could say to deviate him from a path which could only widen the rift.

The following morning Calum lathered his chin vigorously and gave himself a lecture.

Get a grip on things. Your wife of nearly sixteen years has never given you a moment to doubt her, she's been supportive and truthful. And opposite her is your brother, a proven liar. Whose word are you going to take?

Not content with wanting to disinherit Gaby, Andy was trying to drive a wedge between himself and Lizzie. Calum sighed. He remembered good times with his brother, when they were relaxed enough to share a joke or two. Why was that side of Andy's personality so absent these days? But the most important thing in his life was his relationship with Lizzie and he was not going to allow his brother to spoil that. He and Lizzie would have to talk to Edward as soon as possible. He might have some idea what lay behind Andy's accusation.

So why was he feeling miserable when it was straightforward enough? Calum rinsed the foam off his face and dabbed himself dry. He had spent a fitful night and by the time he awoke, Lizzie was already up. The aroma of fresh coffee drifted up the stairwell and after dressing hurriedly he went down to find her in the kitchen.

The sun was shining in from three sides and Calum remembered with affection the day they had decided this was their house. It had dry rot and suspect plumbing but when Lizzie pointed out that they would always have a bright welcoming kitchen, even in winter, they bought it.

Calum kissed the top of her head and picked up a mug of coffee. Automatically she separated the sports section from her newspaper and handed it to him. They sat for a moment or two in companionable silence before he looked up and asked, 'Is the monster up yet?'

'Are you kidding? That girl can sleep for Britain.'

'I used to at her age.'

'Calum, you always stick up for her.'

'I didn't yesterday.'

'I have a nasty feeling that yesterday was just a small hint of what we can expect. We'll have fewer sanctions than we do now. At least we were able to keep her under some kind of control with the threat of cutting off her allowance.'

'She doesn't get a sniff of the money for three years. We have some time to sort her out.'

'Don't kid yourself. She's a wily one, your daughter.'

'Oh, so she's *my* daughter, is she?'

'Well, that's something she gets from you. She's grown up an awful lot this last year.'

'Don't be too hard on her. She wants to be independent.'

'You're defending her again.'

'I'm trying to be fair.'

'You don't see the way she treats me when you're not around. Sometimes she looks as though she hates me. And I don't know what I've done, Calum.'

His shrug was accompanied by a look heavenwards. 'You know teenagers.'

'If someone says that one more time to me or that it's all hormones, I'll scream.'

'Come on, you don't usually let her get you down.'

'You know what,' said Lizzie, buttering a piece of toast and handing it to him. 'I can't say I give a toss that your father didn't leave his fortune to you. We've always managed somehow. But I sure as hell worry what effect it's going to have on that young lady upstairs.'

Calum looked at his watch. 'Do you think we should get her up and have a chat? I'll go with a peace offering, a nice cup of coffee,' he said, and put the kettle on.

'My God, you're brave.'

'I still think it's best to operate on the drip drip principle. One day she'll turn human.' He made the coffee and grinned at Lizzie. 'She's an heiress now and we'll need someone to look after us in our old age.'

As she stirred her coffee, Lizzie reflected that because of his good-tempered approach Calum often acted as a buffer between his two warring women. Perhaps the books were right and Gaby did see her mother as a rival for her father's affections.

She was idly scanning the paper for that night's television programmes when there was a shout from the top of the stairs.

'Lizzie, she's not here.'

Lizzie rushed to the hall and peered up the stairwell.

'There's no sign of her.' Calum turned and went back into Gaby's room. It was impossible to tell from the state of her bed whether she had slept in it or not. As usual the carpet was covered in discarded clothes, reflecting the daily frenzied activity of a teenager unable to decide what to wear. Lizzie joined him.

'Perhaps she got up before us,' suggested Calum, only to meet Lizzie's sceptical gaze. 'What are you thinking?' he asked. 'That she crept out last night when we were asleep?'

'It's possible.'

'But even she wouldn't stay out all night without letting us know.'

'I'm not so sure. This could be her way of showing us that the money has already given her the freedom to do what she wants.'

Calum said quietly, 'We'll have to put her right about that. We'd better ring round and see if she's with any of her friends.'

Gabriella frequently entertained a legion of friends at home, the chief of these being Natasha Sinclair, the eldest child of Lizzie's best friend. She was their first line of inquiry but they met with a negative response. Natasha suggested they try one or two other good friends, but when they did, these teenagers claimed not to have seen Gabriella socially for weeks. That set off more alarm bells.

Lizzie sat back, her mouth dry, trying to keep a sense of proportion. They had drawn a complete blank and Lizzie tried to quell the frightening thoughts that crowded in on her. Recently a teenage girl had been murdered after a particularly savage sexual attack only a few yards from her home.

'Don't let's go off the deep end,' said Calum as she confessed her fears. 'There's probably a perfectly logical explanation. Just because the kid doesn't confide in us where she's off to doesn't mean she's not safe.'

Part of her agreed with him. She told herself that murders made front-page news because they were so rare. She was overreacting. Nevertheless, even at her worst moments Gaby had always checked with them when she wanted an overnight stay.

After another hour of not being able to settle to anything, Calum opened a bureau drawer in the sitting room and began to search through it.

'What are you looking for?'

'That photograph of Gaby we took at your cousin's wedding.'

Her hand went to her mouth. 'So you do think something's wrong?'

'No, no,' he said at once. 'But I think we ought to phone the police as a precaution and if we want them to search for her they have to know what she looks like.'

When they finally made contact with the police they received a sympathetic response and were assured that they had done the right thing in reporting her absence. After outlining what had gone on over the last couple of days and how it had caused a family row, the duty police officer said, 'I'm a dad myself. My guess is she's probably trying to teach you a lesson but we don't mind if we're wasting our time. Can't be too careful with a fifteen-year-old.' He took down the numbers of the friends they had already contacted, saying that the police were not as easy to fob off as parents. 'We'll get onto it right away. We'll contact you at home as soon as we have any news.'

During the fraught hours that followed, every time the phone rang they both sprang to the receiver but all the calls were in connection with Calum's business or from friends. By the time it was dark, all pretence of being unconcerned was abandoned.

47

They made endless cups of coffee which were left unfinished, unable to concentrate on anything.

'Surely she would've phoned by now.' Calum was pacing up and down the kitchen.

'If she was able to,' Lizzie said before she could stop herself.

The arrival of two uniformed police constables, one a woman, sent a spurt of panic through them.

'Oh God, has something happened to her?' asked Lizzie. But the officers quickly reassured her that they had no news and this was normal procedure and they were only in the house to search Gaby's bedroom. They were looking for anything that could help them find her. An entry in a diary, a scrawled note, anything that might give a clue to her whereabouts. They were also looking for evidence of drugs though they omitted to mention this to the agitated parents.

Lizzie hovered behind the police officers as they roamed around Gaby's room. She felt embarrassed about the debris. Downstairs, Calum stationed himself at the living room window, peering out into the street.

The officers found nothing they considered would help the search. Partly to delay them so she could have the opportunity to ask more questions, Lizzie offered them a cup of tea. She was about to pour out the first cup when she heard the roar of a powerful engine at the gate. Calum let out a bellow.

'There she is.'

Lizzie and the officers raced to the window to see Gabriella in the lamplight shaking her hair free from a yellow crash helmet, her leather-trousered legs swinging over the pillion of a large motorbike.

At the sight of her parents standing at the window, she gave a defiant shrug and turned her back on them to begin an animated conversation with her helmeted companion. His lanky figure was enveloped in the black leather uniform of the biker, his face masked by his helmet.

Lizzie made for the door fuelled by a mixture of anger and relief.

'We've been worried out of our minds. Where have you been?'

Gabriella looked over her shoulder at the police officers silhouetted in the doorway. 'Why are they here?'

Calum appeared at Lizzie's side. 'Go inside this minute, I want some answers from you.' He gestured towards the biker who had retreated and looked as though he was about to start up his machine. 'And you too, young man.'

Gabriella shot her father a frightened glance. Then she took the biker by the hand and brushed past him. Lizzie fought down a desire to shake her daughter by the shoulders. It would do no good at all to lose her temper but by God it would help her cope.

The woman police officer caught Lizzie's elbow. 'I think it's best if I talk to your daughter on her own.' When Lizzie looked uncertain she added quietly, 'If you're there she'll tell me what she thinks you want to hear.' After a moment's hesitation, Lizzie nodded.

The young people slumped down on the sofa, apparently unconcerned as the two police officers and the parents formed an uneasy circle round them.

'I suggest you take your helmet off, sir,' said the policeman. 'This could take a while.'

Reluctantly the young man pulled at the visor and took it off. They all watched in silence as he heaved off his gloves.

He was certainly a most striking-looking man with a fine physique but in Calum's view his appearance was marred by the sullenness of his expression. He was around eighteen or so, too old for his daughter, Calum thought. The youth slouched on the sofa, arms folded, long legs akimbo.

The woman police officer shepherded Gabriella into the kitchen, explaining that her mother had given permission for her to be questioned. The other officer asked the biker to go with him to the dining room. After about fifteen minutes, Gabriella emerged. Lizzie heard the woman officer say, 'So I can assume that you haven't been held against your will.'

Gabriella gave her a startled look. 'Course not. He's my boyfriend.'

'Could we be introduced to him, do you think?' asked Calum.

At that moment the dining room door opened and the young man stepped out. The police officer who had questioned him said that he was persuaded no crime had been committed and that this now ceased to be police business.

The youth went to sit down on the sofa once again and Gaby immediately placed herself beside him and laid her hand casually on one of his thighs. Lizzie could feel her face burn and she noticed Calum clenching his fists but the biker gave no sign he noticed anything amiss.

49

'This is Luke,' said Gabriella in an offhand manner. The young man gave a barely perceptible nod in their direction, making no attempt at a polite smile.

Despite strictures to herself to keep calm and give them a chance to explain, Lizzie could feel her anger growing.

'I think we can handle this from now on,' Calum said to the officers.

'Thank you,' said Lizzie, 'and we apologise for putting you to all this trouble and wasting your time.'

The policewoman reassured them that they didn't mind, it was their job and they were glad that Gabriella had come home.

The policeman turned to Luke. 'Can I trouble you to show the papers for that motorbike, sir?'

The young man sighed, lazily unzipped his leather jacket and handed over his licence.

The policeman took some notes before handing it back. 'Thank you, sir,' he said.

Calum showed the officers out. On the doorstep the policeman confided that he would check on the name to see if the youth had any form. 'Just to know who your daughter is hanging round with, sir,' he said blandly. 'After all, she is under-age and if you're worried about anything at all and want to take it further, please feel free to talk to us.'

Calum thanked him but said he didn't think that would be necessary and immediately returned to the sitting room.

Lizzie's eyes were blazing. 'She's offering no apologies for scaring us out of our wits. No explanation about where she's been.'

'Where were you all night?' Calum demanded.

'Were you with him?' Lizzie burst out.

'What if I was?' Gaby folded her arms across her chest. The truth was, she hadn't meant to stay out all night, but had fallen asleep on Luke's sofa.

'You're only fifteen and still in our charge,' said Calum with heat. 'Why did you do it? You knew there'd be trouble.'

'You were horrible to me and I wanted to talk to Luke.' She moved closer to the boy. 'You're so old-fashioned,' she said, a note of asperity in her voice. 'Now I have Grandpa's money I can live the way I want. No stupid curfews. No going on all the time about taking drugs . . .'

'Are you?' asked Lizzie abruptly.

'That's my business.'

'No, it's not,' snapped Calum. 'While you're under this roof you'll obey our rules. So we'll have no more of this nonsense.'

Lizzie could not contain herself any longer. 'Did you sleep with him?'

Luke's arm stretched lazily across the back of the sofa and he lifted up his eyes. 'Nothin' happened,' he drawled.

'Where was she?'

'At my place,' he said.

'Then why didn't you come home? Or at least phone?'

Gabriella sat, lips clenched, silent, and Luke replied, 'She fell asleep, then she said it was too late and she'd get into terrible trouble.'

Lizzie was struck by Luke's blank expression, no guilt, no fear or reaction of any kind.

Calum walked across to the sofa and looked down at his daughter's rebellious face. 'Fell asleep? That's no excuse after you sneaked out in the middle of the night. Do you realise what we've been through? The worry you've caused your mother?'

When Gabriella did not answer Lizzie snapped, 'She's not interested in how we feel, she's only concerned about her precious money. Did you realise she's already promised him some?'

'What? But it's not yours to give yet.' Calum felt a sense of foreboding. The damn will was already causing trouble for this family without a penny of the money being released yet.

'That's what you say,' retorted Gabriella. 'But the money belongs to me and I'm sure I can get some of it. Luke's got a band and he needs studio time for a demo tape. You don't get anywhere without one. And it only costs two thousand pounds.'

Lizzie couldn't contain herself. 'Two thousand pounds?'

'Haven't you been listening?' Calum raised his voice. 'You can't have any of it for *years*!'

Gabriella was unmoved by her parents' outrage. 'Luke's been trying to raise the money for ages,' she said almost conversationally. 'Haven't you, Luke?' He merely compressed his lips and gave an almost imperceptible nod. 'He's been promised studio time because of a cancellation but he needs cash up front. You could lend it to him, couldn't you, Dad? Then I'll pay you back.'

'Why on earth would I bankroll somebody I don't even know?'

'You don't know him but I do,' Gaby retorted. 'We've been going out for three weeks and two days. Luke's mega-talented

51

and he's very clever too. It's an investment. His group will definitely make it and then he'll be able to pay the money back. In buckets.'

Luke sat motionless, his blank expression unchanged.

'Even if I had the money, and I don't, if you think I'd lend it for something like this you're crazier than I thought,' said Calum sourly.

'You two always say no to me,' shouted Gabriella. 'I can do nothing right. This is the one thing in my life I really want. All I'm asking is that you lend it to me. You'll get your precious money back.'

'The answer's definitely no,' said Lizzie.

'If he knew what it was for, Grandpa would want me to have it.' Gaby was beginning to sound tearful.

'Your grandfather worked damn hard to make his money,' said Lizzie. 'He wouldn't want you to waste it on airy-fairy schemes.'

This roused the youth to action. 'So I don't get the money?'

Husband and wife spoke in unison. 'Absolutely not.'

Slowly Luke hauled himself to his feet and made for the door, with Gabriella close behind him.

'Don't worry,' she said to his retreating back, 'I promise I'll get it for you somehow. I will.'

A few moments later they heard the sound of the front door closing.

A white-faced Gabriella reappeared. 'I hope you're satisfied. He'll probably bust up with me over this and it'll be all your fault.'

'If he was going around with you because of money, he's not worth it anyway,' said Calum. Then, always the peacemaker, he added, 'Look, if we'd had the chance to get to know him we might've helped. Why didn't you bring him round?'

'Because I knew what you'd say when you saw him. You're both such snobs.'

'That's unfair,' said Calum. 'And you know it.'

'You hate black people,' said Gaby.

'What have we ever done to make you say that?' asked her mother indignantly.

'You always say you're not prejudiced but do you have any black friends? No.'

'Only because it hasn't happened. It's not deliberate,' Lizzie replied.

Gaby began to cry. 'Luke's kind and good and he's always been there for me. And now you've ruined it.'

Calum rolled his eyes at Lizzie.

'I hate you both!' The words were spat out. 'I hope Luke makes me pregnant, then I'd have an excuse to get out of this dump.' With that she wrenched open the door and ran up the stairs before either of her distressed parents could stop her.

Lizzie sat on the sofa, her head in her hands.

'She's not sleeping with him, is she?' Calum asked, his face anguished. 'The boy said nothing happened. Can we believe him? What were they doing all night?'

Lizzie chose her words carefully, mindful that this would be an unpalatable idea for a doting father. 'I don't know if they had sex. It's possible but it could be bravado, that crack about getting pregnant.' She had a sudden thought. 'I hope she's on the pill.'

'Oh my God. Isn't she too young for that kind of thing?' asked Calum hotly. He stood up and poured himself a whisky. 'She's growing up too fast for my liking.'

'It's our fault,' said Lizzie. 'We've babied her a bit. That's the problem with an only child, and fifteen's quite grown-up these days.'

Calum pushed his hair off his forehead. 'How do we deal with this? She must realise she can't roam about London all night without permission.'

They sat in silence, brooding.

'What if we sit her down and talk to her like an adult.' His voice trailed off.

'Calum, don't you think I've tried? Many times. She freezes me out.'

'Maybe I should have a go.'

'I don't think this is the right time. She needs to cool off.'

Calum gave a lopsided grin. 'So do I.'

For a minute or two they were silent.

'So there's not much we can do,' said Calum.

'Not unless we declare war and take him to court for having sex with a minor,' said Lizzie.

'That's out of the question.'

'In any case they both deny it and Gaby would be on Luke's side fighting us.

'That's all we need.'

* * *

53

The weekend passed with Gabriella spending much of her time in her room, her parents having decided to postpone their talk with her. Calum took a phone call from the police officer who gave him the welcome news that Luke had a clean sheet as far as they were concerned. 'And in case you need to contact Luke for any reason in the future,' the officer added, 'this is his address.'

When Gaby finally did emerge, she surprised them by asking if she could use the phone before they talked.

She hunched over it, apparently trying to track down Luke. Listening in from the kitchen, Lizzie and Calum gathered from the soft murmurings and long silences from Gaby that the taciturn youth of the previous day had turned loquacious. But the conversation seemed to be on a more even keel by the time she put down the phone.

At the sight of her slight body, arms wrapped round herself defensively and lower lip trembling, Calum experienced a surge of pity for his wayward daughter. This was abruptly dispelled when she glared at him.

'Am I grounded?' She made direct eye contact for the first time since the row.

Trying not to show surprise, his response was automatic. 'Definitely,' he said, as firmly as he could.

Incredibly, she seemed to accept this and he asked her to go with him to the sitting room for a chat.

'What's the point?' She stared at him belligerently. 'We're never going to agree about anything.' He began to protest but she stomped back to her bedroom, firing a defensive shot over her shoulder. 'I wish I could get out of this bloody house forever,' she shouted. 'And I will just as soon as I can.'

By Monday morning Lizzie was delighted to get back to school and have laughter and good humour surrounding her from fellow teachers and pupils who knew nothing of her troubles.

Chapter Seven

September was the busiest time of the year for both Calum and Lizzie. A new school term meant hours of extra preparation for her and as a supply teacher she was given tasks that permanent staff were happy to offload. This meant that often she had mountains of paperwork to deal with on her home computer.

For his part, Calum had been forced to meet his bank manager again and admit that the expected injection of fresh capital had not materialised. He was given an extension of a month to present proposals for salvaging the situation, and for the first time he began seriously to consider selling his business. Erik Schroeder had recently been making noises about a merger with FairWinds Inc., his exhibition company based in NewYork. It would mean a lump sum for Calum plus a salary to match his status as head of the British operations. And he would be able to hold on to most of his existing employees. The downside would be answering to someone other than himself. And Erik was a tough business-man. So far Calum had not been desperate enough to consider losing his independence but he wondered if the time had come. Still, he decided not to worry Lizzie with his problem. She had enough on her plate already.

A week passed before Calum contacted Edward Foxton. There had been no further word from Andrew and he hoped this meant Andrew had changed his mind about litigation. Edward thought it more likely he'd been told his case was not winnable. 'Hot air doesn't give you grounds for fighting a case.'

'I suppose he was just acting out of spite,' said Calum. 'Imagine saying I'm not Gaby's father. It's downright wicked.'

During the last few days there had been no major upsets with Gabriella, partly because she was rarely to be seen, protesting that she had already eaten by the time he came home and needed to study for her essays. Happily she appeared to accept the strictures about coming home straight from school and being grounded for the evenings, though she was allowed out with Natasha at the weekend.

Lizzie had been checking Gabriella's movements with her teachers and they had been reassuring about her performance at school. As a peace move, Lizzie had tentatively suggested that Gaby invite Luke for a meal, but this was rejected. She comforted herself afterwards that though her daughter was uncommunicative, she was not overtly hostile. Luke's name had not been mentioned since and Gabriella's time-keeping was proving reliable. Lizzie began to relax, hoping the storms were abating.

Late one afternoon, her mind whirling with ideas and tasks still needing to be done at school, Lizzie took a call from Edward Foxton.

'I haven't been able to contact Calum and there's been a development,' he said. 'I've just had couriered from Andrew's solicitor formal notice of his intention to contest the will.'

Lizzie's heart sank.

'They've applied for a preliminary hearing in three weeks' time, so I have to see you and Calum as soon as possible. Tomorrow morning if you can manage it.'

Damn. Calum had left for Birmingham that morning for the National Exhibition Centre where he was setting up a display for a client and had said he wouldn't be in touch until evening.

'I can come but Calum's away for the next three days. He won't be home until the exhibition's over. Why are they in such a hurry?'

'Where money's concerned people always are.'

'What's Andy playing at, Ed? He must see he hasn't a hope.' She paused. 'Has he?'

To her consternation Edward did not answer her question but said it was imperative that he talk to them together. After tomorrow he had a court hearing which would put him out of action for at least a fortnight. Could she see if it was possible for Calum to manage an early-morning appointment?

Puzzled and anxious, Lizzie spent the next half-hour trying to track down Calum.

'You handle it, darling,' he said when she finally contacted him. The success of the exhibition was crucial to the company's perilous cash flow and he did not dare abandon his client.

'I can't. Ed insists we both have to see him. Calum, he gave me the impression he thinks Andy has a case.'

'That's how lawyers earn their money,' he said wearily. There was a short silence on the line before he added, 'I suppose I could do it. I'm only an hour and a half away on the M1. See if he can make it really early.'

It was a resentful-looking couple who turned up at Edward Foxton's office at seven-thirty the next morning, cursing Andrew for causing so much trouble. Calum had arrived home well after midnight and was in no mood to be messed around by his brother's mischief-making. Though Gabriella was aware that Andrew had been issuing threats, they decided to say nothing of this latest development. There was no point in rousing her and in any case Lizzie wouldn't be able to answer her questions until after they were given details of her brother-in-law's strategy.

Calum was thanking his friend for agreeing to such an early start but Edward did not waste time on the niceties. 'I was sent this yesterday by Blondell's, that's the firm your brother is using. It's a copy of a lab report comparing Calum and Gabriella's blood groups.' He took off his spectacles. 'In my opinion Andrew has no right to use the information from the laboratory. Those blood samples were given for another reason entirely.'

'I thought all that stuff was confidential,' said Calum.

'It is.' He handed over a sheet of paper. 'I can only assume this fell into Andrew's hands because of the testing being done for his baby. Blondell's haven't the best reputation for being too particular about their sources, but we won't be able to complain about how they obtained this document; we can only challenge their information if it contains an untruth.'

Edward began to toy with his spectacles. 'Their claim is based on the blood samples being totally incompatible which they maintain means that Calum could not be Gabriella's father.'

'That's utter nonsense,' said Lizzie, angry that such a fantasy could be taken seriously by her own side.

Calum's eyes were still fixed on the report.

When Edward told them he had asked the lab for the test to be done again, Lizzie's jaw tightened. 'Hold on a minute. You don't believe Andy, do you?'

He reached for a jug of water. 'I can't imagine the other side would go this far unless they were satisfied with the veracity of the test,' he said carefully. 'I suppose my first thought was that Gaby must have been adopted. We lost touch for a couple of years and I assumed you hadn't mentioned it. No reason to, of course.'

'She was not adopted,' said Lizzie, startled. 'She's ours. And when the lab checks its work again they'll find they've made a mistake. In fact, knowing Andy's methods, I'd say he faked the result.'

The two men made no response and infuriated by her husband's silence, Lizzie repeated herself. 'You have my word that Gabriella is our baby, Calum's and mine.'

Edward was busying himself riffling through the papers. 'Quite so. This is upsetting for both of you, I see that.' He shifted uncomfortably in his seat. 'I must admit this case is giving me some anxiety because of your father's emphasis on the bloodline. If I'd had a hand in drawing up his final will I would have insisted he put Gabriella's full name in the document.' He picked up a copy of the will and read a sentence which had been highlighted with a yellow marker. ' "My primary concern . . . is to ensure the continuity of what I consider is the good bloodline of the Lynton family . . ." '

'That may be so,' Lizzie retorted, 'but I'm not concerned about money here. I'm telling you categorically that Calum and I made a baby together and he was there when I gave birth.'

Calum took her hand and gave it a squeeze.

'Then it's fairly straightforward,' said Edward briskly. 'We have already insisted that the test is to be done again. The lab has asked us to supply another sample of your blood, Calum, and Gaby's, of course.'

'We'd rather not involve Gaby in all this,' said Lizzie quickly.

'I appreciate that.' Edward appeared to be avoiding her eyes. 'But you must see that a fresh test is the only way to settle this.'

Lizzie tried to catch Calum's attention but he was focusing on the solicitor's desk. She told herself that sarcasm was no way to handle this but she failed to keep it out of her voice. 'So the word of a mother who you'll accept was definitely present at the conception of her own daughter isn't good enough?'

'The law demands hard evidence,' said Edward gently.

'I find that offensive.' All attempt at restraint was now gone. 'The main reason we married so young was because Gabriella had been conceived,' Lizzie raised her voice, 'by both of us.' She appealed to Calum. 'Tell him.'

Before Calum could answer, Edward, who was now busily

polishing his lenses, interrupted. 'You'll both appreciate that we'll have to fight this with medical proof of our own.' He replaced his spectacles. 'It's a nuisance, I know, but our best defence is to produce our own tests, one from Gabriella and another from Calum. I suggest we send them to the same laboratory so the other side can't make any capital out of a change of testing procedure.'

Lizzie had to concede. They arranged a date for the blood samples to be taken by their local doctor and said their goodbyes to Edward.

They had barely reached the steps outside his office when Lizzie, unable to hide her anger, demanded, 'Why didn't you back me in there? You just sat and accepted this stupid test. You know it must be inaccurate.'

'You shouldn't worry,' said Calum, taking her arm. 'I can't see the point of arguing when we'll soon have the proof.' His voice was soothing, 'And then we can fight back.' As he began to steer her towards the car park he glanced at his watch. 'I'm sorry to leave you but I'll have to shoot off or I won't be on site by the time the exhibition opens. We can work on the affidavits Ed's asked for over the weekend.' He paused, car keys in hand. 'What should we tell Gaby?'

'Nothing,' said Lizzie firmly. 'When they re-check those results it'll kick the case out so there's no need to upset her, is there?'

'Won't she ask why she has to give more blood?'

'Not if I say they need it to help Sebastian.'

She was right. Gaby raised no objection to going to the doctor again to give another blood sample if it meant helping the sick baby.

Lizzie was more unsettled by the potential court action than she would admit. She would have liked their solicitor to have been more dismissive about Andrew's challenge. He seemed to be giving it a credence it did not deserve. And why hadn't Calum agreed with her whole-heartedly that the test, if not a fake, was inaccurate? He had been far less supportive than she would have wished. But maybe she was being too emotional. It was, after all, Andrew and his solicitor who wouldn't settle for less than cast-iron proof, not Calum. Well, proof they would have as soon as the second blood test was done.

* * *

Everyone had warned them that the Japanese rice wine could be lethal. But here she was on her fourth tiny glass and it was having no effect on Lizzie, although Sarah was beginning to giggle.

Calum had arranged to take her and her closest friend, Sarah, with her husband, Hugh Sinclair, to Sushi's, the best restaurant in the district, to celebrate their sixteenth wedding anniversary. Hugh and Calum had met at university and by coincidence had ended up living in the same part of London, in Wandsworth. Their wives had become friends when their children began to attend the local kindergarten and Sarah was a cheering guest at Lizzie's graduation as a mature student. Since then they had become entwined in each other's lives and over the years they consoled each other during the lows and shared the joy of the highs.

When Sarah's husband Hugh had been made redundant, Lizzie was the first person Sarah turned to, and when Gaby was making life intolerable, Sarah was there with sympathy and a gin and tonic. She had been immensely helpful in calming Lizzie after hearing that further blood tests were needed to fight Andy's allegation. 'It's worth the hassle to squash him once and for all,' she said to her friend.

Little seemed to faze Sarah Sinclair. With three demanding children and a husband who rarely kept a job for any length of time, Lizzie admired the way her friend bowled along through life, seeming to rise above her problems. With little money she nevertheless managed to dress stylishly, a relic she used to say of the days when she was a department store window dresser. She was the only woman in Lizzie's circle who could make the same outfit do duty for different occasions by the addition of a few well-chosen accessories. But what Lizzie most envied was Sarah's ability to be tranquil in the face of what she saw as teenage aggression from her daughter. When Natasha was sometimes impertinent, Lizzie would bridle on her friend's behalf but Sarah would ignore the outburst, treating her daughter with unfailing patience. But that policy had paid off because Natasha was now a well-balanced, delightful child. How often had Lizzie wished she had Sarah's temperament, but maybe that difference was the reason they had become such friends.

Lately she had been trying to emulate Sarah's knack of not rising to Gaby's rudeness. And certainly the atmosphere between them had improved. And when these new tests confirmed that Calum was Gaby's father, there would be no further problems with the will. Calum could then concentrate one hundred per cent on rescuing the business, as he always had been able to do in the past, and they could get on with life.

It was the quartet's first experience of Japanese cuisine and they had been amused to be asked to take off their shoes; Sarah in particular made a fuss, complaining that her feet were not her best asset. They had been kneeling on the tatami matting for the best part of an hour and Lizzie wished fervently that she could ask for a nice comfortable chair. But soon the sake was doing its work and although her lower limbs were going numb it ceased to bother her.

Calum started the round of toasts. 'To my beautiful bride, as lovely now as she was when she walked down the aisle sixteen years ago.'

'To Lizzie.' The other three downed their eggcup-sized glasses which were instantly refilled.

'I have a toast too,' said Sarah. She raised the thimble of sake and recited:

> I wish I could drink like a 'lady'
> I can manage two glasses at most
> The third puts me under the table
> The fourth puts me under my host.

Hugh laughed loudest and announced that was why he was careful to monitor his wife's alcoholic intake.

Lizzie then raised her glass. 'Here's to the only man I could have married.'

Another round of sake disappeared.

There was a snort from Hugh, who fancied himself as a comedian. ' "Only man"? Come on, who you marry depends on who's around at the time.'

'Some wives might think this a slur on their unique charms,' said Sarah drily, 'but we all know how Hugh likes to stir up the conversation.' She smiled, totally relaxed.

'You mean if Sarah hadn't begged you to marry her you'd have chosen someone else?' Lizzie's eyes danced mischievously.

'Exactly so,' said Hugh, 'and you might've married Peter Rivers.'

'He didn't have a chance.' Lizzie was used to Hugh's teasing.

'Not with Calum around,' said Sarah, pouring more sake into her glass.

'Don't you believe it.' Hugh downed another drink and held out his glass for more. 'Tiny glasses, aren't they? I remember one party when you and that guy were all over each other.'

'Don't start your stirring,' Lizzie waved a finger jokily in his direction.

Hugh was not to be diverted. 'Peter was pretty keen on you.'

'He was just a big flirt,' she said, noticing that Calum was not joining in the joshing. Surely he wasn't jealous over a flirtation which happened such a long time ago.

'A flirt,' Sarah piped up. 'Like our eldest. If flirting was on the curriculum, he'd get an A grade.'

'That's understandable,' said Hugh, 'He's a carbon copy of me.'

'They all are,' retorted his wife. 'All three of them. I know I must've had something to do with the making of them but who would guess it?' She grinned at Calum. 'As soon as they were born the nurse said, "Here's another little Sinclair. Can't mistake his daddy".' Her hand flew to her mouth when she saw Calum's expression. 'Sorry, that was pretty crass.'

'Sorry for what?' said Hugh, trying to focus.

'Nothing.'

'What's going on?' asked Hugh.

'It's their case,' said Sarah quickly. 'About the will?'

Light dawned. 'Oh yes. Worrying.'

Calum was aware that for years Sarah and Lizzie had used each other as sounding boards. Most times he did not mind but now he wished his wife had not confided the nuts and bolts of their private business. The fewer people who knew about the blood test, the better.

'Andy must be off his rocker,' said Sarah sympathetically.

'The whole thing's absurd,' said Lizzie lightly. 'Calum and I have decided not to let the court case upset us. Haven't we, darling?'

He said nothing. If only that were true. These days he woke up long before the alarm, churning Andy's allegation over and over in his mind. How likely was it that a reputable lab could make such a mistake? When he read the newspapers, the stories that leapt out at him were those involving paternity cases. One in

62

twelve children, they reported, was not born to the man named on the birth certificate. The statistic tormented him.

'It's spiteful to say Gaby's not your daughter, Calum,' said Sarah indignantly.

Hugh was making a clumsy attempt to get his fingers round the tiny glass. 'Wicked,' he agreed. Halfway to his lips the glass halted in midair. 'Pity she doesn't look like you. It'd make the case go away.'

'Yes, she does,' said Sarah, retrieving the glass from his hand.

But Gabriella did not resemble him, thought Calum, re-arranging the chopsticks on his plate. It had not bothered him before and if anyone idly commented on it, they humorously blamed Gaby's dark looks on a genetic throwback, possibly an undiscovered Latin forebear. But right now he did not find the subject amusing. He turned and indicated to the waiter that he would like the bill.

'What's the matter with you?' Hugh asked his wife truculently. 'She doesn't look like Calum. Any fool can see that.'

'You've had enough.' Sarah's mouth was set in a thin line.

'We all have,' said Calum.

Lizzie sat tight-lipped in the back of the taxi on the way home. Calum was making an effort at desultory conversation by commenting on the standard of the cuisine, high, the service, low. Lizzie could not bring herself to respond, she was deflated. The allegations about Gaby's parentage were wicked but what had Calum said to refute them? Nothing. Thank goodness they were with Sarah and Hugh who were practically family. But his lack of support still rankled. And his attitude throughout the evening had been distant. Good God, wasn't this supposed to be a happy anniversary celebration?

'I'm tired,' he yawned, and then giving her a gentle nudge, added, 'but not too tired.' She smiled briefly. That was rich, expecting her to feel loving towards him after an evening like this. She had spent years telling him that for women love-making began first in the mind, but after a few jars of Japanese wine that had gone out of the window.

She could feel the irritation building. Rarely had she turned away from Calum if he made the first move. But tonight . . . She stopped herself. If she spurned him, it could be the first trickle of water through the dyke walls. And she was fearful of where that could lead. It was the night of their anniversary and she had better try. Memories of their honeymoon upset her momentarily. Calum had been tender and sensitive, asking anxiously whether or not it was safe for the baby. In fact they had made love twice, or was it three times, that night. Since then during the sixteen years of living with him Lizzie had never imagined being with anyone else. She had to get over this antagonism. Of course it was temporary. The second blood test would prove Calum was Gaby's father and all would be well again.

Like many long-standing couples, they had settled into a pleasant if unexciting routine, taking their relationship for granted. Disputes were seldom and serious quarrels – well, she couldn't remember a time when they couldn't talk out a problem. Indeed, she pondered ruefully, they never raised their voices to each other except when they disagreed about how best to deal with Gabriella's moods.

They headed straight for the bedroom and as was their custom she took first turn in the bathroom. When she emerged, Calum had already dimmed the lights and was swaying slightly as he endeavoured to untie his shoelaces with one hand. A few minutes later he slipped into bed and rolled over to nestle into her body, murmuring appreciatively as his hands caressed her satin-clad body.

She began to lift the gown but Calum stopped her, 'I'll do that,' and began kissing the side of her cheek while fumbling under the bedclothes to find the hem. He started pulling the nightie over her shoulders and Lizzie tried to make it easy for him by arching her back. But as the material bunched round her neck, a strand of hair was caught by a button and she yelped in pain.

'Sorry, don't move.'

Attempting to extricate the hair, he pulled it more, which made her eyes water and she said irritably, 'Leave it. I'll do it myself.' Great start, she thought.

When the nightdress was finally dumped on the floor, Calum lay back on the pillow, looking crestfallen. Then he leaned over, giving her a soft kiss and suggested that maybe this wasn't their night.

Lizzie was disarmed by the affectionate look on his face. His equable mood seemed to have returned, with no hint of his earlier aloofness. Perhaps if she could reassure him physically that she was the same person he had married, he might recover his good humour.

With an air of mock command she ordered him to relax as she was about to take over, and was rewarded with a beatific smile.

She kissed his body and he groaned with pleasure but a part of her brain would not switch off. Round and round went the thought that Calum was beginning to have doubts about Gaby's paternity. True he had paid lip service to the idea that the lab might have made a mistake but his recent moodiness proved he was not one hundred per cent sure.

She intensified her efforts and Calum, who had always been easy to please in bed, responded eagerly. But she could not equal his excitement and, unselfish lover that he was, Calum seemed to realise this. He broke free and began to stimulate her body in a way that had never failed before. But it was as if he was making love to someone else, the tick, tick of her brain denying her the trip to oblivion. Despite his endeavours Lizzie failed to enter the pleasurable world that foreplay usually induced. She made a rare decision, to pretend to have an orgasm.

Chapter Eight

As he waited for Edward Foxton to finish his phone conversation, Calum gazed round the familiar oak-panelled reception area. The Lynton family had paid for much of that carving but he didn't begrudge it because two generations of this family had been served well by Foxton and Small. When Edward's father had died, it was Calum who persuaded his father to stay with the firm, though he had never told his squash partner the part he had played in retaining this valuable client.

For the umpteenth time Calum chastised himself for being nervous, not about whether the court case would go ahead but about the result of the new test although Lizzie appeared pretty laid back about it, apparently certain that the new test would confirm Gabriella's parentage.

When Edward requested another meeting at short notice, the timing was inconvenient for her. It would cause immense disruption if she were to ask for leave of absence in the middle of a hectic week when the staff were preparing for the dreaded visit of an Ofsted inspector.

'Could Edward make an appointment for later in the week?' she had asked and Calum had told her this was the only time he and the solicitor were both free.

'I'm sorry I can't get away. Phone me the minute you leave him, OK?'

Thank goodness Lizzie had appeared to put aside his ungracious behaviour which had spoiled the atmosphere of the anniversary dinner. He had blamed the Japanese rice wine for his less than inspired performance, though in truth she had not been as enthusiastic as usual. Afterwards she joked that he owed her one.

But it was not the alcohol that had prevented his climax, it was all the uncertainty. How could he doubt he was Gaby's father? It was preposterous. Not Lizzie. Never his Lizzie. Since their romance had begun at university they'd been steadfastly faithful to each other. Hadn't he resisted sleeping with anyone else before they married? And since then there'd been several times when he could have been unfaithful. Hotels shared by exhibition personnel provided fertile ground for adultery and he'd be lying if he said he hadn't been tempted once or twice by stunning models on the promotion staff. And Tess Parker.

Until recently Calum had been assiduous about never being alone with her since a lustful encounter a couple of years ago. It had been after a particularly hectic week in which they had been thrown together from daybreak until late evening. After packing up he had invited Tess to share a brandy in the deserted exhibition suite. He had found himself kissing her enthusiastically and reacting to her ardent response. It had taken every ounce of self-restraint to break away and apologise for losing control.

'I wanted it as much as you,' she had said to him, before making her way to her own bedroom. Alone. Calum had blamed his weakness on being away from Lizzie and an over-indulgence on alcohol. He and Tess had not referred to it the next day or afterwards and he vowed he would be careful not to put himself in that situation again. But recently she had seemed to sense something was bothering him and had made it clear she would not be averse to taking their relationship further. Even before all the problems with the will, her moral support over Premier Promotions' financial difficulties had become almost too personal. She had taken to sending him the occasional e-mail to amuse and distract him from his worries, and some of them were blatantly sexual.

Calum looked at Edward Foxton. Usually when they met there was a minute or two of bragging about who had won their last squash bout, with diaries being consulted to fix the next encounter. Today there was a marked change in the atmosphere and Calum realised at once what it was. Edward greeted him like a professional rather than a friend.

Edward unlocked his desk and extracted a slim buff folder. 'There's no easy way to tell you this, Calum. I'm afraid the original tests have been proved correct. You could not possibly be Gabriella's father.'

'I can't believe that. How can you be so sure?'

Edward shook his head. 'I'm sorry, Calum. Our experts tell

me there's a ninety-nine per cent probability you are not her father.'

Calum gazed at his friend, his heart beginning to pound. 'There must be another explanation. May I see?'

As he looked at the meaningless codes produced by the laboratory, Calum's eyes began to blur and dimly he became aware of Edward sliding a glass of brandy across the desk.

'It's a mistake, it must be. And this test isn't a hundred per cent certain, Ed.' His eyes pleaded for assurance.

'I don't think there's been any mistake.' Edward pointed to a paragraph of the accompanying letter from the lab and quoted, ' "These results conform to the previous ones in every particular".'

'But there's a one per cent chance that I am her father.'

'Calum, I would very much like to offer you hope but I can't. I'm sorry, but you're going to have to accept . . .' his voice tailed off.

Calum stared at the pens on Edward's desk. If he counted them slowly perhaps the pain would recede.

Eventually he asked, 'What am I going to do, Ed?'

The solicitor's face exuded concern. 'I don't think you should do anything, not at the moment. You need to think about it rationally.'

'Rationally! Can you imagine how it feels to be told after all these years of loving her and bringing her up that Gaby isn't mine?'

'Calum, you were there when she was born and you've been with her since then. She's as much your daughter as anyone who . . .' he paused.

'As anyone who gave her life?' Calum's voice was ominously calm as the magnitude of the news began to sink in. 'And what about Lizzie's part in all this? Ed, she's lied to me all our married life.'

Edward hesitated for a second. 'She must've had a good reason, don't you think? A young girl, pregnant, afraid that when you found out she would lose you.'

Calum thought about that for a moment but found he couldn't excuse her so easily. And yet it could all have been different. When Lizzie announced she was pregnant, his first reaction, God help him, was that they were both too young, she ought to consider having an abortion. But before he could bring himself to find the right words, Lizzie had made it clear she wanted to keep the baby. She acknowledged the bad timing and although they had already discussed marriage, her fear was that he might not want to go through with it under these circumstances. When he had caught sight of the apprehension in her eyes he put aside all doubts. This was the woman with whom he wanted to spend the rest of his life and he sure as hell wasn't going to lose her.

They'd been happy in the early years though he'd experienced a little resentment at the sacrifices forced on him. If he hadn't been a newly married man with a young baby would he, a graduate, have taken those dead-end jobs in the sales office because they offered higher salaries than others with better long-term prospects? Other young men were enjoying the single life while he'd been busy working to clothe and feed his family. He and Lizzie had agreed it would be better for Gabriella to have a stay-at-home mother. They'd calculated that the money an unqualified Lizzie could earn would barely pay for a competent childminder.

She had always bemoaned the fact that she had not completed her degree and in the beginning had helped with Calum's fledgling company. He discovered with delight that she had an intuitive feel for style which could be translated into innovative designs for exhibition stands. But when Gabriella grew older she began to express a wish to complete her interrupted university studies. He'd been disappointed when she decided to go into teaching rather than join his company but, as always, had given her his unqualified support.

He could feel Edward watching him and he met his gaze. 'All these years she made me believe Gaby was mine. Can you imagine what it means to know your whole life is based on a lie? Why didn't she trust me enough to tell me the truth?'

Edward said nothing.

'I was sure there was no other man in her life,' Calum said forlornly. 'Just last week she laughed at me for suggesting there was. That's hard to take. Even after sixteen years she didn't have the guts to tell me the truth. I'd respect her more if she had.'

'Calum, I want you to think about your next step very carefully.' Edward stood up and began to pace the room. 'How important is your marriage to you? How you handle this with Lizzie could make or break your relationship.'

This time it was Calum who was silent.

'It's been a good marriage, hasn't it?' persisted Edward.

Still Calum did not respond.

'Whatever happened is history,' Edward went on. 'You can't change it. But,' he took off his spectacles and rested them on the desk, 'what you do now will determine the present and the future.'

Calum bowed his head to try and regain some control. His throat was closing up and he felt perilously close to tears.

'As a father myself,' said Edward, 'I can't imagine what this is like for you but as your lawyer I have to remind you that we're fighting a court case. I'd rather not raise it now but we need to take soundings for a new strategy. I've already consulted a barrister and—'

'Fuck the will. This is my life you're talking about.' Calum felt a surge of anger.

'I'm sorry, Calum, but I also act for Gabriella and I have to put up the best case I can on her behalf, whether or not her paternity is in dispute.'

'Does Andy need to be told about the second test?'

'I'm afraid so but we'll vigorously contest any case he puts up and our strength is the bond between Gabriella and her grand-father. I'm reasonably sure the judge will go with Robert's clearly stated intentions in his will.'

Calum stood up abruptly. 'Do what you have to do.' Before going through the door, he paused and swivelled round to face his friend. 'Who could he be?' he asked agitatedly. 'The man who fathered Gaby?'

Edward raised his shoulders in a gesture of bafflement and Calum went on, 'How can things ever be the same between Lizzie and me?'

As he walked towards the car his first thought was to go straight to Lizzie's school, yank her out of the classroom and force her to admit the truth. All these years he had admired her honesty and courage, willing to shoulder responsibility however much was heaped on her. He had misread her completely. She was devious, scheming and, what was worse, gutless. Why hadn't she been brave enough to confess that she had made a mistake? But to walk brazenly down the aisle, to see him waiting for her at the altar with love and trust on his face and all the time knowing she was carrying another man's child . . . The bile threatened to gag him.

A driver pressed his horn impatiently behind him. Red had

71

changed to green at the traffic lights and Calum had not noticed his car had stopped. As soon as he could he pulled into a layby and tried to steady his shaking hands. Edward's advice had always proved to be wise in the past and he could see the sense of it. Do nothing impulsive. Think of your marriage. Think of Gaby. He had to accept that the advice was sensible and he would try to follow it. The happiness of another person was threatened. Gaby was another victim of this deceit. At least he could try and protect her as much as possible. He would achieve that best by keeping a rein on his anger. And that meant not rushing in to accuse his wife. Anyway, what would she do if he did confront her? Continue to deny everything. It was useless to talk about medical evidence with her. She would dismiss it. The word of a mother was good enough as far as she was concerned.

Although he had a series of appointments for that afternoon, nothing would have induced him to return to the office so he phoned Tess to cancel them. Even in this state, he thought wryly, old reliable Calum would not forget his responsibilities. Tess's voice was full of concern and for a moment he was tempted to confide the whole hideous story to her but thought better of it. She would put his preoccupation down simply to the court fight with his brother. Nevertheless, when the call ended he had a momentary feeling of warmth. Someone out there was on his side.

As he sat staring miserably through the windscreen, the germ of an idea began to form. Starting up the car he went onto autopilot on the drive home. He would have a couple of hours to himself before Lizzie's school day ended. Gaby had swimming lessons and did not usually return home till late afternoon.

At home Calum made straight for the bedroom where he sank to his knees to rummage under the bed. He pulled out two large shoeboxes, covered in a film of dust. He upturned one of them onto the bed and there, in a pile, lay mementos of his youth – letters, school reports, diaries and souvenirs from long-forgotten holidays.

Rapidly he emptied the other box. This one contained hundreds of snapshots, mostly informal pictures of the three of them on picnics, visits to the Tower of London, Buckingham Palace and one with Gaby, covered in pigeons, in Trafalgar Square.

Memories flooded back as he began to place the pictures into two separate piles, those taken in the last sixteen years and, the smaller pile, from his university days. He picked up a photo of a young man squinting into the sun. Geoff Hastelow was always larking about with Lizzie but he had a serious girl friend at the time and Calum hadn't noticed any hint of sexual frisson between them, though they could have hidden it.

Calum frowned as he looked at another young face. He could not for the life of him recall this one's name. All he remembered was that he'd been a great athlete. Once Lizzie had made a comment admiring his physique and Calum's jealousy had sent him to work out at the college gym. Was his first name Ben? He noticed the young man had the same dark colouring as Gabriella, but the timing was all wrong. Ben had switched universities after being awarded a sports scholarship to Berkeley in California long before Lizzie could have conceived.

He sifted through the remaining batch and picked out another photo showing a group of friends at a barbecue. This was the picture which, he now realised, had triggered his dark memories. He sat motionless, remembering.

That was the night he'd gone to look for Lizzie in the garden, with her drink, only to find her half in shadow talking to Peter Rivers who was standing over her in a somewhat proprietorial manner. Rivers had been part of the crowd, about ten of them from college days, but he always seemed to drift, ostensibly casually, towards Lizzie, as several photos showing his tall figure standing next to hers testified. The group had spent much of its summer holidays together.

That night he and Lizzie had had a terrible fight, Lizzie accusing him of mistrusting her. But he had seen the sensuous look on Peter Rivers' face. Lizzie had wept, saying he was behaving exactly like her father who spent his long absences abroad supervising engineering projects constantly picturing his wife with other men. When he was home he made her life miserable with his jealousy, which was unfounded. After enduring this for some time, her mother had rebelled and started the affair which broke up the marriage.

The row that night was a catalyst for straight talking between them and they vowed to be honest with each other and brave enough to discuss problems before they became insurmountable. Lizzie said she would do all she could to avoid imitating the destructive pattern followed by her parents.

What a fool he'd been. All this time his crowd had probably

been laughing at him, they would know all about her and Peter carrying on behind his back. But why the hell hadn't she gone off with him when she'd found she was pregnant? Maybe, he thought bitterly, he had made himself scarce. Although he did not think of himself as a violent man, at that moment Calum felt a desire to destroy everything they'd built up together. Everything had been based on deceit.

What would Lizzie say when he accused her of betraying him? Would she bluster? Imply he was mad? Ask, yet again, whether he placed more trust in the evidence of the laboratory than her word?

As he settled down to wait, Calum was plagued by a thought which increased his desolation. He had never fathered a child.

Lizzie closed down her laptop, pushed it to the back of the desk and gave her arms a good stretch. She was feeling more positive about everything. Today would surely mark the end of a nightmarish few weeks and then, thank God, they would get back to normal.

Gabriella was another reason for her optimistic mood. Since the police incident, she had been surprisingly co-operative and lately Lizzie had experienced a small example of how their relationship might develop. Sitting round the kitchen table, helping her with her English homework, Gaby suddenly went off at a tangent and began talking about her part in the school play.

She did not think she was good enough to take up acting as a career but she was interested in working behind the scenes.

'Who's the head guy when you put on a play or a film?'

'The producer finds the money but the director tells everyone what to do.' Lizzie told her.

'Then I'm going to be a director.' They both laughed, a moment that gave Lizzie hope that one day they could be friends.

It was only four o'clock. Lizzie had been able to sort out the problems with the examination timetables and there were dozens of tasks still to be tackled but she could concentrate no longer. She wanted to hear about Calum's meeting with Edward Foxton. Calum hardly ever phoned her at school because she was difficult to locate and it was hard for her to phone back until break times. When she had finally managed to access a phone in the busy staffroom, Tess had surprised her by saying he would not be coming back to the office that day. No, she could not say where he might be. Was Tess being deliberately obstructive? Lizzie suddenly remembered those crude e-mails Tess had sent Calum. She had meant to tackle Calum about them but Andrew's actions after the will reading had driven it from her mind. She pushed her irritation aside and tried the answering machine at home in case Calum had left a message for her, but there was only Sarah's voice confirming a weekend outing to the cinema. Calum's mobile was switched off and Lizzie wondered whether he could still be at the meeting.

As she walked swiftly from the bus stop she saw with surprise that his car was parked outside the house. What had brought him home this early? Her optimism abruptly disappeared. She opened the front door and made straight for the kitchen. There was no sign of him so she went into the hallway and at the foot of the stairs called out his name. He answered from the bedroom so she made her way up the stairs.

Calum was sitting on the bed surrounded by a jumble of photographs and postcards from the old cardboard boxes holding the lifetime of photographs she always meant to paste into albums one day.

'Are you feeling OK?'

He ignored her and continued to sort through the souvenirs.

'I've been waiting for you to phone all afternoon,' she said in a tone of mild reproof, moving towards him with every intention of giving him her customary kiss. He drew back. Her unease grew. 'What did Ed say?' she asked.

At last he looked at her. 'Is this him?' He held up a photograph.

'What are you on about? Tell me what happened at Edward's office.'

'I want to know. Is this him?'

She took the photograph from him. 'Is this who?'

'Don't try and pretend.'

When she stared at him dumbly, he said, 'Peter Rivers. He's Gabriella's father, isn't he?'

She sank down on the edge of the bed, the photo still clasped in her hand, and stared at her husband's pale, stricken face. Calum lay back on the bed, his arms behind his head, his voice quiet.

'It's quite obvious when you look at him. I don't know why I didn't notice the similarity before.'

Lizzie could not trust herself to speak.

'The second test is exactly the same as the first. I can't be Gabriella's father.'

She stared at his wild eyes. 'Calum, can't you see? The lab's made a mistake again.'

'You never give up, do you? Can you imagine how humiliating it was, sitting in Ed's office, realising how you've made a fool of me all this time?' He snatched the photo back from her. 'Take a look at this. His jaw, his nose, his colouring. It's Gabriella. The evidence was staring me in the face.'

Peter Rivers. Tall, dark-haired, a jester. Master of the bloody universe. Lizzie remembered his ironic sense of humour and how it matched her own. He would single her out with his eyes. There was a spark between them, she had to admit, and like most women she enjoyed his admiration. He paid her extravagant compliments which she could never take seriously because compared with Calum he was lightweight. And she was aware that the twinkle in Peter's eye for her was also there for others.

She recalled the night in the garden when she'd been sorely tempted by Peter, his hands, his lips. Her body had longed to submit but her mind had recognised the difference between lust and her love for Calum.

Calum broke into her thoughts. 'Peter was always hanging around you like a dog on heat. I suppose he wouldn't marry you so you came to the poor sucker who did.'

All the frustrations of the past weeks engulfed her. Her instinct was to go on the attack. She wanted to scream and rant about the unfairness of being accused of such a deception by a husband who was supposed to trust her word above all others, to honour and revere her above all others. But some inner voice urged caution.

'I've lived with you all these years,' she said, trying to keep her voice steady. 'Is this what you think of me?' He did not answer. 'Calum, you've convinced yourself that two and two make five. It doesn't seem important to you that I deny it.'

He gave a derisive snort. 'How can both sets of tests be wrong, Lizzie? Answer me that.'

'I don't know but I do know that you're Gaby's father. Let's go and see Edward together.'

Calum ignored that. 'Why didn't you have the guts to tell me before I was forced to find out?'

Her restraint evaporated. Anger propelled her towards him

76

and she began to pummel his chest with her clenched fists. 'You're the only man I've been with since we met,' she shouted, punctuating each word with a punch of her fists.

He took hold of both of her wrists. 'You were so concerned to find a name for your illegitimate child you didn't care about me.'

My God, he actually believed that, thought Lizzie, dismayed. Unsteadily she pulled away from him and went to the dressing table. Feeling stiff with tension, she stared at her reflection in the mirror, dimly aware that Calum had disappeared into the bathroom.

This was their first real crisis. She did not count problems with the business on the same scale as this and she had no idea how to go about convincing Calum the tests were wrong. If he would not accept her word, what could she do? Right now she was too distraught to think straight. And their daughter – and despite what Calum was saying, she was their daughter – would be home at any moment.

Lizzie tried to compose herself. It would be difficult but she had to keep Gaby in ignorance of the calamity that had befallen them. She and Calum could pretend to be disagreeing about something else for a time but if the court case went ahead Gaby would have to be told about Andy's allegation. Lizzie accepted that Gabriella's relationship with Calum was far closer than hers at present and she dreaded having to try and persuade her daughter this was all a monstrous lie, especially when her own husband thought it was true. For now, it was essential that they carry on as normal. Her instinct was to move out to the spare room but that would be the first time they had slept apart and would certainly alert Gabriella that there was a crisis.

She took refuge in preparing supper, taking her anger out on saucepans and dishes, pulverising the garlic, bashing the tomatoes into a paste, and aggressively slicing the onions to make bolognese sauce, always popular with Gaby.

She jumped when Calum appeared behind her shoulder and calmly took out the shoe-cleaning equipment from under the sink. She turned away and switched on the radio so the silence between them would be less noticeable when their daughter arrived.

'Why are you cooking?' he asked over the radio. 'We have to go to the hockey dinner.'

He was kidding, wasn't he? It had completely slipped her

mind but in any case he couldn't expect her to play the part of the dutiful wife after what had gone on.

'If I'm such a terrible liar, why do you want me there?' she asked.

'Frankly, I don't. But your name's on the invitation, we've sold two hundred tickets and there is such a thing as duty.'

'I hate hockey.'

'You've never made a secret of that. OK, don't go. Gaby and I will say you're ill.' He walked out carrying the cleaning box.

Lizzie ceased her chopping and laid the knife on the board. Gaby? Of course. She was at that moment changing at Natasha's place. The girls were excited at being able to earn a little money as waitresses at the function. Damn and blast. If she didn't go, Gaby was sure to ask why and might be drawn into the drama. Lizzie gazed down at her fingers which reeked of onion and garlic. Her hair was lank after bending over a steaming saucepan. She would have to work miracles to make herself presentable.

Half an hour later she critically inspected the result of her efforts in the mirror and was amazed that her inner misery was not reflected. Indeed the woman she saw appeared not to have a care in the world. It gave her childish satisfaction to have jettisoned her usual classic appearance. The safe navy silk sheath she wore on occasions like this had been rejected in favour of a halter-neck top from Gabriella's wardrobe, which revealed the swell of her generous curves more than usual, as well as the slight tan, which had survived beyond the last rays of summer. Her hair, which she hadn't had time to wash, was slicked back behind her ears. The ankle-strap shoes she hadn't worn for years but had been too expensive to throw out set off the long, sleek, crepe skirt to perfection. Determined to wear none of the jewellery that Calum had given her over the years, round her neck hung the silver heart on a black leather thong which belonged to Gabriella. She had also filched a pair of silver gypsy hoops from her daughter's bedside table. When she descended the stairs on the dot of seven, she was happy to note Calum's surprise at her rapid transformation.

After the hurtful things he had flung at her, she disliked being in such close proximity to him and during the journey she sat determinedly upright, filmy shawl thrown back over her shoulders, eyes firmly fixed on the road ahead. She dreaded the next few hours when she would have to smile, laugh at his jokes and pretend to be the loving, supportive wife.

The fifteen-minute journey passed silently. Calum barely looked to his left to check oncoming traffic and she did not once glance to her right. When they turned into the car park of the hotel he switched off the engine and cleared his throat.

'Don't say how wonderful the Torquay game is going to be to Bruce and Sally. He probably won't be selected.'

'Fine,' she said shortly.

'And remember to thank Mrs Watkins for offering to pay next year's petrol for the coach.'

'Don't worry,' she said with as much frost as she could muster. 'I won't let *you* down.'

He stifled his exclamation of anger as the interior lights in the car beside theirs lit up and four doors opened simultaneously. Two couples, stalwarts of the club, spilled out.

Lizzie forced a smile. 'Hi,' she said brightly, getting out of the car. Amidst the excited chatter Calum, too, was beaming as if he had nothing but this evening's entertainment on his mind.

They walked in tandem through the car park, chatting to the other guests, and throughout the noisy, hot, evening they were able to give every impression of togetherness. A veritable golden couple, reflected Lizzie sadly.

After the dinner, Calum got to his feet to make the keynote speech of the night. Lizzie marvelled at the capacity of men to put their worries so far on the back burner. Calum took the assembled company through the season, sketching in the escapades, the losses, the triumphs in such a jovial manner that club members and their partners creased with laughter. This was the Calum whose life she had shared for so many years. He had been her rock, her teacher, her lover and her friend. How could she allow this crisis to disrupt her marriage? Somehow she had to prove that the damn lab had made a mistake. Again. They were testing the same blood and using the same procedure; obviously they had reproduced their error. Well, she would just have to prove it.

Chapter Nine

The baby wriggled as the cold hands of the doctor touched his stomach. He squealed and rolled over, his large hazel eyes alive with mischief.

'He's doing well, isn't he?' said Edina. 'Since you changed the drugs he's been really lively.'

The doctor's face registered none of her hope. In the seven months since Sebastian had been diagnosed as suffering from leukaemia Edina wanted him to reflect some optimism but he was the pragmatic type. Polite, professional and kind he might be but Edina occasionally wished he would hold her hand and squeeze some reassurance into her system. He was usually careful with his pronouncements and when he showed pleasure at Sebastian's blood count, she would be on a high for days afterwards – only to crash down to earth when the next result was not as good.

Edina had done her homework on the disease in libraries and with information from the Leukaemia Support Group. According to one article in a medical journal, the treatment of childhood leukaemia was one of the great medical success stories over the past thirty years. She was not quite so comforted by the statistic they included that out of every ten children diagnosed with it, three would die. But Sebastian was not going to be one of them. She would do whatever was necessary to make him well again.

Sebastian had been in remission for nineteen weeks and she and Andy had just emerged from the 'holding-the-breath' stage and were about to enter the 'maybe-it's-gone-for-good' level when he had suffered a relapse. The memory of the day it happened would never leave her.

Edina had returned from the hospital after doing some shopping. The computer was down so the nurses had not been able to obtain Sebastian's blood count immediately. As she struggled to open the front door, manoeuvring baby, carrier bags and pram, the phone began ringing. Edina rushed to answer it but twisted her ankle and tripped. Encircled by Sebastian and groceries, she hobbled to the now silent phone and dialled 1471. She recognised the doctor's number at once. Feeling sick with anxiety, she pressed digit three and was instantly connected. Sebastian's leukaemia had returned, the calm voice informed her. Then, for the first time, the doctor mentioned a bone marrow transplant. He had been glancing at the database and thought there might be a couple of potential donors; but it was a hit and miss affair and she could help in the search. Family members were the best sources, they often produced a match. His voice went sonorously on while Edina, not then taking in the words, watched her baby singing to himself as he played with the cheese triangles, squishing them happily in his fingers.

She found herself hugging him with extra ferocity as she pulled him out of the bath that night and wrapped him in a large bath sheet she had first warmed over the radiator. Her poor baby who had suffered so much was to suffer more. It was almost more than she could bear. Later, as he slept, she knelt beside him and kissed his forehead, stroking the fine crop of blond hair which would soon fall out again. Why did this have to happen to her little angel? Why? Anger gave way to uncontrollable grief.

Andrew came rushing back from work and for the rest of the day and night she did little but weep helplessly on his shoulder. He was as upset as she was but he had to go out to work the following day. She had been alone. Then her fighting spirit returned. Was she not the woman who had achieved more than anyone else in her street? Had she not started a promising career as a fashion sales assistant in Selfridges? She might have risen to become a buyer if she had not met and snared the rich Andrew Lynton while serving part-time in his local pub. Correction. She'd thought he was rich; it turned out it was his family who had the money. Still, he had enabled her to transform herself from Edna Williams to Edina Lynton. Not bad for someone from South London – or 'Sauf' London as the media sneeringly described it.

During the first months of their marriage Andrew had been inconsiderate and bad-tempered, especially when his business ventures failed. She had often thought that their marriage would surely not have lasted had it not been for Sebastian's illness. Having a sick child bound you in ways she could not have comprehended. She, whose world had centred around her wardrobe, whose idea of tragedy was snagging a nail, concentrated wholly on one small child and never thought about outward appearances.

Andy had changed too. He often made supper when she'd had a tiring day and, though he worked long hours, insisted on taking over at night when Sebastian was fretful. She was sure that if only Andy's family could see this compassionate and caring side of him, it might change some of their perceptions. But give them their due, all of them offered to help in the search for a bone marrow match the moment she asked. Andrew had at first been reluctant to contact the family but when she'd screamed at him that there was no choice in the matter, he said no more. But he would not approach them himself.

She was woken from her reverie by the doctor who had finished his examination and started packing away his instruments.

'I think we'd better admit him to hospital, Mrs Lynton.' Her blood froze because he actually leaned over and took her hand in his. It scared Edina far more than his words.

'Why?'

'Before we can do the bone marrow transplant we have to get his body ready for it. We need to do transfusions with blood and platelets and these can't be done as an out-patient.'

Sebastian was trying to gouge out the eyes of a fluffy bunny toy as the doctor went on, 'We have to suppress the immunity of the patient when we treat the cancer cells so that the transplant will take.'

Dry-mouthed she had had nothing to say, no questions to ask, and was dumbfounded when he suggested that he could take both of them to the hospital immediately.

'Now?' she had managed to croak. 'Right now?'

'He can't wait much longer, Edina.'

He had called her by her first name. The message could hardly be clearer. He thought Sebastian was going to die.

Lizzie's faith in Calum had been damaged. With her head she could understand his confusion when confronted with the results of the blood tests but in her heart she believed he had let her down.

It was fortunate that Gaby did not seem to notice the extent of her parents' alienation and as her eating times rarely coincided with theirs they were saved having to make polite conversation. They were physically estranged but living in the same house, both suffering yet unable to comfort each other. Calum walked out of the room each time Lizzie attempted to convince him that he was Gaby's father. Incensed after one such incident she began to fantasise about life without him. As a single person she could be more selfish. She need never go to another hockey function. She could eat fish every day of her life if she wanted. And she'd be in sole charge of the remote control. She used to joke that she had been born married and had forgotten what it was like to be an individual rather than part of a pair. But at thirty-six she was no older than many women who had not married at all. Did she want to start again?

The question brought her up short. How could she go down this alley? What had happened to her resolve to force the lab to admit they'd blundered over the tests?

She pulled herself together and decided to talk to Edward Foxton first. Calum had a high regard for him; maybe she could persuade him to intervene on her behalf.

His voice on the phone sounded crisp. 'I have the letter from the lab in front of me. They are adamant there has been no mistake so how could I persuade Calum otherwise?'

Lizzie clenched the receiver. 'Edward, you've known me a long time. In the light of this so-called proof, wouldn't I have admitted my guilt by now?'

'I'm sorry, Lizzie, I'm trained to accept evidence, not someone's word, however fond I am of them.' He sounded distant, not like the friend she had known for years.

There was silence on the line for a second or two before he said, 'I advised Calum not to make any hasty decisions, ones he might regret later on. He may need to think things through before discussing them with you.'

'I see. So he wants to put everything into the deep freeze, me included, until he's ready to act. Well, I'm not happy about that.' She slammed down the phone. If Edward wouldn't help her, she would have to confront the lab herself.

The white-coated laboratory technicians were hard at work on blood samples. It was laborious and time-consuming. For bone marrow work they had to establish the human leukocyte/antigen typing through testing white cells against numerous antibodies.

They were studying the thousandth tissue culture plate that week, always conscious that every day in this job involved life and death. When they joined the lab, they were warned to switch off their emotions. Trouble was, they found it difficult to switch them back on when they returned home.

Today their specific task was to re-check a test in the batch on the Lynton child. They had already handed over the results of a second test to a firm of solicitors for some kind of paternity case. You'd have thought that would've been enough, yet the boss insisted on this third check. They wondered why Dan Hargreaves was in such a bate about this particular client and the buzz around the office was that the boss had kicked Dan's butt and he needed it to prove the lab's accuracy to some woman threatening trouble.

Dan Hargreaves picked up the Lynton file. 'Finished?'

His assistant nodded.

'Come up with anything different?'

'Nope, exactly the same. Why wouldn't it be?'

'People always hope it's an error.'

'They wouldn't be so keen to give their blood if they had any idea of how much one tiny drop can tell us.'

'Too true.'

'And it didn't help that the client read that smart-arsed comment, "Not his kid. Bet he doesn't know".'

Dan did not reply but gazed out at the darkening sky. That note could spell curtains to the promise of a future partnership, not to mention a subpoena from the ethics committee of the General Medical Council. But today all he was concerned about was Mrs Elizabeth Lynton. She was accusing the lab of making a mistake with the tests. She was wrong but he had to mollify her, then steer her away from any idea that Andrew Lynton had decided to contest the will as a direct result of his lab's indiscretion. If the news leaked out that the laboratory was insecure then it would be curtains for the business and certainly for him. As it was he had been verbally flayed alive by his boss for allowing a client access to a confidential report. He hadn't been able to deny it. Andrew Lynton's solicitor had made it perfectly clear why his client required a copy of the lab report on the blood samples given by Calum and Gabriella Lynton. Dan's protestation that it wasn't him who had written the damaging comment was dismissed contemptuously. If the report hadn't been shown in the first place there would be no repercussions, serious or otherwise. The lab's co-operation would be treated with every discretion, the solicitor had assured them. The threat of exposure if they did not co-operate didn't need to be spelt out.

Dan did not anticipate problems with Elizabeth Lynton and hoped it would not take long to get rid of her. A couple of weeks ago a new nurse had started in haematology, a redhead, and she'd already made it plain she would not be averse to bumping into him in the pub frequented by hospital staff after work.

He was always last out of the lab but then he was last to arrive in the morning, a reflection of his social life. It was his thirty-third birthday next week and he decided his way of life was damn near perfect. His income was OK, there was plenty of bread and butter work, thanks to the NHS, but he thought his boss should go after Harley Street and harvest the caviar accounts. It would be his suggestion when he clinched the partnership he felt he already deserved. So far he had not done badly.

He was fortunate enough to have an ex-wife who had a high income, so he enjoyed the real twentieth-century luxury, a divorce with no alimony. He owned the freehold of a two-bedroomed flat in Primrose Hill, although not in the most salubrious section. But his pride and joy was a vintage Morgan on which he lavished more affection than any of the women in his life.

Other than wanting more cash, Dan could not ask more from life. Women told him he was getting better looking as he got older and he was inclined to agree with them. He had taken to wearing pale blue polo neck shirts under his lab coat since one girlfriend had told him that it deepened the colour of his eyes. Dan had acquired them in cotton, silk and cashmere. They seemed to work. Certainly his bed saw a succession of highly-toned, enthusiastic women, several of whom were wives of his colleagues. In his single state, he was coming to the conclusion that married women were less trouble.

One of them, a hugely expensive interior designer, had obliged by giving him her advice without a fee, though that night he had repaid her more than adequately with two orgasms. She had selected the sort of chi-chi furniture that wasn't truly comfortable. His boss had at first vetoed it until Dan persuaded him it looked expensive enough to illustrate success. The office carpet she chose was in an impractical shade of cream. It never failed to arouse some comment from professionals who spent their working hours walking on rubberised flooring and assaulted by dark green paintwork. The lab's premises near Queen Charlotte's Hospital were small by Harley Street standards but had been carefully designed to impress not only hospital trust executives but also the managers in charge of the more lucrative private contracts. So far the decor was not doing its job and Dan's boss constantly put on pressure to bring in more work.

Carefully Dan straightened the pen and ink set on his desk. He had to give the impression of a top professional at work, someone whose laboratory simply could not make a mistake.

As Lizzie walked through the doorway, Dan's business smile was firmly in place but it gave way instantly to genuine pleasure at the sight of this attractive woman. He wouldn't mind a closer inspection of those breasts. How lucky it was, he thought, that women rarely suspected the pornographic thoughts that crowded a man's mind.

'Do sit down, Mrs Lynton,' he said, indicating the chair opposite him. Nice legs, too. 'Would you like some tea? Coffee?' It was an automatic offer not so much to put his guests at ease but rather to show off the delicate green and gold china purchased to reinforce the quality image of the laboratory.

When she refused he asked, 'I believe you're unhappy about a test we did here.'

'I certainly am. It is inaccurate and it's caused me and my family a great deal of trouble.'

He leaned back, swivelling his chair, arms folded, his body language dismissive. He was sorry to hear that, he said, but pointed out it was highly unlikely the lab had made a mistake.

'Are you saying you never make mistakes?'

'No one's infallible but we've done a third test and the results are exactly the same as the first two.' He spent the next few minutes explaining exactly how the tests were done.

When he had finished, she shook her head. 'Dr Hargreaves, Gaby is my husband's child. She cannot be anyone else's. I wasn't a virgin when I met my husband but I assure you that I haven't made love to anyone else since we started going out.'

Dan stopped himself saying what a great waste that was. 'If you tell me you're the mother, that's good enough for me,' he said with a confidence he did not feel. 'But we have established that your husband could not be the father.' She made as if to interrupt and he added, 'Mrs Lynton, you have to accept that the tests are correct.'

Lizzie's face crumpled. 'I don't understand. You say you believe me . . .'

'I do but I'm a scientist. I deal in logic.' He went rapidly through the possibilities in his mind and had a sudden inspiration. He rose and crossed over to a filing cabinet to take out a buff folder. 'There has to be another explanation,' he said. 'You've told me you're telling the truth so it means we need to test for other comparable components.' She looked perplexed. 'Wider tests might give us more clues.'

'Do you think that'll show anything different?'

He smiled at her. 'I don't know yet. Maybe I'll discover something so rare I'll write a paper for *The Lancet* and make my name.'

Lizzie gave him a smile of such radiance that for an instant he could imagine himself as a knight in shining armour. Her husband did not believe her, and if he was honest nor did he. But there was something about her sincerity and her faith in him that touched him. It made him want to help.

'The sensible thing would be for me to take a sample of your blood for testing,' he said. 'I'm surprised no one has asked you for one before.'

'There was no reason. I'm not related to Sebastian and they tested only the Lynton family, not those who married into it.' It was such a relief that at last someone was prepared to help nail the lie, Lizzie would have given him six pints of blood if he'd asked her.

She took off her jacket and Dan applied the tourniquet, pressing her wrist gently to try and raise a vein. Her skin was pale and delicate and smelled of freshly-picked lavender. He wondered if she could feel the electrical charge between them.

'You'll have to be patient for the results,' he said, extracting the syringe carefully from her arm. Finding out what blood group she belonged to was a mere ten minutes' work, he told her, and tissue typing to find a compatible bone marrow match could take up to seventy-two hours. But a DNA comparison, to settle matters of paternity, was far more involved. Lab technicians had to isolate each DNA strand then scrutinise them individually. To collate these could take as long as three or four weeks.

'Will I have to wait that long?' Lizzie asked in alarm.

Dan shook his head. 'The lab's pretty busy but I'll ask them to rush through a preliminary test on your blood. It should be ready in about two or three days' time.'

Dan expected her blood test to have one main result: make her admit the truth. Faced with irrefutable proof, she would suddenly remember a distant, one-night stand, like the actress in the film he'd enjoyed so much. What was its name? The main character had also sworn to the young woman who had contacted her that she couldn't be her daughter because she had 'never gone with a black man'. Then slowly, as she talked, it had dawned on her . . . *Secrets and Lies*, that was it.

Whatever the result of the test, what this desirable, vulnerable woman needed at this moment was to be rescued from a trough of despair. He was just the man to do it.

Calum was not conscious that his hair was standing on end, the result of his fingers threshing through it as he grappled with the balance sheets. He was startled by the touch of a hand smoothing his unruly mane.

Tess started to laugh. 'You look like a rock star who's been plugged into the amplifier.'

He pushed his chair back and grinned at her. She always made him feel better. Lately they had been spending more time together after the others in the office had gone home. She had been offering him practical advice and together they were working on the redrafting of clients' contracts to ensure that late payers coughed up by instalment rather than waiting for the final settlement date.

'I'm fed up with all this,' he gestured to the pile of invoices. 'Let's go to the pub.'

This was another ritual that had developed over the past couple of weeks when Calum had no desire to rush home.

As they walked the few hundred yards from the office, Calum watched the way Tess's dark hair swung this way and that as she strode alongside him. She was not a head-turner like Lizzie but she had good though angular features. Purists might say her nose was slightly too long but he did not agree, it gave her face character. And when she began talking animatedly her looks were upgraded.

As soon as the barman spotted their arrival, he gave a smile of recognition and reached for a bottle of dry white wine. He handed over a glass of wine to Tess and poured a half-pint of Calum's usual brand of bitter. As Tess and he settled into the small booth, she launched into the ramifications of a conversation Calum had had that afternoon with Fair Winds Exhibitions in New York.

The restrained light in the pub highlighted the glisten of her lipstick and her generous mouth moved rapidly as her story gained momentum. Every now and then she would pause to sip from the glass before continuing the story, pursing her lips as she tried to remember the salient points. For a moment he speculated what it would be like to silence her with his own lips. Until now he had stifled all memories of that solitary occasion when he had almost lost control. He wondered whether her mouth would yield to him as it had done all those years ago. Not once since then had she embarrassed him by referring to it. Last time he had a reason to fight temptation. He was enjoying a damn good marriage with a great sex life. Not any more.

He was conscious of Tess looking at him quizzically over the rim of her glass. 'What are you thinking about? You've been miles away.'

'Better you can't read my mind.'

She raised her eyebrows. 'Would I enjoy it?'

Already regretting his provocative comment, he did not respond. He should not go down this road with a woman he had to face every day in the office. What he needed was someone to comfort him, tell him he was not a bad bloke, reassure him that everything was going to be all right with the business and with the court case and most of all with Gabriella. And he wanted this reassurance from the wife he loved. He had not discussed any of this with Tess but she must have guessed all was not well at home from the absence of phone calls between him and Lizzie. And Tess was going out of her way to be solicitous, shielding him from much of the office minutiae, making it clear he could rely on her for extra support.

Tess rotated the stem of her wine glass slowly through her fingers. 'You're having a tough time at the moment, aren't you? And I'm not talking about the business.'

Warmed by the alcohol and needing a sympathetic ear, he made the decision to unburden himself. He found himself telling her about the terrible discovery over Gabriella's paternity. Tess listened, her mobile mouth stilled, her eyes full of compassion. He talked about the tension at home because Lizzie kept on insisting there was some mistake with the test.

'I've always liked Lizzie,' said Tess after a pause. 'She's been a wonderful wife to you.'

Calum was momentarily distracted by her unexpected comment. Then he blurted out, 'I can't understand any of this. Why, when she's been found out, won't she admit the truth?'

Tess gave a deep sigh. 'Haven't you heard the saying "deny, deny, deny"? If the test proves you're not Gaby's father, what else is there for her to say? And she'll probably keep on denying it. She has to.'

'Even after two tests say the same? That's ridiculous.'

'I'd do exactly the same.' She took a sip of wine and stared at him over the rim of the glass. 'If it meant I'd keep you.

Lizzie was dreading the sound of the key in the lock. She prayed that Calum would be late and she would be in bed and could pretend to be asleep. Anything to put off the terrible moment when she had to tell him that the laboratory had been right about his test. No ifs or buts. She had tussled with the idea of not telling him about her visit to the lab. After all, she was confirming what he already knew. And why risk another row? But she wanted to let him know that the doctor she had met for only a few minutes had believed her when her husband of sixteen years had not.

She sat in the kitchen flicking through a home decor magazine. If the will had gone the way they had expected she had planned a conservatory for the back of this room, picturing them at breakfast surrounded by exotic plants.

The phone rang and made her jump. It showed how tense she was, she thought, picking up the receiver. But it wasn't Calum. The hurried voice of Tess Parker asked her to tell Calum she would bring the file he'd left in the pub to their morning meeting.

Lizzie smacked down the phone, irritated that she was in a state of stress waiting for him to come home while he was apparently having a relaxed drink with the attentive Tess. She knew she was being unfair. Calum had no idea she had been to the lab so why should he hurry home when they spent most of their waking moments trying to avoid each other? They exchanged words only when absolutely necessary to discuss domestic matters like the few times Gaby needed transporting.

When at last she heard the sound of the front door opening and Calum came in, it was apparent from the loosened tie and the suspicion of a glaze in his eyes that he'd had more than his customary pint of beer. But she decided to ignore this and asked whether he'd had supper.

'I had a pie in the pub,' he said, walking over to the cupboard to pour a glass of Scotch. He said he was looking forward to a long, hot bath and had some papers to read for a meeting in the morning.

She watched him carefully while she gave him Tess's message but his face gave nothing away.

'I've something important to discuss before you go off to bed,' she said carefully.

He looked at her warily before easing himself into a chair. Lizzie described her visit to the laboratory and her interview with Dr Hargreaves and he straightened quickly, asking if they had found out anything new. When she said the test had given the same result, the light went out of his eyes.

'So there's got to be another explanation,' she went on quickly.

'There is,' he said icily. 'You were pregnant by another man.' Abruptly he got up, turned on his heel and stalked out of the room.

She stared at his back, feeling sick. He hadn't given her a chance to tell him that Dr Hargreaves believed her and was testing her blood to see if that provided any clues to the mystery.

She heard sounds of banging coming from the living room. Puzzled, she went in to find books strewn over the floor.

'What are you doing?'

'Putting everything in alphabetical order.'

'Why?'

He climbed off the chair and looked at her coldly. 'I need some order in my life, something to stop me thinking.' He threw a book on the floor with a force that made her flinch. 'Only it doesn't work. I keep on remembering you standing at the doorway of the church, on your father's arm. I thought I had never seen anyone so beautiful and all the time you must've known you were pregnant by another man.'

I've had enough of this, thought Lizzie. 'Listen to me. Dr Hargreaves is doing a test on my blood. He believes—'

92

'In miracles.'

She gave an exasperated sigh. 'Calum, can't you get it into your head that if I were guilty I'd have given up trying to convince you long ago.' A cynical smile flickered across his face. But she went on relentlessly. 'Hargreaves thinks there could be another reason . . .'

'What other reason?'

'He's not sure,' she faltered. 'But . . .'

'You're clutching at straws,' he said, and moved towards her in such a threatening manner, for a moment she feared he was about to hit her. He prodded her shoulder sharply. 'Deny, deny, deny. That's your strategy, isn't it?' His face was distorted and he turned towards a pile of books and gave it such a savage kick that books were sent flying all over the floor. Lizzie backed away from him.

He wheeled round and said viciously, 'I was right about Rivers. He wouldn't marry you, would he? So then you turned to me, the sucker.'

Her face was ghostly pale, making her eyes seem darker and brighter. With a great effort of will she cleared her throat. 'Peter Rivers has nothing to do with all this and you know it. Having a slanging match isn't going to help.' His expression didn't change but she ploughed on regardless, putting as much control into her voice as she could muster. 'I'm only thinking about Gabriella. And you should be too. To protect her I think we should settle with Andy, try and come to some sort of arrangement with him which wouldn't disinherit Gaby.'

His voice was scathing. 'Anything not to go to court. Why would you want to air your dirty linen in public?'

What was the point in defending herself further? He was so sure of the facts. If he had come to believe she was the kind of woman who could enter a church and take those vows of commitment while intending to deceive him, what kind of future could they have together?

Slam.

The yellow spot ball ricocheted off the scarred wall and the player charged towards it, walloping it at a vicious angle.

The smell of sweat permeated the court but the two men did not notice, so intent were they on the game. Edward Foxton was a wily player, adept at slamming the ball against the side wall, but Calum, whose Bible was Jonah Barrington's book on the championship approach, was the better strategist.

Edward made an unsuccessful lunge.

'Game, third set and champ.' Calum held his racquet above his head in a victory salute. Edward wiped his brow with the back of his hand.

'Adversity suits you. I thought I'd done enough to win, shows what happens when you relax.'

'Relax nothing,' grinned Calum, taking off his wrist bands. 'It's court craft, skill, iron wrists.'

'I'll get you next time. Come on, I owe you a pint.'

Calum slung a towel round his neck and he and Edward made their way towards the showers. As the hot water cascaded down his body, Calum reflected how he conformed to Lizzie's often-expressed criticism that men so easily compartmentalised their emotions. Lizzie would never have wasted time in this way. She would have insisted on hearing the latest development on the court case rather than bide her time until the squash game was over and they were sitting in the clubhouse bar.

But before they could order a ploughman's and a pint of bitter, Calum could restrain himself no longer.

'So tell me.'

Edward shrugged. 'Bit of a problem. It's not straightforward, I'm afraid. I felt sure our barrister, Tim Goodman, would quibble about the way your father expressed himself in the second will and he did.'

'The bloodline?'

'Precisely. Tim thinks it could make for complications because judges' interpretations can vary.' He gave a tut of annoyance. 'I wish your father hadn't drawn up this will behind my back. I could've checked the language so there was no ambiguity.'

The waiter appeared at the table with their order. Calum rolled the glass in his hand and wondered out loud whether his father had acted the way he did because of their friendship. It would have put Edward in an awkward position. Edward reflected on this for a moment and decided he might be right. But he pointed out that when Robert Lynton had drawn up this will himself, without legal assistance, none of them could have foreseen the development. Without the problem of Gabriella's paternity, Andrew would not have had a case.

They supped their pints meditatively.

'Why didn't Dad mention Gabriella's name in the will?'

The solicitor shifted uneasily in his seat. 'Because it wouldn't have occurred to him there were any other granddaughters. Heaven knows what we'd have done if Andy and Edina had a girl child.' He gave a half-smile. 'Now that would've been a case to remember.'

'With all the evidence we're going to present about the bond between Gaby and my father, we must win, surely?'

'Nothing's certain, but I think we have a good chance. Tim Goodman mentioned that the judge might want to talk to Gabriella.'

Calum put his glass down with a thump. 'I hope not. I don't want Gabriella to be put under that kind of pressure. She doesn't yet know about the blood test. Lizzie and I are hoping that Andy will settle so there won't be a case and she won't have to know.' Observing his friend's questioning gaze, he added, 'Yes, we will tell her but at a time we choose, when we think she can handle it better than she can at present.' He told Edward that he had tried speaking to his brother but Andrew would not come to the phone or return his calls. 'Has his solicitor given you any idea how much it would take for him to settle?'

'I don't think there's any chance of his settling out of court,' said Edward. 'His solicitor's response to the idea was that his client wants the will declared null and void. In which case your father would be deemed to have died intestate and then the whole estate would be shared between you and Andy.'

Privately Calum thought he would not quibble with this outcome. Then he felt guilty. It had been his father's expressed desire for his money to go to Gabriella and whatever he thought about the decision, he had to live with it.

'If the judge passes on that one, there's another angle Andy's solicitor could use,' Edward went on. 'They could ask for a comparison between your family's financial situation and his. That's so Andy could make out a case of need.' He recounted a recent case where the grandfather had left everything to his grandson, cutting out his daughter. She had married for the fourth time to a foreigner who could not speak English and the grandfather was determined the man wouldn't get his hands on his money. The woman took her son to court.

'Don't tell me she won,' said Calum.

'She lost. But on appeal she proved she was heavily in debt without the means to pay it off. The judge awarded her half the money.'

Calum thought for a moment. 'OK, you don't think he'll settle. But I'd like you to have one more try. We haven't any cash but when he knows I'm prepared to sell the business, perhaps he'll change his mind.'

'I don't think he will,' said Edward. 'But Calum, that'd be quite a sacrifice. And Lizzie agrees?'

'I haven't talked to her yet about selling the business but I'm sure she will.'

'I'm surprised at that. She was adamant there was a mistake.'

'She's all for sorting out a settlement with Andy. Lizzie's keener than I am to have her past life kept quiet.'

Edward agreed to put another offer to Andrew but warned Calum not to assume his brother would be satisfied with what he could raise. It wouldn't be nearly as much as half the estate. Calum thought Edward was probably right but what he was proposing was a commonsense solution and he hoped even Andrew must see the justice in not wrecking Gabriella's life.

They drank in silence for a minute before Edward gave an embarrassed cough. 'How are things with you and Lizzie?' Calum's expression was so melancholy that he added quickly, 'If you'd rather not talk about it . . .'

'No, you're one of the few people I dare confide in. Ed, every time I look at her I'm reminded I've been living with a liar all these years. The problem is I'm stuck, I can't do anything because I have to think of Gaby. She needs me.'

Edward nodded sympathetically.

'I love her as my own, nothing will change that, and you know the strange thing about all this? The fact that she's not mine doesn't worry me nearly as much as I expected it would.' Calum raked his fingers through his hair. 'It's Lizzie's duplicity that really hurts. I feel cheated.' He appealed to his friend. 'Is that any basis for the future?'

Edina stirred her coffee, aware that Andy was still speaking but too tired to concentrate any more. The doctors had told her that Sebastian was responding reasonably well to the pre-operation tests and if a match could be found they would go ahead immediately. Please God it came soon. None of the relatives had matched up, but the hospital was still testing the hundreds of volunteers who had come forward. She wasn't sure how much longer any of them could put up with the waiting.

The baby's illness had brought her and Andy closer. Other mums in the hospital said the exact opposite, so in that respect she was lucky. Andy didn't appear to care that she looked like hell most of the time. They had changed their priorities. They hardly ever went out when once they used to hire babysitters at least twice a week. There were compensations. Andy didn't seem to mind cuddling up on the sofa to watch telly practically every night.

She had been surprised at how gentle he was with Sebastian. All the love he had inside him spilled out. It was a side of himself he rarely showed to outsiders. Once again she thought what a pity it was his brother didn't see any of it. If they were friends, Calum might have been able to talk Andy out of all this court business.

Andy was in full flow about the court case but as he did not appear to expect her to respond, Edina was able to carry on with her own thoughts, giving him the occasional nod. She did not want any court case. She hated the idea of fighting with the family when they had been so good about Sebastian. She had no legal knowledge but it seemed to her perfectly clear that Robert Lynton wanted his money to go to Gabriella so whatever the solicitors were putting into Andy's head, she did not think they had much chance of winning.

She had never set eyes on the old man. By the time she met Andrew he was not speaking to any of his family but when Sebastian was born Andy's mother came to see him and gave her a cheque for £500. She never came back again. Andy said that was because she was completely under his father's thumb. Edina thought it a shame Robert Lynton had not seen his only grandson. But if he didn't want to acknowledge Sebastian, she didn't want any of his money. She had not the courage to say any of this to Andy.

Money wasn't easy and Andy worked like a slave to keep them all but sometimes through no fault of his own he didn't make a sale for weeks and his commission came in dribs and drabs. She felt too tired to give Andy the attention he needed. He was a baby himself in many ways. She was often impatient with him and too exhausted to take the trouble to tart herself up to look like the girl who snared him. In the past people used to think she was a model or a Page Three girl. Huh, they wouldn't think that now. She had lost a fair bit of weight. These jeans were baggy around the bottom and the tops she wore now were chosen for warmth and comfort, not to show off her figure. It was rare these days that she had time to bother with make-up, unless she was off to the hospital.

When they were first married Andy would joke that they were always at it like rabbits. Well, not these days and she had a conscience about it. Though they did not make love as often as he wanted, Andy had surprised her by being very understanding when she turned away. Spending so much time at the hospital had drained her and seeing all those tubes and things being pushed into her baby was a stressful experience. By the time she got to bed, all her body craved was sleep.

There was a sharp cry from the next room and at once Edina sprang up from the table and ran to attend to her son.

Chapter Ten

The scene outside Gaby's school in the early dawn was chaotic. Parents, trying to be helpful, were hampering the driver in his efforts to load the coach. Baggage was piled everywhere and it was raining, as usual. Invariably the pupils began their annual half-term trip to Lyon with damp anoraks and hair dripping down their backs.

A few weeks earlier Gaby had announced that she had no intention of joining her classmates but since the incident with Luke she had been told by Calum that whether she liked it or not she was going. Apart from the fact they had paid the full amount well in advance, Calum had been adamant that Gaby was to be prised away from Luke's influence. Natasha was also going which sweetened the pill. This had been one of the rare occasions Calum had initiated a domestic conversation with Lizzie and she was thankful to be able to agree on this one subject at least.

The unearthly hour of 4 a.m. had been chosen so that the coach would pick up the Dover ferry in time to make a reasonable start on the French autoroute. But the sight of yawning, ashen-faced youths made Lizzie wonder whether the school shouldn't have insisted on a more reasonable timetable, rather than save a few pounds by using an off-peak crossing. She glanced at her watch. They should be leaving in five minutes. Gaby was sitting in the front seat, headphones already clamped in place, when Lizzie spotted a familiar navy-blue Rover screeching to a halt alongside the bus.

Calum had said his goodbyes to Gaby the night before and had been generous with spending money, so what was he doing turning up here? He had never before come to see her off, especially at this time of the morning.

He tooted the horn twice before climbing out, then came to stand alongside Gaby's seat, waving at her until he caught her attention. A broad smile crossed her face and she hurriedly got up from her seat and clambered off the coach.

'Dad. What are you doing here?'

He clasped her in his arms and held her tight.

'What's the matter?'

Lizzie thought she could see the beginning of tears.

'Nothing, Gabs. Nothing at all. I just wanted to see you.' He let her go. 'You know you're my favourite daughter.'

'Dad,' she laughed, as she always did, 'you've only got one.'

Never had this familiar litany sounded more poignant to Lizzie and she assumed his unexpected appearance was as much a message to her as to his daughter.

The last pupil turned up, his mother apologising profusely, and the driver was finally able to start up. Hands waved frantically until the vehicle was out of sight. There was an awkward moment when Calum, standing rigidly alongside Lizzie, muttered, 'Come on then.' She had to explain to Sarah that she did not need a lift home.

On the journey back Lizzie attempted to discuss Gaby's packed schedule but Calum rebuffed her efforts with a curt, 'I saw Edward yesterday. It seems Andy is determined to go to court.'

'We can't let him do that. We've got to settle.'

'Do you think I haven't tried? I've asked Ed to have another go but he's pessimistic about the chances.'

Lizzie twisted her wedding ring as she always did when she was stressed. The pounds were dropping off her and the ring was now so loose it was in danger of falling off.

'Then Gaby's going to find out everything,' she said dully. So that's what lay behind his appearance at the school.

'Not if I can help it. I think we should sell out so that we can make Andy a decent offer. I intend to leave for America tomorrow to see if Erik Schroeder still wants to take me over.'

'Sell the business?'

'There's no other option open to us. It's still doing well enough to interest Erik and I hope you agree that we should.' Lizzie owned twelve per cent of the shares and when she hesitated, he reminded her that he would still head the British arm.

Lizzie could offer no alternative and reluctantly agreed. She was all in favour of trying to settle with Andy out of court but she was taken aback by Calum's decision to try to sell the business

100

outright without first discussing it with her. Once or twice over the last few days she had ditched her pride and made an attempt to discuss their problems. But, if anything, his hostility seemed to be increasing and each time she made a peace move he would walk out of the room or change the subject. He wasn't just making it difficult; he was making it impossible.

This unravelling of their marriage had happened at such speed, she began to question how solid its foundations could have been. Surely if Calum had truly valued her all this while, he would have tried to find some solution for them, instead of pushing her away. Most evenings they spent in different rooms. It was a horrible way to live. She had lost nearly half a stone in the last three weeks but he seemed to have no trouble with his appetite – not that he wanted her to cook for him any more; he seemed to prefer to live on takeaways. Thank goodness Gaby spent so much of her time out or in her bedroom or even she might have noticed that her parents had taken to grazing rather than sharing a meal.

So much was going wrong. If only they had been able to discuss things together. Calum was willing to sacrifice the business he had slaved to build over so many years and he had come to this life-changing decision without her. If their relationship had disintegrated to such an extent, would they ever be able to put it together again?

Calum kept an obedient eye on the semaphoring stewardess as she indicated the emergency exits. He had an appointment the following day with Erik Schroeder, the egocentric chief executive of Fair Winds Inc., his major overseas client. Working with Schroeder over the years had been a test of patience. He always expected Calum to drop everything to accommodate his demands, but in this instance it had been Schroeder who had agreed to fit in an unexpected visit.

Calum was preparing himself for tough negotiations. He had a rough figure in mind although he doubted it would be enough to satisfy his brother. But Schroeder could not be allowed to guess how much he needed money and his accountant would have to put the best gloss possible on the current trading figures, which were not brilliant.

Damn and blast Andy's interference. In his brother's place Calum would have accepted his father's wishes. He did not share his father's view that Andy was to blame for their mother's early death. Calum had made that plain many times, telling his father that where Andrew was concerned, he was too dogmatic and unforgiving. Ironically Andy had never believed Calum was sympathetic to his plight.

Calum assumed that his brother's motive in all this was to safeguard the future of his son. No other reason could excuse Andrew's actions. But however sorry he was about Sebastian's illness, he would always blame Andrew for dragging Gabriella into this mess.

Calum eased open the seat belt as the overhead sign was switched off. His mind turned back to the business. He had been forced to tell the staff that it needed an injection of cash and this was unsettling for all of them. He had been bad-tempered and distracted and hadn't been able to hint at the real reason. There were eight people on the payroll and Calum was conscious that a number of them had left good jobs to come to him. They were rightly nervous that their jobs were not as secure as they'd once thought. Who could blame them?

Tess appeared to be speaking for them all when she handed him the plane tickets. 'I hope the talks have the result you want,' she smiled at him. 'Is there anything I can do to help? Come with you, maybe?'

Tess with him in America? Certainly not. She was a complication he could not cope with at present. Until lately he had resolutely regarded her as nothing more than a provider of solutions to problems before they became crises. For her sake, and his, it had to stay like that.

He accepted a glass of orange juice from the stewardess, who dipped gracefully in front of him like a geisha. Her lips curved into a well-practised smile, masking any problems she might have. If only he could put on such a good act. That morning when he'd caught sight of his face in the shaving mirror he had been struck by the signs of ageing which seemed to have become visible overnight. The lines around his mouth had deepened, the optimistic gleam usually present in his eyes had been overtaken by a lacklustre expression that made him look older than his years.

He leaned back and tried to blot out the subversive question that had been troubling him since the blood test revelations. Just supposing Lizzie had confessed the truth about her pregnancy at

102

the time, what would he have done? The answer came at once. However much he loved her, he could not have married her.

Lizzie had left home far too early for the appointment with Dan Hargreaves at which he would tell her the result of her blood test. However much she dawdled, the traffic in the Goldhawk Road was unaccountably light and she was in his office forty-five minutes ahead of time. But fortuitously, his last meeting had been cancelled and the instant she saw his welcoming smile, some of her tension evaporated. Surely his relaxed manner must indicate he had good news for her. But her optimism was short-lived.

'I'm really sorry,' he said, 'there's a slight delay and the last few pieces of information are being collated now. It won't be long. Under an hour, I'm told.'

She could not hide her disappointment, nor could she resist asking what he had found out so far.

'I'd prefer to wait for the complete analysis,' he said firmly. 'The final stuff may alter things. While they're doing the last of it why don't I take you to the wine bar round the corner?'

She nodded gratefully. 'A drink is exactly what I could use at the moment.'

Dan Hargreaves was an amusing companion and as they drank their wine she found to her surprise that her worries receded. He was an able conversationalist and he even managed to provoke her into laughter when he described what she supposed was a dramatised version of life within the hospital village.

She noticed the blond tints in his thick, unruly hair which kept falling over his forehead when he talked. She found herself wondering if he was married. Somehow he did not give that impression.

Perhaps it was the combination of a couple of glasses of chilled Chardonnay and the candlelight in the darkened cellar but for the first time in weeks Lizzie began to relax and she found herself confiding in him about Gabriella's inheritance and the fight for the money between the two brothers. He appeared riveted. He was such a sympathetic listener that Lizzie wished she could tell him how serious the rift was between her and Calum. But she was saved from any possible indiscretion when he straightened suddenly and took off the pager attached to his waistband.

'It's the lab,' he said.

Lizzie's heart gave a lurch.

'I'll find out what's happening. Excuse me.'

She watched his athletic figure hurry towards the phones, certain the call was to do with her test. She had no clear idea how it could prove that Calum was Gaby's father, she simply trusted that it would. Why else would Dr Hargreaves have suggested taking a blood sample from her?

He returned to their table and sat down. Lizzie stared at him, her heart pounding in her rib cage. His expression was solemn.

'This is going to be hard to understand. I think we'd better go back to the lab. It's more private there.'

Iron fingers gripped her insides. 'No, please. Tell me now.'

He looked down at the table for a moment. When he raised his eyes, his expression was grim. 'We know your husband's blood type doesn't match your daughter's.' He paused. 'But neither does yours.'

She slumped back in the chair, bewildered.

'It's a scientific fact that a mother's blood always matches that of her child in some respect. Yours doesn't. Which means,' he swallowed, 'there's no possibility that you gave birth to Gabriella.'

Lizzie's face was white. Her body started to shake. 'I saw her being born. They put a mirror at the bottom of the bed. I saw her come into the world and then Calum cut the cord. She's our baby.'

'You saw a baby being born. But it wasn't Gabriella. It couldn't have been.' He leaned over and took her ice-cold hands in his. 'I think there must have been a mix-up somewhere along the line at the hospital and you were given the wrong baby.'

This was not happening. Not to her. She could not speak, could not feel the contact with him. She became aware of the clink of glasses, the buzz of quiet chatter and laughter of people with no problems, intent on having a good time. How could they be unaware of what was happening to her life? She was conscious of her breathing, which was far too rapid. It was ironic that she found herself following the instructions she had learned at childbirth classes on how to manage labour, inflating her diaphragm at regular intervals in an effort to calm herself.

'I'm finding it difficult to come to terms with this myself so I can just imagine how it is for you,' said Dan, watching her anxiously. He poured some bottled water into a glass and handed it to her. Gratefully she gulped it down.

After a few moments she managed to stammer, 'I don't understand . . . how could it happen?'

'That's what we have to find out. What happened to her right after the birth? Tell me exactly.'

Searing pain, she remembered. Labour had lasted for more than eighteen hours. By the time the midwife told her it was time to push, Lizzie had been debilitated, full of drugs, and weepy. Calum had cried tears of joy when he saw the baby. The midwife handed the newborn to Lizzie but she was too weak to hold her for more than a few minutes before Calum took over. He cradled his daughter and began crooning to her as Lizzie sank into exhausted oblivion. When she awoke, the staff nurse told her the baby had been taken away to the special care unit for jaundice treatment.

'How long was she there?' Dan asked.

'For about two days. I struggled up there, with Calum, and held her hand and talked to her . . .' she bit her lip. She must not break down.

'You didn't notice anything different? Her size, her colouring?'

'No, but I'd had only a short glimpse of her when she was born and I was exhausted, full of drugs and in the first few hours they let me sleep.' She added, more defensively than she intended, 'Calum held the baby and he didn't notice anything was wrong either. When I began to count the fingers and toes, it was much later.'

'Did you breast feed?'

'Yes, the following day.'

'And as far as you were concerned it was the same baby that you visited in the special care unit?'

When she nodded, Dan let go of her hands and beckoned the waiter to refill their glasses. He was quiet for a time then asked a question which surprised her. 'What day of the week did you give birth?'

'Sunday,' said Lizzie immediately. She remembered Calum reciting that rhyme to her about Sunday's child being the most favoured of the week.

He seemed satisfied. 'Sunday's the day when a mistake like that could happen,' he said. 'Hospitals are often short-handed at weekends.'

'I suppose that makes sense,' she said slowly. 'They did seem rushed off their feet.'

'Two babies could have arrived in the special care unit at the same time,' he said, 'and the identity tags could have been accidentally switched. Security systems weren't as rigorous then as they are now.'

Surely she ought to have known at once? Wouldn't some instinct have told her that the baby who returned from the special care unit wasn't hers? But when she voiced this thought to Dan he reassured her. 'Don't blame yourself. You bonded with the baby at your breast. Why should it occur to you that she wasn't yours?'

All these weeks, she had asserted her innocence to Calum. She had accused Andrew of faking the medical proof. Yet the truth was simpler and she believed it without a quibble because it answered so many questions. It had been a straightforward mix-up. Human error. But that didn't make it easier to accept.

She would never forget Gabriella's eyes fixed on her face during those close moments of breast-feeding and the feeling of awe at the sight of her dainty toes splashing in the bath. Lizzie masked her face with both hands as a flood of emotion threatened to swamp her.

There were so many memories . . . watching Gabriella's expression as she lay sleeping in her cot, or toddling around the garden, or grimacing at her first taste of carrots – still her least favourite vegetable . . . practising her part in the school play when she played a princess. And all the time, all fifteen years of it, she had been living with and loving the wrong child.

Lizzie let her hands drop into her lap and took a deep breath, nerving herself to ask Dan the question she had been avoiding.

'What,' she asked quietly, 'could have happened to my child?'

He frowned. 'It won't be easy to find out. But you've had a great shock and I'm not sure you should make any decisions about that, not right now. Once you start to search, other people are sure to find out why you're asking questions and you have to think through the consequences before disrupting so many lives.' He paused for a second. 'Why not talk it over with your husband?'

'He's in America.'

'Is there anyone else you can talk to? I don't think it's a good idea for you to be on your own.'

Lizzie nodded, thinking of Sarah, but Sarah was in Norfolk

with the rest of her brood for the half-term holiday. She did not say so to Dan Hargreaves. She was already feeling she had un-burdened herself too much to someone who was a comparative stranger. Lizzie thanked him profusely for his help and promised to keep in touch before making a quick exit.

Of course she had to tell Calum but first she needed time to marshal her thoughts, to work out the full implications of the bombshell that threatened to fragment their lives. Poor little Gaby. She dreaded the moment she would have to tell her she belonged to neither of them. Gabriella's future rested on the way she handled this. Then there was the business of the inheritance. Calum's father had placed such emphasis on the continuation of the Lynton bloodline that Lizzie feared the real grandchild, whoever and wherever she was, might have some claim on the estate. Would Edward Foxton feel duty bound to reveal the findings if he were told? She would have to think about that very carefully. This new development only strengthened Andy's challenge.

Back home Lizzie lay on the bed completely worn out. It was incredible to believe that the hospital had accidentally switched the babies and the little girl she had raised as her own belonged to someone else. Yet nothing else made sense of the blood tests. Dr Hargreaves had told her there could be no other explanation. Rationally she would have to accept the facts but emotionally how could she regard Gabriella as anything other than her daughter?

She levered herself off the bed and began to forage around the top of her wardrobe until she found the small holdall she had taken with her to hospital when her labour had begun. It was many years since she had examined the contents but each item was imprinted on her memory. She reached inside and took out a pair of minuscule white bootees. She remembered putting them on the tiny wriggling toes of her newborn before taking her home.

Lodged in the corner of the bag was a piece of tissue paper containing a souvenir of a milestone in Gabriella's life, her first tooth. Lizzie turned it over in her hand and sighed. Impatiently she turned the bag upside down on the floor, shaking out dozens of congratulatory messages and florists' cards. And then she found it, the doll-sized pink wristband bearing their surname and Gabriella's date and time of birth. She examined it carefully.

How could the hospital have made such a cataclysmic mistake?

Snapshots from Gaby's childhood came into her mind, starting with the eighteen-month-old toddler in a blue swimsuit. She was clutching the hand of her six-foot-three father and Lizzie had photographed the two of them from the back as they walked to the beach. Gaby's curly mop barely reached Calum's thigh and Lizzie's eyes prickled with tears.

This was replaced by an image of Gaby at four on another summer holiday, walking in the hills of Cornwall, her head touching her father's elbow. And so it had gone on throughout her childhood, her father providing the ruler against which they measured her height. There were many other memories, of proud parents holding out protective arms to catch the unsteady toddler attempting her first steps. Hiding the milk tooth under her pillow for the munificent fairy. Christmases when inevitably the tree would have been better decorated without help from willing but clumsy little fingers. All the minutiae of family life.

The one comfort to spring from all this mess was that her attitude to Gaby was unchanged. She hoped she was being honest with herself but at the moment it did not matter, one way or the other, that she was not her biological mother, that they were not flesh and blood. No connection with her or Calum? Rubbish. Fifteen years of nurturing had established a bond between them that could not be broken easily. And whatever criticisms she could make of Calum's behaviour towards her, she could discern no change in his attitude to Gaby since he had been told about the blood tests. Knowing her husband as well as she did, she was certain that whatever his true feelings, Gaby would never be the loser.

Lizzie glanced at her watch and made a rapid calculation about New York time. It was around lunchtime but Americans usually ate early so Calum might be available. Before she lost her nerve she dialled the number of his hotel.

Calum, too, was looking at his watch. He had just left Schroeder's office on the East Side and had an hour to get across the city for his meeting with his accountant and lawyer. He had forgotten an important document in his room and as he hailed a yellow cab he asked the driver if he could wait outside the hotel. The guy was unusually co-operative and Calum decided New York's latest charm offensive was working. Talks had gone well with Schroeder

108

and he was feeling more relaxed than at the start of the trip.

Calum raced into the hotel and up in the elevator to the ninth floor. It did not take him long to find the paper he needed. But when he glanced through it he saw to his dismay that one of the figures was wrong. It could skewer everything. He'd have to phone the office and get them to fax a new copy. As he reached out for the receiver, it rang. Please God let it be the office and he could get Tess onto it right away. But it was Lizzie.

'Is this a good time?'

'Afraid not, I'm rushing off to a meeting. Gaby OK?' If he phoned Tess she could probably fax the new figures to his accountant's office before he arrived. He reached for his electronic organiser to find the accountant's number.

'Yes, she's fine. Look, I wouldn't phone you but I've had the results of my blood test.'

'Lizzie, I'm sorry, I can't talk now. I'm only interested if this changes the picture. Am I Gaby's father?'

'No, but—'

'Then I'll have to phone you back later.'

'Calum, I kept on telling you there had been a mistake and I've found out that—'

'Sorry, Lizzie, I'm going to be late, I really have to go. Bye.'

Lizzie replaced the receiver, fuming. How dare he not listen? Where the hell were his priorities? If the position had been reversed, she would have registered the urgency in his voice and, whatever the schedule, made time to talk.

She sighed but if she knew Calum, he would be intrigued and curious to hear what she'd wanted to tell him. He was bound to phone back. Lizzie cracked open a couple of free-range eggs in a bowl to make an omelette for her supper. The automatic whisking motion was quite soothing and she began to daydream about her child. The baby who had spent nine months in her womb.

The family might have left Britain, emigrated. She could be anywhere in the world. She would be the same age as Gaby, of course. Would she be as tall? As striking-looking? Would she look more like her or Calum?

From here it was a short jump to speculating about the girl's talents. Would she have inherited her love of classical music, something completely alien to Gaby? And then there was Gaby's facility with figures. Her teachers had often said if she worked harder, she could read maths at university. As neither of them had any skill in that direction Lizzie and Calum had been stunned by the news. Now she realised Gaby could have inherited this gift from her natural parents. A disloyal thought crept into her mind, that she and the unknown daughter might relate better to each other than she did to Gaby. Perhaps they could have the kind of relationship Sarah enjoyed with Natasha. And then she had another thought. If she tracked the girl down, she might be the one to save Sebastian. Lizzie would have loved to pick up the phone and tell Edina what she had discovered but it was too early.

It was a perfect omelette, fluffy and the right shade of gold but after two small bites Lizzie's appetite vanished. She poured herself a glass of white wine, took it up to the bathroom and turned on the taps. As she sprinkled some bath salts into the running water, she tried to convince herself that it was in the best interests of everyone if she let things be for the moment. Dan Hargreaves had counselled caution and she was sure he was right.

Relaxing in the hot water did much to soothe her anger at Calum's peremptory manner. Involvement in the negotiations for the sale of the business was all-consuming, she told herself. She was foolish to assume that he would be ready and able to talk just because she was. She played a game with herself. If Calum phoned within the next hour, before she turned off the light, she would tell him everything she had learned today. Once he'd got over the shock of her news, she would discuss everything with him. They would decide what they ought to do and, difficult as it would be, she would wait until he returned to begin searching for their birth daughter.

Early on in their marriage Lizzie had accepted that she could be impatient and often needed instant action to satisfy her restless temperament; but she would always be guided by Calum. They were a well-matched pair; her uncanny ability to go to the heart of his problems was balanced by his more considered approach. She wished he was here right now to thrash things out.

As time passed and still Calum did not ring, her mood changed to one of self-pity. If only her mother were around. At least she could be relied on to listen. But her mother's itinerary was vague. She had promised a contact number when she reached a hotel where she might stay for a while, but so far Lizzie had heard nothing.

She allowed herself to wallow in her misery and, alone in the house, she wept for the life she had lost. She and Calum had been friends and lovers since her formative years and she missed their day-to-day badinage. Never before had she questioned the wisdom of marrying at such a young age. She and Calum had enjoyed learning about life together, although Lizzie had always been regretful that she had not finished her university degree course first time round. Marrying young meant she had missed out on the dating game but that was no hardship. She had always disliked the ritual. But there was no doubt that she and Calum had missed some of the excitement of their contemporaries, like backpacking around India, surfing in Sydney and grape-picking in Israel.

These days she went to work feeling that the person who was performing her duties was some kind of alter ego. Her voice sounded as if it belonged to someone else, and she wondered how this woman could smile at her pupils, hold their attention during the music lessons and converse sensibly with other members of staff. It was almost as if she was outside her own body.

If the days were painful, the nights were worse. She and Calum had been in the habit of reading for a while before switching off the light, pointing out snippets of interest to each other. But now there was complete quiet in the bedroom. Calum positioned himself at the very edge of the mattress, making it clear he could not bear any physical contact. Lizzie wanted to clap her hands over her ears, to scream, to shout, anything to shake the silence between them. If she had been able to go and stay with Sarah, she would have done, to escape the chilly atmosphere. But while Gabriella remained in ignorance they both agreed to act out the charade.

She could get a full-time job. There was a notice on the board at her current school inviting applications for a post which had accommodation offered with it. That would be a neat solution to their problems. Despite their occasional bust-ups, she suspected Gaby would choose to live with her if it came to the crunch.

It was late when Lizzie climbed into bed. Calum hadn't phoned. Miserably she wondered why she'd ever thought he would. Nothing about his attitude towards her lately suggested he was remotely interested in anything she had to say. Well, she would track down their daughter without his help and find out all there was to know about her. He would have to be told eventually but in her own good time. She tried to be honest with herself, recognising that part of her wanted to punish him. Allowing him to continue to think she had been guilty of sleeping with someone else was her revenge for his unyielding attitude. It would make the eventual revelation all the sweeter.

She ached to find the child who had been switched. She would take it a step at a time. First, find them, then see how the family was situated both financially and emotionally. Then move into top gear to try and persuade the girl to help Sebastian. The next step would be to tell Calum. Then Edward Foxton probably. And Gabriella? But this thought proved too much and Lizzie switched off the light. After a few minutes, her brain whirling, she switched it on again.

Calum's sudden trip to America and Gaby's half-term visit to France meant that for the first time in years she was alone. She would not have to explain her movements or account for her absence to either of them. Nor was she expected at the school as sometimes happened during the holidays. It was as if God was saying to her, 'Here is the perfect opportunity. Make the most of it.'

Where would she start? She could imagine the reaction she would get if she marched into St Martyn's Hospital and asked if she could examine their records of fifteen years before. Whatever story she managed to cook up she was certain she would be shown the door. Smartish. She could visualise what would happen at her school should a parent make a similar request. No, she needed the help of an insider.

Would Dan Hargreaves help? She didn't even know if hospitals kept old records available for that length of time. Surely they must have a cut-off period, after which the documentation disappeared into the archives. One of the nightmares at school was finding someone with the energy to look after these old records; it was not a priority for most organisations.

After spending the best part of the night wrestling with the problem she decided that Dan offered the best option. He might say he had no time. On the other hand he might be persuaded if she pointed out it could lead to a bone marrow match for Sebastian. All she wanted from him was to be steered in the right direction.

'Don't ask, don't get,' parroted Lizzie as she psyched herself to pick up the phone and dial his laboratory at the start of the business day. She was surprised and pleased to find that not only was he in but he would take her call right away. And it was clear from his greeting that he did not regard her interruption as a nuisance. And when he heard she had made up her mind to find her, he did not try to dissuade her from the search. On the contrary, he immediately offered to help. She was delighted but also surprised and slightly puzzled. A telephone contact or an introductory letter to the hospital authorities was all she had hoped for. Why would he be willing to give up his time to actively join in the search? Then she chastised herself for being suspicious. Surely it was Sebastian's welfare which was motivating him. And why on earth was she questioning his motives? Whatever it took to find her birth daughter she would do and be single-minded in the pursuit. She accepted his help gladly and they arranged to meet in the hospital's reception area the following day.

'We'll have to be careful about our reason for requesting to see records from fifteen years ago,' he said. 'If there's the smallest sniff of the hospital being to blame for a cock-up, those files will be buried under concrete.'

'I'm not interested in blaming anyone,' she told him. 'I just want to find the child.'

'I know that and you know that but Marty's will never accept that somebody won't want to make money out of this. Trust me.'

The least suspicious way to gain admission to the records department would be to ask the authorities at the hospital, for whom he had done work in the past, if he could examine their files for a research project on teenagers born fifteen years ago. He planned to interview them, naturally with parental permission.

'Wouldn't that put you in a tricky position?' she asked.

He paused for a moment. 'Not really. I can justify the research. That kind of data is immensely valuable in my line of business.'

Lizzie stifled a pang of misgiving. She could think of no other way to obtain the information and he was perfectly capable of assessing his own risks.

'There's no time like the present,' he said. 'Let's try our luck tomorrow afternoon. Your cover can be as my assistant,' he added, smiling, 'although if you were, I think I'd find you too distracting.'

What did he expect as a reward? Lizzie wondered uneasily, and immediately dismissed the thought. He was only trying to keep her spirits up. He had not made her feel the least bit uncomfortable and it was true she was cheered by his response to her quest, feeling more positive and hopeful than for days.

In the taxi to the hospital the next day, Lizzie tried to remember names, faces, anything connected with St Martyn's maternity ward that might help them.

'There were six of us in the ward,' she told Dan. 'We said we'd meet up afterwards but the only thing we had in common was that we all had young babies and lived reasonably near to the hospital, so we never did.'

'What were the other mothers like?' he asked. 'Think. Any small detail might be useful.'

'We were a mixed bunch. A Polish woman was having terrible trouble getting her husband to join her. She had more meetings with immigration people than nurses. Her name was Helga.'

'Go on.'

'Another woman had lost a baby two years before.' Lizzie recalled the strained, white face constantly peering over the cot at her infant. 'She couldn't sleep for worrying that this baby might suffer the same fate. She was the wife of a trade union official and he was trying to negotiate through a strike so he came to see her at odd times, mostly when the rest of us were just about to nod off. But their baby was a boy. They called him Adrian.' Lizzie showed amazement. 'Why I should still remember that I can't imagine.'

'I'm impressed,' said Dan. 'Anyone else?'

'I remember one young girl very well. She was fifteen years old and her baby girl arrived about half an hour after she had been wheeled into the labour ward.' Lizzie gave a little laugh. 'She thought having babies was a piece of cake. I remember someone who'd had hours of hard labour threw a pillow at her.'

The archive section of St Martyn's was attached to the hospital, only a few hundred yards away from Dan's laboratory. It was little visited these days; current data was accessed by computer. They were shown into a basement room by a harassed young clerk, who had been expecting them. He brushed off their explanations and gestured towards a row of daunting-looking cabinets. 'There you go. The files you want are in the second cabinet on the right. We haven't had time to put them onto computer. Mind if I leave you to it?' He quickly vanished.

The first drawer Lizzie looked in contained files dated six months before Gabriella's birthday. Two more drawers brought her no nearer the correct date.

'I can't find anything here, can you?' she asked Dan.

He shook his head, clearly annoyed. 'What was the guy talking about? He doesn't have a clue about which files are where.' He frowned and pulled so hard at the next drawer that the cabinet rocked forward and almost fell on him. Lizzie automatically put out both arms to steady him. Embarrassed, she drew away at once, but not before noticing how muscular his back felt underneath his linen jacket. The nearness of his body had unsettled her and she was made acutely aware that it had been weeks since she and Calum had made love.

Dan half turned and thanked her. The heat was beginning to rise in her cheeks but he did not appear to notice and continued to rummage through the folders.

'Here we are. This is more like it,' he announced triumphantly. 'The week beginning November the eleventh.' He isolated several of the folders before placing them on a nearby desk. 'Your call, I think.'

Now that the moment had arrived, Lizzie had ambivalent feelings about opening this Pandora's Box. Would it be better for her, for Gaby, for Calum to leave the folders undisturbed?

Dan saw her hesitation. Leaning over, he opened the first file. 'You don't necessarily need to act on what you find, do you? If indeed you find anything at all.'

He was right. Having got this far, she should make the most of the opportunity. There might't be another.

Dan divided the files into two piles. They sat down and agreed to consult with each other before discarding any possible candidate. Taking a deep breath, Lizzie began examining her folders. It was hard to recollect surnames but luckily these files were prominently marked in date order. Rapidly she began to sift through them and extracted the ones bearing the date 11 November. Compared with the rest of the week the eleventh had been a busy day, with fifteen babies delivered during those twenty-four hours. Only five were girls. Dan replaced the files containing data on male babies while Lizzie went through the others until she came to the one marked 'Lynton'.

Below the columns in which the time, weight and the length of the baby were recorded was a comment column. In it was a note that an Apgar score taken immediately after birth, then again five minutes later, gave Gabriella seven out of ten for colour, breathing and response. Except for a slight touch of jaundice, Gaby's physical condition was apparently perfect. At the bottom of the page was a scrawled comment: 'Mother emotional and also groggy after epidural'.

After scrutinising the other files she told Dan, 'We can discard two of these right away. I remember this woman. She was a jazz singer and was in a private ward so we didn't see her much. But she and her husband were both from Jamaica, and this baby,' she tapped a file with her fingernail, 'has Chinese parents.'

'Here's one that is a possible,' he said, scanning the folder. 'No, as you were. This child died three days after birth.' Lizzie felt a shiver pass over her body. Dan's eyes darted over the details. 'She wasn't your child, the blood groups aren't compatible.'

Lizzie relaxed but a sobering thought occurred to her. That did not mean her birth daughter was still alive or, thinking about Sebastian, that she was in good health. Well, she would not rest until she had found out.

Only one folder remained unopened on the table. Dan picked it up and Lizzie's breath stopped as she waited for him to check the medical compatibilities.

'Now this looks more promising,' he said, handing her the sheet. The child was the third pregnancy of Nancy Ewing, aged thirty-eight, married to Derek Walter Ewing. His occupation was given as long-distance lorry driver. There was a note that the mother suffered from diabetes. The baby girl had the same birth weight as Gabriella and measured about the same in length. She also had the same Apgar score. But what clinched it was the added detail: 'Respiratory problem. Fluid in lungs. Transferred to special care unit 22.15.'

There was no other file left, no other baby of the right sex and blood group. Lizzie did not need Dan's words, 'This is the one,' to tell her this had to be her daughter. The immensity of what was happening suddenly overwhelmed her and it was some time before she could compose herself. Dan said nothing more but came round the back of her chair and put his hands on her shoulders. There they stayed for several minutes until Lizzie became aware that her wet cheek was resting on one of his hands. She lifted her head abruptly and began to apologise.

'It's completely understandable,' he said quietly, taking out a handkerchief and wiping her face gently. She was embarrassed at showing such raw emotion to a comparative stranger. It should have been Calum by her side, comforting her, assuring her that everything would turn out right. She was conscious of Dan's warm breath against her skin and she broke away, confused, unable to understand how she could be aware of his physical presence when faced with this traumatic discovery.

Dan picked up the folder, appearing not to notice her discomfiture. 'Does the name ring any bells?'

Lizzie shook her head, frantically trying to remember the small room with its six beds. 'I don't think she was in my ward.' Try as she might, she could not fit a face to the sixth bed in the corner, the bed that could have been occupied by Nancy Ewing, nor could she recall any of her visitors.

'According to this file the Ewings lived in Fulham,' he said. 'Here's the address.' He paused. 'I could put this back right now. Tell me what you want.' He walked towards the filing cabinet holding the Ewing folder aloft. 'What do you want me to do? Put it away? Or give it to you?'

If it wasn't for the possibility that the Ewing child could be a match for Sebastian, there were good reasons to forget she existed. When she told Calum, as she had to, he would inform Edward. Would he have to tell the court if Andrew went ahead with this case? If his argument about the bloodline succeeded, wouldn't the girl have a claim? He might gain nothing for himself, or for Sebastian. Either way, the cat would be out of the bag. It might or might not scupper Gaby's inheritance; it would certainly turn her world upside down. Lizzie baulked at the thought. God damn Andrew. Why couldn't he have let well alone? It was obvious Grandpa intended the money for Gaby's welfare, whether or not she was a Lynton.

But then other thoughts crowded in. Where was her baby? What was her name? Did she look like her or Calum? Was she happy? And what about Sebastian? She could be his lifeline.

If she did manage to track down her birth child, Lizzie told herself, she wouldn't have to say anything at first, would she? To anyone. It would be her secret. But wouldn't it be wonderful just to set eyes on her? That's all she asked.

Slowly Lizzie reached out a hand and took the folder.

Chapter Eleven

Sarah heard the desperation in Lizzie's voice on the phone early the following morning and without hesitation agreed to meet her in the park, away from telephones and domestic interruptions. She had just come back from Norfolk and said this was the perfect excuse to get away from the chaos.

Waiting for Sarah to arrive, Lizzie had been wondering how to put into words something she herself was finding difficult to grasp. She needed a sympathetic ear from someone with no axe to grind, someone who could be relied on to keep her lips zipped and who had heard all the ins and outs of Andy's threatened litigation. This was the first step in acknowledging it herself but Sarah would be able to advise her on what she should do about Calum.

She gazed appreciatively at the elegant row of mature beech lining the path. Late October was her favourite time of year, warm enough to enjoy being outdoors but with a hint of autumnal crispness that invigorated the spirits. But this morning nature did not work its usual magic and by the time she spotted Sarah, tugging at the leash of Mungo, her golden-haired Labrador, her mood had not improved.

Lizzie stuffed her hands into her pockets and watched as her friend, with a clink of Mungo's lead, set the dog free.

'Mungo, go, boy. Go,' commanded Sarah. 'No ball today.'

Sarah quickened her pace to catch up with Lizzie and together the friends walked towards a park bench.

'Tell me what's happened,' said Sarah. 'Is it the court case?'

Lizzie shook her head, her eyes downcast. She turned to look at Sarah. 'Calum is definitely not Gabriella's father.'

'But I thought you said—'

Lizzie put up a restraining hand. 'There's an explanation. I had my blood tested and I'm not Gaby's mother either.'

'What?'

The words came tumbling out. 'There must have been a switch in the hospital when she was born. I was given the wrong baby, Sarah. She's not related to either of us.' Her tears, so long held back, spilled over and a stunned-looking Sarah reached over to comfort her.

'Lizzie, Lizzie, how awful for you.'

'I don't think I've taken it in yet. I can't.' Lizzie put her hand over her eyes. 'I feel so stupid. For God's sake, I talked to the baby in the womb. I used to play her Beethoven. And then in those first days after the birth there are so many unforgettable moments, the first time you breast feed, the first time you dress her, when you take her home. I just assumed that every molecule and cell of mine and Calum's was imprinted on her.'

'Why wouldn't you? No one questions whether the child you're taking home from the hospital isn't your own.'

Lizzie didn't appear to hear. 'I didn't sleep a wink that first week, kept on creeping in and putting a mirror under Gaby's nose to check if she was still breathing. I've always believed that a mother has certain instincts about her offspring, so why didn't I sense that she wasn't mine?'

'Don't torment yourself, Lizzie.'

'I used to overhear the other parents in the hospital ward say their baby looked like this aunt or that grandmother but Calum and I could never see any of our relatives in Gaby. And as she grew up I remember Calum asking his mother if Gaby resembled her younger sister who had died young.'

'What did she say?'

'She was vague. But you've never thought Gaby looked like either of us.'

Sarah replied mildly that that was a long way from thinking she was not their biological child. Besides, she added, patting her friend's hand, her views did not count for much. Many kids did not resemble their parents.

'But people often commented on it,' said Lizzie.

Mungo came running up and started sniffing the ground around them.

'Let's walk,' said Lizzie, getting up from the bench. 'I need the exercise.' She picked up a stick and threw it for the excited dog to retrieve.

'What does Calum say about this?' asked Sarah. 'I bet he feels terrible about accusing you of two-timing him. This is proof that you weren't lying.'

Lizzie's mouth tightened and she told Sarah about the rushed phone call. 'I know how business stuff gets him stressed out but he still hasn't phoned back and I'm damned if I'm going to ring him again.'

'I know how you must feel but—'

'Don't try and defend him. You don't know the half of it. He said I trapped him into marriage and that I did it only because I wanted to give "my illegitimate baby" a name. You can't believe how close I was to walking out. The only thing that stopped me was Gaby.'

Sarah took the stick out of her dog's mouth and threw it along the path. 'This is outside of my experience, almost anybody's experience come to that, but,' her voice was grave, 'this concerns him just as much as you. I don't think you can have a proper marriage with this kind of secret between you. Anyway,' she added, practical as usual, 'he'll have to find out some time.'

Lizzie remained indignant. 'It's all very well for you to say that. After all we've been through together and he still wouldn't accept even the possibility that I might be telling the truth. Before he left for New York he played the hurt, innocent party for all it's worth, punishing me with the stony-faced treatment, staring out of the window, sulky silences, that kind of thing. Well, maybe I don't want to make it that easy for him any more.'

Sarah shrugged. 'Every time Hugh comes home and says he's lost a job I feel the same way. I want to make him suffer. But so far I've managed to hold back.'

'I had no idea,' said Lizzie, upset that she had not known about this. 'You always seem so unfazed by everything.'

'If I let his failures get on top of me I couldn't go on with the marriage. Of course I moan at him bitterly but at least we talk about things. And that's what you and Calum ought to do. You can't chuck away all these years of a good marriage, you have to try.'

Lizzie looked sombre. 'I suppose you're right.'

'No suppose about it,' said Sarah briskly. 'What do you intend to do about Gaby?'

Lizzie groaned. 'The last thing I want to do is tell her when she's already so difficult to handle. I'm going to wait till she's older,' then added, with the trace of a smile, 'like forty.'

121

Sarah gave her hand a squeeze. 'God, what a mess. It's like a Grimms fairy tale, you know the princess snatched from her cradle and replaced by the foundling?'

'Yes . . .' Lizzie's expression was anguished. 'Except I know who took my baby home.'

'Oh, my God.' Sarah stopped short. 'Tell me.'

Lizzie recounted what she and Dan Hargreaves had discovered in the hospital archives. Sarah just stared at her.

'What a traumatic time you've had,' she sympathised. 'Why didn't you tell me? I haven't a clue what I could've done but at least you wouldn't have had to go through this alone.' She paused for breath then added, 'But you must tell Calum.'

'Not yet. Not until I find out where the child is.' Lizzie was adamant.

'Oh, Lizzie, you're on dangerous ground. Please be careful.'

'I will. The idea actually petrifies me but I want to know whether she's happy, what she looks like, what her first name is. Wouldn't you?'

'Of course.' Sarah looked troubled.

'And then there's Sebastian. This girl is his cousin. That's another very good reason to track her down.'

'You're going to need the wisdom of Solomon to sort out this mess.'

'I know.'

Sarah looked at her. 'Would you like some help?'

Lizzie kept her eyes wide so the tears wouldn't spill over. 'Yes please.'

Mungo, now muddy and tired, came trotting back and Sarah put on his lead, fastened the collar on her coat and hooked her arm into Lizzie's as they walked home together making arrangements to meet the next morning. Sarah drove Lizzie to Fulham, having once again left Hugh to entertain the children.

As she manoeuvred her car into a rare parking spot off the Fulham Broadway, she asked, 'So what's the plan?'

'We can't assume they still live around here,' said Lizzie, trying to quell her nervousness, 'but I thought we could make inquiries at the local shops, talk to the neighbours, find out something about the family if we can, if her daughter still lives with her, that sort of thing.'

'They'll probably think you're a burglar's moll casing the joint for your man.'

Lizzie appreciated the attempt to lighten the atmosphere. 'I wish,' she said, smiling.

'You could short-cut all this by knocking at the address you were given,' said Sarah.

'Yes, and how do I explain myself without frightening Mrs Ewing to death? I can't just come out and say we were in the same hospital fifteen years ago and I have your baby and you have mine, can I?'

'I didn't say you should. OK, let's go.'

They started at the local newsagent's then next door at the bakery and finally at the corner shop. Their approach was studiously casual. Did anyone know of a family called Ewing? They had been college friends of Nancy's and were planning a reunion but had lost touch.

They drew a blank. Frustrated, they decided there was no other course but to go to the actual street.

Few of the houses showed any sign of life. They were standing across the road from number 53, Lizzie nerving herself to go over and knock at the door, when a heavily-built woman pulling a shopping trolley turned into the gate.

'Could that be her?' Sarah asked quietly.

'Doesn't she look too old?'

Sarah agreed she did but they crossed the street to talk to her before she disappeared indoors. She looked up startled as Lizzie hurried down the path.

'I wonder if you can help me,' Lizzie tried not to sound breathless. 'I'm looking for an old friend by the name of Nancy Ewing, and when I knew her she lived in this house.'

The woman stared from one to the other before shaking her head. 'Never heard of her,' she said curtly, jabbing her key in the latch. 'We've been here seven years and that wasn't the name of the person who sold the house to us.' She opened the door, heaving her trolley over the step, giving every impression of wanting to cut short the conversation.

'Oh please, wait a minute,' intervened Sarah. 'It's very important for us to trace these people.'

The woman halted. 'I've never heard of them.'

'What happened to the people who sold you the house?' Lizzie hoped she did not sound as desperate as she felt.

'Mr and Mrs Hudd? Don't know,' the woman replied in a voice that implied 'don't care'.

'Did they leave a forwarding address?'

'If they did it was seven years ago,' said the woman impatiently.

Sarah again butted in. 'Look, I don't know if you're like me,' she smiled, 'but I never throw away anything. I don't suppose you'd still have it, would you?'

'I might do but I haven't a clue where it could be.' She looked at their crestfallen faces and relented slightly. 'The only thing I can suggest is that you try our solicitor. She handled the sale.'

'Yes, we could do that,' said Lizzie, already thinking how tricky it would be to extract confidential information from a legal firm.

The woman disappeared inside for a moment and came back with a large black book and read out the address and telephone number of the solicitor. In Sheffield. Lizzie and Sarah could not hide their dismay.

'You don't have to go there in person, do you? You could phone,' said the woman sourly.

They thanked her and turned to leave.

'Or you could try the estate agents,' the woman added. 'They're just round the corner.' And with that she went into the hall and banged the door firmly shut.

'That was easy, Dr Watson,' said Lizzie.

'I don't think,' replied Sarah, looking at her watch. 'Let's go. I promised Hugh I'd be back in an hour to feed the kids.'

They soon discovered the estate agent had changed hands twice in the intervening fifteen years but fortunately one of the employees had managed to survive all the buy-outs. But when it became clear that Lizzie was not there to inquire about a property, her welcoming smile faded.

'Sixteen years ago? All those records are somewhere in the basement.' She made it sound as far off as the modules on the moon.

Lizzie allowed her desperation to show. 'Believe me, I wouldn't ask you if it wasn't vital to get the address of Mr and Mrs Hudd.'

'I can't spare the time. It'd take hours.'

'Please,' said Sarah. 'It's life or death stuff.'

'Well, I'll see what I can do. Come back in about two or three weeks.'

Lizzie and Sarah looked at each other in consternation.

'But we need the information now.'

'That's impossible.'

Sarah had an inspiration. 'What if we gave you twenty pounds for your time?'

The woman remained indifferent.

'Fifty,' said Lizzie hastily, fishing around in her handbag, thankful that she had enough cash.

The estate agent looked over her shoulder at her bustling colleagues, none of whom showed any interest in what was going on. Lizzie slipped the cash to the estate agent who took the notes and with a rapid movement put them into her pocket. 'We close at five. Come back then.'

The friends walked back to the car exultant. Sarah had to go home but she lent Lizzie her mobile so she could contact her from the taxi and tell her how she got on.

Five minutes before the office was due to close, Lizzie presented herself at the woman's desk. Unsmilingly the estate agent handed over a photostat of the front page of a house contract. But the surname on the sheet was not Hudd.

'These are not the people I was looking for,' she said, disappointed.

The estate agent was brisk. 'That's the best I can do.'

'But I need the present address of Mr and Mrs Hudd. They may know the whereabouts of the family I'm looking for.'

'You didn't say you wanted me to look up the whole history of the house,' said the woman belligerently.

'I'm sorry,' said Lizzie, hoping humility might be the best way to get this bad-tempered woman to co-operate. 'Is it possible for you to find the Hudds contract?'

The estate agent dropped her voice. 'That'll cost another fifty pounds.'

The Hudds would have to live in Dorset, a good four hours' drive on the motorway. Disappointingly, Sarah had to rule herself out right away. 'Can't you put it off till the weekend?' she asked, before adding with a groan, 'No, dammit. I'm sorry. I can't get away then. I promised the kids an outing and Hugh can't stand in for me.'

'That's a pity,' said Lizzie, 'I don't want to go alone. Maybe I could . . . hang on, there's a call waiting. It's probably Calum.'

'Are you going to tell him?'

'I'll have to.'

But the call waiting was not from Calum. Lizzie recognised the husky voice at once. Dan Hargreaves wanted to know how the search was progressing.

'Quite well,' she said, 'if a trifle expensive.' She explained her tussle with the estate agent.

'So are you going down to Dorset?'

She sighed. 'I suppose I'll have to, but it might be a wild goose chase.'

'You could phone.'

'No, I'll get far more out of them face to face.'

'You're right.' A thought seemed to strike him. 'If you haven't anyone to drive you why don't I come with you?'

Lizzie was suddenly wary. 'Why would you do that?'

'Are you serious? How often do you think I come across a situation as unique as this?'

Lizzie was uncertain how to react. It was a generous offer but she wasn't sure how keen she was to have a stranger involved in something as personal as this search.

'Besides,' he carried on cheerfully, 'unless you've got someone else to go with you it's not something you'd want to do on your own, is it?'

'No, it isn't,' she said emphatically, thinking that a man with his reputation to risk would hardly give up free time for something frivolous and undoubtedly his status as a doctor, planning medical research, was a far better cover when asking personal questions of strangers.

As they made arrangements to meet the following morning, Lizzie felt a surge of excitement. Nor could she put it down solely to the fact that her search had started in earnest. Dan Hargreave's wasn't the kind of man she met at hockey club dances or at school and that gave him added appeal. But only up to a point, she told herself sternly. I'm engaged in serious business, not on the lookout for a quick affair.

When Lizzie put down the phone she hoped fervently that Calum would not call that night. They might not be on good terms but she would still find it awkward explaining why she was planning a trip with a man she had only just met. Normally he wasn't the jealous type though early in their marriage he had confessed that whenever she smiled at another man he'd get the urge to throttle him. She was so lovely, he'd said, warning her that her warmth could be misunderstood. She couldn't remember the last time he'd said anything remotely possessive.

When Dan Hargreaves' vintage racing-green Morgan drew up outside her door, Lizzie was impressed. She and Calum had always regarded their vehicles as workhorses, functional, part of the background of life. This wonderful piece of metal was something else. She slipped onto the calf leather-covered seat, sniffed that distinctive, expensive aroma and almost purred.

'I feel like a princess,' she said.

Dan gave her a dazzling smile. 'Anyone who appreciates this car is definitely on my wavelength.'

The next few miles were spent with an amused Lizzie listening to Dan proclaim his love for a car he confessed he had lusted after for years and worked hard to afford. She risked a sideways look at him; his face was alight with boyish enthusiasm, and she longed to say what she was thinking: you talk about this car as though it was a woman.

As if he could read her mind, he said, 'I know I go over the top about my Morgan but really, when I meet a woman I love more than this thing, then I'll know it's real.'

His exhilaration amused her and she liked him the better for it.

'What does your husband make of this?' he asked, when they had pulled off the motorway to refuel at a service station and have a quick lunch in the snack bar.

'I haven't told him yet. He's still in America, in the middle of business negotiations. They're really important to us and if I tell him he'll come straight back.'

Dan cut his cheese baguette in half. 'Then I'm glad I'm around to give you some company.'

'I'm very grateful,' she said, warming her hands round the coffee cup, and for the first time was full of anticipation about what the next hours would bring rather than nervous about it.

Dan noted that she seemed more relaxed and smiled to himself. He had been ordered by his boss to keep close to her in case she made trouble for them. So far she had not mentioned the lab in connection with the court case and he was there to ensure as far as he could that they were kept out of the frame. He did not know how difficult that would be but his boss's view was that if he was charming and helpful, there was more chance of their keeping one step ahead and away from the ethics committee. At least this way he might find out what she planned to do.

Dan gave Lizzie a disarming smile and suggested it might be easier on her nerves if he approached the Hudds, assuming they were still the occupants of the house. She stifled a surge of annoyance at the idea of him taking over but she agreed because she had no particular wish to see this family. It was simply a stepping stone in the search for her daughter. Dan said all he would do was ask whoever came to the door whether they had any idea where his old friends the Ewings were living now as he had lost touch with them.

It was dusk by the time they located the terraced house in a quiet cul-de-sac in Thurlston but it seemed someone was at home for there were lights shining from a downstairs window.

Lizzie watched from the car as Dan's six-foot frame approached the front door, briefly blocking out the fading sun. His knock was answered by what looked like a short female figure but in the gloom Lizzie could not make out any features. By now her palms were moist and she let out a sigh of relief as Dan was ushered through the doorway. They must be accepting his story.

She tried to occupy her mind during the next few minutes by planning what they could do next if she was lucky and the Hudds were still there and were able to put their hands on the Ewings' address. If the family was living close enough, maybe she and Dan could speed there right away. This time she would insist on making the approach herself.

What would she say? Maybe some excuse that she was in the area and had often wondered how Mrs Ewing and her daughter were getting on. They might think it was odd but they wouldn't be rude enough to turn her away. If the girl – her daughter, she thought with a thump of the heart – was at home she hoped she'd have an opportunity to observe her and get some idea of the family circumstances. That would surely give her some inkling of whether or not the child was happy. On the record sheet it was stated that the Ewings already had two children. The baby born that day was their third so at least this girl was not an only child, like Gabriella.

Lizzie had spent many hours wondering whether her birth daughter was content and settled. If she was, she had come to the conclusion that it would be cruel to tell the family about the switch. What had she to gain by that? What had any one of them to gain, for that matter? She was sure she could find a way to get the family involved in Sebastian's donor programme without them being made aware of the reason why. Edina had told her that many anonymous donors had taken part already.

But if the girl was in any way neglected then Lizzie would be in a dilemma. Her loyalty was first and foremost to Gabriella and she had made up her mind that she would not act on impulse whatever the circumstances in which she found her child. It was better not to say or do anything drastic until she had time to think it through and maybe discuss it with someone she trusted, like Sarah.

As always, money was a large part of the problem. Yet again she cursed her father-in-law for being so stubborn. If only he could have been persuaded to leave Andrew even a portion of his wealth, none of this would have happened, she was sure.

Her thoughts turned to Calum. When he returned from America she must tell him. But could they repair the damage that all this business had caused? She wasn't at all sure they could. Shifting uncomfortably in her car seat, Lizzie thought what an unreal situation she was in. How on earth could this be happening and her husband not known a thing about it? It illustrated better than anything else how far they had drifted apart.

At precisely that moment Calum was in a soulless Manhattan hotel room on 53rd and Lexington. He was shortly due to meet Erik Schroeder again and before he left he decided he'd better call Lizzie. He had not been in touch since her phone call and he wanted to find out whether she'd heard from Gaby. He ought to tell her, as well, how the talks were progressing. It looked as though he would have to stay over longer than he had planned. Erik Schroeder was proving a tough negotiator.

Calum's mood had not softened but not having to be reminded of Lizzie's betrayal by seeing her every day was at least alleviating his despondency. He dialled briskly and no answering machine switched on. Typical. However many times he nagged her about it, she would forget. He would try later. In the meantime he had better find out what was happening at the office.

Tess was at her desk, as he knew she would be. As he heard the sound of her pleased chuckle when she recognised his voice, his mood lightened.

Lizzie's body was stiff with suspense. For the past ten minutes her gaze had not wavered from the entrance to the pebbledash house. She straightened as the door opened and Dan appeared.

He waved his hand in farewell to someone standing inside the house and turned towards her. As he neared the car Lizzie tried to fathom from his expression whether or not the mission had been successful.

Sliding into the seat next to her he seemed distracted. 'Good news and bad. The Hudds do live there but I'm afraid we have to come back in the morning.'

'Why?' Despite her efforts Lizzie's frustration was evident.

Dan put the ignition key into the lock. 'Mr Hudd works nights so he wasn't at home and he's the only one who knows where the papers are. I tried to persuade his wife to phone him at work but she was horrified by the idea. Says she'd only do that if somebody had died.'

'Well, thanks for trying.'

'He'll be there in the morning.'

'What time does he get home?'

'Around half past seven and he goes straight to sleep so you'd better not be late. It might be best if you stayed somewhere here overnight. There must be a decent pub in the nearby village.'

'Yes, I suppose you're right.' She felt a mixture of disappointment and relief that he had not included himself in the plan. It was comforting to have him by her side when she felt so nervous about everything, but at the same time she was beginning to feel awkward with him, wondering what was going on in his mind, trying to fathom what he expected from her. The Morgan moved smoothly forward and nosed its way towards the village.

But however awkward she felt, Lizzie was dreading an evening alone with her thoughts and Dan would be a welcome diversion. With what she hoped was a relaxed and casual tone she asked if she could treat him to dinner as a thank you for driving her down. After a slight hesitation he accepted.

The nearby village of Thurlston on the Green was full of carefully maintained thatched cottages and it was not long before they saw a stuccoed building with a wrought-iron pub sign proclaiming the Prince of Wales. Huge window boxes garlanded the front terrace and tubs containing late-blooming pansies and lollipop-shaped bay trees decorated the entrance. A blue and red plaque pronounced the pub had won a coveted Routiers award for its cooking.

Lizzie stood waiting while Dan fussed over the locking of his car and when he had finally secured it to his satisfaction she muttered, 'I haven't brought any overnight things with me.'

'Don't worry. I've got a spare toothbrush.' He gave a half-smile. 'I was a Boy Scout.'

Casually, he steered her towards the reception area and Lizzie had to suppress a giggle. She had a vision of Calum striding across the green at that moment to see her enter this out-of-the-way pub in the company of an attractive man in a classic sports car. If the position had been reversed she would have sharpened up the scissors.

The Prince of Wales tavern had been built for travellers in the sixteenth century and generations of innkeepers had prided themselves on offering four-star hospitality. The pub landlady was a cliché of her forebears, buxom and comforting, and suggested they had a meal in front of the fire while she prepared their room.

'My room,' said Lizzie firmly. 'Only one of us is staying.'

The landlady examined the register. 'Double or single? We're not busy and you can have your pick for the same price.'

'That's very generous,' said Lizzie, smiling. 'Then let it be a double,' thinking how long it had been since she had spent the night alone in a hotel. The landlady did not seem to think it odd she had no luggage. Obviously this was the way it worked these days.

The cloth on their table was starched white cotton and in the centre was a posy of seasonal flowers and a candle in a pretty silver holder. Lizzie drank the pre-dinner wine more swiftly than she meant. In her heightened state it had more effect than usual. She began to feel uncomfortably warm. She dearly longed to take off her jacket but she worried it might send the wrong signal. Nervously she began to toy with the top button but stopped abruptly when she noticed Dan's eyes fixed on her moving fingers.

From that moment the atmosphere changed. Lizzie sensed an undercurrent between them. She found it difficult to meet Dan's gaze. Even the most prosaic questions seemed to have hidden meaning. When he asked if she'd like to have another glass of wine she found herself colouring. Was she being naive or was he trying to lower her guard? She began to wonder again what he expected from her. Well, if he thought she was going to jump into bed with him he would be disappointed.

By the time the meal arrived she found her appetite had

disappeared. She pushed morsels of food around her plate while Dan quizzed her about her life. Gradually her fears began to subside. He was being charming and she was being ridiculous. She was a well married woman. She reminded herself that an unattached, successful man like him would have the pick of the crop in London. He didn't need anything from her so why was she ruining the moment by analysing it to death? After all, it had been a long time since she had been the centre of attention for a man other than her husband, a man who under any circumstances would be regarded as a catch.

Lulled by the pleasant ambience and fuelled by several glasses of a fine Bordeaux, Lizzie began to relax. She appreciated Dan's skill in diverting her attention away from her problems as he encouraged her to talk about the school, her work and some of her wayward pupils.

At the end of the meal two glasses of dessert wine appeared with the landlady's compliments but Dan refused, saying with a charming smile that he had to drive back to London. Lizzie squinted at her watch and looked brightly at him. 'It'll be quite late when you get back. I feel really guilty, I shouldn't have persuaded you to stay for dinner.' He merely gazed at her, saying nothing, and she hurried on, 'I suppose you have a full day at the lab tomorrow otherwise I'd suggest you stay over as well.'

He spoke so quietly she had to lean towards him to hear.

'This all started out with me wanting to play the great detective,' he said quietly. 'It was a welcome break from my routine in the lab. But now something's changed. I don't only want to help you. I find I'm thinking about you. Often, at the most inappropriate times.

Lizzie was taken aback. With all that was going on in her life how could she cope with extra complications? The light from the fire shimmered on his face and she gazed into warm brown eyes, certain that he would indeed be some complication.

For a moment or two they avoided eye contact then Dan said, 'I didn't mean to embarrass you. I think I'd better get on my way. I'll just have a black coffee.'

Lizzie found herself in a quandary. She did not want him to believe she planned to jump into bed with him but it was late and he had been drinking. If anything happened to him she would never forgive herself.

She surprised herself by saying, 'Now don't be silly, you've had too much wine to drive. You might scratch your car.' His expression registered such shock that she had to laugh and added, 'Come on, let's be grown up about this. Stay the night and we'll go and see Mr Hudd early in the morning. The landlady told us she had plenty of spare rooms.'

It took little more to persuade him and when the coffees turned out to be laced with brandy and cream, he took it as a sign that he should indeed spend the night at the Prince of Wales.

As he sipped the Irish coffee the conversation became more personal. He stared across at her quizzically. 'Let me get this straight. You've been married for sixteen years and you've been faithful all that time?'

Dear God, the way Dan put it he managed to make it sound incriminating. Lizzie just prevented herself from apologising for her fidelity. She tried to sound flippant.

'Don't make me feel like a freak. There are more of us around than you think.'

He grinned. 'Only one lover, eh?' He leaned across the table. 'Don't you ever wonder . . .?'

'Of course. I'm only human. I wouldn't be honest if I hadn't ever thought about making love to another man now and then.'

'Let's think about this in a scientific way.' His eyes were twinkling. 'You married at what? Nineteen, twenty? And you don't seem to me to be the wild child type so I wonder, how much experience would you have had?'

Too dangerous to answer him, thought Lizzie, smiling enigmatically.

'What a challenge,' he said mischievously and held her gaze so long she was forced to look away.

Eventually he went to book himself into a room and the moment came when she had to get up. She walked up the narrow staircase towards the bedrooms, acutely aware of Dan's eyes following her. In the corridor he opened his palm and showed her two large gold keys.

'You choose.'

As Lizzie reached out to pick up one of the keys, his hand closed over hers, trapping it in his grasp. In a sudden movement he pulled her towards him. His lips were soft and the kiss was gentle but her body responded fiercely. Not since her first days with Calum had she experienced such an electrical charge. Every nerve ending tingled and her pulse was racing. The kiss ended and he let her go, which was just as well because she could not have pushed him away.

They stared at each other, short of breath.

'I'll see you in the morning,' she said, trying to sound like a strong-minded married woman instead of a gauche young girl after her first kiss. She turned and quickly opened her bedroom door, locking it behind her. She flung herself on the bed and lay back on the faded coverlet trying to conjure up a vision of Calum's face. What would have happened if Dan had been a trifle more persistent?

She tried to find excuses for the way her body had reacted. Calum and she had always enjoyed a satisfying sex life but it had been several weeks since they'd made love. That was it. Sexual frustration. And the wine. And being away from home.

Lizzie rolled off the bed and walked into the bathroom. She peeled off her sweater and began undressing. Then in the harsh light of the bathroom mirror she peered critically at her body. Clothed she wasn't bad. Naked? Forget it. If only she had time for exercise instead of endless hours in front of a computer doing the admin work full-time teachers gladly jettisoned into her lap. But why did she hesitate before taking off her make-up? And why was she not surprised when only a few minutes later she heard a soft tap at the door?

'Lizzie,' said Dan quietly. 'I've brought you that spare toothbrush.'

She only had to shoo him away and that would be it. Her reflection stared back at her in the mirror, cheeks flushed, eyes deepened in colour.

Quickly she wrapped a towel round her body and made her way to the door, with every intention of taking the toothbrush and saying good night. The face looking down at her was without guile. This man wanted her. Wanted her very much.

As she reached out for the toothbrush he leaned gently against the door. When there was resistance he stepped back and slowly, with a certain amount of regret, Lizzie closed the door on him.

Lizzie lay turbulent on the cool sheets. Having sex with Dan was not the answer to her problems. It would only add to her guilt. Until recently she and Calum had made love every weekend, almost without fail, and usually it was good if a trifle predictable

134

for them both. But that was only to be expected. Knowing each other so well, inevitably some of the passion had died along the way. It couldn't be compared to the excitement of sex with someone new.

It was some time since she and Calum had tried more than a couple of positions and she was as much to blame as he was. Did she not regard their weekly bout more as a duty, an adequate diet for their marriage rather than a gourmet feast? This had never bothered her before. That's what happened in longstanding relationships. Marriage, she told herself, was ninety per cent companionship and the familiar trivia of everyday living, and ten per cent heaving and threshing about in bed. It was only because Calum had made it clear lately that he did not want her physically, could hardly bear to look at her, that she had responded to Dan's flattery. She had always resisted one-night flings and Dan, she was sure, would regard her as just one more notch in his belt. She hoped her refusal would not bruise his ego because it was better to have him on her side.

After a fitful few hours' sleep, she went into the shower. Hoping to shock herself awake, she set the thermostat to cool. They planned to leave in half an hour to see Mr Hudd and she needed to have all her wits about her.

Dan was already at reception when she came down the stairs and was about to take a credit card from his wallet when she laid a restraining hand on his arm.

'I insist on paying. If it wasn't for me you wouldn't be here.'

'That's true, but I'm still not letting you pay for me.'

The landlady observed this interchange with some interest before accepting a credit card from both of them. While she was dealing with the bills, Dan turned to Lizzie and gave her a smile that reassured her he wasn't bearing a grudge.

'If you'd been braver we could've saved the price of a room,' he teased.

But when the landlady gave him the receipt, Lizzie noticed that he aimed that same smile at the woman and she had a slight feeling of irritation. God, she had to stop behaving like a hormonally-plagued teenager. Soft words said at a candlelit dinner about falling for her were part of the game for him – the softening-up game.

There was a definite nip in the air as they made their way to the car park. 'We ought to be in time to catch Mr Hudd before he goes to bed,' said Lizzie, wrapping her coat more tightly round herself.

'Don't worry about that,' said Dan. He produced a slip of paper from his back pocket. 'We don't have to go back. His wife already gave me the name and address last night.'

'Are you telling me you had this all the time?'

'Yup.'

She raised an eyebrow. 'You planned for us to stay overnight.'

' "Planned" is such a harsh word,' he grinned. 'Let's say I hoped.'

Dan used the remote control to release the door locks and opened the passenger side for her. She watched as he strode round to the driver's side. Part of her was flattered, but she was also angry. He was well aware how anxiously she had been waiting for the Ewings' address. She was searching for her lost child, for God's sake, not some sexual adventure. She would have respected him more if he'd been straight with her. Then again, she thought, she would never have spent the night in the same hotel with him if he had been honest. The deception caused the skin-tingling euphoria of the previous night to fade somewhat. From now on she would not be so trusting of him.

Lizzie studied the slip of paper and saw with dismay that the address was in Glasgow. And the Hudds had lost touch with the Ewings seven years ago. As the car sped along the motorway back towards London she began to think about how she could find out if the family still lived in Glasgow without alerting them to her search. It was a long way to go without checking they were still at this address. She would have liked to discuss the Ewings with Dan but she didn't want him to get the idea she was hinting that they should have another trip together. At the same time it was difficult to put away the memory of his kiss and pretend to have a normal conversation.

Dan apparently had no such difficulty. 'I've been thinking that the Glasgow address might be out of date,' he said. 'The Ewings could be living anywhere. They don't even have to be in the country. Wasn't he a long-distance lorry driver?'

'Yes, but at least we have his full name from the hospital records, and we can get a phone number from this address,' she said. It would be a start, she thought. Maybe she could persuade Sarah to go north with her if they found out anything worth following up.

136

Dan pointed to the car phone. 'No time like the present.'

Lizzie drew a blank. The female operator could find no trace of a D.W. Ewing in Glasgow. Lizzie used all her charm to persuade the woman to try and locate the subscriber at another address. Surely there couldn't be too many Ewings with those initials? Some operators are extremely obliging, others go by the book and indeed seem to relish being able to say it was impossible to track down numbers without up-to-date information. Lizzie had logged on to one of these. She admitted that she wasn't sure whether or not the Ewings still resided in Glasgow, and the woman's voice seemed to gloat. When Lizzie suggested she widen the search to the whole of Scotland, the woman almost snorted, saying she was sorry, that was out of the question.

Lizzie switched off, her face disconsolate.

'Cheer up,' said Dan. 'We'll just have to carry on with this detective business.'

'OK, Sherlock, what ideas do you have?'

'It looks as though we're going to be forced to spend more time together.' He gave her a roguish look. 'Fancy some haggis?'

She couldn't help smiling but her answer was swift. 'You've been a great help and I'm grateful, but I don't expect you to come to Glasgow with me.'

Dan slid his gaze to Lizzie's profile. Was he losing his touch? She appeared to be relaxed, not uptight at all. Why then had she turned down his offer to go to Glasgow? It was a pity, because there were worse ways of spending a working day than keeping close contact with an attractive woman. Perhaps he had come on too strong last night. Oh well, he would just have to accept it with good grace. He did not want her to feel uneasy with him. His boss would still want to be briefed about her plans. He would have to find an excuse to see her again.

Chapter Twelve

Back home, away from the magnetic influence of Dan's personality, Lizzie was delighted to find Sarah had managed to persuade her mother to stay with the children so she was free to go with her to Scotland.

On the plane journey Lizzie and Sarah had rehearsed their cover story, that they were tracking down babies born on a certain day in a certain hospital as part of research for a magazine article. Lizzie as the mother of one who had already been interviewed was helping Sarah, a journalist, to try and find the others.

If the Ewing girl turned out to be alive and well, the next step would be somehow to persuade her to give a blood sample, needed as part of the research. Lizzie wasn't sure how they should approach this; she might have to enlist Dan's help once again. Still, one step at a time. They had to find the Ewings first.

Sarah had argued for hiring a car as soon as they arrived at Glasgow airport, expensive as it was, and Lizzie saw the wisdom of not being stranded in the middle of a strange city without transport. Sarah had visited the university years before and insisted they ignore the signs diverting them away from the city centre. After a brief verbal skirmish about which direction the car hire staff had suggested, they soon found themselves crossing the River Clyde, following directions towards the Cathedral. Sarah urged Lizzie to manoeuvre her way through the Merchant City area and as they passed by the imposing Victorian architecture, Lizzie decided the negative impression she'd had of the city had been wrong. 'This reminds me of Paris,' she said. It was not long before they spotted the signpost to Springburn, the last known whereabouts of the Ewing family.

The address proved to be a three-storeyed Victorian house badly in need of a coat of paint. It was distinguished from the others in the rundown terrace only by the name in faded lettering on the window above the door.

'Gallagher's Guesthouse,' read Lizzie as they sat in the car across the road from the house. 'Oh, Sarah. We've come all this way for nothing.'

'Not for nothing,' she said, peering at the window where a sign proclaimed there were vacancies. 'We could always pretend we wanted a room and these people might know where the Ewings have gone to.' She smiled at her friend. 'I feel as though I'm an undercover detective.'

Lizzie started to laugh. It was such a daft situation, cowering in a car outside a seedy boarding house half hoping, half fearing she would meet her birth daughter.

Sarah became businesslike. 'Look, it's possible the Ewings gave this address because they were staying here temporarily.'

'You're probably right but it's all I've got,' Lizzie said, opening the car door and climbing out.

Until that moment she had been able to control the flutters in the stomach. But the idea of being so close to finding her daughter made her shiver with apprehension.

She hesitated at the front gate and Sarah linked arms. 'Courage,' she whispered.

Lizzie had sworn to Sarah that whatever the temptation she would do nothing rash. She was well aware that the minute she said anything significant to Nancy Ewing, there would be no going back. All the way north she had lectured herself that she must show no emotion, whatever she encountered. She would be scrupulously careful not to say anything which would make them suspicious. Until she was clear what was the right thing to do, it would be grossly unfair to the whole family to upset their lives. She must exercise rigid control and be very careful in choosing her words.

After what seemed an age, the door opened abruptly and a whippet of a woman stood in the hallway apologising for the delay. She was probably in her early forties and looked as though she could do with a decent meal and a good haircut.

'Did you want a room?'

Lizzie took in the greying hair, the deeply-etched lines around the faded features but nothing jogged her memory.

'No, I'm sorry. We're actually looking for someone who gave this as their address.'

'A lot of people do that, lady.' The woman grimaced. 'Running

140

away from wives, debts, you name it. Are you bailiffs?'

Sarah immediately reassured her and said they were looking for a family called Ewing.

The woman stiffened and Lizzie added hastily, 'They've done nothing wrong.'

'Then why are you looking for them?'

'Nancy and I had babies on exactly the same day in the same hospital.'

'So?'

'We were looking for the Ewing child because,' Lizzie tried to keep her voice noncommittal, 'we need her help with a magazine feature we're doing.'

The door opened a fraction. 'I'm her mother. I'm Nancy Ewing.' She peered across at Lizzie. 'Come in and tell me what this is about.'

Lizzie took a deep breath and tried to compose herself, hardly able to believe that she might be within touching distance of her daughter.

The interior of the boarding house was as dingy as the outside. The flocked wallpaper had probably been the height of fashion when it was first pasted but now it looked shabby and gloomy.

Nancy Ewing led the way to a sitting room, cheaply and shabbily furnished. A number of ill-assorted chairs crowded the interior; Lizzie guessed that the room was probably used by guests to watch television. Mrs Ewing motioned them to sit down and Lizzie perched nervously on the edge of an armchair.

Tentatively she introduced herself and Sarah and started gently questioning Mrs Ewing about her background. She appeared to be flattered by the attention and lost her air of suspicion.

Apparently she had taken over the boarding house after the death of her mother, Mrs Gallagher. Her two older boys had left home not long after her husband had been killed in an accident while driving a defective lorry. Life had been a struggle for her and her daughter since then, though the boys managed to send money home occasionally. Anna-Maria had suffered from the loss of her father.

Anna-Maria. A pretty name in such an unattractive setting thought Lizzie and ventured the question she had been itching to pose since the monologue started. 'Is she about? Your daughter.'

The woman's face clouded. 'No, I never know where she is these days.'

141

'Isn't she at school?'

Nancy Ewing's expression was bitter. 'Ha. She's been bunking off since she was twelve and finally the school got fed up with her. They asked me to take her away and now she works in a pub. When she bothers to turn up.'

'Working in a pub?' Lizzie tried to make her voice sound neutral.

'She lied about her age, said she was eighteen. I threatened to report the landlord because he didn't check but she said she'd leave home if I did.' Nancy Ewing raised her shoulders in a what-can-I-do gesture. 'Mind, she looks eighteen.'

'Do you have any pictures of her?' asked Lizzie eagerly.

Mrs Ewing shrugged. 'You know what they're like about posing for photographs at that age. I can never get her to look at the camera.'

'My daughter's just the same,' said Lizzie fervently. Strange, she had no recollection of this woman at all.

Nancy Ewing sighed and stood up. 'Maybe I have some from a year or two back.'

She returned with a much-creased envelope containing one of those sterile school pictures. Lizzie had the same type at home of Gabriella posed in front of white cardboard so beloved of school photographers.

The girl might have been described as pretty had her eyes not been staring at the camera with undisguised hostility and if she had been persuaded to smile. As it was, it was difficult to judge from the pale cheeks and the unruly hair what she would be like in the flesh.

A wave of anti-climax engulfed Lizzie as she examined the picture for some sort of family likeness. Apart from the girl's colouring, she could see little of her own parents or grandparents or Calum's. At a stretch maybe that mane was a little like Calum's, rather wiry and quite unlike Nancy Ewing's limp-looking hair. And was there something of Calum about the eyes? But it was tenuous. Perhaps when she saw her in person she would spot a characteristic she could identify. She and her mother used to joke that they had indistinguishable small feet and her grandmother used to attribute Gabriella's less than dainty shoe size to a modern diet.

'Fifteen's a difficult age, isn't it?' said Lizzie, hoping to draw out Mrs Ewing. 'They know everything.'

142

The woman gave a groan of agreement. 'She won't listen to anything I say. I don't know what she gets up to and she comes in at all hours of the day and night. I really worry about her.'

'Is there anybody she does listen to?' asked Lizzie sympathetically. 'Mine seems to take more notice of her friend Natasha than she does of me.'

'What about boyfriends?' asked Sarah.

At this, the woman's expression changed and became sombre. 'I never meet them. She doesn't bring anybody here.'

Lizzie stared at Nancy Ewing with growing despair. How could this depressed, defeated woman cope with a turbulent teenager? And she could be Gabriella's birth mother! As Lizzie looked at the faded, lined features, there was little hint of what she might have looked like at Gabriella's age. But there was a certain something around the cheekbones and the shape of her head which Gaby could have inherited.

Fleetingly she had an image of her own daughter's life. The pony rides, the swimming sessions, the ballet lessons, the trips abroad — at that moment she was probably eating baguettes in a café in France. The bedroom that was regularly redecorated to reflect her changing tastes. The computer, loaded with video games. Her own stereo, a small television and the stacks of compact discs scattered all over the floor. But more than material possessions, Gabriella had grown up with the confidence to believe that whatever she chose to do would be possible. Nothing was barred to her. How different were the limits set on Anna-Maria's life.

'Doesn't she have something she wants to do?' asked Lizzie, 'She can't want to work in the pub all her life, or does she?'

Nancy gave a sardonic laugh. 'Oh, she's got ideas all right. Only to be a film star, if you please. She's been talking about drama school but how can a girl like her get into one of those? She'll be lucky if she isn't pregnant with three kids underfoot by the time she's twenty-one. And I know who the mug'll be stuck looking after them.'

Oh God, thought Lizzie. If she's mine I'll have to get her away. I'd never be able to rest knowing that my daughter is in this dead-end place, in a dead-end job and facing a dead-end future. Her impulse was to scoop up Anna-Maria at once, to help her, introduce her to a different kind of life and imbue her with some desire for a worthwhile future. But she pulled herself up sharply.

How could she presume to judge the relationship between mother and daughter? They could have a real bond. Anyone hearing her moans lately about Gaby would certainly get the wrong impression about their feelings towards each other. And in any case, the deal she had made with herself was to do nothing impulsive. What could she be thinking of when Calum didn't know anything about this? Nor Gaby.

Her conscience began to trouble her. If this was the Lynton grandchild, did she have the right to deprive her of a share of the inheritance? If Edward Foxton were to learn of her existence, he'd feel obliged to do something about it, wouldn't he? On the other hand, since the reading of the will Lizzie had become more and more convinced that it was the bond between Gaby and her grandfather that mattered, not the bloodline. Robert Lynton had definitely intended his money to go to Gabriella. Shouldn't she just leave matters as they were? But Sebastian's needs were more important than any of this. It was vital they persuade the mother to co-operate in getting a blood sample. Inwardly she groaned at trying to reconcile so many conflicting demands. Mrs Ewing was looking at her expectantly.

'About this research we're involved in,' said Lizzie, 'would you mind if I talked to your daughter? Where would she be now?'

'At the pub, I suppose – if she's turned up.'

'We'll go round and see, take our chances.'

'Good luck,' said Nancy Ewing a trifle sourly. Poor woman, thought Lizzie, having to battle with her daughter on her own. Without Calum's good-natured intervention she could well imagine how hard it would be to control Gabriella.

The wind was whipping up the debris on the streets as Lizzie and Sarah made their way, following Nancy Ewing's directions, to the Pack Horse. They had expected Anna-Maria's place of employment to be as rundown as her mother's boarding house and were surprised to discover a turn-of-the-century pub with well-tended hanging baskets; it was out of kilter with the area it served.

Lizzie hung back, smoothing her hair and brushing the shoulders of her jacket.

'Are you OK?' asked Sarah, taking her arm.

She nodded, biting her lower lip. She was about to see her daughter, talk to her . . . oh God.

When Sarah saw her still hold back she said, 'Look, you don't have to go through with this. We could turn right round and go home.'

'No.' She pushed open the swing door. 'It's not only for me. She might be a match for Sebastian.'

The pub had been newly refurbished and had stalls complete with gleaming brass rails and leather-type banquettes, though the Victorian splendour was spoiled by the ear-splitting decibels of Rod Stewart spewing out, 'If ya think I'm sexy' from the jukebox.

Behind the bar was a young woman laughing uproariously. A shaven-headed youth was perching on a stool in front of her. Although she bore little resemblance to the photograph, Lizzie recognised the springy curls. She saw that hair, that colour, every day of her married life. It was losing some of its lustre now but when she had first met Calum, the subtle reddish shade of his hair was what had first attracted her attention.

The girl turned towards them inquiringly and Lizzie ordered two glasses of white wine. As Anna-Maria hunted for a half-opened bottle of Frascati, Lizzie took the opportunity to scrutinise her. She was slim, and above average in height, but then Calum was over six feet. Her narrow-fitting jeans clung to a pair of extraordinarily long limbs. It was one of the best assets of the Lynton family physique, something Lizzie had always wished for Gabriella.

'Large or medium?' asked the young barmaid. Lizzie found herself ridiculously pleased that the Scottish accent, a melodious burr, was pleasant to the ear.

Anna-Maria did look older than her years but that was more to do with her make-up than the uniform of the young – baggy T-shirt tucked into faded jeans. She had spent a great deal of time on her make-up. Each eyelash, curling up in commas, reminded Lizzie of a doll Gabriella had had years ago that Calum had brought from America, called Sweet Sue. When her eyes closed the lashes fanned out like a feather duster. But it was her eyebrows, unusually thick for a young girl, that fascinated Lizzie. She had seen similar ones before, belonging to Robert Lynton. Her nails, too, were unnaturally long, and adorned with tiny starbursts. It was impossible not to be aware of the immaculate talons as Anna-Maria fluttered them across the top of the bar counter, passing over the drinks, her smile firmly in place. There was no hint of the intractable teenager as described by her mother; she was acting the part. With a battery of lights reflected in the mirror behind her, Anna-Maria could pretend to be far away from her real world, in a make-believe setting where she was centre stage.

Lizzie was nerving herself to talk when the young woman pre-empted her and asked, 'I haven't seen you in here before. Are you just passing through?'

Lizzie explained that they were visiting the area and had just come from her mother's house.

The girl's face showed immediate alarm. 'What do you want with me? Are you from the police?'

Lizzie was in a quandary. She did not want to scare her but maybe pretending she was a police officer would be her only opportunity to extract information about her lifestyle before the curtain came down. But she couldn't lie. This was her own flesh and blood.

'No, we're not,' she said.

'Oh, social workers,' the girl said in a rush. 'I should've known. I don't know what the police told you but that stuff was planted on me. I said so at the station and they told me that was the end of it. So why are you bothering me?' Her eyes flicked to the back of the pub. 'The boss'll be here any minute. I'm telling you I don't deal and I don't use the stuff.'

'Don't worry, we're not here about any of that,' said Lizzie, appalled.

'Then what do you want?'

'It's private. Let's have a talk at a table.'

Anna-Maria darted a look at the youth on the bar stool, who was studiously uninterested, then followed them to a banquette where she sat down in the corner and glared at them.

So this aggressive young woman could be her daughter. Try as she might, Lizzie could conjure up no maternal feelings, no instinct that she had given birth to this young woman. She wondered if all the talk about bonding and imprinting was just that, so much sociological claptrap. It worked for most mothers with their newborn but it did not seem to extend to a fifteen-year-old.

'Who are you then? What d'ya want with me?' Suddenly Lizzie glimpsed the girl Nancy Ewing had been describing, pugnacious and hostile.

Trying to appear unruffled by the girl's antagonism, Lizzie

146

explained how she and Nancy Ewing had met in hospital. 'You were born on exactly the same day as my daughter.'

'So?'

Sarah cut in and said she was working on a nation-wide research project. This appeared to evince a spark of interest and she explained that the reason they wanted to track her down was because they were focusing on children born on her birthday.

Lizzie admired the charm Sarah was using to win over the suspicious teenager. But then with three children she had had plenty of practice.

Sarah went on to explain that they were recording all physical and medical details. Anna-Maria seemed intrigued and asked pertinent questions. The girl might have bunked off school but she seemed to have natural intelligence and Lizzie wondered what might have happened if she had been brought up in different circumstances. Nancy Ewing was having trouble coping with her own disappointments. She did not appear to have energy left over to deal with a stubborn, argumentative teenager. Lizzie could well see how the girl would like working in this pub. Compared with home it was glamorous.

Lizzie thought Sarah had done enough softening up and it was time to broach the vital question. Would Anna-Maria be willing to co-operate with the research?

At once she was suspicious. 'What would I have to do?'

'Nothing much. We'd need to take some pictures.'

'That's fine, so long as you pay me something.'

'No problem.' Lizzie took a deep breath. 'And you'd have to give a small sample of your blood.'

'Give blood? No way.'

'It won't hurt, I promise you,' said Lizzie. 'It's just a tiny jab on your thumb. My daughter was the same as you. She hates needles. But now she's glad she did it.'

'Big deal. I'm not doing it.'

'Listen, your doctor will clear it with the laboratory in London and arrange everything.'

'I'm telling you no. I'm not doing it.' She stood up. 'I have customers. I have to go,' she said, stalking across the near-deserted pub to her position behind the bar.

'Dammit, we mucked up,' said Sarah. 'I don't think she's going to go for it.'

'Well, I can't just walk away from her,' said Lizzie. 'We have to try again.' And with that she followed Anna-Maria to the bar, Sarah in her wake.

Anna-Maria turned away from them to rearrange the bottles stored underneath the bar. Lizzie decided the only way to get her attention was to order another drink.

Sulkily Anna-Maria poured two more glasses of wine and held out her hand for the money.

'I don't want to take up too much of your time but this is very important. It's linked to a research project which eventually could help thousands of people.'

Anna-Maria took a cloth and began to wipe the surface of the bar vigorously.

'Look, I don't ask for help. Nobody helps me and that's the way I want it.'

'All the samples are anonymous.'

'I've told you I'm not doing it.'

'Please,' began Lizzie and at this Anna-Maria flared up.

'How many times do I have to tell you people? Stop bugging me. Leave me alone.' She flung the cloth onto a shelf, turned on her heel and disappeared into a back room.

In the car outside the pub, Sarah tried to comfort Lizzie but she would not be consoled.

'I handled it all wrong,' she said despondently.

'No, you didn't. Did you see her pupils? That girl's on something so she's going to overreact whatever we do.'

'I should've spent more time winning her confidence before jumping in like that.'

'It wouldn't have made any difference, she was antagonistic from the start. It's obvious she's scared. It might be she's had a bad experience in the past but my guess is she's afraid of what a blood test might show about whatever drugs she's on.'

'God, Sarah, she's only fifteen.'

Sarah shrugged. 'You heard her first reaction when you said you'd been to her home. She's obviously been in trouble with the police.'

Lizzie took out a handkerchief. 'But I can't just abandon her. Not now I've met her. There must be something I can do for her.'

'You have to be cautious about this. You can't just break the news. "Hello, let me introduce myself properly. I'm your birth mother, I've come to claim you." '

148

'I know that, but perhaps Calum and I . . .' she trailed off. 'We could see she gets some money.' The mention of Calum's name brought Lizzie back to reality. Whether or not her marriage was over, it was imperative to bring Calum into the picture. Anna-Maria was his responsibility too. Anything that needed to be done, any decision that needed to be taken must be decided by both of them.

Sarah glanced at her watch. 'We have a decision to make. If we race to the airport we might just catch the flight.'

Lizzie nodded despondently.

She had invested so much hope in this trip, for her own sake as well as Sebastian's, yet here she was, on her way back to London, little nearer to knowing the truth. But whatever difficulties lay ahead she wouldn't be able to forget the Ewings and pretend none of this had happened.

How could she persuade Anna-Maria to change her mind about the blood test? She had shown an interest in being photographed but Lizzie was reluctant to continue the charade of pretending to work for a magazine. Her instinct was to tell the Ewings everything and to hell with the consequences. But first she would have to talk it over with Calum.

'I'll have to tell somebody about Anna-Maria,' she told Sarah. 'Sebastian's life could be saved.'

'But you'll be handing Andy a gift on a plate.'

'I know that but what alternative do I have?'

'Couldn't Dan Hargreaves organise a blood sample through his medical contacts in Scotland?'

'Yes, he probably could. But I still have to get Anna-Maria to agree.'

Chapter Thirteen

Gabriella arrived back home from Lyon in the early afternoon. She flung a bulging rucksack heavily onto the hall floor and burst through the kitchen door demanding, 'Anything to eat? I'm starving.' Then she darted back out and dragged her rucksack into the kitchen.

She delved into it, throwing out clothes and toilet bag, and Lizzie glowed with pleasure at the sight of her lively face. She had obviously enjoyed her trip to France. Lizzie felt an overwhelming urge to protect Gabriella from unhappiness. She might not be of her flesh but Lizzie could not imagine a situation where she would regard Gaby as anything other than her daughter.

When Gabriella had nearly emptied the bag, she gazed up and spotted the tender smile on Lizzie's face. 'Don't tell me you missed me,' she grinned.

'I did.'

'Good, because I've brought you something – ta-da.' And she unwrapped a bottle of wine and proudly displayed the label, saying that the man in the store had selected it as a particularly good year for Bordeaux. It was wonderful to know that Gabriella was trying to please her and Lizzie took the bottle and said it would be saved for a special occasion. In her highly-charged state Lizzie was afraid she might overreact and start to cry so she busied herself with filling the kettle to make them both a cup of tea. For a while at least she could enjoy having her daughter around and hearing about her experiences in France. They could go out and see a film and have a pizza afterwards, perhaps.

Lizzie had prepared a plate of sandwiches and sat down at the table watching Gabriella munch away. In a perverse way, knowing she was not related made the job of building bridges slightly easier. She could stop looking for similarities, stop moaning about how she hadn't done this or that at Gaby's age. Maybe she could stand back a little and give Gaby more room to breathe.

151

The week in France seemed to have been a challenge. Gabriella discovered she was one of the few girls brave enough to tackle the French in their own language. It was like old times, sitting down together, laughing at the things that had happened on the trip. Lizzie revelled in the feeling of intimacy, something she had not experienced with Gabriella for months.

The telephone interrupted their laughter and, as ever, Gabriella raced to pick up the receiver.

'It's Dad,' she called excitedly over her shoulder and spent the next couple of minutes telling him about her trip. After a moment or two she asked, 'When are you coming home?' As she listened, a puzzled frown flickered across her forehead.

'Surely you have some idea? OK . . . see you then. Want to talk to Mum now?'

Lizzie rose but her daughter shook her head. Gaby's frown deepened and after a few seconds she said quietly, 'OK, I'll tell her,' and replaced the receiver. 'He didn't want to talk to you, said he was in a hurry.' She looked puzzled. 'I've never known you two not to speak, especially when he's out of the country. Have you had a fight?'

'We had a bit of a tiff before he went.'

'It's not serious, is it?'

'I don't think so.'

'You don't think so?' Gabriella's voice rose.

'I don't want to talk about it until Dad and I have discussed it.'

'What's it about?'

What could she say? This was not the moment to be frank, nor could she make light of it because as soon as Calum returned home it would be clear they were on bad terms.

'I've said I don't want to talk about it,' she said, adopting an I'm-the-mother-and-still-in-authority tone.

'Why won't you tell me?' Gabriella was beginning to sound plaintive. 'You always treat me like a child as though I can't understand anything.' When her mother did not reply, her alarm was obvious. 'Are you going to split up?'

Lizzie rose from her chair, opened a cupboard and began rearranging the packets and tins, desperately trying to think of how she could change the subject. She and Calum needed to have major discussions about the baby swap as well as the state of their marriage and she could not talk about it now.

'This'll blow over,' said Gabriella. Her voice sounded firm but she was eyeing her mother apprehensively. 'You and Dad have the best marriage of all the parents I know. You're just going through one of the "downs" they talk about, aren't you?'

'Probably, we'll see,' said Lizzie, moving tins from one side of the shelf to the other.

'I hate it when you say "we'll see".'

Lizzie finished her tidying and turned round. 'I suppose you've got mountains of washing.'

'Forget the washing. Talk to me. Please.'

To her great relief the doorbell chimed and Gabriella took off at great speed to see who it was. If it was one of her friends, thought Lizzie, she would be saved. But when her daughter returned she was carrying an expensive-looking arrangement of lilies and ferns.

'Aren't they beautiful? You see, this is his way of saying sorry or whatever. Dad loves you. You know he does. Forgive him. Go on, Mum.'

Lizzie smiled. It was an exceptionally lovely bouquet.

'Let me open the card,' said Gabriella eagerly. She ripped open the tiny white envelope and with a flourish extracted a gold-edged card. Her mouth formed the words but as she read them silently her animated expression faded. Lizzie was faintly alarmed.

Gabriella's voice was dead as she parroted the message on the card. 'I must see you again. D.'

Lizzie's eyes widened and she began patting the skin at the base of her throat.

'Who is D?' Gaby's voice was dangerously low.

'Nobody.' She corrected herself. 'Nobody important.'

There was a long pause followed by a slow expulsion of breath and Gaby's eyes stared with hostility into hers.

Lizzie said quickly. 'He's a friend. Just a friend.'

'Do you expect me to believe that?' Gabriella's voice was incredulous. 'How old do you think I am? Five?' She did not wait for Lizzie to answer. 'When I think of how you went on when you found out about me and Luke. And all the time you were having an affair.'

'I haven't been having an affair,' said Lizzie, irritated. 'I don't know why this man's sent me flowers, he's got hold of the wrong end of the stick.'

Gabriella let out a sarcastic laugh. 'Oh, really?' She waved the card angrily at her mother. ' "I must see you again?" What's that supposed to mean then?'

'Nothing.' She put a note of finality in her voice. 'There's nothing romantic between us, certainly not on my side.'

'He doesn't seem to think so. And isn't it funny that he's come on the scene when you and Dad aren't talking?'

'This has absolutely nothing to do with the problems between your father and me.' Lizzie's mind was frantically searching for something she could say, an explanation, anything, to stop her daughter thinking the worst. 'All this man's been doing is helping me.'

'Helping you with what?'

'I can't go into it. When you understand what's going on . . .'

'I understand all too well. Dad's the one I feel sorry for. I bet he doesn't know that behind his back you've been having an affair.'

'Gaby, I've told you. There is no affair. I wish I could explain.'

'Then why don't you?'

'Because . . .' Lizzie hesitated. It was tempting to tell Gabriella the truth and get herself off the hook but this was something she needed to do with Calum first. 'I will tell you but not yet,' she said weakly, recognising it was a pathetic comeback.

'You're so horrible. You know you're in the wrong.' Her eyes brimmed with tears. 'And Dad doesn't know . . .' she paused then burst out, 'he doesn't know that his wife is . . . a lying whore.'

Gabriella flung the bouquet on the floor with such force that the lilies burst through their wrapping. With a last furious look at her horrified mother Gabriella stomped up the stairs and slammed her bedroom door.

In the kitchen Lizzie stood rigid, arms held tightly at her sides, fists clenched, staring at the floor where the heads of the flowers lay broken from their stems.

Upstairs in her bedroom Gabriella climbed under the duvet and did some figuring out.

The state of her parents' marriage flummoxed her. Her mother and father were having problems, serious ones too, yet in front of her they'd seemed their normal selves. She had never heard them shouting at each other, unlike Natasha's parents. Not that this worried Tash. She used to say screaming at one another was

154

better than not talking. Gabriella realised her parents must have been putting on a show in front of her. But then she had kept to her bedroom lately; perhaps that was why she hadn't noticed.

Many things were now clearer. Her father had found out his wife was sleeping with another man. That was why Dad had disappeared to America and why he hadn't wanted to talk to her mother on the phone. And that was why he had come to the school to see her off when she went to France. Even then, he hadn't said one word against her mother. He was so loyal.

Gabriella could not control her tears. Her mother didn't seem to think she'd done anything wrong. There was no sign of guilt or sadness even when tackled about the flowers. It was puzzling. But if her parents were going to split up, she wouldn't want to live with her mother. She'd ask to stay with her father.

Poor Dad. Gabriella snuffled into her pillow. She would never forgive her mother for breaking Dad's heart. Never.

Shaken, Lizzie sat on the chair in the hall and tapped number three on the speed dial for Sarah's number.

'I've just had the worst ever fight with Gaby.'

'You must be getting used to that by now.'

Lizzie gave a wry laugh. 'This was different.'

When Sarah heard all the details, she was appalled. 'She actually used those words?'

'I'm quoting verbatim.'

'What are you going to do about it?'

'I intend to give Dan Hargreaves a piece of my mind. Put it this way, after I'm finished with him he won't send me so much as a daisy again.'

Sarah stifled a laugh. 'It's a bit rich to tick someone off for sending flowers. Your husband's away and he couldn't know your daughter would read the note.'

'But why's he done it, Sarah? The more I think about it, the more I reckon it's not because of my tremendous charms but a self-preservation thing. I can't help wondering how on earth Andy got wind of the fact that Gaby wasn't Calum's daughter. Something must have persuaded the lab to send his solicitor the full report of Gaby's blood test.'

'What are you saying, that Dan somehow cocked up and has taken this time off work to trail after you because he's worried about his job?'

'Precisely. If he let Andy see the report, it's a breach of confidentiality, at the very least.'

'He's been very helpful, why are you now so suspicious?'

'Because of the flowers, Sarah. And he didn't need to write such a provocative message.'

'You don't think Gaby will tell Calum about the message, do you?'

'God, I hope not. She's very protective of her father.'

'It's a complication you can do without.'

'Exactly. I have to tell Calum everything soon but he won't even talk to me on the phone now.' Lizzie sighed.

'Are you going to be all right?' Lizzie could hear the concern in Sarah's voice.

'Let's see. My marriage is coming apart because my husband thinks another man has fathered my baby. My daughter's just called me a whore. I'm going to have to tell Calum that yes, he isn't her father but nor am I her mother.' She took a hurried breath. 'And my real daughter's probably a junkie. Apart from that everything's hunky dory.'

'I'm glad you still have a sense of humour.'

'Sarah, only on the outside, believe me, only on the outside.'

He had chosen the same blue shirt she'd admired on their first meeting and the white wine she had enjoyed that night in the pub was already in the ice bucket. As Dan sat waiting in the cellar wine bar he reflected that this invitation couldn't have come at a better time. His boss had been pestering him to find out how far Lizzie had got in her search and what she was going to do about it. He had happily ditched the red-headed nurse when Lizzie said she wanted to see him tonight. Flowers fix everything, he mused. Women were suckers for that kind of thing.

He spotted Lizzie's shapely figure in the doorway, glancing uncertainly at the tables. He half rose and caught her eye. When she arrived at the table, Dan took both her hands in his, giving them a firm squeeze. 'I'm glad you phoned. You look stunning.'

There was no reaction to his greeting and for a moment he was disconcerted. But hell, she had asked to see him, not the other way round. She sat down abruptly, extricating her hands and drawing her chair slightly away from his. He began to pour out the wine then raised his glass. 'To many more occasions like this.'

Her glass hovered in mid-air before she replaced it untouched on the table, her expression stony. He decided to distract her.

'While I've been sitting here, I've had a naughty thought.' He gave his little-boy grin. 'Why don't I book us a room in the hotel across the road?'

'I want you to stop sending flowers, stop thinking about hotel rooms.' She spoke so loudly heads began to turn.

'Come on,' his voice was a gentle banter, 'you're not telling me there's a woman alive who doesn't like being flattered.'

'Why the hell did you send me those flowers? And what did that message mean?'

'It meant what it said – that I wanted to see you again,' he said mildly and when she still did not soften added, 'Lizzie, you affect me in a way I've not experienced before. I've never wanted to help a woman, to support her as much as I do you. That must mean something.'

Lizzie leaned back in her chair and considered him. 'Now, why don't I believe that.'

This didn't sound promising. He frowned. 'Lizzie, do you think I'd give up my time to help just anyone? From the first moment I saw you, that was it.' Pretty good. He almost convinced himself.

'Please, Dan. Stop.' She gave a half-smile. 'Don't go down that road. I know you don't mean it.'

'You're wrong about that, and don't tell me that after what your husband's put you through your marriage is fine and dandy, because I won't believe it.'

She flushed. 'Whether or not it's over doesn't affect you.'

'So the signals I picked up in Dorset meant nothing? Your body responded to me. You can't deny that.' He was aware that they were attracting more stares from other tables and lowered his voice. 'But I respected your wishes not to take it any further and I sent the flowers because I wanted to get to know you better.'

'I'm sorry you did. My daughter read your note.'

Dan forced himself to look contrite. 'That wasn't my intention. But how else could I get through to you that I didn't want our relationship to end?'

She lifted her chin in a gesture of dismissal and for one of the rare occasions in his life Dan Hargreaves felt he was not going to be able to manipulate a woman.

'I don't suppose your protestations would have anything to do

157

with worries about your lab's breach of security?'

So his boss had been right to be concerned. 'I don't know what you're talking about.'

'I'm sure you do. How else could Andrew have found out about Gabriella's parentage except from you? Your mistake has caused all of us a great deal of heartache.' She paused. 'And for that I blame you.'

'I swear it had nothing to do with me or my lab,' he said with as much sincerity as he could muster. 'You're forgetting how many people had access to that report, like the hospital and the bone marrow organisation, to name two.' He was rewarded by the flicker of doubt that crossed her face and pressed home his advantage. 'But that's all past and I don't think we should waste time talking about that. Tell me about Glasgow. Did you find your daughter?'

She nodded.

'What are you going to do about her?'

She looked uncertain. 'I'm sorry but I think it best if I don't tell you.'

Dan tried to mask his irritation. 'But if it wasn't for me you wouldn't have found her.'

'Dan, forgive me. This is intensely private and I don't want anyone outside the family to know our business.'

It was clear he wasn't going to be given any details. The boss would be furious. Could he appeal to her better nature? 'You led me on,' he said without heat. 'You made me believe your marriage was over.'

'Come on, Dan. Don't tell me I'm the first married woman who's turned you down.' Her face had resumed its glacial mien. Lizzie pushed back her chair and stood up. 'I don't want to see you again and I don't want you to contact me either.'

His chair scraped against the floorboards as he stood up hurriedly to have one last throw of the dice. 'We could have something special together. I'd like to give it a try. Wouldn't you?'

This halted her in her tracks. 'You don't give up easily, do you?'

'I care about you.'

'No, you care about the lab.'

'You're wrong. This is personal. Between you and me, and nothing to do with the lab.'

'I'm not sure my solicitor will see it like that,' she said tersely before making her way swiftly to the door.

Dan sank back into his chair. If she planned to exploit that moment of weakness, the one time when, against his better instincts, he had bent the rules, she would be sorry. He couldn't risk waiting around to see if he was fingered in the case. He had to strike first.

Andrew clicked the flashing 'You have new mail' message on his computer to open his mailbox. He had embraced the Internet eagerly. He believed it was designed specifically for wheeler-dealers like him who needed to widen their network. The Inbox heralded five new items. Four were from fellow car dealers hoping to close deals and clinch their commission. Good. The fifth message made his eyebrows swoop in surprise.

'I have new information about Gabriella's parentage. She was the product of a baby switch at St Martyn's Hospital. I can give you the name and location of where I believe the real Lynton granddaughter is living now. It's worth real money, like fifty thousand. I am prepared to divulge this if you guarantee my anonymity. Your call. D. Hargreaves.'

He stared at the words on the screen, hardly able to believe what he was reading. My God, a baby switch? Could it be true? But why would Dan Hargreaves make up such a ridiculous story? Andrew stood up and began pacing excitedly around the room. That sulky Gabriella wasn't Calum's child. She wasn't even Lizzie's. If he could provide proof, this was a bonus his legal team could use to muddy the waters still further. Andrew let out a belly laugh. Dad, leaving his fortune to continue the so-called good branch of the family when the girl was a cuckoo in the nest. Lynton blood? She wasn't even related to him by marriage.

Andrew could smell the inheritance getting closer. How he wished his father was still alive and could be told about his precious Gaby. Then he had a sobering thought, guilty that it had not occurred to him immediately. The girl could be a match for his baby. This thought was closely followed by another which settled like a stone in his stomach. If the court accepted that bloodline, not Gaby, was what mattered to Robert Lynton, this girl's family might try and snatch the whole estate and he could be left with nothing. He would have to be very sure of his facts before he had a conflab with his lawyers. He didn't want them leaping ahead. The situation was threatening to escalate out of his control.

He stared at the screen for a moment or two, thoughts jumbling around his head. Calum couldn't have a clue about this, judging by their last conversation. But what about Lizzie? He decided she probably didn't know either. If she had been aware of the swap she'd have told Calum.

Everything was suddenly clear. He had to get to the girl first. The most important aspect of all this was Sebastian and he would size up the situation before deciding how much of the story to tell the girl. He was sure he could persuade her to help Seb. His lawyers seemed confident that they could win the case on the evidence they had now so maybe there was no need for her to know about the fight for his father's money. Not yet, anyway.

Andrew leaned back, considering his options. Dan said fifty thousand. What a hope. He didn't have five hundred. Edina wouldn't let him near any of the money her committee had raised for Sebastian. There was a tidy sum in the account for publicity and admin, and so far they'd needed far less than that to try and find a donor. He never wanted to see his son suffer and the money was there to secure his child's long-term financial future. Edina had gone off her rocker when he'd only hinted at using it to help finance the court case. In the event he'd managed to persuade his solicitor to take on the case on a no win, no fee basis.

Andrew began typing 'Sorry unable to deal' then stopped. He didn't have a starting point. He had no idea who the girl was and where she might be living. To find her might take weeks.

Then a slight smile played on his lips. Maybe it was time to call in the reptiles. Newspapers, as he had once discovered, had deep pockets for stories like this. To a big newspaper group, fifty grand was a small price to pay for a scoop. He would have a better chance of getting to the girl first if he could squeeze money out of a newspaper to pay his informant.

It was a long shot but who had managed to sell an over-priced Merc, revamped after a massive crash, that had been hanging around in the sale room for over a year?

Andrew began to type. 'Am unable to raise fifty grand though I could, at a pinch, raise twenty. Acceptable?' He pressed the 'SEND' button.

The answer arrived within thirty minutes. 'Unacceptable. Fifty or nothing. Up front, no messing around. This is my bank and account number. Please confirm soonest. When the funds are cleared I'll be in touch with the information.'

Andrew decided he'd better just make sure it really was Dan Hargreaves he was dealing with here. Checking creditworthiness and account details was something you had to know how to do in the car business if you wanted to stay in it.

A phone call later Andrew was satisfied that the account number he had been given was indeed Dan Hargreaves'. But before he took this any further, he decided to jerk Dan's lead a tad. 'How do I know your information is reliable?' he typed.

A few minutes later he got his reply. 'Common sense. I wouldn't risk my career like this on a scam.'

Arrogant sod, thought Andrew. He wasn't above risking his precious career for some straightforward extortion.

Andrew scrolled through his electronic organiser for the name of the journalist he'd helped a couple of years ago on a car fraud story. The newspaper was the *Chronicle* but he couldn't now remember who the man was. Why had he not filed it under the name of the newspaper as well? Because he thought he had such a phenomenal memory and wouldn't forget the investigative reporter who'd given him a nice fat cheque eighteen months ago, that's why.

Andrew had enjoyed every minute of being an integral part of the *Chronicle*'s reporting team. In return for contact names and leads on price fixing he had been promised anonymity and the reporters had been true to their word. It was a good thing his fellow dealers hadn't realised who had finked on them or he'd soon have found himself looking for another career path.

What the hell was the bloke's name? Andrew was irritated with himself. He'd have a better chance of raising the money with somebody who knew him and would accept his story at face value rather than starting from scratch to persuade a stranger.

Since the plum had dropped right into his lap Andrew's mind had been racing, examining the possibilities. Even his lawyer would be impressed. It would give his case legs. Huh. What else did they want? First he produced proof that the girl wasn't from his father's precious bloodline. Then proof that Gabriella had nothing at all to do with the Lyntons. OK, it mightn't affect the case per se but it would be a bargaining counter. Calum wouldn't want his precious Gaby to find out. And he could always pay off this new girl if her family tried to cause problems.

Andy picked up the phone and punched in the *Chronicle*'s number. A bored newsroom secretary reeled off the names of their investigative reporters. His memory was jogged as soon as she mentioned the name. He cut her off then pressed the redial button and asked the switchboard for Craig Garrett.

'Craig? Remember me? Andy Lynton. I helped you with that car scam story.'

'Yeah, it was a good one. I had a splash and a double spread. Got any more like that?'

'Much better than that.'

They arranged to meet at a pub a couple of miles away from the Canary Wharf office.

Andy had learned enough to realise that a reporter never met a contact on home ground because of meddling eyes and ears – and not just from rival papers. He'd discovered that the *Chronicle* was renowned for encouraging competition among its staff, so writers literally battled for space. The executives believed that in this tense atmosphere journalists tried harder and took greater risks to ensure their by-lines were seen regularly.

Craig Garrett was regarded as a bovver boy in the office, with a reputation for stamping on ideas and colleagues in his efforts to remain the editor's current favourite. As a result, his colleagues were always on the alert to try and find ways to get their own back. But Craig's reputation in the office did not matter to Andrew. His sole aim was to come away with the promise of the money he needed to pay Hargreaves.

Andrew had been rehearsing how he could sell his story to put the best gloss on it so the reporter would take the bait. The baby swap was a great story but there was no way he wanted it in the paper yet. That could scupper everything. He had visions of Calum and Lizzie's faces when he produced their real daughter. What a sweet moment that would be. He could imagine the collapse of their case and could already hear the judge's words, 'I find in favour of the plaintiff.' But the girl had to stay on ice, out of the reach of newspapers. He would have to enthuse Craig with the angle of brother against brother. But Craig was a man who was incredibly impatient; he had a low boredom threshold. That was OK, he could deal with that. He would use the same skill with Craig as he did to reel in the suckers that bought cars from him.

In the pub Craig allowed him only one sip of beer before he got down to business. 'OK, what you got for me?'

Andrew loved this bit, the sell, the pitch. 'This is a tale of revenge. It involves a family feud. We're fighting over a fortune.' Succinctly Andrew sketched in the main planks of his impending court case, and that the young heiress was a fraud, not his brother's child at all.

Craig downed his pint and set the glass down on the table with a clunk.

'Sorry, mate,' he said, rising from the bar stool, 'it's not sexy enough for my editor. If there was a celeb involved or there was some sleaze, like the grandfather was giving her one, maybe we'd be interested.'

Trying to hide the desperation in his voice, Andrew said. 'Have another pint. I'm not finished yet.'

Craig looked at his watch. 'I haven't got much time. Get on with it.'

'That little bitch doesn't deserve the family money,' said Andrew. 'My baby's dying of leukaemia. He needs it more than she does.'

The reporter sat down again. 'Dying baby? That's more like it.' He narrowed his eyes. 'What's the kid look like?'

Andrew bought him another pint and then took a family snapshot out of his wallet and was pleased to see the journalist nodding at the sight of Sebastian's smiling face.

'I have to be straight with you. We only take on cases we can win. The *Chronicle* never loses its campaigns.'

Andrew winced. How the hell could he guarantee that? For a fleeting second he had a vision of Edina's wrath if she suspected he was using Sebastian's illness as a lever to prise money out of a newspaper. She would kill him. But wasn't he, in his own way, trying as hard as she was to help track down a donor? And if he recruited the newspaper to find a match, how could she object? If they wanted to pay money for the privilege, well, that was his business. She didn't need to know about that.

Andrew cleared his throat and adopted the tone of voice he reserved for clinching a deal. 'The hospital is very hopeful they'll find a donor match for Sebastian any time now.'

Craig leaned back, his eyes glazing into the distance. 'I have it.

A great headline. "SOS: Save Our Sebastian." Yeah, that's quite good. We haven't done a story like that for a few months.' Andrew breathed a sigh of relief. 'It's a shame this Gabriella whats-hername didn't turn up trumps. She's definitely ruled out as a match, is she?' Andrew nodded. 'Pity. That would've been a real tear jerker. "Heiress loses money but saves baby", that kind of thing.'

'I've got all their photographs,' said Andrew eagerly. 'That'd be useful, wouldn't it?'

Craig didn't appear to hear. 'Yeah, the editor might well go for it.'

Andrew shifted in his seat. 'But I'd like to settle all the details so let's put all the cards on the table, shall we? How much would I get for this story?'

'Money for this? You're joking? We're doing you a favour. We're going to try and save your kid. You ought to pay us.'

'But the last time I got money . . .'

Craig was scathing. 'That was different, you were putting yourself at risk. Anyway, things have changed since then. They don't lash out like they used to. The glory days have gone, brother.'

No money? Andrew hadn't taken that into consideration at all. He decided to call Craig's bluff.

'If you don't think it's worth anything I'll take it someplace else.'

'Fine,' said Craig curtly. 'You'll soon find that all papers operate exactly the same these days.'

Andrew was stuck. If he let Craig walk away he'd have to try and interest another newspaper. But where would he be with that? At least he'd already done business with this guy and he could get through to him. He didn't have contacts with other newspapers. He could not let this fish slither off the hook. What would induce the man to pay good money? Only for something extra, a story which was rare. Like a baby switch at a hospital. He thought hard about whether he dare risk it. But he needed the funds to find the girl's address. Without that information, as he kept reminding himself, he couldn't help Sebastian.

'Would your editor pay money for another twist to this story? Something so unusual I bet your paper's not done anything like it because it hasn't happened in Britain.'

'Can't say till I know what it is,' Craig said.

164

'I told you that the girl, Gabriella, isn't my brother's child, right? I've just found out that there was a baby switch at the hospital – my brother and his wife have been bringing up the wrong child.'

To Andrew's disappointment Craig's expression seemed not to alter. He could not know that a seasoned journalist never let on when he was given pure gold.

'That could be interesting.'

'How much?' pressed Andrew.

'Depends,' replied Craig, 'If it's true—'

'It is,' Andrew interjected eagerly.

'Maybe I could screw the editor for a few grand.'

When Andrew said he needed fifty, at least, to get the address, Craig choked on his beer. He wiped the beer froth off his lips with the back of a hand and said slowly that it might be possible if the story made the front page and the centre spread. With the proviso that not a word about the baby switch would be printed until after the court case, the two men shook hands.

Andrew breathed again. Craig pressed him for the name of his contact but Andrew held out. All that was important was the girl's name and address which he would pass on. He would then get a blood sample from her.

Satisfied he was sitting on an exclusive, Craig ordered a couple more pints and took out his reporter's notebook. Much research had to be done before a word could be printed in the paper.

Back in his office Craig congratulated himself. Andrew Lynton thought he was a smart operator. Fifty grand? Dream on. It was his practice never to let a punter know that he was being ridiculous. For that kind of money they would want photographs of the Queen nude. And not as a baby.

It had been simple to fillet Andrew. The information from his contact was now unnecessary. It had taken him only a few minutes to find out the name of the hospital where the swap had taken place. Craig had every intention of getting his butt down there and obtaining the details himself. If he could do a number and get a shufty at the hospital records for that date and the details of the mothers with their addresses, then he wouldn't have to cough up a cent. Andrew would be pissed off but it wouldn't half get him in good with the editor. And boy, did he need that at the moment.

Unfortunately his bloody boss was trying to suck up to the establishment and had got himself appointed to the Press Complaints Commission. This meant that Craig had to identify himself to the hospital as a newspaperman or risk the sack if he was found out. With his mortgage, no story was worth that.

Unfortunately the administrator at St Martyn's had suffered badly at the hands of the press when a dying celebrity had been under siege by journalists desperate to get into his ward and snatch a photograph. One paper had gone to extreme lengths, hiring a crane to lift the cameraman to the level of the seventh-floor window before being spotted by the police. Craig was given short shrift.

Undeterred, he called in his second gun, a freelancer who specialised in undercover work. He would infiltrate the hospital under the guise of a university researcher, which truthfully he had been, albeit several years ago.

Briefed by Craig, the freelancer unwisely used the same phraseology when asking for permission for a trawl through the records. 'You've been sent by that damn reporter from the *Chronicle*,' admonished the harassed administrator. 'I'm telling you and I'm telling him, I know that whatever this is for, it won't be to the advantage of the hospital. Get out.'

Reluctantly Craig decided the only course left to him was an appeal to his readers. It would have to be carefully worded so as not to alert his competitors to the facts of the story. Nor did he want the Lynton family to get wind of it. Not yet. He would have to take the chance that if they did spot the date they would think it a coincidence. If not, too bad. Would his editor go with that? Craig had not yet proved to his own satisfaction that the baby switch story was on the level, nor had he tracked down the girl but he needed time and expenses to do both. He typed out a memo, taking more care with the words than he'd done for most of the stories he had written lately.

After outlining the main facts of the 'Save Our Sebastian' feature, Craig sketched in the probable baby switch angle and suggested there would be at least three bites at the cherry.

1. First we try and track down the real granddaughter. I have a good wheeze for how we can do this: as one of our come-ons. See the rough draft attached.
2. This might lead us to the girl (though I am following

166

other avenues as well) and when we find her, we can then kick off the 'Save Our Sebastian' campaign with a pic of her holding the sick baby. We don't say this is her long-lost cousin – yet. Instead, she will be just a reader who has come forward hoping to save the baby's life.

3. I've established an arrangement with a local lab to test the blood of any reader who volunteers. (Note: have organised a fifteen per cent discount.) Unfortunately we cannot guarantee this girl will be the match (remember the story of the identical twin who failed to save his brother?). If she isn't, we then splash on the main story: the baby switch. I think we will get at least two or maybe three leads as well as a decent centre spread and I will see to it that this remains our exclusive, particularly as the real granddaughter could be at the centre of a court case. Her uncle is contesting his father's will (see attached notes). The court case is due to be heard any time now and my contact will not allow me to break the baby switch story until then. But I am hopeful we will get maximum mileage out of the SOS story before this one breaks.

4. I'll need money to pay the father and expenses for the search.

Four hours later back came his memo with the editor's note scrawled at the bottom: 'OK but watch budget. £5,000 top whack.' His signature was underneath.

First Craig phoned Andrew to tell him the good news but he warned him there would be no money until the end of the campaign. Craig hoped that as the story gained momentum the editor would cough up more cash but Andrew surprised him with a furious outburst about how he needed money to get his hands on the girl's address. 'No cash, no address,' he shouted.

'Relax,' said Craig and then revealed his own scheme for smoking out the girl, using a teaser in the paper.

Andrew, who had only just finished tucking up his frail son in his cot, was shaken at this double-cross but was slightly mollified when Craig assured him that nothing would be published until the morning of the court case. 'By then we'll have sewn up the girl and there'll be no danger of her falling into the wrong hands.'

In due course Craig would need those photographs of

Sebastian and the other members of his family he had mentioned. A feature writer from the paper would also be phoning him and his wife to check out the background for the story.

Within the hour Craig began planning page five of the next day's edition with his art editor. Under his direction the art editor created a silhouette of a teenage girl, designed to look like a 'Wanted' poster from the Old West. A prominent question mark was inserted above the figure. The type was bold and black. 'Are you a girl in a million?' Below it was another question: 'Were you born on this day and in this year?' The date and year were given, which was Gabriella's birthday. If so, and they phoned a special phone number, they would learn something to their advantage.

At this stage there was not a whisper about who was involved or why, and no mention of possible fortunes. That was a trump card to be used if the girl was found and the family gave trouble. Craig wasn't going to hand over his exclusive to his rivals. In the past his success had been based on finding solutions to most problems before revealing his hand.

The copy explained that the lucky person would have to have been born in a London hospital. Craig dared not mention St Martyn's at this stage. If the Lyntons themselves didn't pick it up, their legal people might.

'If you are one of these lucky girls,' the copy went on, 'you could take part in a fabulous draw. Phone us to hear details of this great mystery prize.' Craig had not then decided what it would be but he was confident the promotions department would come up with something irresistible to teenagers. They would be swamped with offers from beauty and fashion people who would die to reach the target audience provided by the millions who read the *Chronicle*.

The idea was to run this for a couple of mornings to see what response it attracted. Of course there would be crank and bogus calls. The operators had been trained to spot the callers who merely wished to discuss their life story. The switchboard people had been instructed to ask a series of questions to which it was possible to reply either 'yes' or 'no'. It was an effective technique which would weed out most time-wasters. Any likely-sounding callers would be asked at which hospital they were born. If they didn't know, they would be encouraged to ring back. And if the caller wasn't born in St Martyn's they would be compensated with a small prize.

168

The odds against someone ringing up and being the missing heiress were impossibly long but Craig preferred to go down that route on the basis that he was born, as he put it, with 'his bum in the butter'. The technique had proved successful once or twice in the past.

The first morning of publication brought sixty-odd calls, mostly from excited parents. Two of them had been born at St Martyn's and, buoyed up with hope, Craig arranged to meet them, along with a photographer, the following afternoon. The first girl, Tanzi Wilson, was a stunner, legs up to her armpits and perfect features. But they were black, a product of a Nigerian mother and a south Londoner. Craig excused himself as fast as was decent, rewarding the girl with a collection of chart-topping compact discs in return for her time. The second prospect was puzzling. Although at first sight the figure looked and sounded effeminate it was, in Craig's opinion, definitely male. Couldn't these people read?

He had tried to flush out the missing heiress by being mysterious, with no success. Now he would have to nail her by being obvious and hang the consequences. When it came to his livelihood or Andrew's problems, there was no contest.

Craig collected the Lynton file which was locked away in the bottom drawer of his desk and marched purposefully towards the editor's office.

Gabriella's mood was not improved when early the next morning her mother rapped on the bedroom door. After the third knock she snarled, 'Go away.'

'Phone call for you. It's Natasha. She says it's urgent.'

'I'll phone her back.'

Blearily Gabriella looked at the alarm clock and reached to the floor where her dressing gown lay in a heap, wondering why Tash was phoning at this hour.

Her friend sounded agitated. 'Have you seen the paper?'

'Course not. It's only seven. I'm not even up yet.'

'Look at the *Chronicle*. Page five.' She lowered her voice. 'It's not good news. Ring me straight back when you've read it.'

The paper was sticking through the letterbox. Sitting cross-legged in the deserted hallway, Gabriella leafed through till she found page five.

The story was all about Sebastian's search for a bone marrow donor. And there was a picture of her, not a very good one, she thought, annoyed. Where had it come from? What was the bad news? Tasha already knew that she was not able to help her small cousin. Natasha had gone with her to the hospital when the doctors had told her about the result. Gaby had been upset and Tasha had been a great comfort.

Then she began reading the boxed-off story underneath her picture. She drew a breath. This was nothing to do with helping Sebastian. It was about some fight her Uncle Andy was having over Grandpa's will. Gabriella had a sudden flash of memory when she was being hustled out of the solicitor's office by her mother. That must have been what he had been going on about. They always kept things from her. She had to read the effing newspaper to find out what was happening in her own family.

'Heiress challenged in court,' ran the headline.

An heiress. Gabriella was pleased. She would show this to her school friends. Why hadn't her mother told her she would have to go to court? She put the paper down, thinking about the clothes she'd have to buy. She'd need some decent gear, especially if the TV cameras showed up. On the news they always crowded around the entrance to the court. She wondered whether that black pin-striped trouser suit she'd spotted last week would look good on the screen. She'd have to touch up her dad for the money. But that was OK because he usually gave in after moaning for a bit about her spending. She'd have to watch her mouth and shut up about all the money that was heading her way. It seemed neither of them liked her talking about it.

Gabriella walked slowly up the stairs, reading on. She paused midway, shook her head and went back over the preceding paragraphs.

'The will is to be fought in the high court on the grounds that Gabriella Lynton, aged fifteen, is not the descendant of wealthy businessman Robert McDowall Lynton.' What were they on about? 'Blood tests have allegedly established that the deceased's eldest son, Calum Lynton, is not her biological father.'

Gabriella's mouth dropped open. Not her father? How dare they print such rubbish. It was a lie. A stinking, horrible lie.

'This information was discovered during a routine search for a bone marrow match for the Lynton baby. Gabriella was one of many hundreds tested and it was at that time her paternity was called into doubt.'

Newspaper clutched in her hand, Gabriella went up the remaining stairs two at a time and burst into her parents' bedroom. Her mother, bending over the washbasin, her mouth foaming with toothpaste, looked round in surprise.

'What's all this crap about?' shouted Gabriella flourishing the *Chronicle*.

Lizzie swiftly rinsed her mouth, dabbed at her lips with a towel and reached for the paper.

'It's all a lie. Isn't it?' Gabriella asked after a few seconds.

'Give me a moment, darling.' It seemed to Gabriella that her mother was never going to answer.

'Tell me.'

Lizzie dropped the paper onto the floor and sat down heavily on the bed. Gabriella, her fear heightened, waited for the denial. It never came.

Finally she shouted. 'But he is my father, he is, he is.' By this time her mother was in tears and for a moment Gabriella watched her in silence.

'I'm sorry, Gaby,' said Lizzie, trying to compose herself. 'What they say is true.'

Gabriella stared at her wide-eyed. 'Why haven't you told me before? How dare you keep something like that away from me.'

Lizzie hesitated then took a deep breath. 'I didn't know myself until a short while ago and I hoped you wouldn't find out, especially like this.' The two women continued to stare at each other. 'Sit down, darling, and let me tell you what happened at the hospital when you were born.'

White-faced, Gabriella slumped onto a chair.

'Your father was there and he's been with you ever since, so he is your father.'

'That's what you say,' retorted Gabriella angrily. 'Why don't you just answer me straight. How many men did you fuck when you were seeing Dad?' When Lizzie made no reply she leapt up and went to the drawer in the bedroom bureau where all the family documents were kept. 'I'm going to find your marriage certificate because I bet you had to get married.'

'Don't bother looking,' said Lizzie. 'You're right, we did get married because you were on the way.'

Gabriella shot her mother a vitriolic look. 'And Dad wasn't the father. Does he know or will he have to find out from the paper as well?'

171

'He does know.'

Gabriella pointed an accusing finger. 'That's why he's gone off to America, isn't it? To get away from this. You've driven him off.'

Lizzie made a move towards Gabriella but she shrank back. 'Don't come near me. I hate you.'

'I want you to know everything. Let me explain.' Lizzie could hear the desperation in her own voice.

'Explain what? That you've always been a whore?'

'Gabriella! Don't talk to me like that.'

'I'll talk to you however I want. Who is my father?' she asked witheringly, before delivering her parting shot in the doorway. 'I bet you don't even know.'

Gabriella had no clear idea what to do next. She was still only fifteen but as soon as she got the first lot of money she would be off. Then a painful thought struck her. If Dad wasn't her dad, then she wasn't entitled to Granddad's money. She was trapped in a house with a woman she hated. Worse, she didn't even know who her real father was.

Dan checked the date in the *Chronicle* story again. November the eleventh. That double-dealing bastard Andrew Lynton had gone behind his back to the paper. He'd given him seventy-two hours to come up with the money and since then the man had been stalling him. Yesterday's e-mail was the most blatant yet. He had been so busy coping with his sick baby, he wrote, he hadn't had time to round up the cash. Presumably Andrew was taking a chance that he wouldn't read this newspaper, that he wouldn't find out the fink had gone running to them for help. It was obvious what his game was. He was hoping the newspaper would find the girl and he wouldn't have to shell out. If this story today brought forward the right girl then his information would be worth zilch. It was time to cut out the middle man.

Dan rang Craig Garrett, whose by-line was printed above the story.

'About this story on page five. I know the name of the girl your paper's looking for and where you can find her.'

'Yeah?' Craig Garrett's voice sounded bored. This was the fourth caller today who 'knew' the girl they were seeking. 'How do I know you're on the level?'

'Ask the kid's father, Andrew Lynton.'

Now Craig's voice moved up a gear. 'Assuming it is the right information, how much were you wanting for the info?'

'Fifty grand.'

'That's a lot of money.'

'Not if it's worth it to you. But I don't want Andrew Lynton to know about our deal. You'll have to check me out with him without revealing that.'

'That'll be difficult,' said Craig. 'What's your name?'

Dan hesitated a second. 'Do we have a deal?'

'Not without your name, we don't. You have five seconds before I put down this phone. We don't do deals with anonymous callers.'

Reluctantly Dan gave his name. Craig fired questions at him but Dan had no intention of giving even a hint of where the girl could be found until he saw the colour of the *Chronicle*'s money. Nor would he be bargained down; he maintained his demand for the full fifty thousand up front. In cash. To convince Craig he was genuine, he gave full details of the baby switch, but nothing more. It worked. A time and place were fixed to meet.

Tough bastard, thought Craig as he put the phone down. The idea of the editor sanctioning a payment as hefty as fifty thousand was as rare as shit from a rocking horse.

It took Craig a couple of hours to persuade himself that there was no way he could get his hands on such a sum unless he worked a scam. He had done it before, but not on this scale. But he reckoned it was worth the risk; he needed to redeem himself in the eyes of the editor. He had a gut feeling this was the story to do it. There had been no repercussions after the last time so he decided he would once again alter the figure on a demand for money. He was one of the few on the paper for whom the editor would sign an authority to draw up to five thousand pounds to pay an informant. The editor's handwriting was so bad, few could read it properly, and the way he had scrawled the figures, it was a simple matter for Craig to match the colour of the editorial pen and squeeze in an extra nought to the five thousand pounds mentioned above the signature on the memo.

A few hours later Craig met his informant. Dan gave him all he knew about Anna-Maria Ewing in Glasgow and readily agreed to accompany Craig to verify the birth details at St Katharine's House. Other checks confirmed everything Andrew had told him so Craig handed over a large bundle of crisp fifty-pound notes fresh from the paper's cashiers.

Then he booked seats for himself and a photographer on the following day's flight to Glasgow.

Chapter Fourteen

The phone was ringing as Calum walked into his hotel bedroom in downtown Manhattan. He hardly recognised the voice of his wife, she sounded so distraught. But when he started asking what the matter was she interrupted him.

'Gaby has found out you're not her father.'

Calum felt a sense of outrage. 'Why did you tell her? We agreed to do it together.'

'Don't jump to conclusions,' she retorted. 'Of course I didn't tell her. The *Daily Chronicle* did.'

'How the hell did they find out?'

'Andrew, I suppose.'

Calum was silent for a moment and said sadly. 'That's ruined everything. I wanted to tell her myself, in my own good time, when I was ready. But more importantly when she was ready. How she's taking it?'

'Badly. She was hysterical.'

Poor kid. Gabriella was volatile at the best of times. They would have to handle this really carefully and he had spent some time thinking how to do it. He needed to make her understand that there was more to being a dad than the act of making a baby. What bound them together was being there when she needed him, it meant experiencing life with her, sharing the ordinary things that made up day-to-day living. Those were the truly important aspects of fatherhood, not a genetic code.

He was midway through the takeover negotiations but this took precedence over business. He would take the first plane out of New York. Lizzie immediately offered to meet him and he said he would let her know the time of his arrival. Calum's next call was to Tess to tell her he was on his way back and did not need a lift from the airport. Then he flung his clothes into his suitcase and went downstairs to settle the bill.

It was his misfortune that the passenger in the seat next to him had been given the flight to London as a birthday present. She chattered on endlessly about the generosity of her sons, how wonderful it all was and exclaimed with delight each time the pilot drew their attention to landmarks below. Finally Calum took refuge behind a pair of earphones.

When he'd heard Lizzie's distressed voice on the phone his gut reaction had been to respond at once. Whatever had happened between them he could not imagine a time when he would ignore a call for help from her. He was still angry about her deceit but lately he had begun to feel some guilt that he had not given her a chance to give her side of the story. When she'd phoned him to tell him something about having her own blood tested, he was wrong to have cut her off and he should have phoned her back.

Could their marriage be rescued? Only if they could forgive each other. Maybe that was possible, but forget? Never. Did he want to try and make it work? That was something only time could answer. In New York he had tried to imagine himself without Lizzie, even going as far as to plan his life without her. He would buy that forty-foot catamaran he'd dreamed about all his adult life and sail off to the West Indies. He had almost been able to feel the wind on his face as he raised the spinnaker. He'd probably need a crew and with a pang he realised his shipmate wouldn't be Lizzie.

Then a fear he had been trying to suppress ever since the shock of the news about Gaby came back to torment him. If he had never fathered a child, was it because he was sterile?

As the doors from the customs hall parted to make way for his luggage trolley, Calum spotted Lizzie's white, strained face at once. She was leaning over the rail, scanning the crowd.

They greeted each other hesitantly and for the first time after an absence they did not embrace. Walking through the inevitable crush of passengers thronging Terminal Three, Calum was conscious that although they were side by side, their bodies did not touch. They exchanged small talk about the flight, the weather and the traffic conditions almost like strangers. He was desperate to hear about Gabriella but hated the idea of conducting such an important conversation while he was driving, and waiting until they got home would be unbearable. When Lizzie began making her way towards the car park exit, Calum suggested they have a coffee before starting the journey home and at once she agreed.

They found a table in the corner of a large snack bar and Lizzie sat down while he went to stand in line to pay for a four-cup cafetiere. The clinking of crockery, the zoosh of the cappuccino machine, the noise and bustle of anxious-looking travellers pushing unwieldy trolleys laden with luggage all created an air of normality. Waiting in the queue for the cashier, Calum took a brief look at the people sitting at the tables, chatting, joking, eating, and envied their apparent lack of cares.

When eventually he brought the tray over to their table he noticed the dark smudges under Lizzie's eyes. Her face was drawn and instinctively he vowed not to harry her. They started drinking the coffee in silence, Lizzie twisting her wedding ring round and round her finger. At last she said, 'I know you want to talk about Gabriella and she is very upset as you can imagine but right now . . .' still she did not look at him, but addressed the table, 'there's something else I have to tell you.'

He waited apprehensively. What could possibly be more important than Gabriella? Her voice was so low he had to lean across the table to hear.

'Look, there's no easy way to say this.' She stopped. 'We've already found out that Gabriella isn't your daughter. Well, she isn't my daughter either.'

His first thought was that she had lost her mind.

She did not wait for him to respond. 'I had my blood tested and it showed the same incompatibility between our blood types as they found in yours. It proves without a shadow of a doubt that Gabriella could not be related to either of us.'

Calum could hardly grasp what she was saying. He gripped the edge of the table until his knuckles whitened. 'That's not possible. I was there, I watched . . .'

'I know, I was there too.' She gave a mirthless smile. 'And I was as sceptical as you are. There's only one logical explanation. They made a mistake in the labour ward at St Martyn's. Somehow two babies were switched. One of them was ours.'

All he could stammer was a pathetic, 'Are you sure?'

Her voice was gentle as she reminded him of the over-busy labour ward, the short-staffing, the special care unit where two babies could be swapped without the mistake being detected.

Calum rested his forehead on his hand. 'A baby switch. I can't believe it. And we didn't notice?'

'I've asked myself why we didn't a hundred times.' Her face

was a study in misery. 'But we had only a brief glimpse of our baby before she was taken off for the jaundice treatment.'

Calum remembered his blind panic at the time but he had been assured Gaby would be fine. And when he had visited her in the special care unit all he'd been concerned about was seeing if there was the correct number of fingers and toes. Had that been their baby or had she already been swapped? The vivid image of a baby suckling at Lizzie's breast suddenly came into his mind.

'When you started to breast feed . . .' Calum was hesitant. 'I just wondered whether you might have noticed anything was wrong.'

Lizzie shook her head. 'I had no doubt she was ours.' Her coffee remained untouched. 'I couldn't see anything of myself in the baby, and nor could you.' Lizzie shifted in her seat. 'But I remember you saying she looked like those photographs of your mother when she was a baby.'

Calum nodded, recalling those hours they spent scrutinising every feature, every expression of their daughter.

'I'll never forget the way she looked up at me in those early days and the way her fingers curled round my hand,' said Lizzie, rubbing her eyes. Calum could see she was making a supreme effort to hold back tears.

'What does Gaby know about this?'

'Nothing, thank God. That's one of the things I wanted to discuss with you. Should we tell her?'

He couldn't answer her immediately. He had so many memories of Gabriella. She was such a scrawny little thing when she was born but as a toddler he thought she would never be able to balance on those chubby legs. He'd been watching her while Lizzie was in the kitchen and had witnessed her first uncertain footsteps. However much they cajoled Gaby, it took another two weeks before she repeated the achievement.

Then there was that day in the park when he had been trying to teach her to cycle. He'd devised a system all his own by holding on to the back of her neck and she had surprised both of them by pedalling off after only a couple of yards. And just a few weeks ago when she finally managed to beat him at backgammon – he would never forget that scream of triumph.

Gaby had already had a shock, discovering from a lousy newspaper that she wasn't who she thought she was. It would be much worse if she found out she belonged to neither of them.

'Maybe we should keep this latest news a secret from Gabriella for the moment and wait until she's older.'

Lizzie nibbled the edge of her fingernail. 'But what if she finds out anyway? From the newspaper again.'

Calum shuddered. 'The *Chronicle* only found out because of Sebastian. Your blood test wasn't part of that.'

Lizzie looked doubtful. 'I don't think we should wait to tell Gabriella the truth. We ought to do it soon. Today.'

Calum considered the alternatives. 'You could be right,' he said after a while. 'Although she's going to find the truth difficult to accept, at least it makes sense of everything.'

The elderly woman at the next table leaned over and mumbled something. He looked at her dumbly. 'Are you using your salt and pepper?' she repeated more loudly, and he passed them over wordlessly.

'I've heard of baby switches in America,' he said to Lizzie. 'How the hell could such a thing happen here?'

Lizzie was staring into the middle distance. 'Well, it did.' She took a deep breath. 'I've found the baby who was switched. In fact, I've already been to see her.'

'You've what?'

'She lives in Glasgow. Her name is Anna-Maria Ewing.'

'Anna-Maria,' he repeated tonelessly.

Lizzie pushed her cold coffee away from her. She explained how she had gone through the records at the hospital with some lab doctor who had been helpful, finally tracking the family via Dorset to Glasgow with Sarah.

Calum stared at the table. Somewhere out there was their real – his mind veered away from that word – their birth daughter. He was conscious that Lizzie was watching him carefully.

'There was one mistake in the hospital,' he said after a while. 'How sure are you that this girl really is ours?'

'Anna-Maria Ewing was the only girl baby in the unit who was about the same weight and length as Gaby.' Lizzie paused. 'And she has your colouring, your hair. And your long legs.'

Calum was silent. He was oddly pleased to hear that his unknown daughter took after him.

'What are you thinking?' she asked eventually.

'What is she like? As a person, I mean.'

'Bright, lively. A bit suspicious of strangers asking questions.

179

Her mother says she's quite a handful and rarely goes to school. They live in a rather dingy boarding house, just the two of them. Mr Ewing was killed in a lorry crash some time ago. I think Anna-Maria has had a few run-ins with social services – and the police. Sarah reckons she takes drugs.'

'God. And she's only fifteen.'

Lizzie nodded. 'She might be a match for Sebastian, but she absolutely refused to give blood.'

'She could be terrified of needles like Gaby,' said Calum with a weak smile.

'Maybe,' said Lizzie. 'I imagine you want to see her for yourself.'

'I'm curious about her, certainly, but I don't plan to dash off to Glasgow, not yet at any rate. My only priority at the moment is Gaby. She's a good kid and she's part of me – us – even if we didn't give life to her. I love her, probably more now because she needs me more. She needs both of us.' Calum glanced at his watch. 'I suppose we'd better get back and break the news to Gaby.'

Lizzie began to gather up her things. 'Gaby's not at home. She's staying at Sarah's house at the moment because we had a terrible fight after she read the article. She says she never wants to see me again. She thinks I'm such a whore I probably don't even know who her father is.' Lizzie thought Calum ought to know just how serious the row had been between herself and Gaby. His own attitude towards her lately still rankled deeply but she wasn't going to mention it. It was up to him to make the first move towards their own reconciliation, and he'd have to work damn hard for it.

Calum's eyes widened with shock. 'God, I'm so sorry, Lizzie.'

She turned wordlessly and he followed her to the parking bay on the third floor. It seemed the nightmare was only beginning. Somehow he had to hold himself together even though he felt as if he was in the middle of a huge jigsaw puzzle where apparently the overall picture made sense but only some of the pieces fitted. Difficult though it was, he had to accept that he and Lizzie had been bringing up someone else's child.

As he stowed his luggage in the boot of the car, he caught a glimpse of the back of Lizzie's head through the rear window. She seemed to take up so little room in the large car and a surge of sympathy overwhelmed him. He had been in the wrong, catastrophically in the wrong. He could barely imagine the

180

agonies she must have suffered since that first awful session in Ed Foxton's office and winced at the memory of the night he had thrown that photograph of Peter Rivers at her. He had accused her of tricking him into marriage, had claimed that Rivers was Gaby's father. Oh God. He had to make her realise how desperately sorry he was for doubting her.

Calum settled into his seat, making no effort to start the engine. He tried to take her hand but she pulled away. That nearly made him lose courage.

'Lizzie, I should have believed you when you said you'd never had an affair. I was wrong not to trust you from the start.'

She gazed steadfastly ahead and showed no reaction.

A note of desperation crept into his voice. 'The only thing I can say in my defence is that the tests were done twice and they were conclusive. Lizzie, I'm very, very sorry.'

She sat bolt upright, her chin jutting out. 'Sorry,' she said fiercely. 'You think by saying it that's enough? Can you imagine what I've been going through these past few weeks?'

Calum was beginning to feel things were slipping out of his control. He had asked himself in the plane whether his marriage could be rescued and he had mistakenly thought that the answer lay with him. Now he could see quite clearly that unless he was careful, Lizzie was not going to give him the chance to put matters right.

He stared at her anxiously. 'I wish . . . I wish I could put back the clock but I can't. Will you try and forgive me?'

Her eyes seemed to darken. 'I'm not sure I can. You were prepared to chuck away sixteen years of marriage, just like that.' She snapped her fingers. 'After those tests came in you wouldn't even consider any other explanation. Well, there was. And we need to tell Gabriella, so I suggest we just think about that now.'

Miserably Calum switched on the engine, shifted into first gear and soon joined the slow-moving line of vehicles snaking its way along the M25 motorway. They sat in strained silence, both worrying about their coming encounter with Gabriella.

Ever since she had met the Ewings Lizzie had been dreading how to tell Gabriella about the baby swap. She had discussed it with Sarah who had advised having a word with the school psychologist. Lizzie was reluctant to do that. Although they had become friendly through bumping into each other in the staffroom, Lizzie was not eager to tell a colleague all the ins and outs of her personal life. But Sarah persuaded her that there was a right way and a wrong way to impart bad news. 'You might as well listen to what she has to say. After all, you don't have to take her advice.' Which was why Lizzie had found herself the day before pouring out her heart in the cheerless surroundings of the school staffroom when everyone else had left for home.

Breaking the news, she was told, had to be quick, direct and without equivocation, concentrating on facts first and feelings second. She and Calum had to make sure Gabriella understood they would always love, nurture and care for her. Once she had accepted she was loved for herself as an individual, she would feel more secure and therefore better able to deal with the situation.

The psychologist warned Lizzie to be prepared for deep emotional scars which might require a great deal of patience to heal. Gabriella would need time to absorb the shock. After a while she might have a real sense of bereavement and could experience feelings of jealousy towards the unknown child she had replaced. To counteract this they needed to emphasise what defined a family. 'Families have to do with memories even if some of them aren't all pleasant. A family goes beyond genetics; it's far more than biology.'

Lizzie broke the silence in the car and recounted the psychologist's main points to Calum. Total honesty had to be their best course, she said and suggested he take the lead as Gabriella usually behaved less aggressively towards him.

He agreed. At least they were united in their aim to leave Gabriella with one certainty: that though biologically she may not be their daughter, it would not alter their love for her. Nothing should be allowed to rock that secure world.

As Calum inched forward slowly amidst a sea of metal on the notorious stretch of motorway leading to the capital, he glanced across at Lizzie. What all this would do to their marriage had obviously been firmly placed in the 'don't-think-about-that-now' box. He would have to live with that. For now.

182

Chapter Fifteen

However many stories he was sent on, Craig never failed to get a buzz. It was what kept him on the road rather than behind a desk issuing orders. Craig's motto had always been: 'Go in low, go in fast and, if necessary, kill.' That was the difference between the adequate newsman and the brilliant.

This assignment was turning out to be a breeze. The electoral register had given him the Ewings' address. In fact, waiting around in front of Gallagher's Guesthouse was the hardest part. He and the snapper had arrived at lunchtime and by five o'clock, when even Craig was beginning to fret, he saw a figure teetering down the street. His first sight of Anna-Maria had been through the dusk, her swaying figure in a black leather skirt riding high on her thigh, showing an expanse of shapely bare leg.

'That can't be her,' he whispered to the photographer. 'She looks well over fifteen.' But it had been, and he thought moodily that they would have to scrape off some of that pancake stuff to make her look more appealing to readers and less of a tart.

'She won't be able to bend over in that skirt,' grinned the snapper. 'It's so short she'll show next week's washing.'

If he had to say it himself the story he strung together for Mrs Ewing and her daughter was masterly, no other word for it. Sebastian's struggle to survive was given in poignant detail. He spared them nothing. The dashed hopes and the brave little fellow's continuing cheerfulness despite many hospital visits. To pre-empt what should have been their first question – 'What has this to do with us?' – he explained that his newspaper had undertaken the search for a tissue match. Probably they had read about it? They shook their heads. Craig wasn't surprised. *Chronicle* sales in Scotland were not great.

The reason he was there, he told them, was because Anna-Maria might be able to save this baby's life. Wouldn't she want to do that? The girl just sat there staring insolently at him but the mother seemed to wake up and asked why her daughter should be the one to save the kid. Craig parried her question with a series of his own. Did she give birth at St Martyn's in London? Was it on November the eleventh fifteen years ago? Did she share a ward with five other mothers? Yes, yes, yes, she answered with increasing puzzlement.

Was one of those mothers a Mrs Elizabeth Lynton?

Her eyes widened. That women had been in this very room last week, sitting on the chair he was in.

Shit, thought Craig. How had she found the address? But he was too experienced a reporter to show surprise and mildly asked if Mrs Lynton had explained why she'd turned up out of the blue.

The good news was that Elizabeth Lynton had given no clue about the true reason for the visit so the Ewings could have no idea about the switch. Craig was going to have to break the news. Well, he had done worse. Dealing with human beings who could be wayward was what provided the element of uncertainty that gave him his kicks. He arranged his features in an expression of concern and released the cataclysmic news that Anna-Maria had been switched at birth with the Lyntons' baby.

Hardened as he was to watching the raw emotions of others, he found himself stirred by Nancy Ewing's inability to grasp the enormity of the mistake. She kept on shaking her head, saying it wasn't possible, that she would have noticed. Anna-Maria, in contrast, seemed not to lose an ounce of composure and said sharply, 'This explains a lot of things.' Craig caught the photographer's eye. A toughie but that could make her easier to deal with.

With a great deal of effort he spent some time convincing Nancy Ewing that the switch had indeed taken place. There was genetic proof that the Lynton's daughter could not be related to them and no other baby in the special care unit apart from Anna-Maria could have been the switch. Elizabeth Lynton obviously thought so; why else would she pay them a visit? It was this that made Nancy believe it was true.

Thirty minutes later Nancy Ewing was red-eyed from weeping but calm enough to ask questions. 'Does Elizabeth Lynton have my girl? What's her name? Where does she live? Can I see her?'

Craig lied and said he did not know but earnestly promised Nancy that if she and her daughter came to London with him, he would fix it for her to meet the Lynton girl.

'This Lynton woman,' asked Anna-Maria unexpectedly. 'Where does she fit in?'

Was the girl thick? 'She's your birth mother,' said Craig.

'I didn't like her and I don't want to see her again,' snapped Anna-Maria.

Craig moved in for the kill. If they co-operated with his newspaper to help the baby, they could come with him to London today and stay, all expenses paid, at a luxury hotel. He added smoothly that they could leave all the details regarding money to him and that there would be a 'proper contract' between them. What he did not share with them was that they would be under assumed names and that the contract was barely worth the paper on which it was written. Of course he could not prevent them making phone calls and that was usually where the slip-ups started. Which was why he'd see to it that they would have a minder at all times. Himself preferably. 'Our main concern is the campaign to help the baby,' he said. 'And there's big money involved if you co-operate.'

'How big is big?' asked Anna-Maria promptly. Nancy Ewing was silent.

'Could be thousands,' said Craig, watching the girl's eyes glitter. She leaned closer, giving him a nice profile of pert breasts.

'What do we have to do to get the money?'

'Very little. There's a legal matter that has to be sorted out between the family and when that's settled you'll get your hands on the cash.' If she helped Andrew win his case, thought Craig, Andrew could pay her and the *Chronicle* wouldn't have to fork out.

Anna-Maria raised her eyebrows. 'I'm not getting involved in any legal stuff. Anyway, what's it got to do with the baby we're supposed to help?'

'It's all bound up in the same thing. The baby's parents are bringing the court action.' Craig then launched into an explanation about Robert Lynton's will, how unfair it was and how a girl who had absolutely nothing to do with the family had been left a fortune under false pretences. Her father's brother was only trying to obtain his rightful inheritance.

'Why didn't the old man leave his money to this guy in the first place?'

Fifteen years old? Going on for thirty more likely, thought

Craig. She certainly got to the nub of the argument swiftly. He muttered something about father and son having a small fight, nothing serious, which he was gratified to see Anna-Maria appeared to accept. To have this wonderful holiday in London, all she had to do, he told her, was to give a sample of her blood to determine whether she was a match for the baby. It would also establish her paternity.

'No way,' said Anna-Maria. 'I'm not giving blood and that's that.'

'If you don't give blood,' Craig said sternly, 'you won't sniff the money.'

Anna-Maria glared at Craig. He turned to Nancy Ewing. 'I think I'd better have a word with your daughter in private, if you don't mind.'

Nancy protested but she was easy meat to a man like Craig and the photographer hurried her out into the kitchen.

'Right,' Craig said to the girl. 'What's worrying you?'

She shrugged. 'Dunno what you mean.'

'Is it drugs? Aids? What?'

She stared out of the window and did not answer.

'Unless you tell me,' said Craig briskly, 'the deal's off.'

'Look, I just don't want to cause the baby any harm if my blood's not OK,' Anna-Maria told him.

'Hospitals test blood for everything these days. They'll tell you if there was anything wrong with yours and if there was, they would never give it to the baby.'

'Well, OK, but who would they tell if they found anything? I mean, do the police ever get involved?'

The police? What the hell was this girl trying to hide? 'Lab tests are confidential,' said Craig. 'If they weren't, nobody would ever give blood. They just need to test yours to see if you're a match for the baby and to establish paternity.'

Anna-Maria was silent.

'So will you come down to London?' asked Craig. This girl would need a minder to keep her away from drugs and booze, never mind the phone.

After a pause she gave such a slight nod Craig almost missed it, but it was definitely a nod. Great. He could already see the editor nodding approvingly at the headline splashed across five columns: 'We find the girl the whole of Britain has been seeking.'

Top of the Pops resonated through the untidy bedroom. Sprawling on the floor, against the bed, Natasha and Gabriella watched as the star practically castrated himself with his guitar.

There was a firm knock at the door. 'Tasha, I need to come in.'

Gabriella shook her head violently. Raising her voice, Natasha called out, 'Gaby wants to be left alone, Mum, and so do I.'

'Sorry, that's not an option.' Sarah was firm. 'Open up. Now.'

Natasha sighed. 'She'll only carry on,' she whispered. 'She won't leave it alone. Best to get it over with.' She went to the door and unlocked it.

Sarah came into the room and sat on the bed. 'Tasha, could you turn that off, please?' Her daughter muted the sound but left on the picture. 'Gaby, your parents are downstairs.'

The girl's lips compressed and Natasha put her arm round her friend's shoulders.

'He's not my father,' said Gabriella vehemently, 'and I don't want that women to be my mother.'

'I think you ought to see them,' said Sarah. 'They're very upset.'

'Good.'

'I know how you must feel—'

'You don't. No one does,' said Gabriella vehemently.

'If Gabs doesn't want to see anybody,' said Natasha, 'no one should make her.'

'You're very hurt, I know, Gaby,' said Sarah. 'It must have been horrible to find out the way you did but you can't stay in this room forever.'

'I've been left money in Grandad's will and when I get it I could pay you back if you let me stay here.'

'It's not money I'm talking about,' said Sarah. 'You'll have to go home some time. You all need to talk about this, that's the only way.'

'No. They've both been lying to me.'

'No, they haven't. There is an explanation and they want to tell you what it is. You owe it to them to at least hear them out.'

Gabriella stared unblinking at the television.

'Please,' urged Sarah. 'Go and see them. If you don't want to say anything you needn't. Just listen.'

Gabriella picked up the remote control and aimed it at the television. Again the strident mixture of bass guitar and violins, which had been elevated to number one in that week's charts, filled the room.

Sarah strode briskly from the room to join Lizzie and Calum who were sitting at opposite ends of the sitting room.

'She won't come down.'

'I'll go up and talk to her,' said Calum.

'I wouldn't if I were you. Leave her a while. You have a very wounded kid up there. Why not let her stay the night with us?'

Calum looked at Lizzie.

'No,' said Lizzie firmly. 'She needs to be with us.'

With that Calum sprang to his feet and went up the stairs. Sarah gave a nod towards his retreating back and mouthed, 'How are you feeling?'

Lizzie shrugged despondently.

'Would you like a drink?' Sarah offered but Lizzie declined.

Calum reappeared, a sullen-faced Gaby behind him. 'I told her we had something really important to talk over,' he said to Lizzie, 'and I suggested we had a bite to eat on neutral ground. She's opted for McDonald's.' He turned to Sarah. 'Thanks for all your help.'

Never were people so at odds with the relentlessly cheerful atmosphere of the restaurant than Calum, Lizzie and Gabriella. The perky faces of Ronald McDonald lined the walls and in one corner multi-coloured balloons were still in place after some youngster's birthday celebrations.

Calum glanced across at the decorations. 'I remember Mum and I bringing you here for one of your birthdays. I think you must've been about six.'

Lizzie nodded but Gaby continued to stare down at her plate, toying with her hamburger.

Calum took his child's hands across the table and readied himself for the most difficult task he had ever undertaken.

'I'm sorry that you had to find out in the most hurtful way possible that I'm not your biological father. But that doesn't matter a hoot to me,' he said softly. 'You are my daughter and you always will be. It's important you believe it.'

Gabriella's eyes were stretched wide. 'I want to,' she said, 'but why didn't you tell me? It wouldn't have been such a shock.'

'I didn't tell you because until very recently I didn't know.' Calum explained how the facts had come to light as a result of the blood test she had given to help Sebastian. Somehow Andrew

188

had found out and was using it to fight the will. Calum described how upset he had been when he had first found out, how he hadn't wanted to believe it but that now he had to.

Gaby shot a sideways glance at Lizzie. 'Don't you mind? That Mum must've . . .' Her courage failed her.

'I thought the same as you, darling,' Calum came in quickly, 'that your mother must have been with another man. I'm not proud of myself. I should've realised . . .' He paused and his voice became stronger. 'We owe your mother a very big apology because she didn't lie. There was a mistake at the hospital.'

Gaby stared from one to the other.

'What happened, Gaby, was that you were switched with someone else's baby. As far as we can work out, a few hours after you were born, the wrist tags must have been muddled up and then they were put on the wrong babies.' He cleared his throat.

Gaby's breath quickened. 'So I'm not yours?' she said to Calum. Then she turned her pale, almost translucent face to Lizzie. 'And I don't belong to you either?' Her face crumpled and she started to sob, her head bent, her body shaking. A few curious glances were thrown in their direction.

Calum was in agony. 'This place is so . . . public.'

'Yes, but she chose it,' Lizzie mouthed at him, her arms round her daughter.

The three sat motionless in the booth, Lizzie aware that Gabriella would need time to absorb the enormity of what she'd been told. Calum held on tightly to Gaby's hands and squeezed them three times. This was their secret code for 'I love you.' She made no motion to repel him but did not squeeze back as she normally did, though slowly the harsh weeping began to ease.

'Gaby, nothing's really changed,' said Lizzie at last. 'We're still the same people and we love you.' Gabriella did not respond and Calum, clutching her all the while, struggled to contain the choke in his voice.

'Someone once wrote that it wasn't flesh and blood which made us parents but the heart. And no accident in the hospital's ever going to change that.'

At this her face crumpled again. 'But I don't know who I am now.'

Lizzie was trying to control her emotions as she took Gabriella in her arms and gave her a hug. She noticed Calum swallowing hard as he stroked Gabriella's hands.

'Darling Gabs, I'm still your father, still your dad, and Mum's still your mum.' He waited for a moment to see if his words were having any effect. 'We've been with you since the minute you were born, haven't we? In every sense of the word we are your parents.'

Lizzie smiled encouragingly at Gaby's pale face.

'You have to say that, don't you?' Gabriella managed weakly.

'But we mean it,' said Lizzie. 'From the moment you were put into my arms, you were mine. My daughter.' She enunciated each word carefully, hoping desperately that Gabriella could take it in. 'And that's how I still feel.' Her heart was thumping uncomfortably. 'Darling, it's not who your parents are that's important. It's who *you* are.'

'In the end,' added Calum, 'what you make of your life is the only thing that really counts.'

Gaby nodded but then her tears started again. 'Mum, why didn't you tell me before?' Her cheeks were glistening. 'I called you . . . that horrible name . . . but if I'd known . . .' Lizzie began to dab gently at the girl's damp cheeks with a tissue. 'I'm ashamed of myself,' said Gabriella, and suddenly she stood up, making off in the direction of the rest rooms. Lizzie half rose as if to follow but Calum shook his head.

'She needs a bit of breathing space.'

For a few moments husband and wife looked at each other.

'God, this is tough,' said Calum. 'How do you think she's taking it?'

'She's young to have all this on her shoulders. She hasn't started asking questions yet.' Lizzie sighed. 'I'm worried about how she'll cope with the court case, all those headlines and awful publicity. Everybody will know our private business.' She shuddered, 'It'll be horrible for her.'

'For all of us,' said Calum despondently.

'We won't be able to shield her forever but maybe she ought to stay at Sarah's place while the court case is on.'

'Good idea,' said Calum, his eye on the rest room doors.

A few minutes later Gabriella returned to the table, calmer, her eyes reddened but with questions on her mind.

'How did you find out about the hospital's mistake?' she asked, and listened quietly as Lizzie told her the entire sequence of events.

'Have you met the other people? The ones who have your baby.'

190

Calum shook his head. 'I haven't,' he said.

'I have,' said Lizzie. 'I met your birth mother, briefly.'

'What's her name?'

'Nancy. Nancy Ewing.'

'And my . . . father?'

'I'm afraid he was killed in a car crash a few years ago. His name was Derek.'

'And I didn't even know him.' Again the tears began to brim and Lizzie passed her a tissue. 'What's my . . . m-mother like?'

Lizzie told her about Nancy Ewing, her appearance, her home and what she did for a living. She did her best to paint a picture of a homely Scottish widow, omitting the less salubrious details of her surroundings. Her heart twisted as she waited for Gaby to ask about Anna-Maria.

'And what about . . .' Gaby couldn't finish the sentence.

'I met her too,' said Lizzie gently.

'Do you think Grandpa would've left me the money if he'd known this about me?' Gaby asked quickly, as if she couldn't face hearing about her mother's birth daughter.

'Absolutely,' said Calum with all the force he could muster. 'He loved you, Gaby, you made him laugh. And he liked spending time with you. Of course he would've acted in exactly the same way. I'm convinced of it.'

Gaby gazed thoughtfully at Lizzie. 'We fight a lot. Do you think it's because I don't really belong to you?'

For a moment Lizzie was at a loss to reply. 'Don't think that, please,' she said firmly. 'Many people go through bad patches when teenagers struggle to become independent and parents have trouble letting go. It happens to everybody and it passes. We'll all be friends again, you'll see.'

Gabriella nodded. She sipped her soft drink and Lizzie was silently hoping this ordeal was coming to an end when Gabriella asked, 'When can I see her, my mother I mean?'

Lizzie's heart began a drummer's tattoo and Calum exchanged a worried glance with her.

He chose his words carefully. 'I can understand your need to find out everything you can about your birth mother and her family. But I think we should wait a while. I promise to help you meet them but right now we have to concentrate on the court case. And maybe that's for the best.' He patted her hand. 'We all need time to come to terms with what's happened. We'll have to wait till the case is over, it won't be for long.'

'We're going to ask Uncle Andy to settle,' added Lizzie. 'He's been against it so far but we'll go on asking until the last minute because we don't want our private business making headlines in the papers again. And we'd hate you to face that kind of publicity with press people ringing up and trying to snatch pictures of all of us.'

For the first time since they came into the restaurant, Gaby gave a weak smile. 'Sounds exciting.'

'It isn't,' said Lizzie, trying to squash that thought as firmly as she could. 'Imagine what your life would be like at school. It'll be hell for you and for your friends.'

They were able to persuade her of the wisdom of being away from home when the story broke in the newspapers. The suggestion from Calum that she could stay with Natasha had the necessary effect and Gabriella seemed pleased with the chance of being cosseted by Sarah and the rest of the Sinclair family.

They were preparing to leave when Gabriella asked, 'Do I have any brothers or sisters?'

'Mrs Ewing has two other children, much older than you, who live away from home,' she replied. 'Two boys. And then there's Anna-Maria.'

Seeing the lost expression on Gaby's face, Lizzie experienced a surge of fresh pity for this vulnerable girl.

'The one who was switched with me?'

'Yes.'

'I'm really Anna-Maria Ewing, aren't I?' Once more her eyes filled with tears. 'And she's Gabriella Lynton. Your real daughter.'

Chapter Sixteen

Restlessly Calum rummaged through the fridge but nothing tempted his appetite. He poured out a generous measure of whisky and turned on the tap watching the amber liquid changing colour as the water rose in the glass. A wave of sadness engulfed him. Upstairs, the woman with whom he had shared everything, had shrunk away from him when he'd tried to embrace her. How often, in the reaches of the night, snuggled up in bed, had they comforted each other when family or business had worried them? And now when they needed each other, she'd turned away from him. Was he such a bad person? He had made one mistake. All right, a major one. He hadn't trusted his wife when he should have. But did she intend to push him away forever? Had she no capacity to forgive?

Frustrated, Calum took a large gulp of whisky and felt it warming his throat. He drained his glass and began to crush the carton that had housed the whisky purchased on the plane. He pressed the pedal of the waste bin with his foot to drop in the cardboard but the bin was full. Of flowers. Expensive-looking, though with some of the heads lopped off and still wrapped in cellophane. Puzzled, he walked slowly upstairs.

Lizzie was sitting at the dressing table taking off her eye make-up.

'I found the remains of a bouquet of flowers in the bin. Why did you chuck them away?'

She looked round for a second, then resumed what she was doing. 'Gaby and I had a fight. She got hold of the wrong end of the stick, as usual, and ruined the flowers.'

Calum was uneasy. He did not want to press her. Having been proved wrong about practically everything lately, he didn't want to upset Lizzie further yet he couldn't help himself asking the question.

'Who sent them to you?'

'Dan Hargreaves, the doctor at the lab who was so helpful. I told you about him.'

Had she? His recollection of their conversation at the airport snack bar was hazy on the details; he had still been reeling from the shock of learning that their daughter had been switched at birth.

'That was good of him,' he said vaguely, before retracing his steps back down to the kitchen. A puzzled frown creased his forehead. Why was this man sending his wife flowers when surely she was the one in his debt? What exactly had prompted Gaby to destroy the bouquet?

Gabriella's mind was spinning as she lay in the bath. Calum wasn't her dad. Lizzie wasn't her mum. She wondered if she ought to start calling them by their first names from now on. They'd said nothing had changed but her feelings were hard to sort out. However much she tried to come to terms with what she had been told, however much she tried to analyse what had happened, it came back to the same thing. Where had she come from? Who were her parents? She'd been told that her real father was dead but what had he been? Nobel prize winner? Thief? Did her mother have talents she shared, like maths, for example? What did she look like?

All this was muddled up with pictures from her childhood which kept on popping up in her mind. Lizzie taking her to ballet classes and telling her over and over that she was as good as the others. Calum bringing her home a little teddy bear when she had a cold. She had brought Angus Bear with her to Natasha's and that night, as every night, she would sleep with him under her pillow. When she was thirteen, Lizzie had arranged what she called a 'posh party' for her. The invitations said that furs and tiaras were obligatory and her friends had raided their mothers' wardrobes, using the event as a wonderful excuse. It had been cool, especially when her father, well, Calum, had dressed as a waiter and poured white grapefruit juice out of champagne bottles. And she would never forget the look on their faces when she appeared in the school play last year. They couldn't have put that on, could they?

Was it possible for them to meet the daughter they had created together and not prefer her? How could they help but compare this daughter with herself, who was sometimes irritable and often, let's face it, horrible, especially to Lizzie. Anna-Maria was a mixture of both their genes. She belonged to them. She probably took after Calum, even-tempered and sweet and, like Lizzie, loved classical music instead of the rock Gaby preferred. She could imagine the three of them, Calum, Lizzie and Anna-Maria cosily listening to some concerto or other and gave a shudder at the thought.

She'd bet a million pounds that Anna-Maria would prefer Calum and Lizzie to her own parents. Anyone would. But her real mother would probably be heartbroken at the loss of Anna-Maria and wouldn't want a strange daughter to replace her. Anyway, how could she live in Glasgow, away from everything that was familiar to her? It did not occur to her that Anna-Maria might feel the same in reverse.

Gabriella shampooed her hair and dipped underneath the water to rinse off the lather. Then she pulled herself out of the bath and reached for a towel. It would be too painful for her to welcome this real daughter into the house, to share her with Calum and Lizzie. She ought to save herself from a very depressing future. From now on she had to become more independent and she had better start right away.

She would have a talk with Luke. He was clever. He would help her decide what to do.

In the kitchen Calum was taking out the bin liner. He emptied it over the kitchen floor. It did not take him long to find what he was searching for, the florist's card. It was ripped into four fragments but it was easy to piece them together: 'I must see you again. D.'.

Calum stared at the message. Gaby must have seen the card. No wonder she had got the wrong end of the stick, as Lizzie had put it. He massaged his aching forehead but realised that despite his jet lag he would never be able to sleep. Impetuously he dialled Tess Parker's number. He could discuss the last-minute demands from Schroeder and ask her to dig out the last financial data to be needed, anything to divert his mind from what had happened in the last twenty-four hours. But when her answering machine clicked in, he sighed and left a brief message. Perhaps it was just as well. He would have been tempted to unload his troubles on her shoulders, which mightn't be wise in the circumstances. Maybe a drive might clear his thoughts and make his body accept the switch from New York to London time.

As he steered the car aimlessly through the narrow streets, his mind returned to the image of the crushed flowers in the bin. What did Dan Hargreaves mean to Lizzie? Was he the reason she kept pulling away from him? God knows he didn't want to jump to the wrong conclusions again but Lizzie wasn't helping. He couldn't risk asking her outright why Hargreaves was sending her flowers and begging to see her again. Calum's head ached as the questions went round and round in his mind. Would he have been so suspicious about a bunch of flowers if his relationship with Lizzie hadn't already been strained by his lack of trust in her? He didn't think so, but that didn't help. It was almost as if having once allowed doubt to enter his mind, however wrongly, he couldn't now turn the clock back and shut it out again. Well, of course he couldn't. Things had changed. He needed Lizzie to meet him halfway.

He suddenly noticed the lights ahead turning red and slammed on the brakes. This was getting him nowhere and if he wasn't careful he'd end up in hospital.

Suddenly feeling dog-tired, he turned the car and headed for home.

Lizzie lay in the darkness, tossing and turning, waiting for Calum to return. She had heard the sound of his car pulling away from the house and wondered where he could be going at this ungodly hour. Unbidden, the image of Tess rose up in her mind. Lizzie thumped her pillow and resolutely turned her back on that line of thought. Things were complicated enough without getting wound up about imaginary affairs Calum might be having. Assuming they were imaginary.

Two hours later Lizzie heard the click of the front door and Calum's footsteps as he made his way to the bedroom. She pulled the duvet over her head and pretended to be asleep.

Breakfast was an ordeal. They pussy-footed around each other until Lizzie felt like yelling with frustration. She had woken up resolute about one thing: they had to protect Gaby above all else. To that end they needed to make a super-human effort to behave towards each other in a civilised manner.

Thankfully Gabriella dashed down the stairs in her usual rush. She never gave herself enough time to get ready for school. For an instant the three of them were in the kitchen together, Lizzie making tea, Calum scanning the papers and Gabriella drowning a bowl of cornflakes, behaving as if yesterday's emotional exchanges had never happened.

Lizzie came up behind her and put her arms round her. 'Are you all right?'

The warm expression on Gabriella's face as she turned round and nodded reassured Lizzie.

Calum smiled at his daughter. 'Gabs, anything you want to ask, anything that worries you, let us know. I don't want anything to fester.'

She looked across at Lizzie. 'Can I ask about the flowers?'

Aware of Calum's watchful gaze, Lizzie said, 'Of course you can. I told you the truth. I was grateful for the doctor's help and he may have thought there was more to it than that.' She paused. 'There won't be any more flowers.'

Gabriella turned from her to Calum. 'Are you two OK now?'

Lizzie gave Calum a level look. She was under no illusions that their marriage was at a critical point and she chose her words with care. 'There were things said and done that we both regret and I hope we'll be able to get over them.'

Calum's tone was deceptively mild. 'Mum was very upset with me because I didn't believe her and I'm going to have to work hard to gain her forgiveness.'

Lizzie thought he made it sound so simple, as if it was only up to her. Was it? Where did he go last night? She couldn't help adding, 'Gaby, there aren't any ogres, no one's a goodie or a baddie. It's a little more complicated than that.'

'Maybe,' said Gabriella. 'But even when you quarrel I can see that you love each other. This'll turn out happy ever after, you'll see.'

They couldn't help smiling at the fairytale imagery before Calum, with a glance at the kitchen clock, said she'd better hurry or she'd be late for school. Gabriella retorted that she'd cut it finer than this and within minutes she had finished her breakfast, grabbed her rucksack and, shouting goodbyes, rushed out of the door.

Calum retreated to his newspaper as Lizzie started clearing up. Making her voice deliberately casual she said, 'You went out very late last night. Where did you get to?'

He put down the paper and stretched. 'Nowhere, I just got

into the car and drove round and round. I needed to think.' He stood up. 'If you don't mind I'm going to try and have a little more sleep before I go to the office. I'm no good to anyone like this.' He walked out into the hallway and she heard his slow tread up the stairs to their bedroom.

Part of her was grateful he was going off because she was in no mood for a confrontation. Had he gone to Tess? Lizzie was surprised at the dull ache inside when she imagined him and Tess making love. She needed to stop thinking about it. The most constructive thing she could do to occupy her mind was to mark some tests she had set her class.

When the phone rang she jumped.

It was Tess; she needed to speak to Calum. When told he was asleep she asked Lizzie to tell him the figures he asked for last night were on his desk.

Lizzie stopped breathing for a second or two. 'Was he with you last night?'

There was a pause before Tess said softly, 'I'd better not say anything more. I don't want to be involved.'

Calum had lied. Driving around aimlessly indeed when all the time he'd been with Tess. Bastard. If this was the way he was going to play it she would apply for that full-time job which was advertised in the staffroom.

The rest of the papers for Form 2B went unmarked.

Calum reappeared downstairs a short time later, dressed for the office. Lizzie was sitting at the kitchen table and she greeted his smile with a frosty stare. He appeared not to notice and walked over to the sink to fill the kettle. 'Couldn't sleep.'

She only just prevented herself from saying he would not be so tired if he had spent the night in his own bed. 'We have some serious stuff we need to deal with,' she said. 'You lied to me about what you were doing last night.'

'I didn't.'

'Calum, Tess phoned while you were asleep and as much as told me you were with her.'

'I can't think why she would've done that. It's not true.'

'You expect me to believe you rather than her?'

'Yes, I do. Just like I'm expected to believe you.'

'What's that supposed to mean?'

'I read the note with the flowers. I think you slept with that man.'

198

Lizzie turned her back on him. 'You're wrong.'

Infuriated, he strode over to her. 'Tell me what's going on?'

'Nothing.' She paused. 'Just like you say there is nothing going on with you and Tess.'

'There isn't. What I want to know—'

Lizzie raised both palms in a gesture of dismissal. 'I don't have the energy for this at the moment. Please, I want us to call a truce. We have too much on our plate. Let's leave to one side what we're going to decide about us.'

Calum's face was strained. 'Us?'

'You know what I mean.' When he said nothing she sighed heavily. 'All right, I'll spell it out. I still feel bitter that you didn't believe me. I hope I'll get over it but I don't know . . . and now you accuse me of sleeping with Dan Hargreaves after spending half the night with Tess.'

'That's not—'

'Just hear me out. I don't want an explanation. I don't want to hear excuses or reasons. I simply want to concentrate on Gabriella.'

'I agree with that,' said Calum grimly.

'As far as she's concerned things have to appear as normal as possible. However difficult it might be I think we ought to put on a civilised front for the next few weeks. At least until Andrew either settles with us or the court case is over. Agreed?'

'That won't be easy,' said Callum.

'What's the alternative? Or can't you wait to go to Tess?'

'No!'

Lizzie collected up the test papers, tapped them on the table and snapped an elastic band round them.

'No more rushing off in the middle of the night then,' she said tartly.

'You'll have to stop needling me about Tess if you want this thing to work,' responded Calum, glaring at her. 'And I won't say anything about Dan.'

'There's nothing to say.'

There was a short silence.

'What about sleeping arrangements?' Calum asked.

'We'll call a truce on that as well,' Lizzie replied, 'but I suggest we share the same bedroom for Gaby's sake. In a day or two if we find the whole business impossible, one of us could move to the spare room. We could tell her that because of the court case and everything we're sleeping badly. If there's no animosity between us she might accept that explanation.'

Calum's face was impassive. Lizzie had been expecting an outburst, then the phone rang and she seized it gratefully. It was Edward Foxton. Andrew's court case had been brought forward. Another one had collapsed which meant space on the list. He had been told by Zak Blondell, Andrew's solicitor, that the date had been set for the sixteenth of this month. Five days' time. Edward wanted them to come to his office as soon as possible. He had already briefed their barrister, Tim Goodman, and needed to discuss his comments with them.

In the car on the way to Edward's office Lizzie wondered how he would react to the news of the baby switch. Like Calum, the solicitor had never given her the benefit of the doubt.

'Do we have to tell Edward about Gaby?' she said to Calum. 'I'd much rather we kept it to ourselves, for Gaby's sake.'

'I think we should,' Calum replied. 'We can trust Edward to keep it quiet but if it leaks out then we don't want our team to have surprises.'

'I'm afraid your brother's after blood,' said Edward as soon as they had sat down. He fingered the corner of his file, tied up with pink cord, and gave a shame-faced grin. 'No pun intended.'

When there was no reaction from either of them, he went on, 'Andrew wants his day in court. I stressed that you were willing to sell the business, the lot, if necessary, and that you had already begun negotiations to sell. But he said if you gave him every penny you owned he wouldn't make what he stood to gain through the court and it's my impression he won't compromise.'

'I'm not surprised,' said Calum. 'And he's right, I can't come close to matching what he hopes to get out of my father's estate, that much became clear when I was in America.' He glanced at Lizzie before continuing, 'There's been another development which Lizzie and I feel you should know about.'

Lizzie took a deep breath and recounted how she had organised her own blood test, and how it showed she could not possibly be Gaby's mother.

Edward appeared puzzled but not for long. 'There must have been a mistake at the hospital.'

'Yes,' said Lizzie, 'we believe there was.' And you owe me an apology, she added silently.

She didn't get one.

200

'We could sue the hospital, you know,' was Edward's first reaction after Lizzie explained the theory that there could have been a switch in the special care unit. Typical legal mind, thought Lizzie. How could money compensate for the fall-out from the hospital's bungle? It had been an honest error, caused by overwork, not malice. Hospitals were usually punctilious about identity bracelets. The fact that one case had gone wrong did not make the whole system rotten.

'I think we have enough on our plates right now without another money-grabbing court case,' she said coldly.

'As you wish,' said Edward smoothly. 'Tim Goodman, our barrister, is quite clear in his mind about the line to take. In his opinion Robert's intention is what matters and I can't think the fact that there might be another Lynton baby out there somewhere changes that.'

Lizzie caught Calum's gaze and gave him a hard stare. She could see no reason to tell Edward that she knew exactly where the other Lynton child lived. She wasn't sure how it would affect Gabriella's inheritance but she wouldn't risk adding to her difficulties.

'I just want to get this whole bloody business over,' said Calum, ruffling his hair.

'It will be an ordeal but no one expects it to last more than two days maximum,' said Edward. 'I'll brief the barrister about the baby switch but, as I say, in my opinion that won't change our tactics. You've given us terrific evidence of how close Gabriella was to her grandfather. Those home videos will be invaluable should we need to show them and there's plenty of backup in the way of letters and photographs.' He extracted a large birthday card from the folder. 'This is particularly helpful because the inscription, "my dearest granddaughter", is in Robert's own hand and reflects the language of the will.' He took off his glasses and started polishing them absent-mindedly. 'I suppose the judge may want to talk to her about her relationship with her grandfather. You never know what judges might want these days. But with all the ammunition we have, I'll stick my neck out and predict we won't need to call Gabriella into the witness box.'

'Thank God,' said Lizzie. 'I couldn't bear her to stand up in court in front of everyone and be questioned by a hostile barrister.'

'Judges don't usually like dragging young people into court unless it's strictly necessary,' said Edward. 'But there are no guarantees. On the day it depends not only on the strength of the case but what the judge has had for breakfast. You should brace yourselves, it could get nasty. Andrew's solicitors are acting on a no win, no fee basis so they have every incentive to go for the jugular.'

When he saw the effect of his words on Calum and Lizzie he added hastily, 'But we have a very good barrister, an excellent man.' He paused and smiled. 'And it has been known for justice to prevail in British courtrooms.'

Andrew was in full flow, enthusiastically punching the air to emphasise the points his solicitor had just made to him on the phone.

They were still waiting to see if Anna-Maria Ewing could be a match for Sebastian, which was all Edina could think about. But the court case was starting in five days' time and Andy was saying that the girl would be a useful weapon for their side. Edina listlessly poured herself a cup of coffee. Sebastian had been awake most of the night and it was an effort to concentrate on what her husband was saying.

Andy was excited, his fury with Craig Garrett all but forgotten. When Craig had told him that he had found the girl and intended to publish the baby switch story to coincide with the court case whether he liked it or not, Andrew had been appalled and outraged. But his solicitor had reassured him; he had pointed out that the girl's existence was living proof that Gaby wasn't even related to Robert Lynton by marriage, which could only help his case. The bloodline aspect was certainly an important part of their challenge to the will but, his solicitor said confidently, no judge would go so far as to rule that Robert Lynton intended his estate to go to a complete stranger. No, the will would be judged to be null and void on the grounds that Robert Lynton would not have left his fortune to Gabriella had he known she was not related by blood; that being so, the estate would be shared between his two sons.

Edina was uneasy about the way the newspaper was using the girl. She thought Craig Garrett wanted the girl in court only to help his newspaper's circulation. When she'd had the temerity to mention this, Andrew had shouted, 'We needed the publicity.

Without the newspaper we couldn't have found her. They'll make it worth her while, I'm sure, and think what this could mean for Sebastian. We're all winners in this.'

Edina didn't interrupt Andy's monologue. She still wanted him to settle out of court but she felt it was useless to argue the point. She had tried and it only made him angry, brought out all his bitterness about his father and Calum. She simply didn't have the energy for it.

Craig Garrett flung his pen across the desk in a fit of irritation and barked into the receiver, 'For fuck's sake I'm not asking for a cure for cancer. It's a blood test I'm after. You do them day in, day out. We need to find out if this girl is a match for Sebastian.'

He listened for a moment and then said slowly. 'No, I've told you people before, it's only the preliminary test results we need. The DNA test is for the paternity suit in court. Yes, I'm well aware that takes three or four weeks, God knows why when they can put a man on the moon within hours but still. You have everything you need to do this test and if you don't pull your finger out the Save Our Sebastian campaign and possibly the kid as well is going to die on us so I expect you to get results *fast*.' He crashed down the receiver so hard his colleague at the next terminal looked up.

'What's up?' The rookie reporter was the newest recruit to the paper and still thrilled at being there.

Craig was cautious. He was not in the habit of telling his colleagues much of what he was up to. Not after the time somebody picked up one of his phone calls and because he'd been unwise enough to brag about the story the guy was able to chat up his contact and afterwards claim the story as his own.

She was waiting expectantly to be given a few nuggets of information and for a moment he was tempted. God, he would love to shove that tart Anna-Maria and her mother on to her but caution prevailed. He sighed and picked up his contacts book and mobile phone and prepared to return to their hotel and the dreary attempts at friendliness. He had to keep them sweet; the court case was due to start tomorrow. He was desperate to get the story rolling but the lab was proving difficult. He needed the info about Anna-Maria's blood test to sweeten the editor. If only the lab would pull their finger out. He was paying them enough, hoping the expense money would last. If he could pull this story off he was hoping to jump ship and get a better paid job with the *Daily Mail*. But they would only show interest if he could come to them with a first-rate reputation for exclusives.

An hour after he had made his way across to the lifts, the phone on his desk rang again. The rookie answered. It was the laboratory. No, they would not divulge the information to her. Mr Garrett was their client and they would only deal with him. Reluctantly she gave the caller the number of Craig's mobile.

The news, when Craig finally got the call, made him more determined than ever to keep the Ewings the exclusive property of the *Chronicle*. OK, Anna-Maria's bone marrow was not a match for the baby. The lab had found certain similarities, it was close, but not close enough. One knock did not kill the story. Maybe a donor would still come forward as a result of the publicity. In the meantime he would have to fall back on the court case; that would bring him the kudos he needed. He could visualise the publicity his paper would attract, drawing attention to the battle between the warring brothers for their father's hard-earned cash. This had all the ingredients of high drama now that a baby swap was involved, and Anna-Maria would be at the centre of it.

Those other crap hounds wouldn't get a sniff of his exclusive in advance. He was keeping the Ewings under wraps until the afternoon of the first day's court hearing. The other papers might get a snatched picture outside the high court when the Ewings, well covered, were hurried to a car but they wouldn't get a single quote from his side. And who cared about the losers?

Naturally he would write the story from the angle of saving the poor baby. But he would wrap it round every twist and turn of the family feud and the switched babies, how the *Chronicle* had tracked down this humble, unassuming Scottish lass, unaware of her good fortune. It was a classic. Better than a Lottery winner story. But he'd better keep to himself the negative result of Anna-Maria's blood test. Best for the editor, Andrew and the court not to know about it for the present.

God, he was pissed off with the Ewing mother and daughter. All they wanted to do was look at Buckingham Palace or go shopping. He would quit rather than do the sightseeing bit one more day and he was damned if he was going to use up his precious expense account trailing around the shops with them. There was also the question of the nights. He couldn't keep them prisoners and last night Nancy had definitely been covering up for the daughter. First Anna-Maria was downstairs having coffee, then she was in the bath, then some excuse he couldn't remember. Was she scoring drugs? Turning tricks? He wouldn't be at all surprised. Thank God it was for only a couple more days.

As she had to get up early to get to court, Lizzie decided to try and get a good night's sleep before the ordeal. Edward had assured them that with all the evidence that demonstrated the strong bond between Gabriella and her grandfather, it was unlikely she or Calum would be called to the witness stand. But should it be necessary he wanted them to stand by, ready, willing and able. He had also warned them that while the case was being heard, they must make no further approach to Andy or his family.

At their last meeting Edward had not exuded his usual confidence and Lizzie had spent some time trying to reassure Calum that all would be well, although privately she, too, was uneasy. But despite the shared burden of the court case, the atmosphere between them remained frosty. Calum watched Lizzie do all she could to envelop Gaby in warmth and wished she could find it in her heart to direct some of it towards himself and forgive him. She was behaving like a stranger, taking care these days not to let him see her undressing and it seemed like an age since they had last made love. It would make life easier if he were not still aroused by her. But if he accidentally touched her, she did not react, pretending not to notice. And she only really talked to him about the court case, nothing else.

As he sat in the kitchen, toying with a cup of coffee, Calum had a sense of foreboding. For the first time he faced the possibility that Lizzie might walk away from all they had built up together. He tried to settle down and read the newspaper but it was hopeless. The headlines swum in front of his eyes and he noticed a dull ache behind his forehead. Right then he could not care less whether or not the German Chancellor was going to devalue, although it could have an adverse effect on his business.

His eye caught sight of the noticeboard covered in a jumble of paper, mostly belonging to Gabriella. There was an official-looking timetable and he peered at it to discover how close they were to the dates of her exams. He tried to analyse his feelings for Gabriella. She was sometimes moody and difficult but he loved her and, however drawn he might be to his biological child, he could not imagine life without this sometimes infuriating, but often delightful girl. She was staying the night at the Sinclairs and impulsively he picked up the phone and dialled their number. Gaby was a night bird. She was sure to be awake and he very much needed to talk to somebody who loved him.

'Sarah? It's Calum. Sorry to ring so late but could I have a word with Gaby if she's still up?'

A moment later she came on the line.

'Hi, Gabs. You OK?'

'Fine thanks.' There was a pause. 'Are we going to win tomorrow?'

'I hope so. Edward Foxton certainly rates our chances.'

Her next question surprised him. 'If we're successful and I get awarded the money and everything, do you think I could ask the court for an advance?'

'What for?' She hesitated for such a long time he thought she wasn't going to answer.

'It's for Luke,' she finally admitted.

Calum gave an exclamation of annoyance. 'You're not still on about that demo tape of his, are you?'

'He's very talented.' Her tone was wheedling. 'It's only two grand.'

'Gaby, the court won't agree and if they did, we wouldn't.'

'But it means so much—'

'Please drop it.' Desperate to change the subject, he went on, 'We've had several people phoning for you saying they were friends of yours. They wouldn't leave a name so I'm sure they were reporters. And a photographer's been hanging round the house. I'm glad you're out of it.'

'I'm sorry to miss the excitement.'

He laughed. 'Now you be good, young lady, and we'll see you at home tomorrow. Sleep tight.'

' 'Bye. I love you.'

His heart missed a beat. 'I love you too. 'Bye, pussycat.'

Calum replaced the receiver and his eyes began to prickle. Not once had she called him Dad.

Across London, in a Canary Wharf hostelry, Andrew Lynton was having a few pints with Craig, who was twitching with adrenaline.

On the table lay the page proofs for the feature in the next day's *Chronicle*, with a prominent Craig Garrett by-line. Craig had splashed on the story about the baby switch and how a fortune lay at stake.

He took out his wallet from which he extracted a memo and flourished it in Andrew's face. 'My editor actually sent me this hero-gram today. First time he's ever bothered to congratulate me.'

'I thought the girl was quite a hard little piece. How did you track her down?' asked Andrew, examining the large picture of Anna-Maria with his child.

Craig tapped his nose. 'Contacts, my boy. That's why I'm a bloody great journalist and you sell second-hand cars.'

'Well, you got me off the hook. That information was going to cost me fifty grand.'

Craig did not think it a good moment to mention that the same informant had decided to bypass the minnow. The editor had not discovered, nor would he, please God, how the money had been found. But the payout had been worth it. A front-page story and the whole of page five so far. Oh yes, he had hopes of milking this story for a good few more page leads yet.

Much against Craig's better judgement he had allowed the Ewing mother and daughter to have a pub supper with Andrew the previous evening. It was a pain but Mrs Ewing had insisted on meeting the baby's uncle since she could not see her real daughter right away. Craig had been able to convince her this would not be possible until the court case was finished. But that bloody Andrew had used the occasion to smarm up to them.

'When will we know about her test?' Andrew asked.

'Another week or so.' Craig wondered briefly if he ought to tell him that Anna-Maria's test had proved she was not a match. Aw, what was the point? The doctor at the hospital should be the one to do that.

'Craig, I put you on to this story. Don't you usually pay your sources?'

'Ah,' said Craig heartily. 'You gave me half a story. I had to find the address for myself. I'm afraid that cost plenty, the records people and so on. The expense to keep the Ewings in the style to which they are totally unaccustomed are very high. There's virtually nothing left over.'

Andrew frowned and Craig went on, 'I told you, I'm paying you in kind. Look at the help I'm giving you with Sebastian as well as with fighting your case. If it wasn't for me, you wouldn't have access to Anna-Maria at all. And if you win you'll get a whopping payout. You're not going to give me any of that, are you?'

'Craig, I'm grateful for the help you're giving Sebastian but this isn't fair. If I'm awarded money from the court it'll take ages to come through. I was counting on the *Chronicle* money to pay legal bills.'

'Didn't you tell me you had negotiated a no win, no fee deal with your lawyers?'

Andrew was silent.

'There you are then. Sebastian's getting his treatment on the NHS. And you'll win your case. We all score.' Craig fished a twenty-pound note from his wallet. 'But I don't want you to be out of pocket. Buy us another round.'

Andrew, still smarting, had to hold his tongue because this man had so much power over his life. Reluctantly he went to stand at the bar, crammed with hard-drinking newsmen, and tried in vain to catch the eye of the harassed barman.

Craig spotted the figure of a neighbour he had roped in to share the burden of minding the Ewings. She was the wife of a retired printer and knew the ropes and he could trust her not to gossip. She hadn't been difficult to persuade. Her days usually consisted of shopping at the local Somerfield and washing her husband's bowling gear. The Ewings made a change. Right now she was hovering hesitantly in the doorway and he waved his hand in the direction of his table, and shouted to Andrew to add a bitter lemon to his order.

By the time he returned bearing a tray of drinks, Craig was listening with apparent attention to a balls-achingly boring shopping trip the neighbour had organised for the Ewing duo.

'They'd never been to Harrods before,' she was prattling on. 'Anna-Maria bought a Mars Bar so that she could have one of their green bags and a receipt to take home. Isn't that sweet? I hope you don't mind, Craig, but I bought them each an outfit.'

Craig struggled to keep his composure. The woman was saving him from having to spend time with the pair but he didn't want to draw his editor's attention to the spiralling costs. Hero-grams were only valid for one day in this business.

208

'How much did you shell out?' he asked her.

'We were lucky. There was a sale.' She fished in her handbag and took out a receipt.

He drew in his breath. 'This much.'

She delved into her bag again and produced another slip of paper. 'That was for Anna-Maria. This one's for Nancy's suit.'

Craig immediately banned any more shopping trips.

'But what am I supposed to do with them?' she asked, puzzled.

'Tomorrow they'll be going with me to court,' said Andrew, 'so you won't be needed.'

Craig banged his glass on the table. 'I've not paid out all this cash to hand them over to other papers. You can have them in the afternoon only. And they're under strict orders from me not to stir out of their hotel until I come and fetch them. After lunch.'

'But my people want her there from the morning, in case—'

'Tough,' said Craig, tapping the advance copy of the paper. 'Once the others see this story they'll be on the hunt. We've got our follow-up for the following day's paper. I want our rivals to have as little time as possible to get in on the act.'

Andrew could see no point in arguing and took a frosty farewell of Craig. He was in a cold fury. He had every intention of using the Ewings in any way he saw fit and if his lawyers wanted them in court from day one, minute one, they would be.

He made straight for the hotel where the Ewings were holed up. This was going to be like dealing with small children. Anna-Maria might have been a hard nut on her own patch but down here in the big city she was just another kid.

'Go to court in the morning?' asked Mrs Ewing anxiously. 'But we were told . . .'

Andrew said soothingly that plans had changed. They were needed in court merely as window dressing at this stage. He added that the morning was better because everyone would cover the story; TV and the other papers would picture the faces of all those involved in the case. Anna-Maria brightened considerably at the prospect of this publicity.

'All we ask is that you sit in a nearby room during the proceedings so if the judge wants to see the real Lynton granddaughter, he'll be able to. It saves the taxpayer's money,' Andrew added piously, 'if the court does not have to wait for people to be ferried from their hotel.'

Mrs Ewing seemed confused, asking why they needed to go to the law courts at all. Weren't they going to get money just for helping Sebastian?

Inwardly, Andrew sighed. God, these people were so dim. Patiently he explained the situation.

'If I'm the real granddaughter, why don't I get all the money?' Anna-Maria's eyes glittered shrewdly.

'Because the judge will say my father never met you,' replied Andrew tartly. 'I'm not a rich man, as you know, but I've told you that when we win this case we'll be able to give Sebastian a much better life. Hopefully you might prove to be a match for him and I'll make sure you share in his good fortune.'

'How big a share?' asked Anna-Maria.

My God, he was negotiating with a fifteen-year-old. He offered one per cent and she scoffed. Finally he had to settle for five per cent and then she made him write it out and sign it on a piece of hotel stationery. Andrew was astounded when she insisted on calling in a member of the hotel staff to witness their signatures. Where had she learned all this?

Even after he had signed, they insisted that Craig had drummed into them that they should not leave the hotel without his express say-so, and go to court only when he decreed, but Andrew smothered all doubts with the clincher, 'Didn't he tell you? He's changed his mind about you going to the court. Why do you think he arranged for you to have those new outfits from Harrods?'

Chapter Seventeen

The morning of the case was unseasonably bright, judging from the intensity of light coming through her windows. A butterfly flapping its wings would usually be enough to wake Lizzie but she had slept for more than seven hours, a record these days. Emotional exhaustion, she supposed.

Drawing back the curtains she looked into the street and straight into the telescopic lens of a cameraman standing inside the gate. With an angry exclamation she grabbed at the fabric and closed it rapidly. She had better warn Calum.

He was already in the kitchen making coffee and his drawn face suggested he had not enjoyed the same oblivion during the night. Determined not to provide more tabloid fodder if they could help it they agreed to leave the house separately and meet down the road. He would act as a decoy and go through the front door while she escaped through the back garden. He would pick her up on the corner and hope that she could get into the car before being photographed.

They had put on their coats and were about to leave when the phone went.

Calum gave a tut of annoyance. 'Leave it. We haven't time now,' he said. But he was too late. Lizzie had already lifted the receiver.

'It's Sarah,' she mouthed at him. Then her expression changed to alarm. 'No, she isn't here.' More murmurings from the other end. 'I'm sure he didn't say that.' Lizzie looked at Calum. 'Apparently you spoke to Gaby last night and told her she could come home.'

Vehemently he shook his head and took the phone. 'Sarah,' he said, 'I thought we all agreed she should stay with you until the court case was over?'

There was a torrent of words and Calum interrupted. 'I didn't say anything to her about coming back here to sleep. What time was that?' The answer did not please him. 'She hasn't turned up, not last night, not this morning.' He listened again. 'She's a teenager, for God's sake. Sarah, shouldn't you have checked with us before letting her go off?' Immediately his tone changed. 'Sorry, I would've probably done the same thing. No, no, don't apologise. We'll sort it out. Goodbye.'

'Oh God, not again. What's she up to?' asked Lizzie. 'Do you think I should stay put until she comes back?'

She started pacing from the sink to the table to the dresser.

'It might've been my fault,' said Calum slowly. 'Last night when I phoned Gaby brought up the subject of Luke and money for that bloody demo tape. And I told her off.'

'I bet she's with him. Let's go to his house,' suggested Lizzie. 'Where did you put his address?'

'Second drawer in the dresser.' While Lizzie scrabbled through appliance guarantee documents, recipes and other domestic trivia to retrieve the information, Calum looked at his watch. 'Ed will go ballistic if we're not on time.'

'We can't just leave her like that. I won't be able to concentrate on anything unless I know she's all right,' said Lizzie agitatedly. 'It shouldn't take too long, he only lives about half a mile away. Why don't you go on and I'll follow later?'

'No, we have to present a united front,' he paused, 'in court at least.' She coloured but he did not appear to notice. 'Gaby is our priority in this whole stupid business and both of us should go and see her. I'll let Ed know.'

Before leaving, Lizzie scrawled a note to Gabriella explaining they had gone to Luke's house to look for her. 'But in case we miss you, please stay here until we get back.'

Calum added a rider, 'Don't talk to the press or any stranger. They're all reporters pretending to be this and that. If we don't see you we'll phone as soon as we get to court.'

Diversionary tactics forgotten, they went out of the front door together to face the flashlight of one persistent photographer.

Luke's home was in the middle of a small terrace in a poorer part of the borough. Its handkerchief-sized lawn had recently been mowed; the rest of the garden was barren. The house had been freshly painted and Persil-white net curtains were at every window.

A wary-sounding voice answered their knock. 'Who is it?'

Calum leaned towards the letterbox and called out, 'Gabriella Lynton's parents.'

A woman peered from behind the curtain attached to the door. Apparently satisfied, she turned the lock and asked them to come in. She was a slim woman in her early forties and appeared to be assessing them carefully. She introduced herself as Luke's mother, Margaret Abbott, before ushering them into the warm kitchen where there were signs that she had been having breakfast.

Calum apologised for disturbing her so early to which Margaret commented that it was not early for her. Her manner was friendly and Lizzie began to relax. When Calum asked politely if their daughter happened to be in her home, Margaret nodded.

'She's upstairs. I can wake her if you like but are you sure you want me to?'

Lizzie bridled slightly. 'We'd like to talk to her. We'd arranged for her to stay with a friend and we can't understand why she left and came here without saying anything to us.'

Margaret Abbott filled the kettle. 'These young people, you push them in one direction, they go in another.'

'Don't I know it,' said Lizzie.

Margaret Abbott smiled reassuringly. 'When she arrived, quite late last night, I asked if you knew she was here. Come to think of it she didn't exactly answer the question. She told me you wanted her out of the way because you were worried about the press.'

'That much is true,' said Calum.

'It was late so I said she could have a bed for the night. I thought I was doing the right thing,' she added.

'You did,' said Calum swiftly, 'and we're grateful she's safe but of course she's playing two ends against the middle.'

'As they all do. If they can get away with it,' said Luke's mother.

There was an uncomfortable silence before Lizzie said she thought it best to wake Gabriella. Margaret agreed at once and while Calum remained in the kitchen, Lizzie promptly followed the lithe figure up the narrow staircase.

Gently Margaret turned the knob of a room at the side of the corridor and stood back to allow Lizzie to enter.

In the gloom Lizzie saw the familiar sprawl of Gabriella's long hair across the pillow. She looked peaceful, as if she hadn't a care in the world. One leg was protruding from under a blanket on what appeared to be a truckle bed. Lizzie stifled a sigh of relief to see she was alone in the bed and wearing the pink candy-striped pyjamas she had given her for Christmas. The only other piece of furniture in the room was a treadle sewing machine, covered in dozens of bobbins of thread.

Gabriella did not stir as Lizzie approached the bed and arranged the blanket over her daughter's recumbent body. For a few minutes she stood silently watching her and listening to the steady sound of her breathing. Conscious that by now they should have already left for the law courts, Lizzie was in a dilemma. By the time they woke Gabriella up, then waited for her to get herself together, they would get to court very late. Yet she was reluctant to leave Gaby in the care of a stranger, a feeling she knew Calum would share.

She tiptoed out of the room, followed by Margaret Abbott.

'That's Luke's room,' said Margaret, indicating a door on the side of the corridor. 'He's still asleep too.'

As the women entered the kitchen, Calum looked up expectantly. 'She's dead to the world,' Lizzie told him. 'I didn't have the heart to wake her. I think you'd better go to court on your own and I'll wait until she wakes up.'

Margaret was slowly moving a teapot round, swirling the tea leaves. 'I have a suggestion,' she said. 'I could keep an eye on Gaby.' She began to pour out the tea. 'If you'd like to go with your husband, Mrs Lynton, I promise your daughter will be quite safe here.'

'I wouldn't like to miss the hearing,' Lizzie admitted, giving Calum an inquiring look.

'I don't like to leave without talking to her,' said Calum, 'but we certainly don't want her anywhere near the court today. Perhaps it's better we don't wake her up. Anyway, there's a good chance she'll still be asleep when we come back.'

They laughed at this and Margaret, apparently sensing their need for reassurance, said, 'There'll be no funny business in my house. Your girl is far too young and I'm strict about that sort of thing.'

Lizzie looked uncertain.

'Luke's a very clever boy and I don't have any trouble on that score from him or his brothers,' Margaret said firmly.

Lizzie was by no means convinced that her daughter and Luke were not already lovers but she did recognise that for a few hours at least her daughter would be under the supervision of someone whose word was law in her own home. She and Calum agreed to leave Gaby there until they could come back and collect her after the court had risen.

Before they took their leave, Lizzie thanked Margaret Abbott. 'Gaby's young and headstrong. I can't help worrying . . .'

'I don't blame you,' said Margaret. 'I thank the good Lord I only have boys.'

Outside the Royal Courts of Justice a clutch of photographers and television cameramen were pushing and shoving to get the best position outside the wrought-iron gates, as close to the boundary in the Strand as they were allowed. The fine Gothic building, known to the millions of television viewers as the setting of high dramas involving the crooked, the misunderstood and the simply unlucky, was alive with a cross-section of Britain's defendants, litigants, barristers, their cohorts and sundry court personnel, all talking earnestly and all walking at top speed.

The Lynton case was not the main attraction that day. A nationally known sportsman was fighting a case against a fellow golfer alleging libel in a recently published biography. It was expected to drag on for days and would involve several famous sporting faces being called to give evidence. Choice media fodder. But the case of Lynton v. Lynton was also attracting attention. Since the first edition of the *Chronicle* had dropped onto their desks, rival newspapers had been on the trail of anyone connected to the Lynton case and had cobbled together their own version of the story, without any attribution to the *Chronicle*, naturally. So far their attempts to get first-hand information had been thwarted. Lynton family members would not talk, the daughter had seemingly vanished and the *Chronicle* had the Ewings well sewn up. Regardless of how tedious the evidence might be on the first day, the other editors were determined to do more spoilers on the *Chronicle*'s exclusive. Picture editors who'd gnashed their teeth at having missed this one instructed staff photographers to whack off a reel or two of anyone involved, particularly the young heiress Gabriella, who apparently had the most to lose, as well as the girl who was in line for the fortune.

That morning Craig strutted into the Ewings' hotel feeling pleased at the reaction to his story, especially from his peers. But his mood swiftly turned to fury. Anna-Maria was all ready to go to court for the start of the hearing, overriding his command. In no uncertain terms he pointed out that he did not want to risk the other papers photographing her and who the fuck was paying her bills?

But the bitch had apparently done a deal with Andrew who had managed to assure them that it was in their own interest to attend court. He had convinced them that they might get a share of the fortune and, after all, the court was where the decisions about the money would be made. They might not be needed as witnesses but the judge could be told that they were available. Mrs Ewing was a mere cipher, unable to assert any authority over her daughter and short of keeping the girl prisoner in the hotel room, Craig had no option but to climb down. To be bested by this snip of a kid was one of the low points of his career.

He began to bark out instructions, trying to drum into the Ewings that when they went into the portico of the Courts of Justice they were to keep their heads lowered, eyes down, and walk as fast as they were able. 'If you look up, even for a second, that's all they'll need,' he warned them, 'and if they get a snap of you then you can pay your own bills.'

He looked with distaste at Anna-Maria who, with time on her hands, had decided that 'more was best'. Her nails were painted a violent shade of purple and her make-up looked more like a mask.

'Wipe that stuff off your face,' he demanded.

'I won't.' She looked away. 'I've got spots.'

'Good,' he said with a grin. 'The judge will think you're a sweet little teenager instead of what you really are.'

'I think you're wonderful as well,' she simpered at him. But she disappeared into the bathroom and emerged a few minutes later, her naked face shiny from the lashings of cleanser she must have used. The lurid eye shadow and nail polish had vanished. The attractive dress and matching short jacket from the Young Teen range at Harrods was spoilt by the chunky bracelet on her wrist and cheap rings adorning each finger, including the thumbs, so he made her take them off.

Craig scrutinised the final effect. Plain but pricey clothes. No accessories to distract the eye. Simple hairstyle. Her skin looked clean. And she had acne.

Perfect.

★ ★ ★

Calum and Lizzie ditched their car at an underground car park near London Bridge and hailed a taxi, thankful that the detour to Luke's house had not made them late. They instructed the driver to pull up as close as he could to the Strand entrance of the courts. A sizeable crowd was already milling around on the pavement. Edward had assured them that once they were through the gates and into the precincts of the court in the Family Division no press could follow so they prepared themselves for a speedy dash.

There were shouts as Calum paid off the driver and he gripped Lizzie's elbow as a scurrying pack of cameramen and reporters began to race towards them. As they paused, unsure how to get by, an intrepid TV cameraman focused his lens. This footage would be incorporated into the lunchtime news.

'I didn't think there'd be as much interest as this,' muttered Calum. Almost blinded by a continuous flash of halogen bulbs, he and Lizzie swerved round the pack and, ignoring questions flung at them by reporters, dashed up the stairs and into the safety of the high-arched lobby.

Hovering inside were Edward and their barrister, Tim Goodman. Edward ushered them quickly up the stairs. Lizzie wondered if she was being hyper sensitive but Edward did not appear to be his usual equable self. He gestured towards a room off the main hall. 'Andrew and his lot are in there and we're in here.' He showed them into a small, dark room. Once shut, the heavy oak door had the effect of blocking out the high-pitched hum from the hallway.

'We have something pressing to discuss before we go into court,' he said, taking off his gloves.

'Andrew's offered to settle?' asked Calum.

'Afraid not,' said Tim Goodman. 'What did you think of the stuff in today's paper?'

'We haven't had a minute to read anything,' replied Lizzie. 'What's it say?'

Tim opened his briefcase and took out a bundle of newspapers. 'All this is an unfortunate complication but I'm glad we knew about it in advance,' he said, spreading newspapers on the table and picking out the *Chronicle*. He handed it to them.

The first thing they noticed was a page one headline proclaiming, 'Baby Switch Drama'. Calum and Lizzie stared at the paper in dismay.

'How the hell did they find out?' asked Lizzie.

The story gave every detail of the switch, with quotes from a worried hospital registrar and information about the two families involved. The last paragraph was particularly noxious, claiming credit for the great crusading *Chronicle* for tracking down the birth daughter of the Lyntons who could 'Save Our Sebastian'. A further story on the centre pages carried a large picture of a smiling Anna-Maria with Sebastian on her lap and the heading: 'I hope to save this baby'.

One of the pages was almost entirely taken up with shots of all the Lynton family: Calum's father, Andrew and Edina with Sebastian. The paper had even got hold of one of Lizzie and Calum's wedding pictures – supplied no doubt, thought Lizzie angrily, by her dear brother-in-law.

The biggest photographs were on the opposite page, side by side. One was of Gabriella taken at a school concert, above which ran the headline, 'The "fake" heiress?' The other was of Anna-Maria Ewing. Lizzie noticed how intently Calum was studying the photograph. 'She looks different in that photograph,' she commented, 'more approachable somehow.' The headline above her photograph was in the same heavy type and read, 'Is this the real heiress?'

'This is disastrous,' said Lizzie. 'I don't want Gaby to see this.'

'What can we do?' Calum knitted his brows together in a frown.

'Have you got your mobile with you?'

Calum nodded.

'I think I'll ring Luke's mother and warn her.'

Margaret understood at once and promised to keep the newspapers away from Gabriella.

Tim Goodman gestured at the newspapers. 'Can anyone tell me how the *Chronicle* tracked down the Ewing girl and, more importantly, how they knew the two girls were switched at birth?'

'It says here the paper's been on the hunt for a match for Sebastian for some time,' said Edward. 'Perhaps the Ewing family answered their appeal.'

'Possible but I'm not persuaded,' said the barrister.

'I'm positive the Ewings couldn't have told them,' said Lizzie, conscious they were staring at her expectantly. 'When I met them they did not know anything about this and it certainly didn't come from Calum or me.'

Calum broke the short silence. 'I bet you anything you like

that Andy's involved. He worked with the paper once before, I remember. I'd say it's too much of a coincidence . . .'

Lizzie tried to control the flush that was spreading up from her neck and threatening to engulf her cheeks. It might not have been Andrew. Dan Hargreaves was with her when the Hudds handed over the address. It could have come from him, though she was puzzled. Dan was the one who'd advised her to think carefully before following up any leads. At every turn he'd urged caution, even agreeing with her that it would be wrong to destabilise the Ewing family. They had parted on bad terms but would he take things this far simply for revenge on her?

Apparently her discomfiture had gone unnoticed, for Calum was asking whether the newspaper publicity would affect the case.

'Can't see that it will,' replied Tim. 'Not the main issue anyway.' He opened his bag and extracted the horse-hair wig he was obliged to wear in court. He looked up as Lizzie groaned.

She began reading aloud from the *Chronicle*. 'Devastated fifteen-year-old Gabriella Lynton sobbed out loud when she discovered she was the victim of a baby swap at a London hospital shortly after her birth. Pretty Gaby recently found out that she was not the biological daughter of her father. Now blood samples confirm her mother is no relation either. For the past fifteen years, Gaby has been living with parents who were no connection to her at all. Fate has dealt her this blow at a time when she is still reeling over the question mark hanging over the inheritance from her grandfather. Today lawyers will argue that as she is not the birth granddaughter of the late Mr Robert Lynton, she is not entitled to his fortune.'

Lizzie put down the *Chronicle*. 'This is exactly what we didn't want to happen. They make it sound even worse than it is. Thank God we told her everything before this was published,' said Lizzie.

Edward began polishing his glasses and Tim leaned back in his chair fiddling with a gold pen. 'Should the judgement go against us,' the sight of their startled expressions made him add hastily, 'not that it will, I'm confident of that, but hypothetically speaking this so-called true heiress could get her own lawyer and sue the family for your father's money.'

Edward nodded. 'And the media interest will make it more difficult for your brother to settle.'

He and Tim began collecting their papers, preparing to leave for the court room.

'Any idea what the judge is like?' Calum asked Tim conversationally.

'Lord Nash? Decent old soul. Quite sound. We could have got much worse.' Tim adjusted his wig. 'He doesn't like long speeches, tends to doze off in the afternoon if you're not careful.' He looked from one to the other. 'I'm a betting man and I like our odds.'

Across the hall in a room identical to the one being used by Edward Foxton, opposing counsel was having a briefing session with their client. Andrew Lynton could hardly contain his glee. The publicity could not have been better if he had written it himself. There wasn't a word that did not enhance his case.

The day had started brilliantly and could only get better. He had smuggled a bottle of red Bordeaux into the room and was handing out paper cups, much to the alarm of Jocasta Hutcheson, his barrister. There was a strict ban against alcohol on the precincts. Nevertheless, she and Zak Blondell accepted a cup of wine. 'Bit early but what the hell,' he said.

'How do you think this publicity will affect our chances?' Andrew asked.

As the over-acidic liquid hit her throat, Jocasta gave a grimace and coughed. 'There are never any guarantees in this business,' said Zak.

'I agree, but it won't do us any harm,' added Jocasta. 'Whether it does any good remains to be seen. It can depend on whether or not the judge likes the look of your face. But overall I reckon we've come out ahead.'

'I have no intention of giving my brother or his self-righteous wife something else to gloat about,' said Andrew. 'I have to win. They've been working against me a long time and it's my turn to come out on top.'

Jocasta was firm. 'I told you from the beginning, we have to fight this on points of law. You can't allow emotion or ideas of vengeance to cloud the issue, however hard done by you feel.'

'When do we play our trump card?'

'If and when we have to. Once the judge is aware that another granddaughter exists, one that carries on the Lynton bloodline, the case could take a direction we can't control. You don't want to lose the money to her, do you? You are my client and I'm battling on your behalf, not hers. But if I see that things are not going our way I might need to introduce her as evidence into the proceedings.'

She was interrupted by a tap on the door. It was Zak's clerk shepherding Anna-Maria and her tense-looking mother into the room.

'Here you are,' said Andrew heartily. 'Don't you two look smart.'

'I've gone off this,' said Anna-Maria tweaking the folds of the blue crepe skirt. Andrew stifled his irritation.

'Any trouble with the press?' asked Zak.

Anna-Maria brightened. 'Craig was trying to stop the photographers taking pictures of us. I kept my head down like he said but they got one or two.' She gave her mother a conspiratorial smile.

'We can't worry about that now,' said Andrew before introducing them to his barrister, who began to reassure the two women it was very unlikely that they would be called in front of the judge.

'Then why are we here?' asked the girl.

'We didn't want to take any chances,' said Jocasta giving a quick glance at Zak, who seemed to be engrossed in his papers. He had already explained to Andrew that they were going to try a procedure which judges normally frowned upon but he thought if anyone could swing it, Jocasta could.

'Blood tests are all very well but we haven't yet got the full results of your DNA test, which is a weakness in our case,' Zak explained to the Ewings. 'So if the judge happens to request proof of your existence, then here you are.'

Not strictly by the rule book, thought Andrew, but that was why he was with Zak Blondell, a street-fighter, and not some prissy-minded outfit like Foxton and Small.

Mrs Ewing was looking uncomfortable. 'I don't know about any of this. I only agreed to come because I want to meet Gabriella Lynton.'

'You will,' said Andrew quickly, 'when the case is all over.'

'That's right,' said Jocasta, 'it would be unwise for you to have any dealings with the other side at this juncture.' She stared directly at Mrs Ewing. 'Anna-Maria is here simply to introduce a doubt about Gabriella Lynton's lineage into the judge's mind.'

Andrew nodded knowingly. 'I've every confidence you'll do me proud.' Then he added, with a roguish grin, 'I ought to be able to afford a better bottle of wine when this is all over.'

The judge settled himself into his throne-like dais and the slender figure of Jocasta Hutcheson rose to address the court.

Not for the first time she wondered why the place had to be so gloomy. It was obvious no one, other than the weather, ever cleaned the windows, probably because they were so high no one could reach them. With its panelled walls adding to the dark interior, it must be intimidating to those not familiar with its atmosphere. Perhaps that was the idea.

She permitted herself a quick glance at the press benches. They were empty. From a professional point of view she enjoyed having the press around to report her golden words, but this was the Family Division from which they were banned. They would be confined to picking up statements and decisions once it was all over.

Jocasta recognised the judge as a long-serving member of the judiciary who appreciated fine claret, beagles and big-busted women, and who hated histrionics from barristers. He was famous for cutting short any advocate who did other than give him a succinct opening address. Once she was advised who was hearing the case, Jocasta drastically altered both her opening and closing speeches.

After a brief outline of her client's claim, she used reports from the laboratory to prove that Gabriella Lynton was not of the Lynton bloodline.

'My lord,' she said, 'we maintain that Gabriella Lynton has no claim whatsoever on this money because she is proved not to be Calum Lynton's daughter. It is our view that if Robert Lynton had known this, he would undoubtedly have structured his will differently. Our case is that he would have reverted to his original will and split the estate between his two sons Calum McDowall Lynton and his brother, my client, Andrew McDowall Lynton. We maintain that these two are the rightful heirs. I hope your lordship will agree and rule in my client's favour.'

She sat down only a few minutes after she had risen and the judge looked over his spectacles at her, his eyes warm.

'Thank you for that masterly and succinct summary, Miss Hutcheson, for which I, and I'm sure others in this court, are properly grateful.' He beamed expectantly towards Calum's defence team.

Tim Goodman, equally experienced in the foibles of this judge, duly took his cue.

'My lord, I do not deny my lordship's description of my learned friend's words and I, too, will not be taking up much of your lordship's valuable time.'

The judge stared at him and his mouth moved slightly as he dislodged a mint lump from the side of his cheek.

'We are here to defend the provisions of the will of Robert McDowall Lynton. In our opinion it is quite clear what the deceased intended. He planned to leave the bulk of his fortune to, and I quote directly from the will, "my beloved grand-daughter". That, undoubtedly, can refer to only one young person, someone with whom he had the strongest of bonds as we will show in evidence.

'And this girl is the one he knew as his granddaughter in every sense of the word. Gabriella Lynton is the young woman he helped to raise as his granddaughter from the time she was born, until virtually the day he died. He intended his money to go to Gabriella Lynton and no one else and I hope your lordship will grant him his wish.'

Tim Goodman sat down and the judge nodded approvingly – although Edward warned Lizzie it was probably due to the brevity rather than the content of Tim's address.

Jocasta stood up immediately. 'With great respect, my lord, my learned friend conveniently omits to mention another sentence in this will.' She flourished a copy of it. 'May I be permitted to introduce this to the court as document A?'

The judge nodded and turned to his clerk, who handed it up to the bench.

'In the aforementioned will, Mr Lynton clearly states, and I quote, "My primary concern is to ensure that my money will allow the continuity of what I consider is the good blood of the Lynton family".' She paused, removed her spectacles and raised her eyes to the judge. ' "Good blood of the Lynton family",' she repeated. 'My lord, can there be any mistake as to what Mr Lynton intended? He wanted to leave his hard-earned fortune to the person he had every reason to believe had his blood in her veins, the Lynton bloodline. But the sad facts of this case are that there exists a blood test which shows he was mistaken. I have a copy of this test result which I would like to introduce to the court as exhibit B.'

The judge's clerk handed up the document.

'I draw your lordship's attention to the summary at the end of the test result. And I might add, the other side does not dispute the veracity or the findings of this test.'

'Is that so, Mr Goodman?' asked the judge.

Tim rose and agreed it was.

'So noted,' said the judge, busy writing this down.

'I'm obliged to your lordship,' smiled Jocasta. She straightened and raised her voice slightly. 'This test proves beyond a shadow of a doubt that there is a ninety-nine point nine per cent probability that Calum Lynton did not father Gabriella Lynton. In other words, my lord, she is not his child and therefore not of Robert McDowall Lynton's bloodline, one of the main tenets of the disputed will.'

There followed various other legal submissions, including ones relating to the state of Robert Lynton's mind when drawing up his last will. Then Tim Goodman presented his evidence supporting his argument with regard to the close relationship that had existed between Gabriella and her grandfather. The judge was passed birthday cards which he studied closely. Next a television monitor was wheeled into the court room and he was asked to scrutinise a series of short video extracts depicting Robert Lynton playing a game of chess with his granddaughter, batting at a cricket match with Gabriella doing the running between wickets, and finally, Gabriella caddying for him at a local golf tournament. A small bundle of letters was also offered as an exhibit.

Jocasta listened to these submissions impassively, occasionally turning to her assistant to ask a question. At one stage, during the video, she scribbled a note to her assistant, 'This is strong stuff. We'll have to bring in the evidence about Anna-Maria. I'm pretty sure he won't want to see her but have her stand by just in case.'

When she received word that the Ewings were outside waiting, Jocasta stood up and asked politely if she could address the court. She wanted to introduce new evidence.

Jocasta was on shaky ground and she knew it. Judges were extremely reluctant to accept late evidence, particularly when it was sprung on the opposing side. She had informed them of her

224

intentions only that morning. She asserted that this new evidence, though not directly affecting the case, would have repercussions on any judgement his lordship was minded to make.

Tim Goodman attempted to speak but he was silenced with a small movement of the judicial index finger. 'Mr Goodman, before I decide whether this new evidence is admissible I need to hear what it is.'

'As your lordship pleases.' Tim sat down.

The judge's bewigged head moved in the direction of Jocasta. 'Continue, Miss Hutcheson.'

'I'm obliged, my lord.' She paused for maximum effect. 'We believe the case hinges on one simple premise. If the deceased wanted his bloodline to continue, then the beneficiary should be someone who is of his blood. Not Gabriella Lynton who is not related to him in any way, and it is on this point that we wish to introduce new evidence.'

'My lord, I protest,' Tim Goodman sprang up. 'The evidence I have shown supports our claim that the bond between Gabriella Lynton and the deceased was extremely strong.'

'We are not disputing that bond, my lord,' said Jocasta. 'The issue here is bloodline.'

'Bloodline, Miss Hutcheson. That is what I have to consider, the crux of this case, you might say. Please sit down for the moment.'

'As your lordship wishes,' said Jocasta, but her eyes gleamed triumphantly as she took her seat. He would have dismissed her out of hand had he been so minded. She had won this argument.

Lizzie, sitting on a bench behind their barrister, watched anxiously as Tim Goodman began to talk urgently in Edward Foxton's ear.

'I have listened very carefully to what both sides have had to say,' boomed the judge, pausing to take a sip of water, 'and I have decided to accept this last-minute submission from the plaintiff. I'm sure you won't prolong the case beyond its allotted time,' he turned a page over in front of him, 'will you, Miss Hutcheson?'

She gave him a pretty smile.

'You may begin.'

Jocasta stood up and pulled at the wide-shouldered robe which was slipping down her back. 'My lord, as you have heard, Calum Lynton is proved not to be the biological father of Gabriella

Lynton.' The judge nodded. 'We have now been given to understand she is not the offspring of the mother either.'

'Not related to the mother either. I see,' said the judge, writing quickly. He showed not the smallest hint that he was surprised at the turn of events. 'But surely relationship to the mother is not relevant in this case.'

'If your lordship will bear with me.' Jocasta went on to paint a picture of a hospital, short staffed and working at full stretch, on a Sunday, when human error resulted in the identity bands of two babies being switched and the babies being given to the wrong mothers. 'We have managed to track down the child born on the same day in the same hospital as Gabriella Lynton,' Jocasta pressed on, 'and by comparing hospital records, we are given to understand there is the strongest probability she is Robert Lynton's biological granddaughter. She now lives in Glasgow and her name is Anna-Maria Ewing. She is at present in the court building should your lordship request her presence.'

Calum and Lizzie exchanged despairing glances. 'How did she get here?' whispered Calum. 'Andrew?'

'Must be. He's been working with the *Chronicle*.'

They watched Tim and Edward rapidly exchange words. Nervously Lizzie twisted the wedding ring on her finger. Beside her Calum sat perfectly still and she thought it must be agony for him, wondering whether he was about to see his biological daughter for the first time.

Lord Nash tapped his pen rapidly on the blotter.

'There is no need to include that information. Please strike that name from the record,' said the judge sternly. 'Miss Hutcheson, since relationship to the mother is not relevant to this case, as I have already indicated, please confine yourself to what is pertinent. With that in mind, do you have anything further to add?'

'No, my lord.' Defeated, Jocasta sat down. She'd given it her best shot. What more could she do? She kept her gaze resolutely away from Andrew, who was seething.

Tim rose to his feet. 'My lord, we have not altered our view. It has not been changed by anything we have heard in this court room today. Miss Hutcheson would have us believe that Robert Lynton wanted his money to go to some unspecified granddaughter. He did not. He had one particular person in mind. One special individual above all others. She, not anyone else, not some young girl of whose existence he was unaware. My lord, Robert Lynton forged a bond with Gabriella Lynton and she and no one else is the rightful heir to his estate. Robert Lynton made a new will. The new will revokes all previous wills, which is the practice in English law. In our view there is no reason for Robert Lynton's wishes to be disregarded since he clearly intended for Gabriella Lynton to inherit.'

Tim resumed his seat and they waited until the judge had completed his notes. He removed his spectacles and put them in their case. 'I will need time to consider this evidence and I may propose a deferred judgement. I suggest we break for lunch which will give me time to give the matter some thought.' The judge used the arms of his imposing chair to ease himself up and fifty or so bodies rose in an automatic reaction as he shuffled slowly out of the court room.

Chapter Eighteen

Luke's mother would have been hard pressed to recognise her son. He actually looked animated, jabbing a forefinger in the direction of the television.

Before she'd gone off to do a quick shop, Margaret had changed the channel. Instead of the rock music on MTV, which habitually entertained her sons, the lunchtime BBC news was on.

Luke nearly choked on his bacon butty. 'Bloody hell, it's your mum and dad.' Gaby had told him about the mistake at the hospital but she'd said nothing about them making the one o'clock news.

She moved towards the set and watched intently as the camera focused on her parents walking at great speed through a throng of people milling around the courts. So absorbed was Gabriella that she missed the first words of the newsreader. The screen switched to the reporter outside the court who was interviewing a black-robed barrister. 'I can't say any more than I said in court, that we have strong evidence that Gabriella Lynton was switched at birth with another baby girl in the hospital.'

Luke half-turned to Gabriella. 'Why's she saying that?'

'Sssh.' Gaby's eyes were fixed on the screen.

'We have traced this young woman,' continued the barrister, 'and she is the person we consider to be the lawful grand-daughter.'

'And that would be,' the television reporter consulted a notebook, 'Anna-Maria Ewing?'

'Yes,' the barrister answered tersely.

The screen was filled with a picture of a smiling young girl who was cuddling a baby, taken from the pages of that morning's *Chronicle*.

'That's her,' Gabriella's voice was choking. 'That's their real daughter with Sebastian. Look at her hair, it's just like Dad's.'

She began to sob and Luke, who until last night had never seen this girl as other than a cool chick, was disconcerted. Clumsily he tried to take her into his arms but she shoved him away.

'Why does it have to be all over the stinking television?'

On screen the reporter had turned to camera and was explaining that the case would continue after lunch but that the judge had indicated he might defer judgement. 'It seems that the ingredients of this case involving a feuding family and a baby switch will provide fodder for newspapers a while longer.' In signing off, the reporter neatly sidelined any sense that television was as interested in the Lynton battle as the tabloids.

Luke appeared from the kitchen with another cup of tea. 'I've put a lot of sugar in it.'

'What does deferred judgement mean?' asked Gaby, her eyes still glued to the set.

'Dunno. He has to think about stuff.'

'Why wouldn't they let me go to the court? They always treat me like a baby.' She stared sightlessly at the floor. 'It's weird. Ever since they told me, I've been wondering whether I'm still the same person. All this time I've been an only child. Now I find I've got two grown-up brothers as well and I don't know their names, not even what they look like.'

Luke fidgeted with the sugar bowl and said nothing.

'I know why they wanted me out of the way,' continued Gabriella moodily, 'because she was going to be in court. They wanted to see her, probably talk to her. They're not worried what happens to me.'

Luke pushed the tea nearer. 'I don't think that's right,' he said. 'They came here this morning and remember how worried they were when you didn't come home that time?'

For a moment Gaby looked uncertain as memories of Lizzie's troubled face, flanked by that of a police officer, came into her mind. She hadn't meant to frighten them then and when she wanted to say she was sorry somehow the words came out all bolshy and as usual it ended in a row. She didn't always want to fight with them but however hard she tried, the words seemed to turn out wrong. And whatever she wanted to do, give money to Luke for his demo tape, go to court, it was always 'No'.

'You should be there now,' he said.

'Where? At the court? I couldn't face them.'

'It's your money they're talking about.'

'But it's not my money any more, is it?' Gaby said miserably. 'He isn't my grandpa.'

Luke made no reply.

'But Grandpa always said I was his favourite. He used to love it when I beat him at chess, he said I was the brains of the family.'

'See, that's the sort of thing you should tell the judge,' said Luke. 'I'll take you there on the bike.'

Gabriella sat motionless for so long that Luke gave up on the idea. He started to get his things together, pointing out that he had to go to a practise session.

'If I go,' Gaby said softly, 'will you promise to stay with me the whole time?'

The woman tugged at her bra strap which was cutting into her shoulder. As she eased it, there was a sharp ping as the safety pin gave up its unequal struggle. She was watching the television set with unusual concentration, giving up a silent prayer that she was mistaken about what she had seen on the BBC 1 lunchtime news. She had switched channels to catch the later BBC 2 news as well, in case the story was repeated. Urgently she called out to her husband who had promised to be there at the start. As usual he had drifted off, he never sat down for long as there were so many chores to do around the house.

'Ron,' she shouted, 'it's starting. Hurry up, hurry up.'

The door burst open with a whoosh that caused a heap of newspapers on the crowded kitchen table to scatter onto the linoleum.

'It's right at the beginning. Hurry or you'll miss it.' Her voice was sharp and he sat down on the arm of the chair and squeezed her arm affectionately.

'I'm here now, hon.'

Silently they watched while cameras panned across Red Square and the commentator reported on yet another Russian economic meltdown. This was followed by a warning of a famine in a little-known part of Africa, which took several minutes of screen time.

The woman dug her nails into her palms.

Then a well-known face filled the screen, a soap queen who was due to fly out to the afflicted country on a so-called fact-finding mission, which would have the added advantage of

231

boosting her diminishing profile. After several other news items, when the waiting seemed interminable, the woman clutched her husband's sleeve.

'There.'

He craned forward, gazing unblinkingly.

'Am I right? What do you think?'

Slowly the man turned to look at his wife. 'No doubt about it.'

She sagged against the back of the chair. 'What are we going to do?'

He gave a deep sigh. 'Nothing. It'll be much better to leave matters be.'

After lunch, as those in the legal echelons fully expected after his heavy hint, the judge decided he would defer judgement. He added, 'I hope this will not take me long but I will let you know the date on which I will deliver it into court.'

The instant he was out of the chamber a buzz erupted from all sides. Lizzie was visibly trembling and Calum slid along the bench to put an arm round her shoulder. Edward was looking sombre as he conferred with Tim Goodman. Calum decided to approach them.

'Do you think we've lost?' he asked.

'Certainly not,' said Tim, but to Calum's ears he could have sounded more forceful. 'This judge isn't known for making fast judgements, for all his impatience over the court's time. This is an unusual case. And if he doesn't take this new evidence into account, the other side might use his lack of consideration as the basis for an appeal. There's nothing much we can do now except wait for the judgement. We've done everything possible. I'm sure we'll get the right verdict,' he added when Lizzie had joined them.

Lizzie listened with half an ear. It was too late to worry about the case. That was now in the lap of the gods and the judge. She was more concerned for her daughter.

'Calum, we must get to Gaby before she hears about this from the papers or the TV.'

The black-helmeted duo on the Mitsubishi motorcycle came to an abrupt halt in the central reservation of the Strand not far from the Courts of Justice. As they clambered off the machine Luke turned and muttered hurriedly, 'Keep your helmet on.' He gestured to the crowd of pressmen bunched together on the pavement. 'You don't want to be recognised by that lot.'

Cautiously they skirted round the jostling bodies, trying to see what was causing all the commotion. Facing the cameras was Andrew, with his arm round a young girl. To one side stood a thin woman with greying hair and with a pang Gabriella realised she must be the woman who had given birth to her. Her real mother. She stared through the visor at Nancy Ewing but felt absolutely nothing. Perhaps, she thought, her emotions had been all used up because too much had happened in too short a time.

Gabriella's gaze then shifted to the girl at Uncle Andy's side. She recognised her at once, from the television news and the newspaper. This was her parents' real daughter. And then she saw Calum and Lizzie.

As they skirted the crowd of journalists who had pounced on the sports stars giving evidence in the other high profile case, Lizzie scanned the road for a taxi. Calum, she could see, was scrutinising the crowd. He was hoping to catch sight of Anna-Maria, though Edward had warned them both about approaching her. She was, after all, in the enemy camp. Neither of them noticed the two figures in black leather on the far side of the jostling reporters.

Suddenly Calum saw his brother extricating himself from a small group of media people. Andrew and another man were shepherding a young girl and an older woman towards a waiting car and for a second Calum met his brother's eyes.

Andrew pulled up short and shouted over the heads of the crowd, 'I hope you're not feeling lucky, brother, because I reckon you've lost this one.' He had recovered his humour and his confidence when the judge had deferred judgement. He felt sure it boded well for his case, and as Jocasta had said to him afterwards, the judge may have stopped her introducing Anna-Maria but at least he knew the girl existed now.

Calum barely registered the words, so focused was he on the girl he recognised from the photographs as Anna-Maria Ewing. His daughter. She was standing only a few yards from him and seemed to be enjoying the attention, turning from side to side to pose for photographers. He had a strong urge to go across and talk to her but even as he made a move in her direction, Lizzie tugged at his sleeve. 'Not now,' she warned.

Andrew and the other man hustled the two women into a car

which drew away into the dense traffic to the accompaniment of flashing cameras. At the disappearance of this quarry, the press pack turned its attention to Calum and Lizzie, following them down the road as the pair sought out a taxi. Calum spotted the welcome sight of a 'For Hire' sign and hurried Lizzie into the cab where she huddled in the corner. Giving the driver the address, Calum instructed, 'Get the hell out of here as fast as you can.' But the traffic in the Strand was bogged down hopelessly and to their dismay the taxi could only move inch by inch. Two photographers seized their opportunity and began flashing away with their Nikons, half-blinding them.

Until that moment Calum had persuaded himself that he did not want to meet the girl or have anything to do with her or her family. But after seeing her in the flesh, he was overcome by sadness at the thought of her being hijacked by his brother for his own ends. She must regard him, her father, as the enemy. Andrew had probably painted him and Lizzie as a pair of grasping, heartless money-seekers. How could they build up a relationship after such a bad start?

He put his hand to his head. 'Oh my God. A few minutes' mix-up in the hospital and look where it's led.'

Lizzie shook her head and said sadly, 'After this case is over we'll have to make up our minds whether or not we want to get involved in her life.'

'Her mother will have some say in that, presumably. Gabriella's mother, I should say.'

'I get the impression that Anna-Maria will survive all this better than Gaby. I think our girl ought to be our main concern.'

But Calum had an indelible picture of his birth daughter in his mind, which would be impossible to dismiss.

Gabriella stared after Calum and Lizzie. She had seen the way Calum looked at Anna-Maria, had seen his expression as all his attention focused on his daughter.

Luke had seen it too. 'Maybe this wasn't such a good idea,' he mumbled. Gaby's distress was palpable, every line of her body was taut, as if she dared not move in case she fragmented. Luke shuffled uncomfortably. Clumsily he tried to console her. 'It'll be all right.'

That brought a flash of the old-style Gaby. 'No, it won't be all right. You saw the way he looked at her. He wanted to go to her, here, in front of all these reporters and photographers. It's like he wanted to claim her, say she belongs to them and I don't.'

'You know that's rubbish.'

'I don't look like either of them. But she does.' Anna-Maria was their flesh and blood, of course they'd want to meet her. They couldn't just pretend she didn't exist. They'd probably want her to come and live with them. Gabriella was overcome with misery. She'd willingly give up every penny of the damn inheritance and all her plans if she could only put back the clock.

'Come on,' said Luke. 'I'll take you home.'

Luke's motorbike turned the corner and Gabriella saw with trepidation that the family car was already parked outside the house. They pulled up behind it and Gaby got off. Luke stayed where he was.

'Come in with me, Luke?' Gaby pleaded. 'I can't face them on my own.'

'Yes you can,' he said. 'They won't want me there, and I'm supposed to be practising with the band anyway.'

Slowly Gaby turned and walked to the house. To the roar of Luke's departing motorbike she carefully closed the front gate behind her. How many times had her mother told her off for leaving it open because the neighbourhood dogs used the lawn as a lavatory? She glanced around the garden, still showing signs of late summer colour. How many times had her mother asked her to help dig in the autumn bulbs? She never had, and now she supposed she never would. But she had once or twice helped her father to rake up the leaves. She could clearly remember their boisterous leaf fight before scooping the debris into a black plastic bag to take to the bonfire at the back. One year Mum had brought out hot chocolate and the three of them had warmed their hands on the mugs in front of the fire. That had been nice.

Halfway up the path her daydreams were interrupted by the opening of the front door and Lizzie, followed closely by Calum, walked towards her. She opened up her arms and Gabriella found herself sinking into the embrace, something she had not permitted herself to do for the last couple of years. Calum's arms encircled the two of them and for a minute the trio rocked back and forth, not uttering a word. Eventually Calum broke away and Gaby was surprised to see his eyes were wet with tears.

Lizzie continued to hold her arm tightly as they walked through the front door.

Finally, Lizzie let go and went with Calum into the kitchen. Gaby, reluctant to follow, stood motionless in the hallway, her arms crossed defensively across her body. After a few seconds they came back out into the hall. 'Why don't we have a cup of tea?' suggested Calum.

She looked at them mutely and Lizzie said gently, 'Come on, Gabs.' She led her into the kitchen where Gabriella took a deep breath and nerved herself to ask the question that had been tormenting her all the way back from court.

'I saw your real daughter outside the court,' she said. 'What happens to me? Do you still want me here?'

Calum swallowed hard. 'Of course we do.'

Lizzie stood in the doorway, her eyes moist with tears. 'You're ours,' she said, her voice breaking, 'you always will be.'

'I saw you outside the court too. I saw the way you stared at her, Dad.'

'I didn't see you,' said Calum lamely. 'I suppose I was staring. I was curious about her.'

'So what did you think?' asked Gabriella. 'I mean, she looks like you.'

'She has the same colouring, I suppose. But until I can meet her and talk to her, it's hard to form an opinion.'

Gabriella hesitated for a second. 'When I saw Mrs Ewing . . . my mother . . . standing there on the pavement, I didn't feel a thing.'

'It was the same when I met Anna-Maria in Glasgow,' said Lizzie, 'I didn't feel anything either. You'll always be our daughter rather than this stranger.'

'I think I'd like to meet her – Mrs Ewing, I mean,' said Gaby. 'She did give birth to me, after all. Do you think that would be possible?'

'We can try,' said Lizzie, 'but they may not feel the same way about making contact and we can't force it.'

'If it happens, I hope you won't be disappointed,' Calum said.

'Why should I be?'

'Mrs Ewing and Anna-Maria were working with the newspaper against us. And people only do that for money.'

For a minute there was a glimpse of the rebellious teenager. 'How can you say that?' said Gabriella hotly. 'They're probably not very well off and anyway Anna-Maria was with Sebastian in the newspaper photograph. She could be trying to help him as well.'

'Yes, she could,' said Calum quickly.

'And you might be disappointed by your daughter,' Gaby pointed out.

Calum smiled and shook his head. 'You're my daughter.'

Gaby was silent for a moment, then sat up straight. 'I've been thinking about what you both said to me that time in McDonald's: it's who you are that's important, not who your parents are. I think that's right.'

Lizzie and Calum tried not to show their surprise. And Gaby added, 'You two are very nice parents.' She went to the door and looked back impishly over her shoulder, 'Most of the time.'

Lizzie and Calum exchanged a knowing grin. It was too much to expect Gaby to be fulsome, even at this emotional time.

'We handled that well,' said Calum.

'Didn't we.'

He had a glint in his eye that Lizzie had not seen for weeks. 'We're good together, aren't we?'

Lizzie opened the door of the freezer and took out bread to make some toast.

'Most of the time.'

Edina was sitting at the side of the cot, her fingers clutching the rungs. On the other side Andrew took hold of Sebastian's small hand. Sebastian was so weak it seemed an effort for him to open his eyes.

Everything was white, thought Edina. Their faces, the walls, the bed linen. Why didn't they have some cheerful colours, brighten the room up a bit? She tried to concentrate on the combinations she would choose – anything to stop thinking about what was going to happen.

Through the glass partition she saw the doctor. He exchanged a few words with a nurse and hesitated before entering the room. For a few minutes he busied himself with the charts at the end of the cot but she, who was more aware of this man's every expression, who examined his face more minutely than she did her husband's, realised he was trying to tell her something. Something bad.

'I'm afraid we've had the test on the Ewing girl and she isn't a match.'

Edina did not move. Andrew came swiftly round the cot and sat beside her, his arm round her shoulders.

'I know we were hopeful because she was the boy's first cousin but in these cases relatives don't always provide the match.' The doctor put on a cheerful-looking smile. 'We had many people volunteer after that newspaper publicity and the lab's working full stretch so don't think there's no hope. There is. There always is.'

This wasn't the cool, detached medical professional. He was involved, concerned, and seemed to be trying to convince himself. He was scaring Edina far more than he would ever know.

There were no tears left as Edina watched her child slowly dying.

Chapter Nineteen

Only a few days ago she had been in the high court, the focus of a great deal of attention, reflected Lizzie. Now she was trundling a supermarket trolley past the bakery section, totally ignored by her fellow shoppers. She gave an ironic smile as she pondered the diversity of her life. From the high court to Tesco's. She caught a glimpse of her drawn face in the reflection of the glass cabinet. She looked haggard. Hardly surprising as the three of them had marked the ending of the case by talking until the early hours, thrashing over everything that had happened over the last few weeks.

One thing they had all agreed. The horrendous problems thrown up by the case had been put into context. The money and who ended up with it was far less important than whether they were still a family unit. Calum was more relaxed about the business; Erik Schroeder had made a reasonable offer and Calum had decided to go ahead with it to pay off his debts. He had thought seriously about doing this before Andrew's legal challenge had stirred him to action, so the decision to go ahead wasn't too difficult. He had come to terms with the idea that someone else would be in effect running the business. He was having to face up to much more serious matters in his private life.

It had changed them all. Lizzie couldn't imagine going back to how they were. She realised with satisfaction that she had been forced to become more independent, had to be responsible for her actions without first discussing them with Calum. Sarah had remarked how much more assertive she was these days, and that wasn't a bad thing. The teacher-pupil relationship between her and Calum had shifted gear.

Gabriella, too, seemed to be more mature. She certainly gave every impression of being as confident of their love for her as she was before all the revelations.

As she tore off a number at the delicatessen counter, Lizzie experienced a pang of guilt remembering how she had turned her back on Calum's tentative overtures in bed last night. When he began to stroke her bare arm she had shifted to the side of the bed. He had not made another move towards her. They had spent the last few weeks skirting around each other, avoiding contentious subjects, treading water. But it had been a strain. The reward was that they had managed to convince Gabriella that all was well between them.

Lizzie waited while the assistant carefully measured out scoops of Greek houmous and vine leaves for another customer. Gaby hated all that so to please her Lizzie was going to try and transform a small haunch of boiled ham with fresh pineapple and apricots.

She couldn't deny she still had feelings for Calum but however much he tried she wasn't able to overcome her hurt. Would she ever be able to see it all in a different light? Perhaps in time, for he had apologised profusely, often. She was certain he was truly penitent. So why couldn't she forgive him? Because she could not banish the vision of him making love to Tess from her mind, that was why. His denials and explanation that she meant little to him did not ring true.

Lizzie could not bring herself to talk about her future plans but she knew she couldn't postpone it much longer. She had applied for the full-time teaching job with flat attached, and the governors had promised a decision within the week. If she were offered the post, that would definitely bring things to a head because she would have alternative accommodation for herself and Gaby. Did she want that?

She was startled out of her reverie by a shopper who accident-ally bumped into her trolley. She wheeled it hurriedly to the check-out. As always there was a queue snaking up each aisle. She dithered between moving to another counter, the usual roulette of shopping which she never managed to win. She always ended up with the trainee or behind the woman who packed every item then suddenly realised she needed to pay and scrabbled to the bottom of her bag to find her purse. This time Lizzie was lucky and managed to manoeuvre ahead of a man walking purposefully towards the same counter.

She began to unload the groceries, glancing at her watch. She had to get to the hospital as soon as she had dumped the shopping at home. She had promised Edina to go and sit with her at Sebastian's bedside. Luckily, Andrew wouldn't be around so she wouldn't have to talk to him. Sebastian was getting weaker and still waiting for a bone marrow donor to turn up and save his young life. His mother needed all the support she could get.

Lizzie had given him no cause for hope since the court case ended and Calum couldn't blame her. What was it she had said to Gaby? That there had been a lot of things said and done that they both regretted. Perhaps she was coming round to the idea that the rift had not been all his fault. Was she beginning to see that she might have handled it differently too? But this truce was difficult to sustain. He had tried his best but came up against a brick wall whenever he tried to bring up a discussion about their marriage. And if you couldn't talk about problems then you couldn't begin the process of curing them.

Calum took stock. After the initial bewilderment Gabriella seemed to be handling all that was thrown at her with remarkable maturity. He was reasonably confident that the bond between them would not be broken by the events of the last few weeks. Naturally she wanted to meet up with her new family. So did he. He had been desperately sad that he could not cross the court precincts and introduce himself to Anna-Maria. But that would happen in time.

Erik Schroeder had indicated that the deal for the business would include signing him up for a three-year contract as a consultant in the UK. Calum was happy with that. It would give him more time to pursue other interests. Sailing, maybe. But how much longer could he and Lizzie postpone a decision about their marriage? What did he want? He had said to Gabriella he hoped it would be OK. Were those just placatory words or did he really mean it? There was a long string of questions which he didn't feel capable of answering. Could any marriage be the same after what had happened? He remembered his bitter accusations about Peter Rivers, flourishing his photograph in front of Lizzie's face. 'You needed a name for your illegitimate child, so you had to marry me.' Calum flinched. How could any woman be expected to get over that?

And when she had tried to tell him about her blood test he was ashamed to remember how he had frozen her out because he thought she was insulting his intelligence by continuing to insist there was another explanation. But no apology from him, for this missed opportunity to hear the truth as well as the original sin of not believing her appeared to assuage her sense of grievance. Did he want to go on trying? He thought he did. She had been so much part of his adult life, every high, every low. She had been there to share the pleasures and the pain. But he couldn't imagine being the supplicant, being figuratively speaking on his knees, for the rest of their married life. She would come to despise him and love couldn't survive that.

He longed for an evening with someone who understood him and could pamper his bruised ego. He thought of Tess, as he did too often these days. Lizzie was convinced he'd been having an affair with her. Tess had made it clear she would wait as long as it took. She knew how distant Lizzie had become. Calum had confided in her not long after Lizzie had accused him of being with her that night he'd gone for a drive, jet-lagged and shell-shocked from hearing about the baby switch. He had turned to Tess partly for sympathy and comfort, but also because he was puzzled by Lizzie's insistence that Tess had told her he had been with her that night.

'Did you tell Lizzie that?' he'd asked outright.

'Of course not,' said Tess. She'd seemed genuinely shocked. 'I only said the figures you asked for last night were on your desk. I didn't tell her your message was on the answering machine. Why would I? Lizzie obviously thought I'd seen you.'

It made sense, but Lizzie just wouldn't listen. Every time he tried to convince her she'd misunderstood Tess, she cut him off. Something about Tess riled her. He was attracted to Tess, he couldn't deny it, and Lizzie obviously sensed that. The fact was that lately the temptation to do something about the attraction had been growing, and if Lizzie continued to turn away from him, what was the point of resisting?

Mrs Ewing kept up a constant bleating about how Craig Garrett had double-crossed her. 'He promised I could meet my daughter as soon as the case was over.'

'And so you will, I'll make sure of that,' said Andrew absently, keeping an eye on the central information board. Only another half an hour to go before the departure of the Glasgow train. He had insisted on taking the Ewings to Euston station instead of putting them in a taxi because he wanted to see for himself the train doors closing behind them.

'We can't do a thing until the judgement is announced,' he said firmly, 'and that might take weeks. When I win, and my legal people are pretty confident that I will, I'll organise your trip back, all expenses paid.'

Nancy Ewing still looked doubtful and he added swiftly, 'Gabriella's as keen to meet up as you are.'

Nancy's face lightened. 'So she knows about me?'

'Certainly. She'll probably rush up to Glasgow before you get a chance to come back here.'

Andrew gave a sideways glance at Anna-Maria. She'd been quiet so far. What was going on in that conniving mind? The longer she remained in London the greater the danger that she would somehow contact Calum and his family. He couldn't allow that to happen; she was just as capable of striking some deal with them if they won and dumping him. In the unlikely event that he did lose, Andrew intended to fight on, using Anna-Maria as his chief weapon.

'We should stay down here until it's all over,' she muttered.

'There's nothing I'd like better,' he replied, forcing a smile, 'but I can't afford it and Craig's newspaper won't pay anything more.' The truth was the *Chronicle*'s editor had washed his hands of the story and was off to fresh pastures.

Andrew took out an envelope containing a hundred pounds and handed it over to Mrs Ewing. 'This is to take care of your expenses on the train and the taxi home.' He intended to deduct this amount from the five per cent share of the inheritance he had promised Anna-Maria.

He then helped them into the carriage with their suitcases and settled them into a non-smoking compartment. The last glimpse Andrew had of the Ewings was a half-hearted wave from the mother while the daughter ostentatiously turned her head away. When the train disappeared round the corner he heaved a sigh of relief.

Edward Foxton rang to say that the judgement was due in two days' time. Gabriella was on tenterhooks. She spent much of her leisure time on the phone to Natasha and Luke, swaying from one extreme to the other, certain of her inheritance in one phone call, convinced she'd lost it in the next. Lizzie's fear about what the money would do to Gabriella's life was countermanded by a deep desire not to see it end up in Andrew's pockets.

Of the three of them, Calum was probably the least exercised. He wanted Gabriella's future to be financially secure but he could manage this if the judgement went against them. Declaring the will null and void would, according to Edward, render Robert Lynton as having died intestate. The money would then be equally divided between the two brothers. Emotionally he had let go of the business and inheriting the money would not change his decision. His thoughts were more preoccupied with the Ewings. So far neither he nor Edward had been able to persuade the other side to arrange a meeting. He would insist on this once the case was over.

Andrew greeted the news of the judgement date with little interest. Sebastian's deteriorating condition was his sole concern. Whether or not he won the case was now totally irrelevant. He wouldn't be going to the court to hear the judgement. Money couldn't save Sebastian's life and he had lost all interest in the Ewing girl when she turned out not to be a match for Sebastian.

The Lynton family made their way to the high court in a state of high tension. During the night Gabriella had been at her most irritating, leaping in and out of bed to get water, toast, any excuse she could think of to postpone sleep. Calum and Lizzie, after a night of fragmented dreams, had woken up heavy-eyed and fuzzy-headed.

Then Gabriella had driven Lizzie demented churning up her wardrobe in her usual frenzy of indecision. Predictably, she eventually chose a long black cotton skirt which, she said, would look well on camera. The remark sent a jolt into Lizzie's stomach as she had momentarily forgotten there would probably be cameramen waiting outside the court. She had better make more of an effort. She discarded her favourite black suit in favour of a newer one in pale blue wool, bought with the interview with the school governors in mind, and fished about until she found earrings that she felt struck the right balance between decorum and fashion.

They were late starting off so they had to take the car but the journey began badly. Lizzie had left the front door keys in the hall so they had to stop half a mile down the road and turn back. The timing could not have been worse. The morning rush hour was made more unbearable by a tailback all along the

Embankment caused, they discovered after a mile or so of crawling along, by a broken-down car on the approach to Battersea Bridge.

But nothing seemed to faze Gabriella who didn't show any of the ravages of lack of sleep. She kept up a steady stream of conversation about what she would do with the inheritance, seemingly impervious to Lizzie's attempt to douse her expectations.

But it was the mention of Anna-Maria Ewing and Gabriella's declaration that she wanted to visit her birth mother the very next day, whatever happened in the court, that caused Calum to turn to look at her and say, 'Pussycat, can we get the court case over, please?'

At that precise moment the traffic lights changed and Calum's bumper connected with the silver Mercedes coupe in front. Calum groaned and wound down his window. The other driver had already leapt out of his car as if catapulted by elastic and was waving his arms around and pointing to his bumper.

'I've only just picked up this car from the showroom, not an hour ago,' he screamed, almost dancing with rage.

Calum, unnerved by the ferocious reaction, undid his belt and went to inspect the damage. He could see nothing, as he pointed out to the gesticulating driver. Cars were swerving around them as Calum tried in vain to pacify the man. He claimed that the bumper was out of alignment and would need to be replaced. Despite Calum's apologies, the man could not be mollified and insisted on a lengthy exchange of names, addresses and insurance company details. By the time Calum climbed back into the car, twenty precious minutes had elapsed and they arrived in court number five with only minutes to spare. They were barely seated when the clerk called for silence to announce the arrival of the judge.

The leather banquettes in front of the dais were deserted except for the two legal teams and Lizzie remembered that Edward had told her that, again, no press would be allowed inside. They would have to rely on statements from both sides later.

The seats behind Andrew's legal team remained empty. The only reason for Andrew's absence must be that he was needed at the hospital. Lizzie sent up a silent prayer for the sick baby.

To her surprise the judge caught her eye as he made his way

to the dais; she was reminded of a medieval king seated on his throne dispensing justice and wisdom to his loyal subjects below.

'From the beginning this case seemed to be fairly straight-forward yet the more I thought about it the more labyrinthine it became. Paramount, surely, must be that Robert Lynton's wishes be carried out. What were those wishes? That his beloved granddaughter, his bloodline as he put it, should be his heir. But what was the importance of that term, "the bloodline"?'

Lizzie's spirits nose-dived. Edward had warned that if the judge concentrated on that aspect he must find in Andrew's favour.

'I had to make up my mind whether it was the biological granddaughter he was concerned with or the child he knew as his granddaughter, Gabriella Lynton.' Lord Nash paused, gazing around the court room over his half-moon spectacles. Then he looked again at his notes and turned the page.

'The evidence that was put before me painted a picture of a man closely involved with the life of a young girl, interested in her hobbies and keen to interest her in others – chess, for instance. But, I had to ask myself, did this man show affection towards Gabriella Lynton simply because she was the product of his bloodline? That, of course, is the nub of the case.'

A slight movement from their barrister caught Lizzie's atten-tion. Tim Goodman was turning towards Edward, eyebrows raised.

'I was reassured by the evidence presented to me that the deceased was impressed by Gabriella Lynton's intelligence and robust attitude to life.' Gabriella, who had seemed subdued by the authoritarian atmosphere in the court, perked up at these words. 'But did the fact that she had considerably brightened his later years give me to understand that he intended to reward her with his entire fortune? That is what I had to decide.' Gaby's shoulders drooped.

'My conclusion is that the bond between the deceased and Gabriella Lynton was such that the continuation of the bloodline was of secondary importance.' The judge paused. 'I therefore find against the plaintiff and in favour of the defendant.'

Calum reached over and patted Gabriella's shoulder.

'Dad,' she whispered urgently. 'Which one are we?'

At this Lizzie let out a laugh which she quickly stifled when she found the judge staring at her.

'An order for costs will be made against the plaintiff.' The judge banged the gavel and stood up.

Tim Goodman leapt to his feet, as did the others, as the judge majestically left the stage. The door to his chamber was barely closed when Tim turned round and clapped Calum on the back. 'We won. Of course I was always confident we would.'

'Congratulations,' said Calum, 'and thank you very much.'

'Well done, young lady,' said Edward to a bemused Gabriella. 'You'd better come and see me in a couple of years' time and I'll give you some advice.' She smiled shyly and he added, 'I like the idea of a dynastic legacy. You'll be the third generation of Lyntons that our firm has served.'

Lizzie squeezed her daughter's arm. 'I suppose I'll have to start being nice to you from now on.'

Gabriella returned her mother's smile. 'Oh Mum, don't be daft. Let's go to eat so that we can talk about going up to Glasgow.'

Andrew was given the bad news by his solicitor and his instinctive reaction was to instruct them to start appeal proceedings. Gently the solicitor informed him that in the opinion of their barrister that would be a waste of funds. They could not accept a further brief on a no win, no fee basis. The judgement was unequivocal, and in Jocasta's opinion there were no grounds on which they could make an appeal.

Andrew went to drown his sorrows with the person who would be able to pay for the drinks. He waited at Craig's usual pub, nursing a much-needed brandy until the reporter appeared. But instead of commiserating with Andrew he began cursing him. According to Craig, Andrew had single-handedly destroyed his career and if Andrew ever dared approach him with a story again he would be booted to kingdom come.

'I'll be lucky to be in charge of paper clips,' Craig snarled, 'and it's all your fault.'

'I did all this to save my kid,' Andy stuttered.

'Like hell you did. You were in it for the money,' said Craig, raising his voice, 'just like the Ewings. I'm glad to see the back of them.'

Andrew was choking with anger. 'Money was not my first priority. You might have thought it was. But saving Sebastian was why I went to you in the first place.'

247

'Give it a break, Andy,' said Craig. 'OK, you might've used some of the money for Sebastian but, let's face it, your greed got the better of you.'

'That's not true. You're such a shit, so self-obsessed, you judge everybody by your own standards.' Andrew was shouting now. 'You couldn't have the least idea about how I feel about my kid. Everything I've done – everything – has been with him in mind. How dare you say it was for the money?'

'OK, leave it out,' said Craig who couldn't care less what Andrew's motivation was. They had both failed. 'You don't know what's it's like,' he ranted. 'I have to produce exclusives day after day and then when one falls apart, like this fucking story, what does my editor do? Tells me I've cost the paper thousands and we didn't get a result. He expected what he always does, a happy-ever-after story.'

Andrew was seething. 'At this moment my child is lying in hospital, clinging to life. How do you think I feel finding out that Anna-Maria wasn't a match? Something you didn't bother to mention, by the way.'

Craig was momentarily repentant. 'Yeah, sorry about that. It didn't pan out for any of us. And I'll probably be out on my ear.'

Andrew stood up and stared down at Craig with a look of such distaste on his face that the newspaperman was temporarily silenced.

'You can always get another job. I can never get another Sebastian.'

Across the road from the courts, in the Wig and Pen club, the judgement was being mulled over by the opposing counsel, Jocasta Hutcheson and Tim Goodman. Over a bottle of fine Bordeaux, Tim Goodman was congratulating his rival on many points well made.

'Not well enough,' she smiled. 'When the judge went doe-eyed over the videos I reckoned we were sunk. That's why I tried to introduce the Ewing girl but it was always a long shot.'

'Another one before you go?'

'Why not?' As he topped up their glasses she asked, 'Do you have a view on how Taylor versus Taylor affected this case?'

'Ah yes, a most interesting question, Jocasta. I most certainly do,' he said and prepared to settle in for a long session.

★ ★ ★

A memo landed on Craig Garrett's desk an hour after the Press Association's report on the judgement was sent down the lines. It requested his presence in the editor's office. An unauthorised payment of fifty thousand pounds had come to light and an explanation was required.

Craig decided there was no point in keeping the appointment and started to assemble the belongings he had accumulated over the past eight years.

As they sat round the kitchen table that night, Calum opened a bottle of newly-chilled Veuve Cliquot and raised his glass in a toast.

'Here's to you, Gabs.'

She took a sip. 'Wait until I get the money,' she said and lifted her glass. 'To all the great things I'm going to do for everyone, you two and Sebastian and, oh, lots of others.'

The three of them clinked glasses and Lizzie grinned. 'Are you including Luke in that? I wonder if you'll still know him when you get the first instalment.'

'Probably. He's been a good friend to me. But he doesn't need money for that demo tape any more. He's given up the idea.'

'Why's he done that?' asked Calum.

'He's got a scholarship to Oxford. Isn't that wonderful?'

Calum spluttered, 'Good for him!' Lizzie remembered Luke's mother mentioning that he was clever. It had obviously been more than just the partial view of a proud mother.

The three of them began talking about the money in a way that gave Lizzie hope for the future. Until recently Gaby had deserved her reputation in the family as a spendthrift, never being able to save up for anything and wasting her pocket money on objects she seemed to tire of after a very short time. Now she was making more sense about her finances. Even before the verdict, when she thought she was not going to get Grandpa's money, she had declared that she was prepared to knuckle down and do part-time work to help with the cost of university fees. And if by chance she was awarded the money, she had agreed that her grandfather had been wise to stagger the payments over so many years.

Gabriella spent a happy half-hour discussing what she wanted to do with the money when she got her hands on it. First of all she wanted to help Mum and Dad. Calum brought her up-to-date with the state of his negotiations with Schroeder and told her that thankfully they didn't need to be bailed out. Well then, she would certainly like to help the Ewings. 'We could ask the court if Grandpa's money could be split between the two of us, me and Anna-Maria. That would be fair,' said Gabriella.

'I don't think it's as easy as that,' said Calum. 'Ed wouldn't agree, for a start, and as he's the executor of the will he has some influence. But certainly there's a way you could help, perhaps with the interest on the capital.'

As for Sebastian they were still desperately anxious about him but he was getting the best possible medical treatment and did not need money at this point in his life. Andrew had told them that the events of the past few weeks had shown him that family was more important to him than money. Now that the case had ended, he was determined to heal the breach with his brother.

'Perhaps I should have been more understanding,' said Calum. 'There's no doubt that Dad favoured me, maybe because he saw too many of his own faults in Andy. In his position, who's to say I wouldn't have behaved badly. I'll fix up a meeting and try and make peace. Maybe later, Gabriella, you could set up a trust that would protect Sebastian's future, which would give Andrew less to worry about.'

Gabriella agreed enthusiastically.

When the first instalment of the fortune came through, Lizzie hoped Gaby would still be as amenable. As it was she had difficulty in keeping her face straight. Listening to Gabriella discuss finance, trust funds and interest payments was a first. What would she want to talk about next? Pension plans?

Chapter Twenty

Since Sebastian had been rushed to hospital Lizzie had promised Edina she would visit as often as she could; she had already been there once this week.

Lizzie had seen a pair of twin toy dogs in the toy shop window which, she decided, had Sebastian's name written all over them. The sales assistant had informed her with a straight face that the bigger of the toy dogs had already been named Colin. 'Pronounced Cole-lin, like the American war general.' Lizzie immediately christened the smaller brother Sammy Cole-lin. Perhaps it might make Edina smile.

Lizzie had made her way down the corridor to Sebastian's ward so many times she could do it blindfold but when she opened the door, there was no sign of Sebastian. Heart racing, she went to look for a nurse, fearing the worst. She saw a nurse she recognised from previous visits hurrying towards her.

'Where's Sebastian?' she asked breathlessly. 'He isn't . . .'

The nurse broke into a beaming smile. 'Oh no. He was operated on an hour ago. They found a donor. Isn't it great?'

'That's wonderful news,' said Lizzie, overjoyed.

'They had to operate immediately,' said the nurse. 'Poor little mite was sinking fast and they couldn't wait. Thank God they found a match at last. His mother's been with him all the while but she's just gone for a coffee.'

Excitedly Lizzie raced down the stairs to the canteen where she found Edina slumped over her arms, fast asleep, at a Formica table. She must be worn out, thought Lizzie, deciding it was kinder to leave her to rest. She returned to the ward and found the friendly nurse sitting at a desk at the entrance to the ward.

'How is Sebastian doing?' Lizzie asked her.

The nurse smiled at her. 'The early signs are promising. He's stable but we won't know for a few days yet whether or not the match will work.'

'Could I see him?'

'I don't see why not. He's in an isolation unit. But I'm sure the ward sister will allow you to peep at him through the window. Go to the third floor, second door on the left, then the first room on the right.'

Lizzie smiled gratefully and set off up the stairs, trying to remember the nurse's directions. All these corridors looked exactly the same. Left then right. She peered through the small window of the isolation room. A couple of nurses obscured the view of the bed. She hovered outside until they came out.

One of them noticed her and said pleasantly, 'Are you the mother?' Without waiting for a reply she said, 'You can only stay for a minute. Those drugs make them very groggy.'

Lizzie was surprised that she was apparently being allowed into the room only hours after the operation and without a sterile gown or mask but they must know what they were doing.

Carefully she turned the handle and stood hesitantly in the doorway. The overhead light had been dimmed and the curtains were drawn. Lizzie walked over to the bed towards the slight figure beneath the covers. Why wasn't he in a cot?

She stared at the sleeping face, head resting on the pillow, at times moving restlessly from side to side, transfixed. She was looking down at a mirror image of herself.

Down in the bowels of the hospital the bustle of the late-morning shift workers storming in for an early lunch awakened Edina from her troubled doze. With a start she grabbed her handbag and hurried to the call box. Again she tried, without success, to contact Andrew at the garage. Again his boss assured her that he would give the message as soon as he saw Andrew. She dialled the solicitors for the second time. No, he had not been with them and no, they could not offer any ideas as to where he might be.

Sighing, she left another message on his mobile, which unaccountably was still switched off, and went back upstairs to the isolation ward to keep vigil over Sebastian in his cot, surrounded by myriads of tubes and life-supporting machines, and prayed that his father would arrive soon.

It was like looking at herself twenty years ago. Hardly able to believe the evidence of her own eyes, Lizzie's legs gave way and she sank onto the chair by the side of the bed, her gaze still on the face of the young girl lying comatose. The same wayward tuft of hair at the forehead, the same texture, the same skin colouring and the same features. Nose, shape of face. Hers.

Every now and then the girl would murmur incoherently and Lizzie experienced a wave of compassion that she could not explain. Who was this young person? What was she doing here? Lizzie was determined to sit there all day if necessary until the girl was able to open her eyes and speak.

A nurse arrived and glanced at her before taking out from her pocket an electronic thermometer. She inserted it briefly into the girl's ear.

'Good, she's doing well. She's been so brave, we're very proud of her.'

Lizzie did not trust herself to speak and the nurse said brightly, 'I've just come on duty. Are you her mother?'

Mutely Lizzie shook her head and the nurse looked puzzled. 'You must be a relative, you look so alike. Wasn't it a miracle she was a match for Sebastian?'

Lizzie was trying to frame a reply when the door opened again and a plump, anxious-looking woman with short greying hair put her head round the door. Lizzie was sure she had never met her before but she found herself thinking that the face looked somehow familiar.

'Is it all right to come in now?' the woman asked, and the nurse beckoned her in before leaving to continue her rounds.

The woman leaned over and landed a soft kiss on the forehead of the sleeping girl. 'Alison, darling, I'm here and Dad's on his way.' She straightened and shot Lizzie a penetrating glance. 'You're Elizabeth Lynton. I read about you in the papers and saw you on the telly.'

Lizzie swallowed. 'Who is this?' indicating the slight figure in the bed. 'Your daughter?'

The woman hesitated. 'No, she's yours. Haven't you realised that?'

Incapable of speech, Lizzie stared dumbly at her and the woman began to explain.

'It was on the news. They were talking about this court case and they mentioned a mix-up with babies at the hospital. Then I saw you with your husband, in front of the court room. You were only on the screen for seconds but when I saw your face I thought I was looking at our Alison. I only had to see you to know the truth. The resemblance is uncanny. I made Ron, that's my husband, look at the next news bulletin and he saw it immediately, too.' She put out her hand. 'Let me introduce myself. I'm Angela Simmons.'

Lizzie's eyes began to mist over and, seeing this, Angela Simmons took hold of Lizzie's hand. After a while Lizzie said, 'I'm very pleased to meet you.' She took a deep breath. 'By the "truth" you mean you've been bringing up my daughter and I've been bringing up yours?'

'It seems like it, doesn't it?' said Angela Simmons quietly.

Lizzie looked again at the still figure lying in the bed and was overwhelmed by a strong, sure instinct that this girl, who was her double, was the daughter who had been taken from her all those years ago. The child she and Calum had conceived. It wasn't only the physical resemblances; Lizzie felt a contact, a bond which she could not fully explain. It had certainly not been present when she first set eyes on Anna-Maria. She took out a handkerchief and began wiping her eyes.

Angela said sympathetically, 'I'm sorry to break the news to you like this. It took me days to come to terms with it. Actually, I haven't really but I've had a little longer to take it in than you.'

Lizzie gulped. 'I'd got used to the idea of another girl being our child. We were making plans to go and see her. But I don't under-stand this. Why didn't I discover her right at the beginning?' She described the start of her search to Angela and added, 'I checked those hospital records myself, meticulously. There were fifteen babies born on November the eleventh and I'm positive there was no Simmons among them. How could I have missed you?'

'Easily.' Angela Simmons' face lightened. 'It's a great joke in our family. When she was little, Alison used to make me repeat it regularly. You see, she wasn't actually born in the hospital. Alison,' Angela paused for half a second, 'my baby, I mean, arrived in the taxi on the way there. She wouldn't wait, the little minx.' Angela rubbed her forehead. 'I won't forget that night in a hurry. This was my third and the others were all quick births too. But with this baby I didn't feel I was going into labour until I went to the toilet and suddenly I wanted to push. I called Ron to phone for an ambulance but the poor man was in such a state he just ran into the street and flagged down a taxi.

'And there I was, on all fours on the back seat when after a few moments I felt the baby slide out. And I told Ron, "I've had the baby." He could hardly believe it and he shouted for the taxi to stop. We had nothing to wrap her up in so the driver took off his shirt. That's why we called her Alison. It was the name of the driver's wife. He still sends us a Christmas card every year.'

'I didn't see any Simmons baby registered in the records,' said Lizzie.

'Presumably you were only looking for babies born on November the eleventh.'

'Of course, that's the only day I was interested in.'

'My baby was born on November the eleventh but just before midnight. By the time we arrived at the hospital it was half past twelve and it was chaos. They didn't expect so many babies to be born and they'd had a terribly busy time. I only got up to the ward past one o'clock. So my baby's birth was registered as the twelfth, the following day. I always tell her she's twenty-four hours older than she is.'

'Was she sent to the special care unit?' Lizzie asked, and Angela nodded. 'Bingo,' said Lizzie. 'I'm sure that's where our babies were switched.'

Angela patted her hand. There was a moment or two of quiet between them before she asked quietly, 'Do you have a picture of Gabriella?'

Lizzie opened her handbag and took out a small photograph. 'It's not very good, she always turns her head away.'

Angela Simmons studied the features for some time, and her square, rather stern face became much softer.

'Very striking,' she said after a while. 'Reminds me a bit of Ron's mother. She was a beauty. Tell me, what sort of girl is she?'

Lizzie's face puckered. 'We've had our ups and downs. I suppose I'd call her spirited. Takes no prisoners. Speaks her mind. Typical teenager, can't tell her anything.'

'Stubborn. Just like Ron's mother.'

'She does well at school,' added Lizzie. 'Her teachers think she'll go to university. She's really good at maths.'

'So are my boys. That comes from Ron.' Angela's gaze returned to the photographs. 'Does Gabriella have a little dent on her small finger?'

Lizzie's eyes widened and she nodded.

'All mine do, apart from Alison. It comes from my side of the family.' Angela tried to smooth her untidy hair and gave a glimmer of a smile. The face was careworn but Lizzie realised what was familiar about it. The shape and colour of the eyes reminded her of Gabriella.

'And Alison,' she asked, almost shyly. 'What's she like?'

Judging by Angela's description, Alison had much the same interests as Gabriella. She was popular at school, interested in art and music – like my father, thought Lizzie – and was very impetuous. 'She just scampers off without thinking sometimes and it gets her into trouble.' Like me, thought Lizzie. Anyone else would have waited to tell their husband that their baby had been switched before haring off to track down what turned out to be the wrong girl.

That worry was beginning to penetrate Lizzie's thoughts. She had been so positive Anna-Maria was the one. Well, she and Dan Hargreaves had decided there was no other possible explanation, never taking into account the possibility of illogical human circumstances. Though she was certain this time, Lizzie suggested to Angela that it would be sensible to do a DNA test on both families. Angela nodded but commented that Gabriella's little finger persuaded her that the girl was a Simmons all right. As for Alison, she was such a lookalike, could there be any doubt of her parentage?

Lizzie contemplated the pale face lying motionless on the pillow and could not help but agree. 'I have some photos of me at this age at home that I'd like to show you. You'd think they were of Alison.'

Alison murmured and Angela poured out a glass of water and began to moisten her lips. The women watched her in silence, but the girl's eyes did not open.

Angela smiled. 'Seeing you sitting there is like looking at an older version of Alison. My husband and I have always been puzzled at the differences between her and the boys. All those years of wondering who she took after suddenly make sense. But I don't think we'd have done anything about finding you for fear it would upset her.'

'So why did you?'

'It was that poor Sebastian. When we heard about him and how he might die, we felt we had to help in case Alison was a match. We contacted the donor unit and they found out she was.'

Strange world, thought Lizzie. If it hadn't been for Andrew, they wouldn't have gone to court, wouldn't have been on television and this family would never have contacted the donor unit. Whatever the emotional cost to her family, the whole trauma had been worthwhile if Sebastian's life was saved.

'But we want to remain anonymous,' said Angela. She hesitated for a moment. 'We're doing this for the baby and we don't want our names in the papers.'

Lizzie was forming an answer in her mind that she fully understood and that she, too, didn't want any more publicity but found the words would not come. She was overwhelmed that this family would choose to turn their lives and the life of their child upside down to help a stranger. She hoped she would have been able to make the same sacrifice.

'Does Alison know anything about the circumstances of her birth?' Lizzie asked.

'No, she doesn't. Ron and I didn't have a wink of sleep thinking about what was the right thing to do. Eventually we persuaded the whole family to volunteer to be tested so Alison didn't think it was unusual to be picked out.'

So the girl didn't know. Should she offer to leave before she regained consciousness? Somehow Lizzie couldn't bring herself to make the offer, though if Angela Simmons had suggested it at that point, she would have agreed to go.

Lizzie prayed for the girl to wake so she could hear her talk but it would be a mistake to force things. This good woman was as much in a quandary as she was and if she hadn't come wandering into the ward maybe they wouldn't ever have told her the truth.

Really they all needed time. How would Calum react? He still believed Anna-Maria Ewing was their child. So did Gabriella. And hadn't they made a pact that they would never again keep her ignorant of anything connected to her parentage? Gabriella had found out that neither she nor Calum were her parents in the most hurtful way possible and Lizzie was determined that wasn't going to happen again.

There was movement from the bed and Angela bent over the prone figure. 'Darling? Alison, can you hear me? It's Mum.'

At the words, Lizzie's eyes filled with tears. For Angela was her mother, as she was Gabriella's, and whatever happened in the future, Angela needed to be alone with her child right now. As silently as she could, Lizzie crept out of the room into the corridor and watched with a thudding heart as a nurse hurried in to attend to her patient.

Still shaking, she made her way to the cloakroom. As she splashed her face with cold water she tried to think how she could get Calum over to the hospital to get a glimpse of the girl. She glanced at her watch. Right now he would be with Gaby at home and this was certainly not something she could blurt out over the phone. But before she set out on the drive, she wanted to talk to Edina.

The canteen was almost deserted; there was no sign of Edina. Lizzie ordered a double espresso and sat down at one of the corner tables. She had been there for only a minute or so when Angela Simmons appeared at her shoulder.

'I hoped you might be here,' she smiled. 'I didn't want you to dash off before we'd at least exchanged telephone numbers.' She sat down and Lizzie, her hands still trembling, began to write down her telephone number and address while Angela gave details of her home in Bromley in Kent.

Nervously Lizzie gazed around the canteen and asked, 'Have you met the baby's parents?'

'I saw the mother briefly,' said Angela. 'She was the only one allowed to see Alison as she was being prepped.'

Lizzie began to fret. The likeness was so obvious, there was a danger that others would make the connection. Like Andrew and Edina.

'Do you think she noticed the similarity between Alison and me?' she asked.

'I don't think so. She was in such a daze and thrilled about finding a match, I don't think she was concentrating on anything else.'

Lizzie sighed. 'Nobody else in the family, apart from us, should see Alison if we want to keep this quiet.'

'I agree. We don't want any fuss. I know the parents are very grateful but I don't think it's a good idea for us to talk to them. They think we came forward as a result of the story on the telly, nothing more.'

'That's good,' said Lizzie, relieved. She explained about the court case. 'The father was involved with the *Chronicle* and he might reveal to the journalists who you are.'

Angela looked alarmed. 'My family doesn't want to see itself splashed all over the newspapers. We made anonymity the main condition of helping.'

'Then you shouldn't have anything to worry about.'

Angela straightened, two tiny spots of colour in her cheeks. 'We're not doing this to get any of the money they talked about on the television.'

'I never thought that for a moment,' said Lizzie quickly.

'It was only to save the baby's life,' said Angela. 'We're fine as we are.'

'I'm sure,' said Lizzie, and Angela's hunched shoulders relaxed. She had a strong conviction that whatever decision she and Angela made about the future they would make together and it would remain within their two families. 'Angela, what are we going to do now?' she asked, feeling that after what Alison had done for Sebastian, the older woman should be allowed to make the running.

'Ron thinks we should leave things as they are. I'm not sure. What do you think?'

Lizzie gave a deep sigh. 'So much has happened, some day I'll tell you about it. But my family's been damaged by trying to keep secrets and I don't want that to happen again.'

'We four parents have to think carefully what to do,' said Angela. 'Once you know something like this you can't just shove it back into the cupboard. First of all we'll have to decide whether or not to tell the girls.'

'Gabriella's already been told she was switched at birth, but she thinks it was with the Ewing baby. She wants to go and see them. It wouldn't be right to do that now.'

Angela looked downcast. 'Alison will be so upset, I don't know how we're going to break the news. I wonder if we ever should.'

'Only you and your husband can make that decision. We thought it best not to keep secrets but then we had a court case to face.'

Angela gave Lizzie a steely look. 'I would like to meet Gabriella but it's not as if we're going to switch them back, are we?'

'Certainly not. That's the last thing I'd want to do,' said Lizzie. 'But having said that, there's nothing to stop our families from becoming friends, is there?'

At this Angela leaned over and clutched Lizzie's hand. The two mothers smiled at each other and, overwhelmed by events, their eyes filled with tears.

One or two at nearby tables looked at them sympathetically. Unfortunately the sight of tears was not a rare occurrence in that canteen.

When they had regained control, Lizzie smiled. 'I think I need another coffee. Can I get you one?'

'Yes, please.'

As she queued at the coffee urn, Lizzie looked round idly and saw to her dismay that Edina was making straight for her. Lizzie smiled at her, hoping she would not betray her anxiety.

'Thanks for coming.' Edina's face was transformed and she appeared to be in a state of euphoria. 'Isn't it wonderful news? I've just come from the isolation ward. Of course it's too early to say, but they're hopeful and you know what? I think he has some colour in his cheeks.'

'I'm so happy for you,' said Lizzie.

'I know he's going to be all right,' said Edina with delight. 'Other babies have been cured and I'm sure Sebastian will be too.'

Lizzie prayed that Edina would not notice Angela Simmons sitting in the corner. The last thing she wanted was for the three of them to have a cosy chat and for Edina to find out that the donor was born on the same day and in the same hospital as Gabriella.

'Here's your two coffees, love,' said the canteen assistant to Lizzie.

'Sorry,' said Lizzie, flustered. 'I only wanted one. Unless you'd like it, Edina?'

She shook her head, apparently unaware of Lizzie's confusion. 'Just water, please. I daren't have any more caffeine. I've been drinking coffee all day.'

The canteen lady was fingering the second cup, already poured. 'You did say two,' she said mildly into the air, before throwing it into the sink.

Lizzie risked a glance towards Angela. The corner table was empty. Smart woman.

'The people here have been incredibly supportive,' said Edina, 'especially that nice doctor, the one who gave us the good news. He was as pleased as if it had been his own child.'

'That's understandable,' said Lizzie. She paused. It would be natural to ask who was the donor and she was anxious to learn how much Edina had been told. 'Who was the donor?' she asked, heart pounding.

'It's a young girl. I saw her briefly before the operation but I don't know anything about the family. Would you believe it, they heard about it on television and came forward. It's a miracle. I've sent them a letter. I'll never be able to repay them, never. Just shows, doesn't it, there are good people around.' She sipped her glass of water. 'Of course Dr Hargreaves said they were prepared to carry on trying to find a match for as long as it took.'

Dr Hargreaves? Lizzie felt a shiver pass over her skin. Had Dan Hargreaves met Alison? Had he spotted the likeness? Their last meeting had been so antagonistic, what would he do if he had and put two and two together?

Edina was unstoppable. She painted Dan Hargreaves as a cross between St Francis of Assisi and Albert Schweitzer. 'He's been a great help all along. I shouldn't tell you this but when he saw Andy at his lab he couldn't have been more sympathetic but then they were at med school together, you know.'

Alarm bells clanged in Lizzie's head as Edina prattled on, walking ahead to find an empty table.

'Dr Hargreaves was the one who first put us onto that girl in Glasgow,' Edina went on.

Lizzie tried to quieten her pounding heart. 'Dr Hargreaves told you about Anna-Maria?'

'Yes, he saw the article in the *Chronicle* and went straight to them with his information. Andrew says he needed money for his lab. Apparently they paid him fifty thousand pounds. I don't mind, it's in a good cause.'

Lizzie's eyes narrowed. She wondered how much of that money had gone into Dan's own pocket.

'You can imagine how I felt when the girl turned out to be no use for Sebastian.' She clapped her hand to her mouth. 'I'm sorry. I shouldn't have said that. Not about your real daughter. But then, without him you wouldn't have found her. You should thank him as well, Lizzie.'

'Yes,' murmured Lizzie. 'I should.'

'What are you going to do about her?' asked Edina. 'And what about Gaby?'

'There's a lot we have to think about,' said Lizzie. 'We haven't made any decisions yet.' That bloody Dan Hargreaves, she thought, going behind her back to the *Chronicle* instead of going to the parents. All this agony, this publicity, because of his greed. She would report him to the British Medical Council. And they would have to strike him off. His lab would close down. He'd be broke, he would have to sell everything. Even that bloody car he loved so much.

261

Edina was talking about the court case. 'I've been so upset about it. I did try to persuade Andy to settle, Lizzie.'

'I know. It's all sorted out now. Where is he, by the way?'

'I wish I knew. Things happened so fast I've not been able to tell him about the operation.' Her face began to crumple. 'He's never around when he's needed.'

Lizzie patted her hand. 'Hang in there, Edina. Once the baby's on the road to recovery you'll be able to think straight. Anyway, I don't want you to worry about money. Whatever we end up with we'll make sure Sebastian is all right.'

At this Edina began to sob, tears coursing down her cheeks. 'Thank you. I've done so much crying recently I didn't think I had any tears left. I've had to put on a brave face for so long.'

Lizzie consoled her as best she could until, unexpectedly, Edina's face brightened. She was staring into the middle distance and pointed to a tall figure making for the counter. 'Look, there he is.'

'Andy?' asked Lizzie who had her back to the counter and was wondering how she could make a hasty departure without upsetting Edina.

'No. The doctor,' smiled Edina, waving vigorously to catch his attention. 'Dr Hargreaves, over here.'

For a moment Dan hesitated, then, tray in hand, made his way towards them and sat down at their table. As he and Edina began to discuss Sebastian's progress, Dan unloaded his cup of coffee, sandwich and an apple and aimed a dazzling smile at Lizzie.

'I'm forgetting my manners,' said Edina. 'Dr Hargreaves, this is my sister-in-law, Lizzie.'

Seeing him basking in Edina's unalloyed admiration, Lizzie was filled with a desire to inflict physical pain on him.

'What a pleasure to meet you,' he said, stretching out his hand. He had the temerity to give it a squeeze and her anger increased. This Judas was responsible for much of the agony her family had suffered. She wanted to wipe that self-satisfied smile off his face.

'Edina's been telling me how wonderful you were. It was good of you to help Sebastian,' she said coolly.

'All in the line of duty,' Dan smiled.

'You went way beyond that,' she said sweetly. 'Fancy being able to find out Anna-Maria's address. So clever of you.' She paused as if to think. 'And that national newspaper who did the story about them, how on earth do you think they got to Glasgow so quickly?'

Abruptly Dan put down his sandwich, his eyes wary.

Bull's eye, thought Lizzie.

'It was so brave of you,' she said, 'risking your professional reputation like that.'

Edina was looking puzzled. Lizzie leaned forward and dropped her voice. 'By releasing information about Anna-Maria this man has jeopardised his entire career for Sebastian.'

'I didn't realise.' Edina's eyes were shining with adoration.

'I think you're exaggerating my part in all this, Mrs Lynton,' said Dan, his smile long disappeared. 'It was a case of all pitching in to do the best for Sebastian.'

'Oh, don't be so modest. You know very well, Edina, doctors have to keep their records confidential. If anyone reported you to the BMA, you'd be struck off.' She paused. 'Instantly.'

Dan flinched and she felt a surge of pleasure. She was getting through to him nicely.

'Don't worry, Dr Hargreaves,' Edina's voice was practically a whisper. 'Nobody will find out anything from us.'

'Let's hope none of us features in any newspaper article from now on,' said Lizzie briskly. By now Dan Hargreaves' skin had taken on a satisfying greenish pallor.

Lizzie was undecided about whether she would act on her threat. In a way it was better not to do anything so that every morning Dan would wake up and wonder if this was the day he would get the dreaded call. It was enough revenge, wasn't it? Not quite.

She rose from her chair. 'I must be off.' As she reached under the table to pick up her handbag, her elbow jutted against the edge of Dan Hargreaves' coffee cup. Piping hot liquid flooded across the table and down onto his expensive trousers. He leapt up, holding his groin, shouting in pain.

'Oh, how stupid of me,' she gushed, handing him a paper napkin. 'I'm very, very sorry.'

Chapter Twenty-one

Lizzie could hardly contain her jubilation when she returned from the hospital and burst into the living room to find Calum and Gabriella transfixed by the concluding episode of a television whodunnit. They barely acknowledged her, eyes determinedly on the screen.

'I've got some great news.'

'Wait, wait.' Gabriella picked up the remote control and activated the video. Calum switched off the set.

'They've found a donor, fingers crossed, it looks as if Sebastian's going to be OK.'

She could not tell which of them was the more delighted.

Calum asked the crucial question. 'Who was the donor?'

'Someone who heard about the story on the television and volunteered a blood sample.'

'That's amazing,' exclaimed Gabriella.

Calum nodded. 'So that publicity was helpful after all.'

Tentatively Lizzie confessed she had not told them the entire story. She began by describing her feelings on catching sight of a girl in the hospital who was a mirror image of her when she was a teenager and ended, without interruption from either of them, with the decision that they should await a DNA test before doing anything.

There was a silence and Lizzie and Calum exchanged nervous glances before Gabriella said, 'But you don't need that test, do you, Mum?'

Lizzie shook her head. 'And when you meet the family you'll understand why. You have the same shaped face as Angela Simmons and exactly the same kind of eyes.' Lizzie then faithfully dredged up every syllable of her conversation with Angela Simmons and described her and Alison's features as carefully as a portrait painter.

Gabriella's curiosity appeared to outweigh everything else and she asked eagerly, 'Is she still at the hospital? Can we go there now?'

'Her mum wants Alison fully recovered before she breaks the news. You can understand that, Gaby.'

'Yes, yes. You're right. In a way this makes everything simpler somehow,' she went on. 'I mean with the Ewings.'

'And it explains why I didn't feel anything when I met Anna-Maria,' said Lizzie.

'But Mum, you were so sure she was the one.'

'Because there was no other baby it could have been. Of course I didn't know about a certain taxi driver who acted as a midwife. If I had, there might have been a slight doubt in my mind. Thank God we didn't jump in and get involved with the Ewings' lives.'

Later, once Gabriella had gone to her room, Lizzie and Calum sat in front of the fire, staring into the flames. The clock might have been put back, Lizzie was thinking. It was almost like old times, although there had not been any physical contact between them.

Since his return from America when she had made it clear she needed time to concentrate on Gabriella's welfare he had not instigated conversations which might have threatened the fragile truce between them. And they had managed to maintain a civilised presence before Gabriella. Realising how much of a strain it must be, she gave him full marks for his restraint.

As if he could read her thoughts, Calum asked suddenly, 'I didn't want to bring this up before but . . . what's going to happen to us?'

She hesitated for a fraction. The morning's post had brought a letter offering her the full-time job.

'I've been offered a job. It's full time.' He seemed pleased but before he could say anything more she added quickly, 'It's in Hampshire so it would mean moving from home. There's a two-bedroomed flat to go with the job.'

'And you're going to take it,' he said bleakly.

Yes, she thought, she was. She had put off the decision but now she was sure. Calum had failed her and that would always haunt their relationship. The question was whether or not she could rise above it and Lizzie did not think she could. Significantly, Calum had made no mention of Tess the few times they had had a normal conversation about the office.

'I don't want my stupidity to break us up. Can't you give me another chance?'

'I'm not sure I can.' Lizzie rose and picked up the tray of tea.

He started to say something, then appeared to change his mind and said quietly, 'And I'm not sure you can expect me to hang around while you decide my future.'

He made no attempt to stop her as she made her way to the kitchen.

When the envelope arrived from the laboratory confirming what the two mothers already believed, Lizzie was at home alone, having a free morning from school. While Anna-Maria had no genetic characteristics in common with the Lyntons, Alison's matched theirs in every important particular. Lizzie's immediate reaction was to ring Angela Simmons and the two women spent an hour on the telephone, eventually deciding two things. That Alison must be told as soon as possible. And that the parents did not have the right to make decisions about the future without the girls being fully consulted. They both admitted they were afraid of the situation running out of control. Once the girls had set eyes on the blood parent, would one or both want to share their lives with them? And if they did, what then? It was a question neither parent wanted to confront.

In the event it was Alison who resolved the dilemma. She refused point blank to meet the Lyntons and no amount of persuasion from Angela would make her change her mind. She did not want to meet her so-called birth parents, she wanted nothing to do with their lives and thought it far better if the family pretended the mix-up had never happened. Ron Simmons, far from supporting his wife, had backed Alison's stand, saying he, too, thought it unwise to 'muck around' with people's lives.

Angela was distressed as she desperately wanted to meet Gabriella but told Lizzie it was best to leave matters awhile. In time, when the girls were a little older, and she had been able to win Alison and Ron over to their way of thinking, perhaps then they could organise something.

When she put down the phone, Lizzie was struck by the sudden realisation that the emotion uppermost in her mind was not disappointment or distress but immense relief. Thank God it wasn't going to happen. She could sympathise with Alison. Perhaps it was not wise to open up this particular can of worms.

Curiosity had impulsively forced her forward. So, she had to admit, had her ego, wondering if the child had her personality as well as her looks. She had once been plagued by the thought that her incompatibility with Gabriella was more to do with genetics than nurturing. But she had since found out that it was more to do with the traumas of being a teenager. All it had needed from her was a bit more understanding and to treat Gaby in a more adult way. These past weeks had taught her that it wasn't a crime to rebel and untidy rooms did not threaten the love that existed between them.

Gabriella was very disappointed by the decision but decided not to worry her parents with it. However, the next day, when she came home to an empty house, she decided this was the opportunity to give fate a little push. She fished in her satchel to find a number then punched it in. When the receiver was picked up at the other end and the voice identified itself, Gabriella took a deep breath. Now or never.

'Hi.'

'Who's that?'

'Gabriella.'

'How did you get my number?'

'I dialled one four seven one after your mother's call last night. I love using it.'

A giggle. 'So do I.'

A long pause followed, before Gaby said she was sorry that they weren't going to meet. There was no response and Gaby summoned up her courage. 'Isn't the whole thing scary?' she asked. 'It's like something on the telly, not real life.'

'You feel like that? So do I. It was horrible finding out. I cried my eyes out.'

'So did I.'

There was another pause.

'So you're never going to meet us?' said Gaby.

'What's the point?'

'Aren't you dying to see if you look like one of them?'

'In a way. But Mum's told me the kind of person Mrs Lynton is and . . .' she stopped.

'And what?'

'My family's very different to yours. My dad isn't a company director.'

Gabriella laughed. 'Actually neither is mine now.'

There was an answering laugh down the line which broke more ice between them. Alison seemed to feel bolder because she began to confess that she had been unwilling to meet her birth parents because they were bound to be disappointed by her. Exactly what she'd felt, Gabriella told her.

And, Gabriella asked, what had she done that was so terrible? It boiled down to the fact that Alison thought the way she had been brought up was different, that the Lyntons would find everything about her inadequate, the way she talked, the way she dressed, even the way she stood. 'Mum's always going on about my posture.'

This was going to be easy, thought Gabriella. She began telling Alison about Luke, about running away and staying overnight at his house, about how she had called her mother a whore. 'Tell me you're worse than that.'

This time Alison gave a full-throated laugh and sensing that the opposition was softening, Gabriella set about drawing out from her what she called the teenage junk, boys, school and clothes, in that order.

'I just want to ask you one other question,' Gabriella went on. 'Do you like classical music?'

'No,' the voice was vehement. 'I'm into the Manic Street Preachers.'

Gabriella could hardly hide her satisfaction. 'So am I and Mum and Dad hate them.'

'So do mine.'

They agreed to keep their conversation secret and made arrangements to talk again later in the week. 'You're the only one who really knows how I feel,' said Alison.

'Ditto.'

Sebastian was sitting up in the hospital cot babbling his entire repertoire of eight words, smiling and rosy-cheeked.

Edina beamed at the nurse. 'I realise we'll have to wait at least four weeks before we know whether the transplant has worked but look at him. He hasn't been this perky for months.'

Andrew had been mortified that his cell phone had been switched off at the crucial time. He explained to his wife he had been in such turmoil he had taken a walk along the Embankment to try and clear his head. The phone had been buzzing with business calls and he had needed a rest from it.

'I'm sorry you weren't here,' said Edina. 'It was amazing to see this life-saving pink liquid being injected into him. After waiting months for this to happen it was all over in under an hour.'

The nurse, who had spent the morning briefing the hospital's admin office on the baby's progress, picked up a toy from the dozens that had flooded in when news of his operation had been leaked to the press and dangled it in front of the baby. The hospital had been inundated with calls from the media alerted to the plight of the child through the publicity in the *Chronicle*. Every edition of the tabloids carried variations of the headline: 'Brave youngster has bone marrow op after appeal for donor.' So far the hospital had managed to protect the identity of the donor and the Press Complaints Committee had issued a statement saying they would take a dim view of any media outlet which infringed the right to privacy. The appeal, as well as giving new hope to Sebastian and his family, had given a huge boost to the register of donors, which shot up by thousands.

Andrew turned to the nurse. 'I can't tell you how grateful we are. I'd like to thank the donor.'

'She's already gone home,' said the nurse, smiling at Sebastian, 'but she and her family were insistent that they didn't need thanks. But I'll let her know that you'd like to see her, if you want.'

Andrew said he'd be grateful if she would. After the nurse left he told Edina he'd been wondering about whether or not to phone Calum. 'The excuse could be Sebastian but even then I wonder if he'll take the call. He must be very angry with me.'

'I wish you'd make the effort because I want Sebastian to grow up as part of a family. It's been difficult for me and Lizzie. I haven't really told you how lovely she's been, even during the court case.'

Andrew looked chastened. 'I wish I'd behaved as well as that.'

His wife stood up and stroked his hair. 'Never mind, that's in the past. We could all go to supper once you've sorted things out with him, couldn't we?'

'I will phone. In time.'

They held hands, watching avidly as their son tried to chew off the ear of a small hand-knitted panda.

Chapter Twenty-two

The date of the meeting was pre-ordained – November the eleventh, the sixteenth birthday of Gabriella Lynton and Alison Simmons. It came about as a result of countless telephone conversations, between Calum and Alison, Lizzie and Alison, Gabriella and Angela, Gabriella and Ron, as well as marathon sessions between the two girls. Gabriella had long assuaged Alison's fears that she would be swallowed up by a new family, or found wanting by them, and when Gaby offered their home as the venue, Alison accepted at once. They also agreed it would be easier for Gaby if Alison's brothers were not there in the beginning. They would be introduced to everyone the next time.

Once she had established a friendly relationship with Gabriella, it was Alison who finally persuaded Ron Simmons that she would be happy to meet the Lyntons. Always protective of the youngest member of the family, Ron needed more urging from his wife, but finally he succumbed.

A stream of photographs had been exchanged between the houses, the girls as babies, the girls as toddlers, the girls without their front teeth. Calum had scrawled on one letter, 'Gaby was the most photographed baby in the borough of Wandsworth. There are thousands more here for you to wade through!'

It was the season for fireworks and Gabriella suggested they have a bonfire and serve sausages and baked potatoes. Calum and Lizzie agreed, thinking a less formal event would be a useful ice-breaker.

The Simmons were due at six. An hour before, Gaby decided she must change her outfit. For the third time. Lizzie, as nervous as her daughter, did not try and persuade her that the cropped leather skirt was perfect but just urged her to hurry up. She and Calum had decided the best way to put their guests at ease would be to dress informally. The weather forecast was for a clear but cold evening and in view of the temperature outside, each had donned freshly-pressed jeans and a fleece jacket.

The cake had been iced and took pride of place in the centre of the table. Gabriella had squeezed the slogan in pink icing. 'Happy Birthday To Us!' and Lizzie allowed herself to hope that the event might be less of an ordeal than she feared.

Remembering how long it took for briquettes to turn to ash, Calum set off down the garden to light the barbecue. While he busied himself with the practicalities – his way, she supposed, of coping – Lizzie began to worry about other delicate matters like how she would actually greet her long lost daughter. With Gabriella watching, should she give Alison a kiss on the cheek, a hug or what? There was no prescribed etiquette for such a situation, no handbook of rules on how to greet a natural daughter after sixteen years. After all, she had no idea whether Alison was reserved or like Gabriella tactile and explosive. Lizzie had not been able to sleep the night before and it was hard to realise that after all this time she would finally talk to the girl she thought she would never get to know.

As she watched Calum joshing with Gabriella, pouring out a glass of white wine and soda for her instead of the usual soft drink, Lizzie reflected on how this turmoil had affected Gaby. She seemed to have undergone some kind of metamorphosis. They had even been able to have a non-heated talk about whether she should think about going on the pill. Gabriella had admitted that her threat about Luke making her pregnant was a fib and nothing had happened between them. Still, after her encounter with Anna-Maria Ewing, Lizzie thought it wise to broach the subject. Gabriella might then not be shy to discuss it with her. She hadn't exactly become the perfect darling daughter but the truculence and hostility towards her mother had been diluted. Indeed, she and Gaby had been able to plan this party together without a single cross word. Almost.

When the Simmons family finally rang the doorbell, all three of them rushed to open it. When they reached the door, Calum took Gaby's hand and gave it a reassuring squeeze.

It was a cold night and the first thing Lizzie noticed about Alison was how pink her cheeks were. As Alison stepped shyly into the hallway, Lizzie heard a faint intake of breath from Calum. She could understand his amazement at seeing a younger version of herself because the first sight of the girl had affected her in the same way. Alison stood hesitantly and, unable to speak, Lizzie folded her into her arms but the girl's body tensed and Lizzie broke away quickly. She mustn't overwhelm her.

Angela was not having quite the same reaction from Gaby, who was hugging her birth mother joyously. Though happy at the warmth of Gaby's welcome, Lizzie couldn't help but feel the merest twinge of jealousy.

When Gabriella finally prised herself away from Angela's embrace, Ron came and patted her awkwardly on the shoulder. During the weeks when she had been making friends with Alison over the telephone, Gabriella had been steeling herself for the traumatic moment when she faced her natural parents, but she felt it was turning out OK, less embarrassing and upsetting than she had feared. She supposed it was because Angela and Ron were pretty down-to-earth, they weren't crying and wailing all over the place, although she herself at that moment was finding it hard to hold back the tears.

Calum made no move towards Alison, busying himself hanging up coats and shepherding his guests into the sitting room. He was being pulled both ways, by the attachment to the child he had helped raise and curiosity about what he would feel when he grew to know his biological daughter. To himself he excused his hesitancy as a cover for his nervousness and in any case he wanted to give Lizzie every opportunity to put the young girl at her ease before it was his turn. She did look the image of Lizzie when he had first met her but the thing that tore him up was the colour and texture of her hair. It was his mother's, his aunt's, his grandmother's, that rich brown with the reddish tints that he was told was the legacy of his Celtic forebears.

Finally, he nerved himself to approach her and politely asked what she would like to drink. Alison looked up at him shyly and smiled. He stepped back. 'You look so much like my wife.'

At this the room grew silent and Ron, noticing Gabriella's disquiet, said in a booming voice, 'No need for that, my girl. You're the spitting image of my mother. God rest her soul.'

The tension was broken and the chattering started in earnest then and never faltered for the rest of the evening. The hot food and wine were replenished at regular intervals, contributing to the celebratory atmosphere. Photograph albums were spread across the floor, all of them exclaiming over the likeness of the girls to relatives, many long dead. Angela Simmons took hold of Gabriella's hand and examined her little finger. 'There it is,' she

273

said, and went on to explain how many female members of her family shared the same physical trait, a slight curve in the finger. 'It's meant to be very lucky, you know.'

Gabriella became even more vociferous. 'Look at this,' she exclaimed, pointing to a sepia photograph of a young woman, her great-grandmother, in a high-buttoned Victorian dress. 'I've got her nose. I really have.' She started crying and Alison immediately burst into tears as well. Instinctively the Lyntons went straight over to Gabriella while the Simmons comforted Alison.

Lizzie and Angela exchanged understanding glances. It was one thing to see photographic evidence of the continuity of the family. But it did not negate sixteen years of hard labour, unsociable hours with no time off for good behaviour and the outpouring of emotion lavished over the lifetime of these two young women.

The fireworks had been taken from the hall cupboard and the two fathers went outside to set up the display. All smiles, the rest spilled out to watch the Catherine wheels and rockets cascading into the night air. Lizzie, her gaze rarely leaving the transfixed faces of the teenagers illuminated by the light from the golden showers, had an immense feeling of wellbeing. She was reminded of something she had read recently about the family resembling a dear octopus from whose tentacles they could never quite escape. Crucially, what had to emerge from this was for both the girls to remain secure within their existing family units. The circle in which they had grown and developed would not change; it would only grow larger.

The display over, they trooped back inside and Ron began making moves to take his wife and Alison home.

'Before you go, we have a little present for the girls.' Lizzie beamed conspiratorially at Angela who went over to the table to pick up two small boxes. They were identical in size and wrapped not in traditional birthday paper but the kind used to welcome babies.

The girls began to giggle when they saw the oversized cherubs decorating the cardboard box inside. Alison was the first to rip open the lid. For a moment she stared at the contents, before squealing with delight. Lizzie held her breath as Gabriella tussled to open her box. A second or two later she held aloft a tiny plastic wristband, the sort used to identify newborn babies. Alison waved hers in front of her.

'Isn't it tiny?' she cried.

'I can't believe we were ever as small as this.' Gabriella's face was full of wonder. 'Mine says Simmons.'

'And mine says Lynton,' Alison laughed.

'We thought it was about time you had proper name tags,' smiled Angela.

'Only sixteen years late,' said Lizzie.

There was silence in the room for a moment, broken by Calum. 'But you are who you are. You'll always be Gabriella Lynton,' he said, glancing at her.

Ron put his arm round his daughter. 'And you'll always be Alison Simmons.'

'Absolutely,' agreed Angela. 'You should think of yourselves as sisters from now on. And Gabriella, you have two brothers as well. We'll fix up for you to come and meet them at our place.'

Lizzie raised her glass at the giggling girls and clinked a spoon against it. 'A toast – no, two.' Obediently they all fell silent. 'First to Sebastian who brought us together and who's making wonderful progress, thank God.'

They cheerfully drank to that, and then she said, 'And to Gabriella and Alison. We haven't lost a daughter, both families have gained one.' Lizzie looked fondly from one young face to the other. Alison's face was glowing, no doubt with the unaccustomed wine and the excitement of being central to the celebrations. Her graphic eyebrows added to the animation of her face. Her smile was dazzling, lighting up features which gave a hint of the beauty which would emerge with maturity.

Lizzie longed to have a proper conversation with her newly-found daughter but this noisy gathering was not the right time. Observing her over the past few hours had convinced her that Alison did not have Gabriella's confidence or brio. But eventually, little by little, she hoped to establish a good relationship between them. She would not allow it to affect her closeness to Gabriella. In any case she was reasonably certain that the growing bond between herself and Gaby was strong enough to withstand the introduction of this new girl into their lives.

Across the room Calum raised his glass towards Alison and she gave him a shy smile of acknowledgement. He looked forward to talking to her about her new family, particularly her paternal grandfather and how the old man's sweat and brains had built up the Lynton fortune. He would set out to make her proud of her

275

ancestry and Calum began to daydream that someday she might be persuaded that for the sake of Robert McDowall Lynton she should add his surname to hers. And if she did, the last wish of his father would have been honoured. The bloodline of the family and the Lynton name would continue.

The Simmons family was long gone and Gabriella had trundled up to bed exhausted. Without the conversational shield provided by their guests, Lizzie and Calum were skirting around each other in edgy silence as they cleared the debris of the evening's meal.

'We should get Alison over for a meal on her own,' said Calum, putting the glasses into the cupboard. He turned abruptly. 'That's if you're still around.'

Lizzie went quite still. She searched for inspiration to answer him without spoiling what had been their first pleasant evening for months.

'Will you still be around?' Calum asked into the silence.

Lizzie frowned. 'It's too late for this kind of conversation.'

He stared at her for a second then asked quietly, 'Too late in the evening or too late in the marriage?' When she did not respond he went on, 'How long do you want me to wait, Lizzie? We can't still go on pretending everything's OK for Gaby's sake.'

'I know you're right but I can't help the way I'm feeling. It's not something I can switch on and off.'

'There's a limit to the number of times I can say how sorry I am,' said Calum with heat.

She turned her head away.

'So you can never get over it? Is that what you're telling me? Because if you are,' he said, his voice rising, 'I can't see how we can go on.'

Why couldn't he leave it alone for now? Her voice sounded snappier than she intended as she said, 'If you push me you'll get an answer you won't like.'

'I'm tired of being the supplicant,' he replied, slamming shut the cupboard door.

That did it. She flung a tea towel onto the draining board and told him she fully intended taking the job in Hampshire and that she and Gabriella would be living in the flat. Seeing the fright in his eyes she added hurriedly that he would be welcome to visit

Gabriella any time he wanted, every day if he liked.

'Why are you doing this?' he shouted.

'I think we need time to evaluate our lives.'

His mouth twisted. 'Don't tell me. You need, horrible expression, "space".'

'Calum, we married very young, with little experience of places, people,' she hesitated, 'or other lovers. This gives us the opportunity to live on our own and see whether we can function as a separate entity, as individuals.'

'This is what you've decided, is it?'

'Perhaps marriages have a shelf life . . .'

'Like yoghurt?'

She disregarded this. 'And maybe we've come to the end of ours.' Warming to the theme she had mulled over many times in the preceding weeks she added, 'Who knows, we may find we prefer being married to each other. If that's a mutual decision, we could get back together again. But for now, yes, I think it's best for us to lead separate lives.'

Calum's eyes took on a glitter that Lizzie had never seen in all the years of their marriage. He stared at her with such anger that a thrill of apprehension ran through her body.

'How dare you chuck this marriage on the scrapheap!'

Lizzie stared at him, her eyes wide, unable to think of an adequate reply. In every row they had ever had, Calum had been measured, unemotional, always looking for the compromise, and she used to joke that without the balance their marriage would have been far more fiery.

'You're going to give up everything we've built up without making the smallest effort?'

She bridled at this but in the face of his fury thought it best not to retaliate.

'Is it that bloody man who sent you flowers? Are you going to him?'

'Definitely not. There's no one else involved in my decision. But what about you? You and Tess?'

'We've never had an affair. She's been very supportive – no more than that.'

'I bet.'

'She's always been there for me, Lizzie. I admit there might have been a time . . .' He paused.

'You lied to me, you said you were driving around the night

277

you came back from New York but Tess told me you were with her.'

'You misunderstood her. She—'

'She's in love with you, isn't she?' Lizzie interrupted.

'Yes, I think she may be.'

Lizzie took a deep breath. 'Then I'm happy for you. This is your chance to make a fresh start. Let's face it, things have been said and done between us that I'm not sure can be undone.'

His jaw tightened. 'You think this marriage is at an end, do you?'

'Don't you? I think we both need a fresh start.'

This seemed to push him over the edge and he moved swiftly towards her, grabbing her by the shoulders and swivelling her round. Panting with fury, he pressed his face close to hers.

'You're a fool, Lizzie, if you don't see how much you mean to me. I don't want you to leave me.'

She tried to speak but couldn't because he began to shake her angrily and, despite herself, Lizzie was moved by his passion. This was a man who at last was prepared to show deeply felt, raw ardour.

'I've always had to be the peacemaker, the comforter and I'm fucking fed up with it! I'm not going to let you walk away without a fight.' He shook her roughly again. 'A big fight.'

For several seconds they faced each other, their breath intermingling, then with a low groan he pulled her towards him and kissed her with such a force that she reeled back.

Calum's kisses had always been gentle, soft, sensuous. This one was full of anger and desperation but the force of feeling behind it excited her. As the kiss continued, he began to pull at the lapels of her blouse until the studs gave way and it dropped. With a sudden movement, he pushed her impatiently onto the kitchen floor where he continued to undress her, muttering, almost incoherently, how much he loved her.

Lizzie's body began to respond and she found herself clutching his hair as he entered her now complacent body.

It was the best damn orgasm she'd ever had.

Afterwards, as she lay back, her head almost under the kitchen table, breathing heavily, Lizzie was overcome by shyness. It was almost like being with someone new. She felt a little awkward.

Calum propped himself up on his elbow.

'It's good to have my lover back.'

'Ditto.' She smiled at him, moved at the intensity of love shining from his eyes.

Calum surveyed the crumpled clothes scattered around them. 'I don't know how that happened.'

'Don't apologise. I liked it.'

'It was the thought of another man making love to you. It sent me demented.'

'You should talk. I've had a few bad moments over Tess.'

He leaned over her. 'I don't think I encouraged her.' Lizzie's eyebrows shot up. 'Well, not much.'

'I don't blame her for trying,' said Lizzie. 'I suppose it looked to her as though we were finished and I wouldn't have left a tasty morsel like you lying around.'

He traced his forefinger around her cheeks. 'You're not bad yourself, Mrs Lynton, and if you thought I'd step back and let that Dan feller whisk you away then you were very much mistaken.'

For a brief second Lizzie was tempted to make a joke about Dorset and how she had to double lock her bedroom door but caution prevailed. These long weeks of being at war, hiding her emotions, having to watch everything she said could not be wiped away with one act of love-making, however passionate. No matter how carefully she worded it, Calum was certain to be suspicious about an overnight stay with an attractive man. Her fingernails would have to be pulled out before she would confess how sexually aroused she had been. And how close she had come to opening that door. Instead she told him about her last encounter with Dan. When she described the scene of him hopping about the canteen with hot coffee all over his trousers, Calum let out a bellow of laughter.

'I haven't heard you laugh like that for ages,' she said, pleased.

'There's going to be a lot more of that from now on.' Then he became reflective. 'The good thing that's come out of this is that it's taught us about priorities. For me it's you and Gaby.'

'And our other daughter.'

'Of course. In time. We'll have to get to know her.'

She agreed with him that the Simmons were excellent people, hard-working, upstanding, and they were both thankful that their birth daughter had grown up in that loving environment, even though it was apparent that she had not enjoyed Gabriella's material advantages in life.

'We'll have to find out what she wants to do with her life,' said Lizzie. 'And if we can help, it'd be good, but we must be careful. It's her decisions, all the way.'

'Agreed. But I'd love her to add the name of Lynton to hers.'

'Dream on,' said Lizzie. 'Why on earth should she do that? Would you like Gaby to be called Simmons-Lynton?'

'If she wanted to I wouldn't object.'

'Let's see what the girls say.'

They went up to bed and lay in companionable silence, Calum continuing his theme about Alison's lack of confidence. He thought if she could spend more time with Gabriella, she'd be able to draw the girl out.

'I think you ought to try and get to know your brother too. I think Sebastian has made him examine his priorities as well.'

Calum frowned. 'That's going to take time. I'm not sure I can forgive him for what he's put us through. If he'd come and talked to me we could've sorted it all out.'

'I'm not excusing what he did, but Sebastian was dying. We all concentrated on him and Edina, but Andy must've been nearly mad with worry as well. I wonder how we would have reacted in those circumstances.' Calum looked away but Lizzie gently turned his face towards hers. 'We should make the first move, for Edina's sake. She wants Sebastian to grow up as part of a family. I thinks we owe her that, don't you?'

'I know family rifts seem unimportant when a kid is seriously ill, but I kept on offering the olive branch right the way through and he just laughed at me.'

'He's been a fool but there's a chance this experience has changed Andy, made him examine his priorities.'

Calum said nothing and she went on, 'What's the solution? To let this feud fester on?'

'I suppose I could make an effort,' he paused, 'because you want me to.'

'You have to want to yourself, but I suppose that's better than nothing.' She smiled at him. 'I'll ask them over for a meal.'

Lizzie snuggled into the crook of his arm and as neither of them felt sleepy they spent the rest of the night talking about the future. They were brave enough to admit that life over the past few years had become somewhat stale and that they had been neglecting each other's needs. They came to the conclusion that one of the things that had gone wrong was that they had few shared interests. Calum's absences on business and for hockey coaching had driven Lizzie to spend her leisure time separately from him and this inevitably had led to a breakdown in communication.

As a start he volunteered to dispense with most of his hockey duties. She suggested they choose a hobby in which they could both participate. As one of his mad ideas for the future was to sail in a catamaran to the West Indies, she wondered if they might take up sailing when Gabriella had gone off to university, an idea he seized upon enthusiastically. As for Lizzie, she wouldn't take the job which would have meant leaving home, but she would look for another full-time post.

One lesson Lizzie had learned from the last few months was that she enjoyed being more independent, while Calum felt he had been too placid and needed to assert himself more in order to avoid the feelings of resentment that sometimes built up. More importantly they both agreed to turn the page and firmly place retributions and accusations where they belonged, in the past.

It was as if their marriage had been reborn, as if they had together found the roots of their relationship. And she reminded him of the saying they both admired: 'Good timber does not grow in ease. The stronger the wind, the tougher the trees.'

'This *will* make us stronger,' he said. 'We've been given a second chance.'

Although there would no doubt be problems ahead, this was a moment to savour and Lizzie lay back smiling and lifted up her face for her husband's kiss.